HIDEAWAY

By Nora Roberts

Homeport	Blue Smoke	Chasing Fire
The Reef	Montana Sky	The Witness
River's End	Angels Fall	Whiskey Beach
Carolina Moon	High Noon	The Collector
The Villa	Divine Evil	The Liar
Midnight Bayou	Tribute	The Obsession
Three Fates	Sanctuary	Come Sundown
Birthright	Black Hills	Shelter in Place
Northern Lights	The Search	Under Currents

The Born In Trilogy:
Born in Fire
Born in Ice
Born in Shame

The Bride Quartet:
Vision in White
A Bed of Roses
Savour the Moment
Happy Ever After

The Key Trilogy:
Key of Light
Key of Knowledge
Key of Valour

The Irish Trilogy:
Jewels of the Sun
Tears of the Moon
Heart of the Sea

Three Sisters Island Trilogy:
Dance upon the Air
Heaven and Earth
Face the Fire

The Sign of Seven Trilogy:
Blood Brothers
The Hollow
The Pagan Stone

Chesapeake Bay Quartet:
Sea Swept
Rising Tides
Inner Harbour
Chesapeake Blue

In the Garden Trilogy:
Blue Dahlia
Black Rose
Red Lily

The Circle Trilogy:
Morrigan's Cross
Dance of the Gods
Valley of Silence

The Dream Trilogy:
Daring to Dream
Holding the Dream
Finding the Dream

The Inn Boonsboro Trilogy:
The Next Always
The Last Boyfriend
The Perfect Hope

The Cousins O'Dwyer Trilogy:
Dark Witch
Shadow Spell
Blood Magick

The Guardians Trilogy:
Stars of Fortune
Bay of Sighs
Island of Glass

The Chronicles of the One Trilogy:
Year One
Of Blood and Bone
The Rise of Magicks

Many of Nora Roberts' other titles are now available in eBook and she is also the author of the In Death series using the pseudonym J.D. Robb.

NORA ROBERTS

HIDEAWAY

piatkus

PIATKUS

First published in the United States in 2020 by St Martin's Press
This edition published in 2020 by Piatkus

1 3 5 7 9 10 8 6 4 2

A CIP catalogue record for this book
is available from the British Library.

ISBN: 978-0-349-42195-7 (hardback)
ISBN: 978-0-349-42196-4 (trade paperback)

Printed and bound in Great Britain by
Clays Ltd, Elcograf S.p.A.

Papers used by Piatkus are from well-managed forests
and other responsible sources.

Piatkus
An imprint of
Little, Brown Book Group
Carmelite House
50 Victoria Embankment
London EC4Y 0DZ

An Hachette UK Company
www.hachette.co.uk

www.littlebrown.co.uk

To family,
of the blood and of the heart

PART I

INNOCENCE LOST

Daughters are the thing.
—J. M. BARRIE

A little child loves ever'body, friends,
and its nature is sweetness—until something happens.
—FLANNERY O'CONNOR

CHAPTER ONE

Big Sur · 2001

When Liam Sullivan died, at the age of ninety-two, in his sleep, in his own bed with his wife of sixty-five years beside him, the world mourned.

An icon had passed.

Born in a little cottage tucked in the green hills and fields near the village of Glendree in County Clare, he'd been the seventh and last child of Seamus and Ailish Sullivan. He'd known hunger in the lean times, had never forgotten the taste of his mother's bread and butter pudding—or the whip-swat of her hand when he'd earned it.

He'd lost an uncle and his oldest brother in the first Great War, had grieved for a sister who'd died before her eighteenth birthday delivering her second child.

He'd known from an early age the backbreaking work of plowing a field behind a horse named Moon. He'd learned how to shear a sheep and slaughter a lamb, to milk a cow and build a rock wall.

And he remembered, the whole of his long life, the nights his family sat around the fire—the smell of peat smoke, the angel-clear voice of his mother raised in song, his father smiling at her as he played the fiddle.

And the dancing.

As a boy he'd sometimes earn a few pennies singing in the pub while the locals drank their pints and talked of farming and politics.

His soaring tenor could bring a tear to the eye, and his agile body and fast, clever feet lift the spirit when he danced.

He dreamed of more than plowing the fields and milking the cow, much more than the pennies gathered at the little pub in Glendree.

Shortly before his sixteenth birthday, he left home, a few precious punts in his pocket. He endured the Atlantic crossing with others looking for more in the cramped confines belowdecks. When the ship rolled and rocked in a storm, and the air stank of vomit and fear, he blessed his iron constitution.

Dutifully, he wrote letters to home he dreamed of posting at the end of the voyage and kept spirits up by entertaining his fellow passengers with song and dance.

He shared a flirtation and a few eager kisses with a flaxen-haired girl named Mary from Cork who traveled to Brooklyn and a position as a maid in some fine house.

With Mary he stood in the cool, fresh air—fresh at last—and saw the great lady with her torch held high. And thought his life had truly begun.

So much color and noise and movement, so many people squashed into one place. Not just an ocean away from the farm where he'd been born and reared, he thought. A world away.

And his world now.

He was bound to apprentice with his mother's brother Michael Donahue as a butcher in the Meatpacking District. He was welcomed, embraced, given a bed in a room he shared with two of his cousins. While in only a matter of weeks he grew to hate the sounds, the smells of the work, he earned his keep.

Still, he dreamed of more.

He found the more the first time he turned over a bit of that hard-earned pay to sit in a movie theater with Mary of the flaxen hair. There he saw magic on the silver screen, worlds far beyond everything he knew, worlds holding everything a man could want.

There the sounds of bone saws, the *thwack* of cleavers didn't exist. Even pretty Mary faded away as he felt himself pulled into the screen and the world it offered.

The beautiful women, the heroic men, the drama, the joy. When he surfaced, he saw all around him the enraptured faces of the audience, the tears, the laughter, the applause.

This, he thought, was food for a hungry belly, a blanket in the cold, a light for the damaged soul.

Less than a year after he saw New York from the deck of a ship, he left it to head west.

He worked his way across the country, amazed at its size, at its changing sights and seasons. He slept in fields, in barns, in the backs of bars where he traded his voice for a cot.

Once he spent the night in jail after a bit of a dustup in a place called Wichita.

He learned to ride the rails, and evade the police—and as he would say in countless interviews over the course of his career—had the adventure of a lifetime.

When, after nearly two years of travel, he saw the big white sign spelling out HOLLYWOODLAND, he vowed that here he would find his fame and fortune.

He lived on his wits, his voice, his strong back. With the wit he talked his way into building sets on back lots, sang his way through the work. He acted out the scenes he watched, practiced the various accents he'd heard on the trip from east to west.

Talkies changed everything, so now soundstages needed building. Actors he'd admired in their silence on-screen had voices that screeched or rumbled, so their stars burned out and fell.

His break came when a director heard him singing while he worked—the very tune the once-silent star was supposed to romance his lady with in a musical scene.

Liam knew the man couldn't sing worth shite, and had his ear to the ground close enough to have heard there was talk about using another voice. It was, to his mind, simply being sure he was in the right place at the right time to be that voice.

His face might not have appeared on the screen, but his voice held the audience. It opened the door.

An extra, a walk-on, a bit part where he spoke his first line.

Building blocks, stepping-stones, forming a foundation fueled by the work, the talent, and the Sullivan tireless energy.

He, the farm boy from Clare, had an agent, a contract, and began in that Golden Age of Hollywood what would be a career that spanned decades and generations.

He met his Rosemary when he and the pert and popular Rosemary Ryan starred in a musical—the first of five films they'd make together in their lifetimes. The studio fed the gossip columns stories of their romance, but none of the hype was necessary.

They married less than a year after they clapped eyes on each other. They honeymooned in Ireland—visiting his family, as well as hers in Mayo.

They built a grand glamour of a home in Beverly Hills, had a son, then a daughter.

They bought the land in Big Sur because, as with their romance, it was love at first sight. The house they built facing the sea they named Sullivan's Rest. It became their getaway, then as years passed more their home.

Their son proved the Sullivan-Ryan talent spanned generations, as Hugh's star rose from child actor to leading man. As their daughter, Maureen, chose New York and Broadway.

Hugh would give them their first grandson before his wife, the love of his life, died in a plane crash returning from a location shoot in Montana.

That son would, in time, place another Sullivan star on the screen.

Liam and Rosemary's grandson Aidan, believing, as with Sullivan tradition, he'd found the love of his life in the silky blond beauty of Charlotte Dupont, married in glittery style (exclusive photos in *People* magazine), bought a mansion in Holmby Hills for his bride. And gave Liam a great-granddaughter.

They named the fourth-generation Sullivan Caitlyn. Caitlyn Ryan Sullivan became an instant Hollywood darling when she made her film debut at twenty-one months playing the mischievous, matchmaking toddler in *Will Daddy Make Three?*

The fact that most reviews found little Cate upstaged both adult leads (which included her mother as the female love interest) caused some consternation in certain quarters.

It might have been her last taste of preadolescent stardom, but her great-grandfather cast her, at age six, as the free-spirited Mary Kate in *Donovan's Dream*. She spent six weeks on location in Ireland, and shared the screen with her father, grandfather, great-grandfather, and great-grandmother.

She delivered her lines in a west county accent as if she'd been born there.

The film, a critical and commercial success, would be Liam Sullivan's last. In one of the rare interviews he gave toward the end of his life, sitting under a flowering plum tree with the Pacific rolling toward forever, he said, like Donovan, he'd seen his dream come true. He'd made a fine film with the woman he'd loved for six decades, with their boys Hugh and Aidan, and the bright light of his great-granddaughter, Cate.

Movies, he said, had given him the grandest of adventures, so this, he felt, was a perfect cap for the genie bottle of his life.

On a cool, bright February afternoon, three weeks after his death, his widow, his family, and many of the friends he'd made through the years gathered at his Big Sur estate to—as Rosemary insisted—celebrate a life well and fully lived.

They'd held a formal funeral in L.A., with luminaries and eulogies, but this would be to remember the joy he'd given.

There were speeches and anecdotes, there were tears. But there was music, laughter, children playing inside and out. There was food and whiskey and wine.

Rosemary, her hair as white now as the snow that laced the tops of the Santa Lucias, embraced the day as she settled—a bit weary, truth be told—in front of the soaring stone fireplace in what they called the gathering room. There she could watch the children—their young bones laughing at winter's bite—and the sea beyond.

She took her son's hand when Hugh sat beside her. "Will you think I'm a crazy old woman if I tell you I can still feel him, as if he's right beside me?"

As her husband's had, her voice carried the lilt of her home.

"How can I, when I feel it, too?"

She turned to him, her white hair cut short for style and ease, her eyes vivid green and full of humor. "Your sister would say we're both crazy. How did I ever produce such a practical-minded child as Maureen?"

She took the tea he offered her, winged up an eyebrow. "Is there whiskey in it?"

"I know my ma."

"That you do, my boy, but you don't know all."

She sipped her tea, sighed. Then studied her son's face. So like his father's, she thought. The damnably handsome Irish. Her boy, her baby, had silver liberally streaked through his hair, and eyes that still beamed the bluest of blues.

"I know how you grieved when you lost your Livvy. So sudden, so cruel. I see her in our Caitlyn, and in more than the looks. I see it in her light, the joy and fierceness of her. I'm sounding crazy again."

"No. I see the same. I hear her laugh, and hear Livvy laugh. She's a treasure to me."

"I know it, and to me as she was to your da. I'm glad, Hugh, you found Lily and, after those long years alone, found happiness. A good mother to her own children, and a loving grandmother to our Cate these past four years."

"She is."

"Knowing that, knowing our Maureen's happy, her children and theirs doing well, I've made a decision."

"About what?"

"The rest of my time. I love this house," she murmured. "The land here. I know it all in every light, in every season, in every mood. You know we didn't sell the house in L.A. mostly for sentiment, and the convenience of having it if either of us worked there for any stretch of time."

"Do you want to sell it now?"

"I think no. The memories there are dear as well. You know we have the place in New York and that I'm giving it to Maureen. I want to know if you'd want the house in L.A. or this one. I want to know because I'm going to Ireland."

"To visit?"

"To live. Wait," she said before he could speak. "I may have been reared in Boston from my tenth year, but I still have family there, and roots. And the family your father brought me is there as well."

He laid a hand over hers, lifted his chin to the big window, and the children, the family outside. "You have family here."

"I do. Here, New York, Boston, Clare, Mayo, and, bless us, London now as well. God, but we're far-flung, aren't we, my darling?"

"It seems we are."

"I hope all of them come to visit me. But Ireland's where I want to be now. In the quiet and the green."

She gave him a smile, with a twinkle in her eyes. "An old widow woman, baking brown bread and knitting shawls."

"You don't know how to bake bread or knit anything."

"Hah." Now she slapped his hand. "I can learn, can't I now, even at my advanced age. I know you have your home with Lily, but it's time for me to give back, we'll say. God knows how Liam and I ever made so much money doing what we did for the love of it."

"Talent." Then he tapped a finger gently to her head. "Smarts."

"Well, we had both. And now I want to shed some of what we reaped. I want that lovely cottage we bought in Mayo. So which is it for you, Hugh? Beverly Hills or Big Sur?"

"Here. This." When she smiled, he shook his head. "You knew before you asked."

"I know my boy even better than he knows his ma. That's settled then. It's yours. And I trust you to tend to it."

"You know I will, but—"

"None of that. My mind's made up. I damn well expect I'll have a place to lay my head when I come visit. And I will come. We had good years here, me and your da. I want what came from us to have good years here as well."

She patted his hand. "Look out there, Hugh." She laughed as she saw Cate do a handspring. "That's the future out there, and I'm so grateful I had a part in making it."

While Cate did handsprings to entertain two of her younger cousins, her parents argued in their guest suite.

Charlotte, her hair swept back in a chignon for the occasion, paced the hardwood, her Louboutins clicking like impatient fingersnaps.

The raw energy pumping from her had once enthralled Aidan. Now it just made him tired.

"I want to get out of here, Aidan, for God's sake."

"And we will, tomorrow afternoon, as planned."

She whirled on him, lips sulky, eyes sheened with angry tears. The soft winter light spilled through the wide glass doors at her back and haloed around her.

"I've had enough, can't you understand? Can't you see I'm on my last nerve? Why the hell do we have to have an idiotic family brunch tomorrow? We had the goddamn dinner last night, we had this whole endless deal today—not to mention the funeral. The endless funeral. How many more stories do I have to hear about the great Liam Sullivan?"

Once he'd thought she understood his thick, braided family ties, then he'd hoped she'd come to understand them. Now they both understood she just tolerated them.

Until she didn't.

Weary to the bone, Aidan sat, gave himself a minute to stretch out his long legs. He'd started to grow a beard for an upcoming role. It itched and annoyed him.

He hated that, at the moment, he felt exactly the same about his wife.

The rough spots in their marriage had smoothed out recently. Now it seemed they'd hit another bumpy patch. "It's important to my grandmother, Charlotte, to my father, to me, to the family."

"Your family's swallowing me whole, Aidan."

She did a heel turn, her hands flying out. So much drama, he thought, over a few more hours.

"It's just one more night, and there'll only be a handful of us left by dinner. We'll be home this time tomorrow. We still have guests, Charlotte. We should be downstairs right now."

"Then let your grandmother deal with them. Your father. You. Why can't I take the plane and go home?"

"Because it's my father's plane, and you, Caitlyn, and I will fly home with him and Lily tomorrow. For now, we're a united front."

"If we had our own plane, I wouldn't have to wait."

He could feel the headache growing behind his eyes. "Do we really need to go there? And now?"

She shrugged. "Nobody would miss me."

He tried another tack, smiled. He knew, from experience, his wife reacted better to the sweet than the stern. "I would."

And on a sigh, she smiled back.

She had a smile, he thought, that just stopped a man's heart.

"I'm being such a pain in the ass."

"Yeah, but you're my pain in the ass."

On a quick laugh, she walked over, cuddled on his lap. "I'm sorry, baby. Almost sorry. Sort of sorry. You know I've never liked it up here. It feels so isolated it makes me claustrophobic. And I know that doesn't make sense."

He knew better than to stroke that shining blond hair after she'd had it styled, so he lightly kissed her temple instead. "I get it, but we'll be home tomorrow. I need you to stick just one more night, for my grandmother, my dad. For me."

After letting out a hiss, she poked his shoulder, then offered him her signature pout. Full coral lips, sulky and soft crystal-blue eyes dramatically lashed. "I better get points. Big points."

"How about a long weekend in Cabo points?"

On a gasp, she grabbed his face with her hands. "You mean it?"

"I've got a couple weeks before I start production." So saying, he rubbed a hand over his scruff. "Let's say we hit the beach for a few days. Cate'll love it."

"She has school, Aidan."

"We'll take her tutor."

"How about this?" Now she circled her arms around him, pressed her body, still in mourning black, against his. "Cate has a long weekend with Hugh and Lily, which she'd love. And you and I have a few days in Cabo." She kissed him. "Just us. I'd love some just us, baby. Don't you think we need some just us?"

She was probably right—the smooth patches needed tending as much as the rough. While he hated leaving Cate, she was probably right. "I can make that work."

"Yes! I'm going to text Grant, see if he can do some extra sessions this week. I want a perfect bikini body."

"You already have one."

"That's my sweet husband talking. We'll see what my hard-assed personal trainer says. Oh!" She hopped up. "I need to shop."

"Right now we have to get back downstairs."

The flicker of annoyance marred her face before she smoothed it away. "Okay. You're right, but give me a couple minutes to fix my face."

"Your face is gorgeous, as always."

"Sweet husband." She pointed at him as she started toward her makeup counter. Then stopped. "Thanks, Aidan. These past few weeks, with all the tributes, the memorials, it's been hard on all of us. A few days away, well, that'll be good for us. I'll be right down."

While her parents made up, Cate organized a game of hide-and-seek as the final outdoor game of the day. Always a favorite when the family gathered, the game had its rules, restrictions, and bonus points.

In this case, the rules included outdoors only—as several of the adults had decreed no running inside. The It got a point for every hider found, with the first found designated as the next It. If that hider, now It, was five or under, he or she could choose a partner on the following hunt.

If a hider went three rounds without being found, that meant ten bonus points.

And since Cate had been planning this game all day, she knew how to win them.

She darted off when Boyd, age eleven, started the countdown as the first It. Since Boyd lived in New York like his grandmother, he only visited Big Sur a couple times a year at most. He didn't know the grounds like she did.

Plus, she had a fresh hiding place already picked out.

She rolled her eyes as she saw her five-year-old cousin Ava crawl under the white cloth of a food table. Boyd would find Ava in two minutes.

She nearly backtracked to show Ava a better spot, but it was every kid for herself!

Most of the guests had gone, and more were taking their leave. But a lot of adults still milled around the patios, the outdoor bars, or sat around one of the firepits. Remembering why, she felt a pang.

She'd loved her great-grandda. He'd always had a story to tell, and lemon drops in his pocket. She'd cried and cried when her daddy told her Grandda had gone to heaven. He'd cried, too, even when he told her Grandda had had a long, happy life. How he'd meant so much to so many, and would never be forgotten.

She thought of his line from the movie they'd made together, while he sat with her on a stone wall, looking over the land.

"A life's marked along the way, darlin', by the deeds we do, for good or ill. Those we leave behind judge those marks, and remember."

She remembered lemon drops and hugs as she scurried to the garage, and around the side. She could still hear voices, from the patios and terraces, the walled garden. Her goal? The big tree. If she climbed to the third branch, she could hide behind the thick trunk, in the green leaves that smelled so good, ten feet up.

Nobody would find her!

Her hair—Celtic black—flew behind her as she ran. Her nanny, Nina, had tucked it back at the sides with butterfly pins to keep it out of her face. Her eyes, bold and blue, danced as she flew out of sight of the multitiered house, far beyond the guest cottage with its steps leading down to the little beach, and the pool that overlooked the sea.

She'd had to wear a dress for the first part of the day, to be respectful, but Nina had laid out her play clothes for after. She still had to be careful of the sweater, but knew it was okay to get her jeans dirty.

"I'm going to win," she whispered as she reached up for the first branch of the California bay, put her purple (currently her favorite color) sneaker in the little knothole for purchase.

She heard a sound behind her and, though she knew it couldn't be Boyd, not yet, her heart jumped.

She caught a glimpse of the man in a server's uniform, with a blond beard and hair pulled back in a ponytail. He wore sunglasses that shot the light back at her.

She grinned, put a finger to her lips. "Hide-and-seek," she told him.

He smiled back. "Want a boost?" He nodded, then moved forward as if to give her one.

She felt the sharp needle stick on the side of her neck, started to swat at it as she might a bug.

Then her eyes rolled back, and she felt nothing at all.

He had the gag on, zip ties on her wrists and ankles in seconds. Just a precaution, as the dose should keep her out for a couple hours.

She didn't weigh much and, as a man in excellent shape, he could have carried her the few feet to the waiting cart had she been a full-grown woman.

After shoving her into the cabinet of the service cart, he rolled it toward the caterer's van—outfitted for just this purpose. He pushed it up the ramp, shut the cargo doors.

In under two minutes, he drove down the long drive, wound to the edge of the private peninsula. At the security gates, he entered the code with a gloved finger. When the gates opened, he drove through, made his turn, then hit Highway 1.

He resisted pulling off the wig, and the fake beard.

Not yet, and he could handle the annoyance of them. He didn't have far to go, and expected he'd have the ten-million-dollar brat locked inside the high-class cabin (owners currently in Maui) before anyone even thought to look for her.

When he turned off the highway again, started up the steep drive to where some rich asshole decided to build a vacation paradise stuck in with a bunch of trees, rocks, chaparral, he was whistling a tune.

Everything had gone smooth as silk.

He caught sight of his partner pacing on the second-story deck of the cabin and rolled his eyes. Talk about an asshole.

They had this knocked, for Christ's sake. They'd keep the kid sedated, but wear masks just in case. In a couple of days—maybe less—they'd be rich, the kid could go back to the fucking Sullivans, and he, with a new name, new passport, would be on his way to Mozambique to soak up some sun in style.

He pulled the van around the side of the cabin. You couldn't see the cabin from the road, not really, so he knew no one would see the van blocked by trees around the side.

By the time he hopped out, his partner had run down to meet him.

"Have you got her?"

"Shit yeah. Nothing to it."

"Are you sure nobody saw you? Are you sure—"

"Jesus, Denby, chill."

"No names," Denby hissed, pushing up his sunglasses as he looked around as if somebody waited in the woods to attack. "We can't risk her hearing our names."

"She's out. Let's get her upstairs, locked in so I can get this crap off my face. I want a beer."

"Masks first. Look, you're not a fucking doctor. We can't be a hundred percent she's still out."

"Fine, fine, go get yours. I'll stick with this." He patted the beard.

As Denby went back inside, he opened the cargo doors, hopped in to open the cabinet doors. Out, he thought, as in o-u-t. He rolled her out onto the floor, dragged her back toward the door—not a peep from her—then hopped out again.

He glanced back when Denby appeared in his Pennywise the Dancing Clown mask and wig, and he laughed like a loon. "If she wakes up before we get her inside, she'll probably faint from fright."

"We want her scared, don't we, so she'll cooperate. The little spoiled rich bitch."

"That'd do the trick. You're no Tim Curry, but that'd do the trick."

He slung Cate over his shoulder. "Everything ready up there?"

"Yeah. The windows are locked down. Still got a hell of a view of the mountains," Denby added as he followed his partner inside the rustic plush of the entryway, the open living area. "Not that she'll enjoy that, since we're keeping her out or the next thing to it."

Denby jumped as "The Mexican Hat Dance" played from the phone clipped to his partner's belt.

"Goddamn it, Grant!"

Grant Sparks only laughed. "Used my name, nimrod." He carted Cate up the stairs to the second floor, open to the first with its cathedral ceiling. "That's a text from my sugar. You gotta chill, man."

He carried Cate into the bedroom they'd selected because it faced the back and had its own bathroom. He dumped her on the four-poster

Denby had stripped down to sheets—cheap sheets they'd bought, and would take away with them.

The en suite was to avoid dragging her out of the room, avoiding a potential mess neither of them wanted to clean up. If she made one, they'd wash the sheets. Once they'd finished they'd remake the bed, nice and tidy and with the original bedding, and remove the nails hammered into the window locks.

He looked around, satisfied that Denby had taken out anything the kid could use as a weapon—as if—or bust out a window with. She'd be too drugged up for that, but why take chances?

When they left, the house would be exactly as they'd found it. No one would know they'd ever been inside.

"You took out all the lightbulbs?"

"Every one."

"Good job. Keep her in the dark. Go ahead and clip those ties, take off the gag. If she wakes up, has to piss, I don't want her doing it in the bed. She can beat on the door, scream her head off. Won't make a diff."

"How long do you figure she'll be under?"

"A couple hours. We bring her some doctored soup when she does, and that'll keep her out for the night."

"When are you going out to call?"

"After dark. Hell, they're not even looking for her yet. She was playing fucking hide-and-seek, as advertised, and headed straight for the grab spot."

He gave Denby a slap on the back. "Smooth as silk. Finish up, make damn sure you lock the door. I'm getting this crap off my face." He pulled off the wig, the wig net under it, revealing a short, stylish mop of sun-streaked brown hair. "I'm going for a beer."

CHAPTER TWO

As the guests dwindled down to family, Charlotte did her duty, sat with Rosemary, made conversation with Lily, with Hugh. She reminded herself the reward made the effort worthwhile.

And it did take effort. Lily might see herself as a big-deal actress because she'd gotten a couple of Oscar nominations (didn't win, did she!), but however nice she played it, Charlotte could feel her dislike.

Hell, she could taste it whenever she got within five feet of the old hag with her stupid southern belle accent.

But she could play nice, too, and did, forcing a smile when Lily let out that brassy laugh of hers. A laugh Charlotte figured was as fake as Lily Morrow's trademark red hair.

She sipped a cosmo Hugh had mixed her at the bar on the far side of the gathering room. At least the Sullivans knew how to make a decent drink.

So she'd drink, smile, act like she gave a shit when someone told another Saint Liam story.

And wait it out.

As the sun dipped down toward the ocean, a ball of fire sinking toward the blue, the kids came inside. Dirty, noisy, and, of course, ravenous.

There were hands and faces to be washed, and in some cases, clothes to change before the children had their dinner, had their baths. The older ones could vote on a movie to watch in the theater, while the adults had their meal and the younger children their bedtime.

In the kitchen, nannies put approved meals together—taking into account this one's peanut allergy, that one's lactose intolerance, another being raised vegan.

Nina, busy preparing fresh fruit, glanced around, counting heads. She smiled at Boyd as he grabbed some baked chips.

"Isn't Caitlyn hungry?"

"I dunno." He shrugged, tried some salsa. "She didn't win. She can say she did, but she didn't." Because his nanny—like he needed one!—was busy with his little sister, Boyd snuck a cookie even though they were off-limits before dinner. "She didn't come in when we called the game, so that's default."

"She didn't come in with the rest of you?"

A smart boy, he made short work of the cookie in case his own nanny looked his way.

"Nobody found her, so she'll say she won, but she defaulted. Maybe she snuck in the house before, and that's cheating. Either way, she didn't win."

"Caitlyn doesn't cheat." Wiping her hands, Nina set off to look for her girl.

She checked Cate's room, in case she'd come in to change or to use the bathroom. She glanced around the second floor, but many of the doors were closed, so she walked out on the wide, cantilevered terrace.

She called out, more impatient than concerned, walked down the railed bridge that led to the pool side of the house, then back again before she took the steps down.

Cate loved the walled garden, so she looked there, wandered through the little orchard beyond it, calling, calling.

The sun dipped lower; the shadows lengthened. The air began to chill. And her heart began to thump.

A city girl, born and raised in L.A., Nina Torez had what she considered a healthy distrust of the country. She began to imagine poisonous snakes, cougars, coyotes, even bears as her calls for Cate rose to desperate.

Silly, she told herself, all that was just silly. Catey was fine, had just . . . fallen asleep somewhere in the big house. Or . . .

She rushed to the guest cottage, burst inside, calling for her charge. The sea side of the guest cottage was a sheer wall of glass. Staring out at the sea, she thought of all the ways a little girl could be swallowed up.

And thinking of Cate's love for the little beach, she raced out, down the steps, called and called while the sea lions reclining on the rocks watched her with bored eyes.

She raced up again to try the pool house, the garden shed. Sprinted inside to the lower level to search the theater, the family room, the rehearsal space, even the storage areas.

She raced back out the other side to check the garage.

"Caitlyn Ryan Sullivan! You come out right now! You're scaring me."

And she found the butterfly barrette she'd tucked into Cate's long, lovely hair that morning on the ground by the old tree.

It meant nothing, she thought even as she clutched it in her hand. The girl had been doing handsprings, racing and running, doing pirouettes and jigs. It had just fallen out.

She told herself that over and over as she ran back to the house. Tears blurred her eyes when she dragged open the huge front door, and all but ran into Hugh.

"Nina, what in the world's the matter?"

"I can't—I can't—Mr. Hugh, I can't find Caitlyn. I can't find her anywhere. I found this."

She held out the barrette, burst into tears.

"Here now, don't you worry. She's just tucked up somewhere. We'll find her."

"She was playing hide-and-seek." The trembling started as he led her into the main living room, where most of the family had gathered. "I—I came in to help Maria with little Circi and the baby. She was playing with the other children, and I came inside."

Charlotte, sitting with a second cosmo, looked over as Hugh led Nina in. "For God's sake, Nina, what's going on?"

"I looked everywhere. I can't find her. I can't find Catey."

"She's probably just upstairs in her room."

"No, ma'am, no. I looked. Everywhere. I called and called. She's a good girl, she'd never hide away when I called for her, when she could hear I was worried."

Aidan got to his feet. "When did you last see her?"

"They started, all the children, to play hide-and-seek. An hour—more now. She was with the other children, so I came to help with the babies and little ones. Mr. Aidan . . ."

She held out the barrette. "I only found this, by the big tree near the garage. It was in her hair. I put it in her hair this morning."

"We'll find her. Charlotte, check upstairs again. Both floors."

"I'll help." Lily rose, as did her daughter.

"We'll start checking this level." Hugh's sister patted Charlotte's shoulder. "I'm sure she's fine."

"You're supposed to watch her!" Charlotte shoved to her feet.

"Ms. Charlotte—"

"Charlotte." Aidan took his wife's arm. "Nina wouldn't have any reason to watch Cate every minute while she's playing with all the kids."

"Then where is she?" Charlotte demanded, and ran from the room calling for her daughter.

"Nina, come sit with me." Rosemary held out a hand. "The men are going to look outside, every nook and cranny. The rest will look through the house."

Rosemary tried a comforting smile that didn't reach her eyes. "And when we find her, I'm going to give her a good talking-to."

For more than an hour, they looked, covering every inch of the sprawling house, its outbuildings, the grounds. Lily gathered the children, asked when they'd last seen Cate. It came down to the game Cate herself had instigated.

Lily, her flame-red hair disordered from the search, took Hugh's hand. "I think we need to call the police."

"The police!" Charlotte shrieked it. "My baby! Something's happened to my baby. She's fired! That useless woman's fired. Aidan, God, Aidan."

As she half swooned against him, the phone rang.

On a deep breath, Hugh walked over, picked up the phone.

"This is the Sullivan residence."

"If you want to see the girl again, it'll take ten million, in unmarked, nonsequential bills. Pay, and she'll be returned to you unharmed. If you contact the police, she dies. If you contact the FBI, she dies. If you contact anyone, she dies. Keep this line open. I'll call with further instructions."

"Wait. Let me—"

But the phone went dead in his hand.

Lowering the phone, he looked at his son with horror. "Someone's got Cate."

"Oh, thank God! Where is she?" Charlotte demanded. "Aidan, we need to go get her right now."

"That's not what Dad meant." His soul sank as he held Charlotte tight against him. "Is it, Dad?"

"They want ten million."

"What are you talking about?" Charlotte tried to struggle out of Aidan's arms. "Ten million for . . . You—she— My baby's been kidnapped?"

"We need to call the police," Lily said again.

"We do, but I need to tell you . . . He said, if we did, he'd hurt her."

"Hurt her? She's just a little girl. She's my little girl." Weeping, Charlotte pressed her face to Aidan's shoulder. "Oh God, God, how could this happen? Nina! That bitch is probably part of this. I could kill her."

She shoved away from Aidan, rounded on Lily. "Nobody's calling the police. I won't let them hurt my little girl. *My* child! We can get the money." She grabbed a fistful of Aidan's shirt. "The money is nothing. Aidan, our little girl. Tell them we'll pay, pay anything. Just give us back our baby."

"Don't worry, don't worry. We're going to get her back, get her back safe."

"It's not the money, Charlotte." Terrified, Hugh rubbed his hands over his face. "What if we pay, and they . . . they still hurt her? We need help."

"What if? What if?" When she turned back to face him, Charlotte's carefully styled chignon tumbled, spilling hair around her shoulders.

"Didn't you just say if we didn't pay, they'd hurt her, if we called the police, they'd hurt her? I won't risk my daughter. I won't."

"They might be able to trace the call," Aidan began. "They might be able to find out how someone took her away."

"Might? Might?" Her voice pitched up, a shriek like nails on a blackboard. "Is that what she means to you?"

"She means everything to me." Aidan had to sit as his legs shook. "We have to think. We have to do what's best for Catey."

"We pay whatever he wants, do whatever he says. Aidan, dear God, Aidan, we can get the money. It's our baby."

"I'll pay." Hugh stared into Charlotte's tear-ravaged face, into his son's terrified one. "She was taken from my father's house, a house my mother has given to me. I'll pay."

On a fresh sob, Charlotte threw herself into his arms. "I'll never forget . . . She'll be all right. Why would he hurt her if we give him what he wants? I want my little girl. I just want my little girl."

Reading Hugh's signal as Charlotte clutched at him, Lily moved in. "Here now, here now, let me take you upstairs. Miranda," she said to her youngest daughter, "why don't you help keep the children occupied, maybe take them down to the theater, put on a movie, and have someone bring Charlotte up some tea? Everything's going to be fine," she soothed as she pulled Charlotte away.

"I want my baby."

"Of course you do."

"Put on some coffee," Rosemary said. She sat, face pale, hands linked tight, but back straight. "We need our wits about us."

"I'll make some calls, start arranging for the money. No," Hugh said when Aidan started out. "Leave her to Lily for now. It's best to leave her to Lily. There's more to consider than getting the money, and how in God's name they took Cate from under our noses. They're amateurs, and that scares me to death."

"Why do you say that?" Aidan demanded.

"Ten million, Aidan, in cash. I can find a way to get it, and I will, but the logistics after? How do they expect to transport such a large amount? The practicalities. It's not smart, son, it's not. Having the money wired, having a way, an account, that's smart. This isn't."

As everyone in the room started talking at once, voices raised in anger and anxiety, Rosemary got slowly to her feet. "Enough!" And with her power as the matriarch, the room fell into silence. "Have any of you ever seen ten million dollars, all in cash? Hugh's right on this. Just as he's right we should be calling the police. But—" She held up a finger before the din started up again. "It's Aidan and Charlotte who have the say on that. We all love Caitlyn, but she's their daughter. So we'll get the money. Hugh and I. It's for us," she said to Hugh. "My house still, and soon to be yours. So we'll go into your father's office, and do what we need to do to get it, and quickly.

"Get some tea up to her," Rosemary continued. "And I've no doubt someone around here has a sleeping pill or two. Given her personality, and her state of mind, it might be best to convince her to take a pill and sleep for now."

"I'll take the tea up," Aidan told her. "And Charlotte has her own pills. I'll see she takes one. Before I do, I'll try again to convince her to call the police. Because I agree with you. Yet, if something happened . . ."

"One step at a time." She went to him, gripped his hands. "We'll get the money, your dad and I. And we'll do, all of us, whatever you and Charlotte decide."

"Nan." He brought her hands up, pressed them to his cheeks. "My world. Cate's the center of it."

"I know it. You'll stay strong for her. Let's get these bastards the money they want, Hugh."

Cate woke slowly. Because her head hurt she squeezed her eyes tight, hunched into herself as if to push off the pain. Her throat felt sore, and something inside her tummy rolled like it wanted her to puke it out.

She didn't want to throw up, didn't want to.

She wanted Nina, or her daddy, or her mom. Somebody to make it stop.

She opened her eyes to the dark. Something was really wrong. She was really sick, but she didn't remember getting really sick.

The bed didn't feel right—too hard, with scratchy sheets. She had a lot of beds in a lot of rooms. Her own at home, her bed at Grandpa and G-Lil's, at Grandda and Nan's, at—

No, her grandda had died, she remembered now. And they'd had a celebration because of his life. Playing, playing with all the kids. Tag, and tricks, and hide-and-seek. And . . .

The man, the man at her hiding place. Did she fall?

She bolted up in bed, and the room spun. But she called out for Nina. Wherever she was, Nina was always close. As her eyes adjusted, as nothing looked right, she climbed out of bed. In the dim light from a scatter of stars, a slice of a moon, she made out a door and rushed to it.

It wouldn't open, so she banged on it, crying now as she called for Nina.

"Nina! I can't get out. I feel sick. Nina. Daddy, please. Mom, let me out, let me out."

Thinking it might come in handy later, they recorded her pleading cries.

The door opened so fast it smacked against Cate, knocked her down. The light outside the door burned into the room, illuminated the face of a scary clown with sharp teeth.

When she screamed, he laughed.

"Nobody can hear you, stupid, so shut the hell up or I'll break off your arm and eat it."

"Chill, Pennywise."

A werewolf came in. He carried a tray, walked right by her as she scrambled back on her heels and elbows. He set it on the bed.

"You got soup, you got milk. You eat it, you drink it, otherwise my pal here will hold you down while I pour it down your throat."

"I want my daddy!"

"Aww," the one called Pennywise made a mean laugh. "She wants her daddy. Too bad because I already cut your daddy into pieces and fed him to the pigs."

"Knock it off," the wolfman said. "Here's the deal, brat. You eat what we give you when we give it to you. You use that bathroom over there. You don't give us trouble, you don't make a mess, and you'll be back with your daddy in a couple days. Otherwise, we're going to hurt you, real bad."

Fear and fury rose together. "You're not a real werewolf because that's made-up. That's a mask."

"Think you're smart?"

"Yes!"

"How about this?" Pennywise reached behind him, pulled a gun out of his waistband. "Does this look real, you little bitch? You want to test it?"

Wolfman snarled at Pennywise. "Now you chill. And you—"

He added a second snarl for Cate. "Little smart-ass. Eat that soup, all of it. Same with the milk. Or when I come back, I'll start breaking your fingers. Do what you're told, you go back to being a princess in a couple days."

Leaning down, Pennywise grabbed her hair with one hand, yanked her head back, and pressed the gun to her throat.

"Back off, you fucking clown." Wolfman grabbed his shoulder, but Pennywise shook it off.

"She needs a lesson first. You want to find out what happens when little rich bitches back-talk? Say, 'No, sir.' Say it!"

"No, sir."

"Eat your fucking dinner."

He stormed out as she sat on the floor, shaking, sobbing.

"Just eat the soup, for Christ's sake," Wolfman muttered. "And be quiet."

He went out, locked the door.

Because the floor was cold, she crawled back onto the bed. She didn't have a blanket, and couldn't stop shaking. Maybe she was a little hungry, but she didn't want the soup.

But she didn't want the man in the clown mask to break her fingers or shoot her. She just wanted Nina to come and sing to her, or Daddy to tell her a story, or her mom to show her all the pretty clothes she bought that day.

They were looking for her. Everybody. And when they found her, they'd put the men in the masks in jail forever.

Comforted by that, she spooned up some soup. It didn't smell good, and the little bit she swallowed tasted wrong. Just wrong.

She couldn't eat it. Why did they care if she ate it?

Frowning, she sniffed at it again, sniffed at the glass of milk.

Maybe they put poison in it. She trembled over that, rubbed her arms to warm them, to soothe herself. Poison didn't make sense. But it didn't taste right. She'd seen lots and lots of movies. Bad guys put stuff in food sometimes. Just because she was kidnapped, she wasn't stupid. She knew that much. And they didn't tie her up, just locked her in.

She started to run to the window, then thought: Quiet, quiet. She eased out of bed, padded to the window. She could see trees and dark, the shadow of hills. No houses, no lights.

Glancing behind her, heart thumping, she tried to open the window. She tried to unlock it, felt the nails.

Panic wanted to come, but she closed her eyes, just breathed and breathed. Her mom liked to do yoga and sometimes let her do it, too. Breathe and breathe.

They thought she was stupid. Just a stupid kid, but she wasn't stupid. She wasn't going to eat the soup or drink the milk that they'd put drugs in. Probably.

Instead, she took the bowl and the glass, picked her way carefully toward the bathroom. She dumped it in the toilet first, then peed because she really had to.

Then she flushed it all away.

When they came back, she'd pretend to be asleep. Deep, deep asleep. She knew how. She was an actress, wasn't she? And *not* stupid, so she slipped the spoon under the pillow.

She didn't know what time it was, or how long she'd slept before. Because he'd—one of them—had stuck her with a needle. But she'd wait, just wait, until they came to take the tray away. And she'd pray they wouldn't notice the spoon wasn't there.

She tried not to cry anymore. It was hard, but she needed to think about what she had to do. Nobody could really think when they were crying, so she wouldn't.

It took forever, it took so long she nearly did fall asleep. Then she heard the locks click, and the door open.

Breathe slow, steady. Don't squeeze your eyes, don't jump if he touches you. She'd pretended to sleep before—and even fooled Nina—when she wanted to sneak and stay up and read.

Music played, and nearly made her jump. The man—the wolf because she knew his voice now and recognized it from when he helped boost her up the tree—said a bad word. But he answered in a different kind of way.

He said:

"Hi, lover. You're calling from the idiot nanny's phone, right? So if the cops ever check it, she'll get blamed? Good, good. What's the word? Yeah, yeah, she's fine. I'm looking at her right now. Sleeping like a baby."

He gave Cate a sharp poke in the ribs as he listened, and she lay still. "That's my girl. Keep it up. Don't let me down. I'll go make the next call in about thirty. You know I do, lover. Just a couple more days, and we're home free. Counting the hours."

She heard something rustle, didn't move, then heard him walking away.

"Morons," he muttered with a kind of laugh in his voice. "People are fucking morons. And women are the biggest morons of all."

The door shut, the locks clicked.

She didn't move. Just waited, waited, counting in her head to a hundred, then another hundred until she risked letting her eyes slit open.

She didn't see him or hear him, but kept breathing her sleeping breaths.

Slowly, she sat up, took the spoon from under the pillow. As quietly as she could, she crept to the window. She and her grandpa had built a birdhouse once. She knew about nails, and how you could hammer them in. Or pry them out.

She used the spoon, but her hands were slippery with sweat. She nearly dropped it, nearly started to cry again. She wiped her hands and the spoon on her jeans, tried again. At first it wouldn't move, not even a little. Then she thought it did, and tried harder.

She thought she had it, nearly had it, when she heard voices outside. Terrified, she dropped down to the floor, her breath coming out in pants she couldn't stop.

A car started. She heard wheels on gravel. Heard a door slam. The house door. One in the house, one going somewhere. She eased her head up, watched the taillights weave away.

Maybe she should wait until they were both in the house again, but she was too afraid and, teeth gritted, went after the nail again.

It popped out, flew up, then hit the floor with a *click* that sounded to her ears like an explosion. She jumped back on the bed, fought to lie still, to breathe deep, but she couldn't stop shaking.

No one came, and tears of relief spilled out.

Her hands had gone sweaty again, but she set to work prying out the second nail. She put it in her pocket, wiped her sweaty, hurting fingers. She managed to turn the lock on the window. As she opened it a crack, it sounded so loud. But no one came, not even when she opened it more, opened it enough to stick her head out and feel the cool night air.

Too high, too high to jump.

She listened, listened, for sounds of the ocean, of cars, of people, but heard nothing but the breeze, the call of a coyote, the call of an owl.

No trees close enough to reach, no ledge or trellis or anything to help her climb down. But she had to climb down, then run. She had to get away and get help.

She started with the sheets. At first she tried to tear them, but they wouldn't tear. So she tied them together as tight as she could, then added the pillowcases.

The only thing to tie them to in the room was one of the bedposts. It would be like Rapunzel, she thought, except sheets instead of hair. She'd climb out of the tower.

Nerves made her need to pee again, but she held it, set her jaw as she worked to tie the knot around the post.

Then she heard the car coming back, felt the knots in her stomach pull tighter than any she could tie with sheets. If one of them checked on her now, they'd see. She should have waited.

Trapped, she could do nothing but sit on the floor, imagining the door opening. The masks. The gun. Her fingers breaking.

Rolling herself into a ball, she squeezed her eyes shut.

She heard the voices again, carrying through the window. If they looked up, would they see she'd opened it?

One said—the wolf voice: "Jesus, asshole, you think this is the time to get high?"

The clown laughed. "Damn straight. They getting the money?"

"Smooth as silk, especially once they heard the recording," the wolf responded, and the voices trailed off. The door slammed.

Too scared to worry about quiet, she dragged the makeshift rope to the window, tossed it out. Too short, she could see that right away, and thought of the towels in the bathroom.

But they might come in, any minute, so she wiggled out the window, gripped the sheets. Her hands slid helplessly a few inches, and she had to bite back a scream. But she gripped hard, slowed the slide.

She saw light—windows below her. If they looked out, saw the sheets, saw her, they'd catch her. Maybe just shoot her. She didn't want to die.

"Please, please, please."

Instinct had her wrapping her legs around the sheet, easing herself down until she reached the end. She could see right into the house, a big kitchen—stainless steel, counters like dark brown stone, green walls, not bright but light.

She closed her eyes, let go, let herself fall.

It hurt. She had to hold back another cry when she hit the ground. Her ankle turned, her elbow banged, but she didn't stop.

She ran toward the trees, believing with all her heart they wouldn't find her if she got to the trees.

When she did, she kept running.

Aidan slipped into the bedroom he shared with Charlotte. Exhausted, sick down to his soul, he walked to the windows. His Catey was out there, somewhere. Frightened, alone. Dear God, don't let them hurt her.

"I'm not asleep," Charlotte murmured, and shifted to sit up. "I only took half a pill, just to calm down. I'm so sorry, Aidan. Being hysterical didn't help anyone. It doesn't help our baby. But I'm so scared."

He walked to the bed, sat, took her hand. "He called again."

She sucked in a breath, gripped hard. "Caitlyn."

He wouldn't tell her he'd demanded to speak to her daughter, to be certain she was all right. He wouldn't tell her he'd heard his child scream and sob she wanted her daddy.

"They have no reason to hurt her, every reason not to." Ten million reasons, he thought.

"What did they say? Are they going to let her go? Are we getting the money?"

"He wants the money by midnight tomorrow. He won't say where yet. He'll call again. Dad and Nan are arranging it. He says when he gets the money, he'll tell us where we'll find Cate."

"We're getting her back, Aidan." She wrapped around him, rocked. "And then we're never letting her go again. When she's safe, with us again, home again, we're never coming back to this house."

"Charlotte—"

"No! We're never coming back to this house where this could happen. I want Nina fired. I want her gone." She pulled back, eyes filled with tears and fury. "I've been lying here, sick, scared, picturing my daughter trapped somewhere, crying for me. Nina? At best she was negligent, but at worst? She could be part of this, Hugh."

"Oh, Charlotte, Nina loves Cate. Listen now, listen. We think it must be one of the catering or event staff, or someone who got through posing as one of them. They had to have a car or truck or van to get her away. They had to have it planned out."

Tears sheened over the arctic blue of Charlotte's eyes, spilled down her pale cheeks. "It could've been someone in the family, a friend. She'd have gone with someone she knew."

"I can't believe that."

"I don't care about that." Charlotte brushed it away. "I only want her back. I don't care about anything else."

"It's important we find out who and how. If we contacted the police—"

"No. No. No! Is the money more important to you than Caitlyn, than our baby?"

He'd forgive her for that, he told himself. She looked ravaged, looked ill, so he'd forgive her for that eventually.

"You know better. I don't give a damn how upset you are, don't you say such a thing to me."

"Then stop talking to me about police when calling them could get her killed! I want my baby home, I want her safe. She's not safe here. She's not safe with Nina."

Heading toward hysterical again—he recognized the signs. He couldn't find it in him to blame her.

"All right, Charlotte, we'll talk about all this later."

"You're right. I know you're right, but I'm terrified, Hugh. I'm letting myself get wound up again because I can't stand thinking about our baby, alone and afraid. Oh God, Aidan." She dropped her head on his shoulder. "Where is our baby?"

CHAPTER THREE

Running, until she couldn't run any more, until she had to sit on the ground, shivering, shaking. She'd tripped a couple of times when the trees blocked out the moonlight and now her hands bled a little, and she'd torn her jeans. Her knee hurt, and her ankle, her elbow, but she couldn't stop too long.

She couldn't see the lights anymore from wherever she'd been, and that was good. How could they find her when they couldn't see her?

The bad? She didn't know where she was. It was so dark, and she was so cold.

She heard coyotes off and on, and other things that rustled. She tried not to think about bears or wildcats. She didn't think she was high enough in the hills for that—Grandpa told her they lived higher, and stayed away from people—but she didn't know.

She'd never been in the woods, alone in the dark before.

All she knew, for certain, was that she had to keep going in the same direction. Away. But she wasn't even sure of that because at first she'd been so scared she hadn't paid attention.

Instead of running, now she walked. She could hear better when her own breath wasn't whistling in her ears. She could hear if someone— or something—came after her.

Tired, so tired, she wanted to curl up and sleep. But something might eat her if she did. Or worse, she thought, worse, she might wake up back in that room.

Where they'd break her fingers and shoot her.

Her stomach hurt from hunger, and her throat clicked from thirst. When her teeth chattered, she didn't know if it was from fear or cold.

Maybe she could sleep, just for a little while. She could climb a tree, sleep in the branches. It was so hard to think when she was so tired, so cold.

She stopped, leaned against a tree, laid her cheek on the bark. If she climbed a tree, slept, maybe when the sun came up, she could see where she was. She knew the sun came up in the east, knew the ocean was west. So if she saw the ocean, she'd know . . .

What? She still wouldn't know where she was because she didn't know where she'd been.

And they could find her when the sun came up.

She trudged on, head drooping with fatigue, feet shuffling as she just couldn't lift them anymore.

Half dreaming, she walked. And smiled a little at a sound. Then shook herself awake, listened.

Was that the ocean? She thought, maybe . . . And something else.

She rubbed her tired eyes, stared ahead. A light. She saw a light. She kept her eyes on it, walked on.

The ocean, she thought again, getting louder, closer. What if she missed a step and fell over a cliff? But the light, it was closer, too.

The trees opened up. She saw a field in the moonlight. Wide and grassy. And . . . cows. The light, well beyond the edge of the woods, the edge of the field, came from a house.

She nearly walked into the barbed wire that kept the cows inside.

She cut herself a little getting through it, ripped her new sweater. She remembered from making the movie in Ireland that cows grew a lot bigger for real than they looked in books or from a distance.

She stepped in cow poop, and said "Gak," with a ten-year-old girl's disgust. From there, after swiping her sneaker on the grass, she tried to watch her step.

A house, she saw now, that faced the ocean, with decks up and down, with a light through the lower windows. Barns and stuff that meant ranch.

She navigated the barbed wire again—more successfully.

She saw a truck, a car, smelled manure and animals.

After stumbling again, she started to run toward the house. Some-one to help, someone who'd take her home. Then stopped herself.

They could be bad people, too. How could she know? Maybe they were even friends with the people who locked her in the room. She needed to be careful.

It had to be late, so they'd be asleep. She only had to get inside, find a phone, and call nine-one-one. Then she could hide until the police came.

She crept toward the house, onto the wide porch in front. Though she expected to find it locked, she tried the front door, nearly dropped with relief when the knob turned.

She eased inside.

The lamp in the window burned low, but it burned. She could see a big room, furniture, a big fireplace, stairs leading up.

She didn't see a phone, so she walked back toward a kitchen with green things growing in red pots on a wide windowsill, a table with four chairs, and a bowl of fruit.

She grabbed an apple, shining green, bit in. As it crunched be-tween her teeth, as juice hit her tongue, her throat, she knew she'd never tasted anything so good. She saw the handset on the counter beside a toaster.

Then she heard footsteps.

Because the kitchen offered no place to hide, she rushed into the dining room open to it. Clutching the apple, more juice dribbling down her hand, she squeezed herself into a dark corner beside a bulky buffet.

When the kitchen lights flashed on, she tried to make herself smaller.

She caught a glimpse of him as he walked straight to the refrigera-tor. A boy, not a man, though he looked older than she, taller. He had a shaggy mop of dark blond hair, and wore only boxers.

If she hadn't been so terrified, the sight of a mostly naked boy who wasn't a cousin would have mortified and fascinated her.

He was pretty skinny, she noted, as he grabbed a drumstick out of the fridge, gnawed it while dragging out a jug—not like a store carton—of milk.

He chugged milk right from the jug, set it on the counter. He sang to himself, or hummed, or made *ba-da-ba-dum!* noises while he pulled a cloth off what looked like some kind of pie.

That's when he turned, still ba-da-daing, pulled open a drawer. And saw her.

"Whoa!" When shock had him jolting back, she had an instant to run. But before she gathered herself, he tipped his head to the side. "Hey. You lost or something?"

He took a few steps toward her; she cringed back.

In what would seem like a thousand years later, she would think back and remember exactly what he said, how he said it, how he looked.

He smiled at her, spoke easily, like they'd met in some park or ice-cream shop. "It's okay. You're okay. Nobody's going to hurt you. Hey, are you hungry? My gram makes totally excellent fried chicken. We got leftovers." He wagged the drumstick he still held to prove it.

"I'm Dillon. Dillon Cooper. This is our ranch. Me and Gram and Mom."

He took another couple of steps as he spoke, then crouched down. When he did, his eyes changed. Green eyes, she could see now, but softer, quieter than Grandda's.

"You're bleeding. How'd you get hurt?"

She started to shake again, but she wasn't afraid of him. Maybe she trembled because she wasn't afraid of him. "I fell down, and then there were sharp things where the cows are."

"We can fix you up, okay? You should come sit down in the kitchen. We have stuff to fix you up. What's your name? I'm Dillon, remember?"

"Caitlyn. Cate—with a *C*."

"You should come sit in the kitchen, Cate, and we can fix you up. I need to get my mom. She's cool," he said quickly. "Seriously."

"I need to call nine-one-one. I need the phone to call nine-one-one, so I came inside. The door wasn't locked."

"Okay, just let me get my mom first. Man, she'd freak if the cops came when she was asleep. It would scare her."

Her jaw wobbled. "Can I call my daddy, too?"

"Sure, sure. How about you come sit down first? Maybe finish your apple, let me get Mom."

"There were bad guys," she whispered, and his eyes widened.

"No shit? Don't tell Mom I said 'shit.'" When he reached out a hand, she took it. "Where are they?"

"I don't know."

"Man, don't cry. It's going to be okay now. You just sit down, let me get Mom. Don't run off, okay? Because we'll help you. I promise."

Believing him, she lowered her head, nodded.

Dillon wanted his mom more than anything and anyone, and ran for the back stairs. Finding a kid hiding in the house during a fridge raid was cool—or would've been if she hadn't had cuts and bruises. And looked scared enough to pee her pants.

Then it turned cool again because she wanted the cops, and the bad guys, more cool. Except she was just a kid, and somebody hurt her.

He dashed into his mother's room without knocking, shook her shoulder. "Mom, Mom, wake up."

"Oh God, Dillon, what?"

She might've brushed him off, rolled over, but he shook her again. "You gotta get up. There's a kid downstairs, a girl kid, and she's hurt. She said she wants to call the cops because of bad guys."

Julia Cooper opened one bleary eye. "Dillon, you're dreaming again."

"Nuh-uh. Swear to God. I have to get back down to the kitchen because she's scared, and she'll maybe run. You have to come. She's bleeding a little."

Now fully awake, Julia shot up in bed, shoved her long blond hair back from her face. "Bleeding?"

"Hurry, okay? Jeez, I have to get some pants."

He bolted into his room, grabbed the jeans and sweatshirt he'd tossed on the floor—even though he wasn't supposed to. On the run, he stuck a leg inside of his jeans, hopped along, shot in the other. His bare feet slapped the wood stairs as he dragged on the shirt.

She still sat at the table, which had him letting out a whoosh of relief. "Mom's coming. I'm going to get the first-aid kit out of the pantry. Then she'll know what to do. You can eat that drumstick if you want." He gestured to the one he'd dropped on the table. "I only had one bite."

But she hunched her shoulders together as someone came down the stairs.

"It's just Mom."

"Dillon James Cooper, I swear if you . . ." She stopped when she saw the girl, and the sleepy irritation dropped away from her face. Like her son, Julia knew how to approach the hurt and frightened.

"I'm Julia, honey, Dillon's mom. I need to take a look at you. Dillon, get the first aid kit."

"I am already," he muttered, and took it from a shelf in the big pantry.

"Now a clean cloth and a bowl of warm water. And a blanket. Light the fire in the kitchen hearth."

He rolled his eyes behind her back, but obeyed.

"What's your name, sweetie?"

"Caitlyn."

"Caitlyn, that's pretty. I'm going to clean this cut on your arm first. I don't think it needs stitches." She smiled as she spoke.

Her eyes had a lot of gold in them, but there was green, too, like the boy's. Like Dillon's, Cate remembered.

"While I'm fixing you up, why don't you tell me what happened. Dillon, pour Caitlyn a glass of that milk before you put it away."

"I don't want milk. They tried to give me milk but it was wrong. I don't want milk."

"All right. How about—"

She broke off as Cate jolted. And Maggie Hudson came down the stairs. Maggie took one look at Cate, tipped her head. "I wondered what all this noise was. Looks like we've got company."

She had blond hair, too, but lighter than Dillon's and his mom's. Blue streaked through it on its way to her shoulders.

She wore a T-shirt with a picture of a woman with lots and lots of curly hair that said JANIS under it and a pair of flowered pajama pants.

"This is my mom," Julia told her as she cleaned the slices on Cate's arm. "Put the blanket over Caitlyn's shoulders, Dillon. She's cold."

"Let's get a fire going in here, too."

"I'm working on it, Gram." The aggrieved boy came through, but she only gave his hair a stroke as she stepped toward the table. "I'm Maggie Hudson, but you can call me Gram. You look like a girl in need of hot chocolate. I've got my own secret recipe."

She reached in a cupboard, took out a package of Swiss Miss, then sent Cate a wink.

"This is Caitlyn, Mom. She was about to tell us what happened. Can you do that, Caitlyn?"

"We were playing hide-and-seek after the life celebration for my great-grandda, and I went to the tree beside the garage to climb it and hide, and there was a man and he stuck me with something and I woke up somewhere else."

The words tumbled out as Maggie put a big mug in the microwave, as Julia dabbed ointment on the cuts, as Dillon, crouched down to light the kitchen fire, goggled.

"They had masks like a mean clown and a werewolf, and said they'd break my fingers if I didn't do what they said. And the clown one had a gun, and he said he'd shoot me. But I didn't eat the soup or drink the milk because it tasted funny. They put drugs to make you sleep in things, bad guys do that, so I poured it down the toilet and pretended to sleep."

"Holy crap!"

Julia merely shot Dillon a look to shut him up.

"That was smart. Honey, did they hurt you?"

"They knocked me down when they opened the door hard, and the bad clown pulled my hair really, really hard. But then they thought I was asleep, and one of them—it was the wolfman—came in and talked on the phone. I kept pretending and fooled him. I kept the spoon from the soup, and I used it to get the nails out of the window lock. One of them drove away. I could hear them talking outside, and he drove away, and that's when I got the window open enough to get out, but it was too high to jump."

The microwave went off, but Caitlyn kept looking right into Julia's eyes. It seemed safe there in the gold and the green. In the kindness.

"I tied the sheets together. I couldn't tear them, but I tied them, and then the one came back, and I was scared because if he came in, he'd see and he'd break my fingers."

"No one's going to hurt you now, baby girl." Maggie set the hot chocolate on the table.

"I had to climb down, and my hands kept slipping, and there were lights on downstairs, and the sheets weren't long enough so I had to jump. I hurt my ankle a little, but I ran. There were trees, a lot of trees, so I ran there and ran, and fell and hurt my knee, but I ran. I didn't know where I was."

Tears rolled now, tears Julia gently wiped away.

"Then I heard the ocean, a little, then more. And I saw the light. You had the light on, and I followed the light, and saw the cows, and the house, and the light. But I was afraid you were bad guys, too, so I snuck in. I wanted to call nine-one-one. I stole an apple because I was hungry, and Dillon came downstairs and found me."

"That's one hell of a story." Maggie put an arm around Dillon. "You're the bravest girl I've ever met."

"If the bad guys find me here, they'll shoot me, and everybody."

"They're not going to come here." Julia brushed Cate's hair back from her face. "Do you know the house where you played hide-and-seek?"

"My great-grandda's house. He named it Sullivan's Rest."

"Sweet girl." Maggie sat down. "Are you Liam Sullivan's great-granddaughter?"

"Yes, ma'am. He died, and we had a celebration of his life. Did you know him?"

"I didn't, but I admired him, his work, and his life."

"You drink your hot chocolate, Caitlyn." Smiling, Julia brushed back Cate's disordered hair. "I'm going to call nine-one-one for you."

"Can you call my daddy, too? Can you tell him how to find me?"

"Absolutely. Do you know the number? If not, I can—"

"I know it." Cate rattled it off.

"Good girl. Mom, I bet Caitlyn could use a snack."

"I bet she could. Dil, you sit down with Caitlyn, keep her company while I scramble up some eggs. Nothing like scrambled eggs in the middle of the night."

He did. He would have just because she was a guest, and that's what you did. But he did it more because he found her seriously awesome.

"You made a sheet rope and climbed out of a window."

"I had to."

"Not everybody could. That is awesome. I mean, you were like kidnapped, and you outsmarted them."

"They thought I was stupid. I could tell."

Since she didn't seem to want it, Dillon picked up the drumstick, took another bite. "You're really not. Was it like a house?"

"I think. I was in the back, I think, and all I could really see were trees and the hills. They kept the room dark. I saw the kitchen when I climbed down. It wasn't as nice as this one, but it was nice. It's just . . . I couldn't tell where I was, and I got all turned around in the trees, so I don't know. And I don't know how long I slept from what he had in the needle."

She sounded scared still, but more tired. To give her a boost, he wagged the drumstick. "I bet the cops'll find the house and the bad guys. We're friends with the sheriff, and he's pretty smart. Maybe the bad guys don't even know you escaped."

"Maybe. He said, on the phone to somebody . . ." She frowned, tried to remember. Then Julia came over with the phone.

"Caitlyn, somebody wants to talk to you."

"Is it Daddy?" Cate grabbed the phone. "Daddy!" The tears came again, spilling down her cheeks as Julia stroked her hair. "I'm all right. I got away. I ran and I'm with Julia and Gram and Dillon. Will you come? Do you know where to find me?"

Julia leaned down, kissed the top of Cate's head. "I'm going to tell him exactly."

"Gram's making scrambled eggs. I'm so hungry. I love you, too, Daddy."

She handed the phone back to Julia, swiped at her tears. "He cried. I never heard him cry before."

"Joyful tears." Gram put a plate with eggs and toast in front of Cate. "Because his little girl's safe."

The little girl plowed into the eggs while Gram plated up the rest.

She ate all the eggs, the toast, and had just started on the pie Julia put in front of her when someone knocked on the door.

"The bad guys—"

"Wouldn't knock," Julia assured her. "Don't you worry."

Still Cate's chest hurt as if someone pressed on it when Julia walked to the front door. When Dillon took her hand, she squeezed it hard. And held her breath even though it made her chest hurt more when Julia opened the door.

Then everything fell away, everything, when she heard her father's voice. "Daddy!"

She leaped out of the chair, ran out of the kitchen, ran to him as she'd run toward the trees. He caught her, swung her up, held her tight, tight, tight. She felt him shaking, felt his scratchy whiskers on her face. Felt his tears blur with her own.

Other arms went around her, folded her in—warm and safe.

Grandpa.

"Cate. Catey. Oh, my baby." Aidan drew her back, and his eyes filled with more tears as he looked at her face. "He hurt you."

"I fell, because it was dark. I ran away."

"You're safe now. You're safe."

As Aidan stood, swaying with her, Hugh turned to Julia, gripped her hands. "There aren't words to thank you." He looked beyond her to where Maggie and Dillon stood watching. "All of you."

"You don't need them. You have a smart, brave girl here."

"Dillon found me, and his mom fixed my cuts, and Gram made me eggs."

"Ms. Cooper." Aidan tried to speak, simply couldn't get words out.

"Julia. I put on coffee. The sheriff's on his way. I felt it best to call him, though I realize you probably want to take Caitlyn home and deal with that there."

"I'd love some coffee. I just want to call my wife, let her and the others know we have our girl." Hugh stroked a hand down Cate's hair. "If it's not imposing, I think talking to the sheriff here and now would be best."

"There's a phone in the kitchen." Maggie stepped forward. "We don't get decent cell service here. Maggie Hudson," she added and offered a hand.

Ignoring the hand, Hugh embraced her.

"Well, this has been a day, and the sun's not up. We meet the bravest girl in California, and I get a hug from Hugh Sullivan. Come on back, Hugh."

"Cate's mother finally took a sleeping pill not long before you called," Aidan explained. "She's going to be so happy, Cate, when she wakes up and sees you. We were so scared, so worried." He lifted her bandaged arm, kissed it.

"Why don't you and Cate sit down, catch your breath. I'll go help with the coffee. How about some more hot chocolate, Cate?"

Still cuddled close to her father, she nodded. "Yes, please."

But even as she said it, headlights swept across the front windows. "That should be the sheriff. He's a nice man," she told Cate.

"Will he go after the bad men?"

"I bet he will." Julia walked to the door, opened it, stepped out on the porch. "Sheriff."

"Julia."

Red Buckman looked more like a surfer than a cop. He may have cruised past forty to inch his way toward fifty, but when time allowed, he still grabbed his board and hit the waves. His hair, a short, sun-bleached braid, fell just over the collar of his jacket. His face, tanned and lined from his hours on the beach, on the water, often held a deceptive "whatever" expression.

Julia knew him to be smart, sharp, and dedicated. Just as she knew he and her mother had an easygoing friends-with-benefits relationship.

"I don't think you've met Deputy Wilson. Michaela, this is Julia Cooper."

"Ma'am."

Beside Red, the dark-skinned beauty with the honey-glazed eyes looked all spit and polish in her khaki uniform. Barely old enough to drink, Julia thought, and standing like a soldier in her high-shine shoes.

"Caitlyn's in the living room with her father. Her grandfather's here, too."

"Let me ask you first. Are you sure the kid didn't just run off from home?"

"There's no question of that, Red. You'll see for yourself when you talk to her. She's settled down, but that child was terrified, and she'd damn well been terrorized. She wanted to call nine-one-one and her father."

"Okay then. Let's get to it."

He went inside, his deputy a half step behind him.

From Aidan's lap, Cate gave him an unblinking once-over. "Are you really the sheriff?"

"That's right." He pulled a badge out of his pocket, showed her. "It says so right here. Red Buckman," he said to Aidan. "You're Caitlyn's dad?"

"Yes, Aidan Sullivan."

"And you're okay with us talking to her?"

"Yes. You're okay to talk to Sheriff Buckman, aren't you, Cate?"

"I was going to call nine-one-one, but Dillon found me before I could. So Julia did."

"That was the right thing. Take a seat, Mic," he told the deputy—who shot him a look at the "Mic" but complied. Red sat on the coffee table so he'd be face-to-face with Cate. "How about you tell me what happened, right from the start?"

"We had lots of people at Sullivan's Rest because my great-grandda died."

"I heard that. I'm sorry about your great-grandda. Did you know the people who were there?"

"Mostly. After people got up to talk about him, to tell stories and everything, I got to change into play clothes, and play outside with my cousins and the kids. And after a while, we were going to play hide-and-seek. Boyd was It, and I had my hiding place picked out."

She frowned at that, just an instant, then told her story.

Red didn't interrupt, only stood a moment when Maggie came in with Hugh Sullivan. He took his coffee, nodded at Cate. "You keep going, honey."

He saw Aidan's stricken face when she spoke of the threats—broken fingers, the gun—watched the father of the child battle tears.

In her chair, Michaela took meticulous notes, and watched everyone.

"Then I saw the light. I heard the ocean first," she corrected, then told the rest.

"You must've been really scared."

"Everything kept shaking, even inside. I had to make it stop when I pretended to sleep or he'd know."

"How'd you think to use the sheets to make a rope?"

"I saw it in a movie. I thought it would be easier, but I couldn't tear them, so they were big and thick to tie."

"You never saw their faces."

"I saw the one by the tree for a second. He had a beard and he had blond hair."

"Would you know if you saw him again?"

"I don't know." She cringed back against her father. "Do I have to?"

"We won't worry about that. How about names? Did they ever say a name?"

"I don't think so. Wait— On the phone, when I pretended to be asleep, he called the person he talked to 'lover.' That's not really a name, I guess."

"Do you know about how long it took for you to get here from when you climbed out of the window?"

She shook her head. "It seemed like forever. It was dark, and it was cold, and everything hurt. I was afraid they'd find me, or maybe a bear would come and eat me." She laid her head back against Aidan. "I just wanted to go home."

"I bet you did. How about if I talk to your dad and grandpa for a bit. Maybe Dil can show you his room."

"I want to hear. It happened to me. I want to hear."

"She's right." When she crawled from Aidan's lap to his, Hugh stroked her. "It happened to her."

"All right then. We're going to need a list of everyone at the house. Guests, staff, outside vendors."

"You'll have it."

"When we've got that, we're going to go over when people left, how they left. For right this minute, tell me when you first noticed Cate was missing."

"It was Nina, her nanny."

"Full name?"

"Nina Torez. She's been with us for six years—nearly seven," he corrected. "When Catey didn't come in with the other kids, Nina went to look for her. When she couldn't find her, she came to us. Everyone looked. I think it was after six, maybe close to seven, I think, when Nina came in, worried."

"Just before seven," Hugh put in. "We spread out in groups, to look through the house, the outbuildings, outside. Nina had found Cate's hair clip over by the garage."

"I lost my barrettes."

"We'll get you new ones," Hugh promised.

"We were about to call the police," Aidan continued, "when the phone rang."

"Which phone?"

"The house phone."

"What time?"

"About eight. Yes, close to eight. It was a man's voice. He said he had Cate, and if we called the police, the FBI, if we told anyone, he'd . . . hurt her. He said it would cost ten million, cash, to get her back, unharmed, and he'd call with further instructions."

"Some of us still wanted to call the police." Hugh continued to stroke, then turned Cate's face to his. "We were so afraid for you. But my daughter-in-law was near hysterics by then, and she was adamantly against it. We decided to wait—the hardest thing I've ever done. To arrange for the money, and wait." He kissed the top of Cate's head. "And pray."

"The second call came in about ten-thirty. He said we had until midnight tomorrow—that would be tonight now. He'd contact us again to say where to bring the money, then he'd tell us where to find Cate."

"Aidan and I talked, and we agreed to demand we speak to Cate, to be sure . . ."

"She screamed. She called for me." Aidan dropped his head in his hands.

"Cate, you said one of the men drove away for a little while?"

"He did. They went outside. I heard them through the window. I saw the taillights."

"Do you know how long he was gone?"

"I don't know, but when he left I got the nails out of the window and started to make the sheets. And he came back before I could get out."

"But you got out right after."

"I was afraid they'd come back to the room and see I had the window open, and the sheets. So I climbed out."

"You're a smart kid. Hey, Dillon, what time did you come down and find Cate?"

"I don't know exactly. I just woke up hungry, and thought about the fried chicken."

"I can tell you Dillon woke me up right before one."

"All right then." He had the timeline in his head, got to his feet. "I'm going to let you take this girl home. We're going to need to talk to the nanny, and the others still at the house. I'd like to do that this morning."

"Whenever you want."

"Let's say around eight? Give you all time to settle in, get a little sleep." He looked back at Cate. He had brown eyes, and put a smile in them for her. "I might need to talk to you again sometime, Cate. That okay with you?"

"Yes. Will you catch them?"

"That's the plan. Meanwhile, you do some thinking, and if you think of anything—any little thing—you let me know." He pulled a card out of his pocket. "That's me, and the number at my office, and the number at home. Got my email, too. You keep that."

After giving her leg a pat, Red got up, eased around the table. "We'll be there around eight. We're going to need to look around the place, especially where Cate saw the man who took her. And we'll need to talk to everyone in the household. Get that list of guests and staff and so on."

"We'll have it ready." Hugh passed Cate back to her father, got to his feet to shake Red's hand. Then he walked to Dillon, did the same. "Thank you for doing everything right."

"Oh, that's okay."

"It's more than okay. Thank you all. I'd like to come back again in a day or two."

"Anytime," Julia told him.

"We're just going to give you a police escort home." Red winked at Cate. "No sirens, but how about we run the lights?"

She grinned at that. "Okay."

Outside, Red got behind the wheel, waited for Michaela to get in beside him. Hit the lights.

He headed down the ranch road behind the fancy sedan. "We've got us an inside job, Mic."

"Michaela," she muttered, then blew out a breath. "Yes, sir, we sure do."

CHAPTER FOUR

Snuggled in her father's arms, Cate fell asleep before they reached the end of the ranch road.

"She's exhausted," Aidan murmured. "I want to have a doctor look her over, but . . ."

"She can sleep first. I can get Ben to come to the house. He'd do it for us."

"I was afraid . . . I know she's only ten, but I was afraid he—they—might—"

Reaching over, Hugh squeezed his arm. "So was I. But that didn't happen, they didn't touch her that way. She's safe now."

"She was close all the time. Just a few miles away. God, Dad, she was so brave, so damn clever and brave. She saved herself, that's what she did. My fearless little girl saved herself. And now I'm afraid to let her out of my sight."

Hugh slowed when they approached the gates securing the peninsula, waited until they opened for him. "They had to have a way in and out. They couldn't have done it without the security code, or clearance. All the people coming and going today of all days."

Lights bloomed along the road winding up, winding away from the sea toward the multileveled house on the rise.

A house, Hugh thought, his parents had built as a sanctuary for themselves, their family. Today, on the day they'd honored his father, someone had invaded that sanctuary, despoiled it, and stolen his grandchild.

The sanctuary would be his now, and he would do whatever he could do to make certain no one ever marred it again.

"Let me get your door," Hugh began as he pulled up, but family already streamed out of the house. While his wife, his sister, his brother-in-law rushed to the car, Hugh walked to where his mother stood, at the entrance portico.

She looked so frail, so tired.

He caught her face in his hands, used his thumbs to brush away tears. "She's safe, Ma. She's sleeping."

"Where—"

"I'll tell you inside. Let's go inside, and let Aidan get her upstairs to bed. Our girl's had a hell of a time, but she's safe, Ma, and she's not hurt. Some scrapes and bruises, nothing more."

"My legs are shaking. It's always after my legs start shaking. Give me a hand."

He helped her inside, into her favorite winter chair by the fire, with the view of the sea beyond the wide window.

When Aidan carried her in, Cate's head on his shoulder, her body loose in that rag-doll way of a sleeping child, Rosemary pressed a hand to her lips.

"I want to put her to bed," Aidan said quietly. "I need to stay with her in case she wakes up. I don't want her to be alone when she wakes up."

"I'll bring up some tea, some food," Maureen told him. "I'll look in on Charlotte to make sure she's still asleep. If she's awake, I'll bring her right in."

"Let me help you get her settled, Aidan. I'll turn the bed down— and I'll check on Charlotte, Mo, while you see Aidan gets some food." Lily hurried to the stairs and up ahead of Aidan.

"We'll wait until Lily and Maureen are back," Rosemary decreed. "Then I think we need to hear the story from Hugh before we try to get some sleep."

"It's a hell of a story. I just want to let everyone know the police are on it—and they'll be here to talk to us in a few hours. So yeah, we'll need to try to get some sleep."

While Aidan slipped off Cate's sneakers, Red and Michaela drove up another steep road on the hillside.

"You have to figure, if she hit the field, the fence, the cows coming out of the trees, she was likely coming from south of the Cooper place."

"Or she got turned around, circled around, even ran down from higher up."

"All possible," he agreed. "But up this road? There's a high-class, two-story cabin. Not much else for another mile south, and the Cooper place about three miles north. It's worth swinging by."

"You know the owners, who lives there?"

"When you work this area, it pays to know who's who. Just like I know the people who live there are in Hawaii right now."

Michaela shifted in her seat, looked up the snaking road. "So it's unoccupied. That would be damn handy."

"That's my thought on it. I don't see any outside lights on, and right there's a little buzz. They'd have left the security light on."

He slowed, silhouetting the cabin in the headlights.

"Looks like a light on in the back. There's a truck under that carport on the north side. Theirs?"

"One of them. They've got an SUV. Probably drove that to the airport. Keep your weapon handy, Mic."

She unsnapped the safety on her holster as they got out of either side of the car.

"Let's do a little circle around first. The kid said they had her in a room in the back, facing the hills."

"And she could see taillights when he left. The way the cabin's situated, the switchback down to Highway 1? Yeah, she could've seen taillights."

"If this is the place, they're likely long gone, but . . ."

Red paused, looked up at the white cloth rope hanging out of the window above. "Looks like this is the place. Christ on a crutch, Mic, look at what that kid pulled off."

Shaking his head, he approached the back door. "Unlocked. Let's clear it."

Weapons drawn now, they went in the door, one heading right, the other left.

She noted an open bag of Doritos—Cool Ranch—a cardboard box holding some empty beer bottles. She smelled weed in the air as she cleared a laundry room, a powder room, a kind of hobby room before she crossed with Red again in the living area.

They went upstairs, cleared the front-facing master suite with its big walk-in closet, its really big en suite. A guest room—with its own bath. A second guest room, then the last.

"Smallest of them," Red observed, "facing the back. They aren't completely stupid."

"And long gone." Michaela checked the windows. "They took off as soon as they realized she got out. One window here's still nailed shut." She pointed to the floor. "And there's the one she pried out, with the spoon. Spoon's bent and scratched. She worked at it."

Red holstered his weapon, looked out the window at the drop. "If that kid was of legal age, I'd buy her a beer. Hell, I'd buy her a god-damn keg. That's guts right there, Mic. Let's do her proud and catch these fuckers."

"I'm on board with that."

While Aidan dozed in the chair beside the bed, the sun crept through the window. And Cate tossed in her sleep, began to whimper.

He woke with a jolt, struggled through the layers of fatigue that weighed down on his mind, his body. He rose quickly, sat on the side of the bed to take Cate's hand, to stroke her hair.

"It's okay, baby, it's okay now. Daddy's right here."

Her eyes flew open, wide and blind for a moment. On a little sob she lunged into his arms.

"I had a bad dream. I had a scary bad dream."

"I'm right here."

She curled into him, sniffling, snuggling. Then went stiff as she remembered. "It wasn't a bad dream. The bad men—"

"You're safe now. Right here with me."

"I got away." On a long, long breath, her body relaxed again. "You and Grandpa came to bring me home."

"That's right." He tipped her head back, kissed her nose. It broke him a little more to see the bruise on her face, the shadows under her eyes. "I'll always come for my best girl."

After pressing her cheek to his shoulder, she frowned. "I tore my sweater. And it's dirty, too."

"It doesn't matter." To soothe both of them he ran his hand up and down her back. "I didn't want to wake you up, but since you're awake now, why don't I help you get a bath, get some clean clothes?"

"Daddy!" Genuinely horrified, she pushed back from him. "You can't help me take a bath! I'm a girl, and you're not. And I like showers now."

So normal, he thought, and found his throat clogged with tears. So completely normal. "How could I have forgotten? Tell you what, I'll go check if your mom's awake. She was so scared and worried, I finally made her take a pill to sleep. She's going to be so happy to see you."

"Look at this!" Lily, a cashmere robe over tailored pajamas, beamed from the doorway before she went in to gather Cate in a hug. "Wide awake, are you, sweets?"

"And too big for baths and my help."

Lily arched those bold red eyebrows. "I would say so. I was just coming in to spell you for a bit, Aidan. Let me and our girl deal with our girl things."

"I ruined my sweater, G-Lil."

Since Cate still wore it, Lily trailed a finger down the tear. "I call that a badge of honor. Come on, sweets, let's get you cleaned up." Again, she arched her eyebrows at Aidan, put a little exaggeration on southern lady. "You will excuse us, sir."

"I've been dismissed."

He gave Cate a big grin that fell away once he left the room. Would his little girl wake with nightmares now, and cling to him shaking from them?

How much of her childhood innocence had those bastards cost his baby? And how much deeper than the cuts and bruises did the wounds go?

He stepped into his own bedroom, found Charlotte still sleeping. He'd pulled the curtains over the windows himself so the rise of the sun wouldn't wake her, and found himself relieved she'd taken the pill, still slept.

When she woke, Cate would be showered, dressed. Here. They could celebrate that, hold that, before they talked about what to do next. A private detective if the police didn't find the kidnappers quickly? A therapist for Cate—for all of them, he corrected as he walked quietly into the bath for his own shower.

A reevaluation on security at their home, at Cate's school, whenever they traveled.

He felt sick and sorry they'd have to let Nina go. He didn't believe, not for an instant, she'd been careless, deserved blame. But Charlotte wouldn't rest easy until she was let go.

As he showered, as he let the pulse of hot water pummel the worst of his fatigue away, he considered the new project he'd signed onto.

The location shoot in Louisiana, in just two weeks.

Should he back out of the film? Should he pull Cate out of school, take her and the tutor with him?

Should he simply clean his plate, stay home, until he could feel certain Cate was safe, stable?

When in uncharted territory, he thought, take one careful step at a time.

He dressed in jeans and a sweater before he slipped back into the bedroom. No romantic long weekend in Cabo, he thought. Not now. No quick getaway without their daughter right there with them.

Charlotte would say exactly the same.

He left her sleeping, quietly closed the door behind him.

It lifted his heart to hear a quick giggle behind Cate's bedroom door, and the quick rumble of an answering laugh from his stepmother. Thank God for Lily, he thought, as he went downstairs.

Thank God for family.

Even thinking it, it surprised him to see his father out on the back terrace, drinking coffee, studying the hills. Aidan poured a cup for himself, went out.

The breeze, whipping through the chaparral, the redwoods and pines, brought the scent of both hills and sea. Snow iced the tops of the mountains, and morning fog crept along the ground below.

"A little cold out here yet, Dad."

"I needed the air. I sometimes forget to appreciate the mountain view. Cate?"

"Lily's with her. She woke up scared, but . . . resilience."

"Did you get any sleep?"

"Some. You?"

"Some."

"Dad, I want to thank you for what you were prepared to do. It's not just the money, but—"

"You should know better than to thank me."

"That it'll irritate you. Yeah." The smile didn't come so hard this time. "But I have to anyway. Just like I have to say I love you, Dad."

"That doesn't irritate me." Hugh clamped a hand on Aidan's shoulder. "There's nothing I wouldn't do for family. You're the same."

"I'm trying to figure out now what the best thing to do for family is. I'm supposed to leave for New Orleans in two weeks to start on *Quiet Death*. Even if I brought Cate and Charlotte with me—or Charlotte for part of it, as she's got *Sizzle* shooting in L.A. next month—the long hours . . . I'm thinking of backing out."

"Ah, Aidan, I hate to see you give up that role. It's a gem. I know why you're considering it, I just hate it. All of this. You know Lily and I would keep Catey with us while you're on location."

"I don't think I can go without her, not now."

No, he thought, he *knew* he couldn't go without her. As much for himself as for his daughter.

"Charlotte worked so hard to land *Sizzle*," he continued. "I can't ask her to give it up and base in New Orleans while I shoot."

Hugh stared up at the peaks, at the way the clouds hovered over them as if they'd drop and smother them.

"You're right. I'd do the same in your place."

"I'm thinking of taking six months off, maybe a year. I could take Cate to Ireland, help Nan settle in. They'd both love that."

Though it hurt his heart, Hugh nodded. His mother, his son, his precious granddaughter, an ocean away. "That might be best."

"I want to hire a private detective if the police don't find these bastards, find them quick. I could offer a reward."

Hugh turned to his son. He hadn't shaved, and more gray than black grizzled his chin and cheeks. "There our thoughts align."

"Good. Then I'm on the right track. And I want a good family therapist. Resilient or not, I think Cate needs to talk to someone. All three of us do."

Aidan looked at his watch. "The police will be here soon, and that's the next step. I need to wake Charlotte." When he turned, he saw Cate at the breakfast counter, her ankles hooked together as she watched Nina sift flour into a bowl.

"Take a look," he told his father.

"Squeezes my heart," Hugh murmured. "In the best way."

Hugh walked to the door, opened it, walked in with Aidan.

"Here's my girl."

He stepped over to kiss the top of her head, sent a grateful look at Lily, who leaned against the big fridge with her own cup of coffee.

She'd pulled Cate's now shiny fall of hair into a high, bouncing ponytail, helped her pick out jeans with flowers on the pockets, and a bright blue sweater.

She would have looked like any pretty ten-year-old girl, except for the bruise on her temple, the dark circles under her eyes.

"Nina's making pancakes."

"Is that so?"

"Caitlyn asked for them, so . . ." Nina sent a pleading glance toward Aidan, one out of shadowed and tear-swollen eyes.

"I'm all about the pancake."

So he'd wait just a bit longer to get Charlotte.

He caught a signal from Lily before she stepped out of the kitchen. He followed her out, and into what had been his grandfather's study.

Liam Sullivan's Oscars and awards gleamed; framed stills from his movies, candid shots with actors, directors, Hollywood luminaries graced the walls.

The wide glass doors led out to the garden he'd loved.

"Aidan, you know I love Cate more than I love red velvet cake."

He had to smile. "Yes. And I know how much you love red velvet cake."

"Nina," she began, in her blunt way. "She'd moved to the room off the kitchen because she knew Charlotte didn't want to see her. But she heard us when we came down. She just wanted to see Cate, to have a moment. I'm going to say Cate was so happy to see her, and before you know it asked for pancakes. Aidan, that girl wasn't careless, she wasn't irresponsible, she—"

"I know it."

At the interruption, Lily drew in a breath. Topaz eyes against her milk-pale skin managed to transmit both relief and disappointment. "But you're still going to let her go."

"I'll try talking to Charlotte again, but I don't see her changing her mind. And the fact is, Lily, I don't think Nina's ever going to be comfortable working for us again."

"For Charlotte again." The southern drawl only added to the bite of the words.

He adored his stepmother. And knew he couldn't claim Lily and Charlotte shared that same level of affection.

"Okay, yeah. I'm going to do what I can to help her get another position, and give her a good severance."

"I'll throw my weight into getting her another job. People listen to me."

"Because you don't give them a choice."

She poked her finger in his chest. "Why would I?" Then she kissed his cheek. "Cate's going to be all right. Some time, some love, she's going to be just fine."

"I'm counting on it. Want some pancakes?"

"Honey, at my age in this profession, I shouldn't be in the same room as a pancake." She tapped her own ass. "But this morning I'm making an exception."

Aidan kept an eye on the time as she ate in the kitchen, quietly sliding away.

"I'm going to go wake up your mom, baby. It's going to be like Christmas morning for her, and you're the best gift under the tree."

Cate smiled a little, pushed at the pancakes still on her plate. "Is Nan still sleeping, too?"

"Probably, but I'll check. Aunt Maureen and Uncle Harry are still here. And Miranda and Jack, some of the kids, too."

"Are we going home today?"

"We're going to see. You remember Sheriff Buckman from last night? He needs to come talk to everybody."

Putting down the fork, Cate gripped her hands together under the counter, stared at her plate. "Did he catch them?"

"I don't know, Catey, but you're safe."

"Are you coming right back? After you go upstairs, are you coming right back?"

"Right back. And G-Lil and Grandpa will stay right here with you."

"And Nina?"

"Nina's a little busy right now," Lily said easily. "Why don't we get out one of those jigsaw puzzles you like so much that make me say all those bad words."

That brought a smile. "Can we do one in the living room so we can see the water, and have a fire?"

"Great idea." Hugh stood. "But I pick the puzzle."

"Not an easy one!" Cate scooted off the stool to scramble after him. Then stopped, her eyes imploring her father. "You'll come right back."

"Right back," Aidan promised.

"Time and love, Aidan," Lily reminded him as he looked after his daughter.

He nodded, and walked back to the stairs, went up. In the bedroom, he opened the curtains, let the light wash through the room.

He moved to the bed, sat where Charlotte lay, her hair like a luxurious tangle of that sunlight. Gently, he brushed it back from her face, kissed her.

She didn't stir—even without a pill she tended to sleep deep—so he took her hand, kissed her fingers. Said her name.

"Charlotte. You need to wake up."

She stirred then, and would have rolled over if he hadn't stopped her. "Charlotte, wake up now."

"Just let me sleep for another . . ."

Her eyes popped open, instantly filled with tears. "Caitlyn!" Already weeping, she flung herself into Aidan's arms. "God, God, how could I have slept when my baby's gone? How could I have—"

"Charlotte. Stop. Stop. Catey's here. She's safe. She's right downstairs."

"Oh, why do you lie to me? Why do you torture me?"

"Stop!" He had to pull her back, give her a little shake to cut off the rise of hysteria. "She's downstairs, Charlotte. She got away. She's safe, and downstairs right now."

Her eyes went blank. "What are you talking about?"

"Our girl, Charlotte?" Tears clogged his throat again. "Our brave little girl climbed out a window. She got away, she got help. Dad and I brought her home last night after talking to the police. She was asleep by the time we got home, and you were under, so—"

"She—she climbed out a window? Oh my God! Did they— The police, you called the police?"

"The family who helped her did. Sheriff Buckman and his deputy will be here in about ten minutes to—"

"They're coming here? Did they catch them? Did they catch the men who had Caitlyn?"

"I don't know. They wore masks. Cate didn't know where she was. It was a gift from God she found this house, this family who helped her, took care of her until we got there. Charlotte, she's downstairs. You need to get up."

"Oh God, oh God, I—I'm so groggy from the pill. I'm not thinking straight." She tossed the covers aside, leaped out of bed. Since she wore only a silk nightshirt, Aidan stopped her before she could run from the room.

"Sweetheart, you need a robe at least. The police are co.

"What do I care about—"

He took the one laid over the foot of the bed, helped her put it on.

"I'm shaking, I'm shaking. This is all like some terrible dream. Caitlyn."

Weeping again, she ran from the room, rushed down the stairs. She let out a wail when she saw Cate sitting on the floor working on a puzzle.

She leaped again, fell to her knees and pulled Cate close and tight against her. "Caitlyn, Cate. My Catey. My baby! I can't believe you're—"

She cut herself off, showering kisses over Cate's face.

"Oh, let me look at you, let me look. Oh, my darling, did they hurt you?"

"They locked me in a room, but I got away."

"Oh, how could this happen?" She dragged Cate to her again. "When I think what might— That Nina! I want her arrested!"

"Charlotte." Even as Hugh tried to speak, Cate wiggled free, pushed away.

"Nina didn't do anything! You can't be mean to Nina!"

"She was supposed to watch you, take care of you. I trusted her. Oh, I'll never forgive her. For all we know she was part of this. My sweet baby girl!"

"It's not Nina's fault." Again, Cate pushed away from Charlotte's reaching arms. "You told me where to hide. You told me to play hide-and-seek and hide up in the tree where nobody would find me and I'd win!"

"Don't be silly."

Before Aidan could speak, Hugh held up a hand, got slowly to his feet. "When did your mother tell you where to hide, Catey?"

"Stop badgering her! Hasn't she been through enough? Aidan, it's time we took our daughter out of this house. Time we took her home."

"When, Caitlyn?" Hugh repeated.

"In the morning before the celebration." While her voice shook a little, Cate kept her gaze steady on Charlotte's face. She didn't look at her mother as if studying a stranger, but as if finding something she'd always known.

"She said let's go for a walk, even before Nina got up. Early. And she said she had the best hiding place, and when she showed me, she said not to tell anybody. It was our secret, and to make hide-and-seek the last outside game."

"This is ridiculous. She's confused. You come with me right now, Caitlyn. We're going upstairs to pack."

"'Them.'" Pale as death, Aidan moved forward, stood between his wife and daughter. "When I told you Cate was here, was safe, first . . . It was shock, not relief. I see that now. And you said 'them.' Did the police catch them, the men who took her."

"For Christ's sake, Aidan, what difference does that make? And I was coming off a sleeping pill. And—"

Her father's voice, so cold when he spoke, had Cate shivering. Lily drew her back.

"Because when you took the pill, we only knew of one. One man. But it was two. It was two. How did you know that, Charlotte?"

"I didn't!" Her robe swirled around her as she turned, as she pressed a hand to her heart. "How could I! It's just a figure of speech, and I was groggy and upset. Stop it. I want to go home."

Something in Cate's belly shook, but she stepped closer again. "I couldn't remember when I talked to the police, but now I do."

Lily took Cate's hand. "What do you remember?"

"He said, when I pretended to be asleep, when he talked to somebody on the phone. He asked are you using the nanny's phone? And how if they ever checked, she'd get blamed."

"Caitlyn's confused and God knows what they did to her when they—"

"No, I'm not." Tears spilled down her cheeks, but the eyes that shed them stayed hot. "I remember. You told me where to hide. You said make it the last game. And he asked if you were using the nanny's phone. Because it was you. I knew it. I knew it inside, G-Lil, so I didn't want to see Mom this morning. I only wanted Daddy."

"You stop this nonsense right now." As Charlotte made a grab for Cate, Lily blocked her.

"Don't you dare touch this child."

"You get out of my way, you washed-up bitch." Charlotte's a shove didn't move Lily an inch. "You get your fat ass out of my way or—"

Eyes glittering, Lily pushed her face into Charlotte's. "Or what? You want to take a shot at me, you soulless excuse for a mother? You couldn't act your way out of a room with one door if the door stood open, and you're not acting your way out of this, you low-rent never-will-be. You go right on and take a poke at me, and you'll be waking up on the floor with that nose Aidan paid for spouting blood."

"Stop!" Throwing up his hands, Aidan pushed between them while Hugh drew Cate away. "Stop this. Charlotte, Lily, I need you both to sit down."

With a toss of her hair, Charlotte jabbed a finger toward Lily. "I'm not staying in the same house with her. I'm going up to get dressed. Aidan, we're leaving."

He gripped her arm before she stormed out. "I said sit down."

"Don't speak to me that way. What's wrong with you?" Sobbing, she fell against him. "I can't stay here! Aidan, oh, Aidan, that woman hates me. She always has. Did you hear? Did you hear what she said to me? How can you let her insult me that way?"

"I've got plenty of other ways to insult you," Lily tossed out. "I've been saving 'em up for years."

Aidan sent Lily a silent plea that had her holding up a hand, gesturing peace.

"Sit down, Charlotte," Aidan repeated.

"I will not sit in the same house, much less the same room with that woman."

"This isn't about Lily. This is about Caitlyn. It's about you being a part of what happened to her."

"You can't believe any of that. I'm Caitlyn's mother! Our baby's upset, confused."

"No, I'm not."

Charlotte whipped her head around, struggled for a moment as Cate stared at her with those hot, streaming eyes. "We're going to get you the help you need, Catey. You had a terrible ordeal."

"You told me where to hide. You said, 'Let's go for a walk before anybody gets up, and I'll show you a secret hiding place.'"

"I did not! You're mixed up. You must've gone for a walk with Nina, and—"

"She went with you." Rosemary, trembling a bit, stood in the wide entranceway. "I saw you. Yesterday morning, I saw you and our Cate outside when I stepped out to smell the sea."

"You're dreaming. You're all conspiring against me! You—"

"Be quiet. Be quiet and sit the hell down." Sick, sick to his bones, Aidan pulled Charlotte to a chair, pushed her into it. "Nan. What did you see?"

"I saw them walking together, and I thought, how sweet, the two of them walking together so early, when the sun's still rising over the hills, when it's starting to glitter on the water. I almost called out, but I didn't because I wanted the two of you to have that moment to yourselves."

"What have you done?"

"I haven't done anything! It's just like you," she spat at Aidan. "Just like you to take everyone's side against me."

"No," he murmured. "In fact, it's not."

He glanced toward the window as the gate signaled. "That should be the sheriff."

"I'll open the gate." Lily walked out to the controls.

"If you try to get out of that chair," Aidan warned as Charlotte started to push herself up, "I'll just put you back in it."

"If you put a hand on me—" She broke off, cringed back when he took a step toward her. "You've lost your mind."

Covering her face with her hands, she fell back on her usual defense. Tears.

CHAPTER FIVE

"Sit here, Catey girl. Ma, come sit with Cate."

"You believe me, don't you, Grandpa?"

"I do." He gave her a hard hug before giving her butt a light pat to send her toward a sofa. "I'm sorry to say, I do."

He went to his mother, put an arm around her as he walked her to Cate.

"Lily," he said when she came back, "would you go ask Nina to come in, bring her phone?"

"Don't you dare bring that liar in here."

"Shut up. Spill all the fake tears you want, but shut up. I'll get the door," he told Aidan.

As he started for it, his sister rushed down the steps. "What's going on? We heard the shouting."

"It appears Charlotte had a part in Cate's kidnapping."

"You— What?"

He scrubbed his hands over his face. "Do me a favor, see if you can get someone to put coffee together. The police may want some. Then you should get Harry, come down and listen. Ask, for now, Miranda and Jack to make sure the kids stay upstairs, or go down to the theater. It's going to be a hell of a show here, and one they shouldn't see."

"Hugh, why would you think she'd— All right," she said when he just shook his head. "I'll take care of it."

When Hugh opened the door, Red and Michaela were just getting out of the car.

"Good morning, Mr. Sullivan. How's Caitlyn?"

"Hugh," he said. "Please, both of you, make it Hugh. We've had some . . . developments this morning. Cate's remembered something. She remembered more details."

"That's helpful." But Red studied Hugh's face, saw the terrible strain, the terrible anger. "Did they do more harm to her than we knew of?"

"No, no, nothing like that. It's . . ." He had to uncurl the hands he'd balled into fists at his sides. "You'd better hear for yourself. Please come in."

Under the soaring ceilings, in front of the panoramic view of sky and sea, Red studied the fascinating tableau.

The little girl with the tear-streaked face and angry eyes sitting under the protective arm of her great-grandmother. The curvy red-head he recognized from the movies perched on the arm of the sofa to flank the girl.

Like a guard on protective duty.

The stunning blonde in the white silk robe weeping while her husband—because he recognized the blonde, too—stood behind her chair. Not in comfort, but another guard.

"My mother, Rosemary," Hugh began, "my wife, Lily. And, ah, my sister, Maureen."

"Coffee's coming. Harry's getting dressed." One glance at Hugh had her going to the sofa, to sit at her mother's other side.

United front, Red thought. With the blonde most definitely cut out.

"This is Sheriff Buckman and Deputy Wilson. And here's Nina, Caitlyn's nanny."

"Get that woman out of my sight!"

At Charlotte's explosion, Nina took a stumbling step back. "Miss Lily said I needed to come in, and bring my phone."

"You're fired! Do you understand the word?"

A small woman, barely twenty-five, she'd always acquiesced to Charlotte. Had always been intimidated by her. But now Nina squared her shoulders. "Then I don't have to listen to you or do what you say."

Charlotte—and Red thought it fascinating how quickly tears

turned to temper—started to spring up. Aidan gripped her shoulder, shoved her down again.

"Don't you touch me. Sheriff, you have to help me."

And, Red noted, how quick tears came back.

"Please, please, they're abusing me. Physically, verbally, emotionally. Please." That beautiful face with its brimming eyes turned up to Red. The hands lifted in a plea.

"We're here to help," he said easily. "How about everybody takes a seat?"

Another woman rolled in a trolley. He could smell the coffee.

"Thanks, Susan." Maureen popped up. "I've got it from here. Susan helps my mother take care of things around here. Susan, you can go on back. Here's my husband. Harry, this is Sheriff Buckman and Deputy Wilson. You should sit down," she murmured to him.

Before he did, he walked over to Cate, bent from his height of six-five to give her an exaggerated kiss. "You were a sleepyhead when I saw you last night."

He took a chair, stretched out his long legs.

Since there was plenty of seating, Red took a chair that gave him the best angle on the blonde and the child. Mother and daughter. Because something very wrong simmered between them.

"How are you doing today, Cate?"

"I'm not scared anymore. And I remembered she told me where to hide."

She lifted her hand, pointed that accusatory finger at her mother.

"She's confused. Those monsters must have given her something that's warped her memory. She doesn't know what she's saying."

"I know." Cate stared straight into her mother's eyes.

Charlotte looked away first.

"She woke me up early yesterday for a surprise, she said. She doesn't get up early unless she has a call, but she was already dressed, and she had my jacket, and my shoes."

"I did not!"

"You did, too."

"Charlotte," Rosemary said with a sigh. "I saw you. I saw them walking, out front, about a half hour after sunrise."

Red held a hand up before Charlotte could interrupt again. "I'd like to hear what Cate has to say."

"I won't have you interrogating my child."

"I don't believe that's what I'm doing." Red barely flicked Charlotte a glance before giving Cate his full attention. "What I'm doing is listening. Tell me what you remember, Cate."

"She said we're going for a walk, and we did. And I was excited because it was a secret, she said."

Though her voice sounded fierce, she knuckled tears from her eyes.

"She said she had the best hiding place, and I should play hide-and-seek as the last outside game, and use that place—the tree by the garage—and no one would find me. So I'd win."

"Yoga," Aidan murmured. "God, how could I be so stupid, so blind? I woke, and you were just coming into the bedroom. You had on yoga pants, a tank, and said you'd taken your mat out by the pool to do some yoga."

"Which is exactly what I did, or is that a crime now?"

"Black yoga pants," Rosemary said, shutting her eyes, bringing it back. "A black-and-white flowered tank."

"Yes." Aidan nodded.

"Obviously, Rosemary saw me coming back from the pool, and she's confused."

"Seems to be a lot of 'confused,'" Red said easily. "Cate seems pretty clear on it."

"She's still in shock, may still be under the influence of whatever those monsters gave her."

"That would be the monsters who took her to the Wenfield cabin, about three miles from here as the crow flies." He kept his eyes on Charlotte's as he spoke. "Maybe you figure they're confused, too."

He watched her pale, watched her fingers dig into the arms of the chair. Smelled the lie before she spoke it.

"They're criminals, liars. They're working with that heartless bitch." She flung a hand out at Nina. "Turning my own flesh and blood against me, and for money."

"I'd cut off my hand before I'd hurt or let anyone hurt my Caitlyn.

I'll take a lie detector test," Nina said to Red. "I'll do anything you want."

"She talked to him on the phone—not Nina," Cate insisted. "He asked if she'd used the nanny's phone, and said good. He called her 'lover.' And his phone, when it rang, it was 'The Mexican Hat Dance.' I know because we learned it in dance class."

Nina's hand flew to her mouth, but didn't quite smother the gasp.

"See, she's guilty."

"I did nothing." Nina took out her phone as she rose, put in the code, handed it to Red. And leaning down, whispered, "I have something to say, but I don't want to say it in front of Caitlyn."

He nodded, shifted to smile at Lily. "Ma'am—and I want to say I've sure enjoyed your movies over the years—I wonder, since we all have this fine coffee, if you'd take Cate back, maybe get her a drink."

"You want to say something you don't want me to hear. It happened to me. I should hear."

She had a stubborn line between her eyebrows when they came together. He had to respect that. "That may be so, honey, but I need you to give me just a couple minutes first. I'd really appreciate it."

"Come on, sweets. Let's get us a Coke."

"I don't allow my child to drink carbonated sugar!"

"Well, bless your heart." With that eyebrow arch for Charlotte, Lily took Cate's hand. "Guess who's not in charge today?"

Red waited a minute, then nodded to Nina. "What do you want to say?"

"I don't want to say it. I wish I didn't have to, and I'm so sorry, Mr. Aidan. I'm so sorry, but Ms. Dupont . . ." Embarrassed color flooded Nina's cheeks. "She's been having sex with Mr. Sparks."

"Liar!" Surging up, a flurry of white silk, Charlotte slapped at Aidan when he tried to stop her. She leaped at Nina. She managed to get a swipe of nails down Nina's cheek before Michaela restrained her.

Even then, she struggled, kicked back.

"You're going to end up in cuffs," Red warned her in the same tone he might've used to comment it looked like rain. "Assault, and assaulting an officer. You better sit back down before you end up cooling your temper in jail."

"My lawyers will sue you both out of your jobs. And bury you," she told Nina.

Slow, calm, Red got to his feet. "Sit down. Or I'll charge you here and now, have you taken in, booked. Nina, do you want medical attention?"

"It's all right. I'm not lying."

"Why don't you tell me why you think Ms. Dupont's having an affair with this Mr. Sparks?"

"I don't think, I know, because I walked in on them. I'm so sorry, Mr. Aidan. She said she'd fire me and see I'd never get another job if I said anything."

"Aidan, you can't believe that." Now Charlotte reached for his hand, her face filled with love and sorrow. "You can't possibly believe I'd be unfaithful."

He pulled his hand free. "Do you honestly think I'd give a goddamn at this point about you having sex with your personal trainer? Do you think I give any kind of damn about you now?"

"Oh, oh, Aidan!"

"You can turn off the fucking tears, Charlotte. That scene's played out."

"Nina, why would it matter right now about Ms. Dupont and Mr. Sparks?"

"His ringtone. I've heard the ringtone on his phone. It's that one Cate said. The hat dance one."

"As if Grant's the only one in the world who—"

"Shut up," Aidan snapped.

"He called her 'lover,'" Nina added. "He called her that right in front of me. Cate and I were visiting her grandparents, and she really wanted this story she'd written for school, to show them. They don't live far, so I said I'd run back and get it. She was so proud of it. I thought they—Ms. Dupont and Mr. Sparks—were in the gym, downstairs. I never thought about it, but just ran right upstairs. The bedroom doors—the master's—were wide open. I heard them first. I heard them, then I saw. They were in bed together."

She let out a breath. "I guess I made some sound—I was so shocked. When she heard me, she got up, and came right out. Naked. She told me if I said anything, I was done, and she'd tell the police I tried to steal her jewelry. I didn't want to lose my job, I didn't want to leave Caitlyn. I didn't want to go to jail. I didn't say anything."

"Not a word," Aidan said quietly when Charlotte started to deny. "Not a single word. Is there more, Nina?"

"I'm sorry, Mr. Aidan. I'm sorry. After that she didn't bother to hide it so much, not from me. And he called her 'lover.' Like, 'Lover, she'll keep her mouth shut. Come on back to bed.' Or when she had me bring a bottle of wine down to the gym, he called her that. He always called her that."

"Let me ask you, Nina, do you always keep your phone with you?"

Clasping her hands together, Nina nodded at Red. "Yes, sir. Almost always. Except when I need to charge it, but I try to do that at night."

"And yesterday, after you realized Caitlyn was missing?"

"I had it with me when I looked for her. Later, after Ms. Dupont blamed me for it, Miss Lily and Miss Rosemary said I should move downstairs for the night, to the room off the kitchen so Ms. Dupont didn't get more upset. I did, and I left my phone in there, on the charger when we were all waiting for the kidnapper to call back."

"Ms. Dupont waited with everyone, too?"

"No, sir, she was upstairs. Lying down. I think she took a sleeping pill, and was sleeping when he called back."

"Okay, Nina. Ma'am," he said to Rosemary, "is there any way to get to that bedroom, the one down here, from upstairs without going by where you all were waiting?"

"Several ways."

"What we're going to do is take your phone in, Nina. With your permission, since it's a cell phone, we can use the computer to bring up the actual calls."

He saw the slightest flicker in Michaela's eyes at the bluff, but Red always figured when you bluffed—or lied outright—you should do it with casual confidence.

"First thing is, if the call Cate's told us about came in when you were in the room with witnesses, we'd know right off it wasn't you who made it. Next, even if they didn't use names, we'd run the voices on the phone through voice recognition. Since this is a kidnapping, we'd get the FBI to help with that. Their equipment's amazing."

Playing along, playing well, Michaela nodded. "It'll be a simple matter to match the voices, since we have the two men already."

"Yep. Mic, why don't you go upstairs with Ms. Dupont so she can get dressed."

"You're not taking me to jail. I'm a victim. I'm a victim. You have no idea what I've been through."

"I think I get the gist, but if you want to make a statement, that's just fine. I'm going to record that. But I'm going to read you your rights first." He took a recorder out of his pocket, turned it on, set it on the table. "That's how we do it."

Calculation, that's what Red saw as he recited the Miranda. "You understand all that, Ms. Dupont?"

"Yes, of course I do. I'm appealing to you for help. I made a terrible mistake, but I was being blackmailed."

"Is that so?"

"I did have a fling with Grant. Another terrible mistake. I was weak, Aidan, I was lonely and foolish. Please forgive me."

His face, his eyes, his voice held no emotion. Not even disgust. "I don't care."

"Are you claiming Grant Sparks blackmailed you over the affair?"

"It was a paparazzo. He got pictures of us. It was awful, just . . ." Lowering her head, she covered her mouth with her hand. "He demanded millions, or he'd publish them. I wanted to protect my marriage, my family, my little girl. All of us. I didn't know how to get the money."

"Staging a kidnapping was the solution?" Red demanded.

"Grant had the idea. If we faked a kidnapping . . . I lost my mind. I wasn't thinking straight. The stress. I knew Grant would never hurt her. We'd pay, and she'd be back home quickly. It was insane, I see that now. I was insane. I was desperate."

Aidan walked away from her now. Had to walk away.

"What was the blackmailer's name?"

"He said his name was Denby. Frank Denby. After the first time, Grant met with him. I just couldn't. I couldn't bear it. Please believe me, after Caitlyn . . . I was terrified. I started thinking of everything that could go wrong, and—"

"Did you know where they'd taken her?"

"Of course! She's my daughter. I knew where she was, but—"

"And being afraid, worried something would go wrong, you didn't call it off?"

"I couldn't!" Imploring, she clutched a hand under her throat, reached out toward Red with the other. "I didn't know what to do! I made that call because I needed to be sure Caitlyn was all right."

"They drugged her."

Charlotte looked over at Aidan. "It was just a little sedative, just so she wouldn't be afraid. She'd just sleep through it until—"

"They terrified her, put bruises on her face, threatened her with a gun."

"They weren't supposed to—"

"You did this for money, for sex. She climbed out a second-story window, wandered lost in the dark, in the cold, for God knows how long. You used your own child, risked your own child over a god-damn affair."

"She was supposed to sleep! It's her own fault she didn't drink the milk!"

"How did you know the drug was in the milk?" Michaela asked, still taking meticulous notes. "Did you tell them to use milk?"

"I—I don't know! You're confusing me. She wasn't hurt. She was supposed to sleep. When we had the money, they'd have me drop it off."

"That was part of it? You make the drop?"

"Yes, and then they'd take Caitlyn to the turn onto the peninsula, leave her right there."

"And you, you could play the shattered, loving mother through it all." Hugh got to his feet. "You'll never see that child again if I have any say. You'll never see a penny of Sullivan money. You'll never step foot in this house again."

"You don't have any say!" Charlotte hurled at him. "You can't keep me from my own daughter."

"That'll be up to the courts. Charlotte Dupont, you're under arrest for child endangerment, accessory to kidnapping a minor, accessory to child abuse, accessory to extortion."

"Did you hear me? I was victimized, blackmailed."

"Well, I've got some doubts about that. But we'll talk more. Right now, Deputy Wilson's going to escort you upstairs, unless you want us to take you in like you are."

"I want my lawyer."

"That would be my lawyer," Aidan corrected. "You'll have to find your own."

"Oh, I will." Now the loathing poured free. "And I'm not the only one who knows how to talk to the press. I'm going to ruin every one of you."

"What you're going to do right now is come with me."

She jerked away when Michaela walked over, took her arm. "Don't you touch me."

"Do that again, we'll be adding resisting arrest. It's already a long list."

Charlotte rose, tossed back her hair. "Fuck every one of you fucking Sullivans."

Rosemary closed her eyes when Michaela escorted Charlotte upstairs. "A pathetic exit line for a pathetic human being. Aidan, I'm so very sorry."

"No, I'm sorry. I loved her. I looked the other way so many times because I loved her. Because she gave me Cate. Her own child, she did this to her own child. I need some air. I just want to step outside, is that all right?"

Red gave him a nod. "Sure."

"What happens now?" Hugh asked as Aidan went out the front door.

"Now we find Grant Sparks and Frank Denby."

"You said you had them . . ." With a shake of his head, Hugh let out a short laugh. "You lied. Well done."

"It's going to take some time to sort all this out. I'll probably need to talk to all of you again, and to Cate. What I'll say, right now, is it's not all that likely Ms. Dupont's going to make bail anytime soon.

What I expect, after she settles some, and if she hires a decent lawyer, is her to work for a deal. That she'll probably get."

"I should've told Mr. Hugh about Mr. Sparks."

"Don't you blame yourself for that, for any of it." Maureen got up, walked over to hug Nina. "Come on with me. I'm going to get those scratches cleaned and treated. Rabid cat scratches are nasty."

"Will they let me stay with Catey?" Nina asked as Maureen led her out.

"I know my nephew. You've got a job for life."

It didn't take long for Michaela to bring a stone-faced Charlotte back down.

"We want to add attempted bribery of a police officer, Sheriff. She offered me ten thousand to let her go."

"That's a lie!"

"Figured it was coming. I had my phone on record. She's cuffed as she didn't like hearing no."

"Let's load her up. I'll be in touch," he told the others. "If any of you have any questions, you know how to reach me."

When the door closed behind them, Hugh brushed his mother's shoulder. "I'm going to go back so Lily knows to bring Cate in."

"Yes, do that. Aidan's going to need Cate, Cate's going to need Aidan. And they're both going to need all of us."

He bent down to kiss the top of her head. "Sullivans stick together. That includes you, Harry."

"She was never one of us."

A quiet man with quiet ways, he unfolded himself from the chair to go sit by his mother-in-law. She patted his hand.

"You never liked her much, did you, Harry?"

"I never liked her at all, but Aidan loved her. You can't choose family, Rosemary my own. I just got lucky with the bulk of mine. There now."

He put an arm around her when Rosemary turned her face to his shoulder and finally wept.

Aidan walked off the sick, walked off at least the top notes of his rage. For Cate's sake, he reminded himself as he kept walking, kept breathing in the cool, salty air, for her sake he had to find his calm, find his steady.

But beneath it, that rage lived, a feral animal that craved blood. He feared it would live and crave forever.

And under that, even under the snarling and pacing of that beast, lay the shattered pieces of his heart.

He'd loved Charlotte with all of that heart.

How could he have not seen? How could he have not known the grasping, selfish, immoral woman beneath the facade? Even, he had to admit, when that facade had thinned and he'd gotten glimpses, he'd dismissed them.

He'd loved her, trusted her. He'd made a child with her, and she'd risked that child, used that child, betrayed that child.

He would never forgive her for it. He'd never forgive himself.

But when he went back inside, he'd coated on layers of that calm and steady. Coated them thick so they couldn't crack—not even when he went in through the back and saw Cate burrowed against his father.

His eyes met Hugh's over Cate's head.

"I think Cate and I need to talk."

"Sure you do." Hugh drew Cate back, smiled at her. "Everything's going to be all right. All right can take a little time, but we'll get there."

He gave her a last squeeze, then left them alone.

"How about we sit and talk in the library? Just you and me?"

When he held out a hand, she took it with such unquestioning trust, his heart broke just a little more.

Because he wanted privacy for both of them, he took her the long way around, through the formal dining room, past the conservatory, around what they called the music room, and into the library.

Its windows faced the hills, the gardens, gave glimpses of a little orchard. They, with the pale winter sun drifting in, offered a quieter view than the roll of sea. Under a coffered ceiling of mocha and cream, shelves of books, of bound scripts, lined the walls. The chestnut floor gleamed under an Aubusson carpet of elegantly faded greens and roses. He knew his grandmother sometimes sat at the antique library table shipped from Dublin to write actual letters and notes.

He pulled the double pocket doors shut, guided Cate to the big leather sofa. Before he sat, he lit the fire.

Then he sat beside her, took her face in his hands. "I'm sorry."

"Daddy—"

"I have to say this, then I'll listen to whatever you need to say. I'm so sorry, Catey, my Cate. I didn't keep you safe, I didn't protect you. You're everything to me, and I promise you I won't ever fail you again."

"You didn't. She—"

"But I did. Never again. Nothing and no one is as important to me as you. Nothing and no one ever will be." He kissed her forehead, and found saying the words to her helped settle him.

"I knew it was her when I was in that room. She told me where to hide. She took me there and showed me, so I knew. But only inside because . . ."

"She's your mother."

"Why doesn't she love me?"

"I don't know. But I do, Cate."

"Does . . . does she have to live with us?"

"No, and she won't. Ever." It carved at him again, the shaky breath of relief his little girl let out.

"Do we have to live where we did? I don't want to go back there anymore, and live where she did. I don't—"

"Then we won't. I think, for now, we could live with Grandpa and G-Lil. Until we find a place for just you and me."

Hope, sweet and bright, lit her face. "Really?"

He made himself smile. "Sullivans stick together, right?"

She didn't smile back, and her voice trembled. "Do I have to see her? Do I have to talk to her? Do I—"

"No." He prayed he could make that the truth.

Her eyes, so blue, and now so robbed of innocence, looked into his. "She let them scare me, and hurt me. And I know what 'lover' means. She scared you, too, she hurt you, too. She doesn't love us, and

I don't ever want to see her again. She's not really my mother, because mothers don't do that."

"You don't have to worry about that."

"I don't feel sad about it," she claimed, even as tears started to roll. "I don't care. I don't love her either, so I don't care."

He said nothing; he understood completely. He felt exactly the same. Torn to bits, desperate not to care. So he just gathered her close, let her cry it out, cry herself to sleep.

And while she slept, he sat alone with her, watching the fire.

CHAPTER SIX

Deputy Michaela Wilson had pursued and accepted the job in Big Sur because she wanted a change, because she wanted community. And, though she wouldn't admit it, because the man she'd lived with for two years, the man she thought she'd live with for the rest of her life, decided that being with a cop equaled too many complications.

She, a woman who believed to the marrow in law, order, rules, procedure, in justice, could admit she'd put the job ahead of their relationship more than once.

But to Michaela, that was the job.

She'd been an urbanite all her life, so the change of locations, of culture, of pace equaled an enormous personal challenge.

She'd wanted just that.

She wouldn't deny that her first few weeks had tested her. She wouldn't deny she thought of Red Buckman as Sheriff Dude. The man had a bikini-clad (well-endowed) woman riding a wave tattooed on his biceps.

He often wore an earring. Not to mention the hair.

All that added into the too laid back, in her opinion, too unbuttoned, and—she'd thought—too damn slow.

It wasn't an easy matter for Michaela Lee Wilson to admit a mistake, especially one of judgment. But in the past eighteen hours or so, she'd had to admit this one.

He might look like a middle-aged surfer, but he was all cop.

She got another good dose of that cop when they sat in interview with Charlotte Dupont and her high-priced lawyer.

She didn't know much about Charles Anthony Scarpetti, but she knew he'd flown up from L.A. in his private jet, wearing his sharp suit and Gucci shoes. And she knew—because Red had warned her—Scarpetti was the type who'd play to the media and pop up on Larry King.

Red sat placidly while Scarpetti pontificated in his slick lawyer way about motions for dismissal, about harassment, intimidation, filing for full custody of the minor child, spousal abuse.

Apparently he had a lot of rabbits in his lawyer hat. Red just let them hop around awhile.

Even twenty-four hours before, that placidity would have had Michaela metaphorically pulling her hair out. Now she saw it as carefully crafted strategy.

"I've got to say, Mr. Scarpetti, that's a lot, and some really fine, shiny words in there, too. If you're finished for now, I'll tell you why you and your client are going to be disappointed."

"Sheriff, I intend to have my client back in her home in Los Angeles, with her daughter, by this evening."

"I know it. I get that clear impression. It's not going to happen, and that's a disappointment for both of you." He leaned forward, but in a friendly way. "I have a really strong suspicion your client hasn't been honest and forthright with you, Mr. Scarpetti. I could be wrong—lawyers gotta do what they gotta—but having some little experience with your client's ways and means, I have to figure she served you up a whole platter of bullshit."

"Charles!" Charlotte turned to him, managed to look beautifully indignant in her orange jumpsuit.

He just patted her hand. "My client is distraught—"

"Your client is an accessory to her own daughter's kidnapping—by her own admission."

"She was distraught," Scarpetti repeated. "Confused, groggy from the sleeping pill her husband forced on her. Her child, also distraught, told you what her father had coached her to say."

"Is that so?" Red shook his head as he studied Charlotte. "Man, you are some number. Deputy, why don't you play back the recording on your phone, from when you took Ms. Dupont upstairs to dress."

Michaela set her phone on the table, cued it up.

Charlotte's voice, a little breathless, but very smooth, flowed out. *"Police don't make much, especially women police, I imagine."*

In contrast, Michaela's voice hit clipped and dispassionate. *"You're going to want shoes, ma'am."*

"I've got money. I can make your life easier. All you have to do is let me go. Tell them I ran out, give me ten minutes' head start. Ten thousand for a ten-minute head start."

"You're offering to pay me ten thousand dollars to let you escape from custody? How are you going to get me the money?"

"I'm good for it. You know who I am! Look, you can take this watch. It's Bulgari, for Christ's sake. It's worth more than you pull in in ten years."

"You're going to want to put on shoes, ma'am, or go out barefoot."

"Take the watch, you idiot! Ten minutes. I'll get you cash, too. Take your hands off me! Don't you dare put those things on me."

"You attempted to bribe a police officer, and have shown yourself to be a flight risk. Sit down. Since you're now cuffed, I'll get you some shoes."

Michaela cut off the recording during the stream of curses.

"I bet she didn't tell you about that one." Red scratched the side of his neck. "Now, before you start saying that was just a desperate plea from a desperate woman, let me save you the breath. It's bribing a police officer, period. I also have your client's confession on tape— including the Miranda warning before she gave it. We have BOLOs out now for her two partners, and we will apprehend them."

"You said you already—"

Red just smiled when the lawyer cut Charlotte off.

"Had them?" Red finished. "You might've gotten that impression. We will have them. You know, they were both mostly careful about wiping things down, but it's hard to get everything. Especially when you're moving fast because, hey, the kid got loose, and the cops might be coming. We got prints."

"We're not disputing the child was abducted," Scarpetti replied. "Ms. Dupont had no part in this terrible crime."

"I guess she didn't know where they took the kid, where they held her. She would never have been there."

"How could I know! I don't even know what I said on that recording of yours. I was so loopy from the pills Aidan made me take. It's not the first time he's forced me to . . . do things."

She turned her head away an instant after she let a single tear slide down her cheek.

"I guess you didn't know the Wenfields. The people who own the cabin."

"I don't know them. I don't know where the damn cabin is. I only go to Big Sur when Aidan makes me. Charles!"

"Charlotte, you need to be quiet. Let me handle this."

"Doesn't know the Wenfields, has never been to the cabin. So saying that," Red considered, "you wouldn't have any idea they'd be out of town, that the house would be empty."

"Exactly! Oh, thank God."

"Now I'm confused. How about you, Mic? Are you confused?"

She kept her stony face on, but smiled a little inside. "Not really."

"Just me then. I'm confused how it is, when you don't know the Wenfields, don't know where their cabin is, how your fingerprint—right index finger—ended up on the light switch of the downstairs powder room."

"That's a lie."

"I guess you got a little careless. How I see it, you checked the place out with your partners, needed to use the facilities. And just didn't think about tapping that switch."

"They planted it. Charles—"

"Quiet now."

Michaela saw the change in his eyes. Whether or not he cared if his client was guilty or not, he cared when the evidence piled up.

"Your story's so full of lies and holes and shifts, it's hard to keep up. But I'm damn good at riding the wave. The blackmail? It's bullshit. Extortion's one thing, and getting caught at it's going to mean some time. But drugging and abducting a minor? Use of a deadly weapon? That's a whole different level. A man's after a pile of money. I don't see him risking that different level by helping grab Caitlyn. That's not his job, not his play."

"He had pictures!"

"Charlotte, stop talking. Don't say another word."

"She's not loopy from a sleeping pill now, and she's back to black-mail. Another shift back from her daughter being coached to accuse her. They stuck a needle in her."

Laid back vanished as Red slammed a fist on the table. "You picked the spot where they could grab her, and they stuck a needle in your ten-year-old daughter."

"For money," Michaela added. "For more Bulgari watches."

"For love!"

This time, Scarpetti reached over, gripped Charlotte's arm. "Not another word. I need to consult with my client."

"Surprise, surprise." Red got to his feet, stopped the recording. "He's going to tell you the one who rolls first gets the best deal. He's not wrong. You want a Coke, Mic? I could use a Coke."

When they walked out, he signaled another deputy to take the door, then gestured to Michaela to follow him through the interview area, the bullpen area, and into his office, where he kept a cooler stocked with Cokes.

He got out two, passed her one before sitting down and putting his high-top Chucks on his desk.

"Okay, so let's tell the state's attorney it's about that time. Fancy lawyer's going to look for a fancy deal."

"How much time is she going to get? Whatever it is, it's not enough, but how much do you think?"

"Well." He scratched the side of his neck again. "You got kid-napping a minor, for ransom. You got the use of drugs on the kid, the gun. Thing is she can carry on about how she didn't know about the gun, so we'll let that slide. And her being a parent, she can use that. But the ransom, that's going to sting even when she rolls."

"And she will. There's no loyalty in her."

"Not a bit. Five to ten, I figure. Her lover and the other? Twenty to twenty-five, easy. Depending on how stupid they are, they could get a full life sentence. But I figure the three of them are going to throw enough shit at each other, plead it down, get the twenty to twenty-five. If we can prove who waved the gun around? That one's twenty-five to life."

He took a long, long gulp of Coke. "But that's the lawyers and court. Us? We gotta catch them. She's going over, and if Sullivan has a brain—and I think he does—he's already filing for full custody, for divorce, and getting himself a restraining order in the possible circumstances she makes bail."

He took another swing. "You did good, Mic."

"I didn't do that much."

"You did the job, and you did it good. You go on, let the state's attorney know we're going to play *Let's Make a Deal*."

Michaela nodded, turned toward the door. "That little girl? The media's going to swarm like flies, Sheriff."

"Yeah, they are. Nothing we can do there but give a statement when it comes to that, then go into no-comment mode, and stay there. She doesn't deserve what's coming next."

No, Michaela thought as she went out. None of them did.

Five minutes after Charlotte began to spin shaded truths, outright lies, and self-serving excuses, Scarpetti cut her off. He told her with stone-cold clarity he needed the truth, all of it, or he'd walk away.

Because she believed him, Charlotte spilled her guts.

While she spilled, Frank Denby lounged on the bed of his motel room just south of Santa Maria, watching porn while he iced down his black eye and swollen jaw.

His ribs ached like a mother, so he'd driven as far as he could before calling it. Now after a pop of Percocet, some weed, some ice, he figured he'd head out again in a couple hours.

Sparks had kicked the shit out of him when they'd discovered the brat had gotten out. Like it was his fault. Not that he hadn't gotten a couple of shots in. Yeah, he'd landed a couple.

But he understood Sparks might have killed him if Sparks hadn't known he shared the blame.

So the job had gone to shit—all that money blown—and now he, down to a few hundred cash, one stolen credit card he wasn't ready to use, what remained of the nickel bag in his duffle, had to lie low.

Not that the kid could ID him, but when a job went south, so did he. Mexico felt right. Cruise on down south of the border. A little grifting, a lot of beach time. Hit the tourist spots, make a few bills.

Sparks might have a sweet gig going with his personal training game and banging a movie star mark, but for himself, Denby preferred short, simple cons.

He crunched into a handful of barbecue chips, sulked a little because the guy on the crappy motel TV was getting a blow job and he wasn't.

He should never have let Sparks talk him into the game, but it had seemed so damn easy. And his share of the two million those rich assholes would pay?

Jesus, he'd live like a king in Mexico with a million bucks. And all he'd had to do for it was help set up the cabin and watch the kid for a couple days.

Who'd've figured the brat would climb out the damn window and go poof?

But the brat hadn't seen his face, or seen Sparks without a disguise, and the movie star couldn't blab unless she wanted to trade in her Armani for prison blues.

Besides, the bitch was hot for Sparks.

Good old Sparks knew how to string the rich ones along.

He took another toke on the joint, held that sweet, sweet smoke in his lungs, then expelled it, watched it drift away and take most of his worries with it.

Sun, sand, and señoritas, he thought.

Things could be worse.

Then the cops broke down the door, and they were.

Grant Sparks was neither as sanguine nor as stupid as his sometime partner. He'd worked on the blackmail/kidnapping game for nearly a year. Getting Denby on board had been as simple as dangling a million-dollar payoff. Denby thought small, was small, so he'd swallowed that they'd split two mil without a doubt or question.

Which would've—damn well should have—left the brains of the game with nine million.

Then he'd take his payoff, spend a couple of years in Mozambique—no extradition—living off the fat.

He knew Charlotte wasn't quite as stupid as Denby—and was a better liar. He knew how to read women, how to play them. He made his living at it.

Obviously, and it pissed him off, he hadn't read the damn kid. Maybe a part of him admired how she'd conned him—she had to have flushed the fucking milk. Damn smart kid. And that meant she'd been awake when he'd been in her room, when Charlotte had called.

He'd gone over the conversation—his side of it—a dozen times while he packed up. Nothing there, nothing to lead back to him, or to Denby, or to Charlotte.

Except . . . he'd asked about the nanny's phone. If the kid remembered that, repeated that, it might be trouble. Still, for all he knew, the kid wandered around in the dark, fell off a damn cliff.

Maybe he hadn't intended to hurt her—more than necessary—but he wouldn't be sorry if she'd ended up dead on the rocks.

But dead or alive, he couldn't take chances. Because women, *those* he could read, and he knew Charlotte would screw this up. If anything went wrong, she'd flip to save her own ass.

He'd have done the same.

Better, he thought as he packed the TAG Heuer Charlotte had given him, to play it safe. Take a little trip, get out of L.A. before they found the kid—or the body—and she fumbled it all.

He had money. The personal-trainer-to-the-stars gig paid well enough. And the tips paid even better.

He had a Rolex as well as the TAG, Tiffany cuff links and more gifted to him over his eighteen months running this con. Charlotte had stood out, so he'd focused on her.

She didn't give a crap about the kid, so the kidnapping idea had blossomed. She despised the Sullivans, had a shitpile of envy going for their status—and their money.

Soaking them for millions—she'd loved the idea. Thinking back, he probably hadn't needed Denby and the blackmail scheme to get her on board.

It should've worked.

He packed up his laptop, tablet, prepaid phones, took a last look around the apartment he'd lived in for nearly three years. A long stretch for him, he thought, but the pickings had been good.

Time to head out, head east, he decided, swing through the Midwest. Had to be plenty of rich, bored housewives, sex-starved widows, divorcées to pluck from.

He shouldered the strap of his computer case, rolled the first of his two suitcases to the door. He'd come back for the other.

When he opened the door, he recognized cop in the eyes of the men, one of them with a fist raised to knock.

And he thought: That fucking kid.

Throughout the day, Red sent deputies out on calls, answered a couple himself. He tackled paperwork, had a burrito for lunch at his desk.

Until the lawyers finished hammering out what they hammered, he didn't want to stray far.

He answered his phone, listened to a colleague with the state police. Nodding, he made notes. Then hung up and called Michaela into his office.

"Staties just picked up Frank Denby at a motel outside Santa Maria. He was watching porn, getting high. Just another genius."

"Do we get him?"

"I have to admire your straight-down-the-channel focus, Mic. Happened in our jurisdiction. It's going to be federal, so we'll pass him on, but the state boys will transport him up here so we can have our swing."

"Good." She wanted the swing. "That's fast work."

"Well, genius. He had a nine-mil S&W on him. What?" Red reared back, blinked. "Wait, hold on! I believe that's a smile I see. I believe I see the beginnings of a smile."

"I can smile. I do smile." Amused, she immediately sobered her face to rag on him. "See?"

"You're a smiling fool, Mic. As we learned after Dupont started naming names, our friend Denby has another few months of parole on his previous conviction as a half-assed shakedown artist. I use 'artist' liberally in his case. The firearm's a parole violation, which just adds some cream to the coffee."

He held up a finger when his phone rang. "Hold on. Sheriff Buckman. Yes, sir, Detective." A fresh grin spread over his face. "Well, isn't that sweet news? We sure are grateful to you for your quick work on this. Is that so? Uh-huh. Well, hard to blame him. I'll be here. And I'll inform the family. This is going to be a big load off their minds. That's good work."

"They got Sparks."

"Wrapped right up," he agreed. "Just before he carted his belongings out of his apartment in L.A. He didn't skedaddle fast enough."

"They didn't know we had Dupont, didn't know we had the BOLOs."

"The one good thing here, Mic, about the Sullivans not calling in law enforcement? No leaks. No media. You add the Coopers to that. They're too decent to run out and call up reporters to brag out their story."

He swung his Chucks off the desk, got up. "Do you want to take a ride with me out to the Sullivan enclave?"

"I absolutely do. First, I want to say it's been an education watching how you pushed this through, every step of it."

"It's the job, Mic. Just a few things in this life I take seriously, that I figure you have to focus in and do right. Sex, surfing, and the job. Let's go give the Sullivans the good news."

The sun painted sky and sea with a symphony of color as it slid toward the horizon. Gulls wheeled and cried as the tide rolled out from the quiet strip of beach on the Sullivan peninsula, leaving bits of glittering sea glass, hunks of shells strewn on the verge of sand and foam.

On the rocks, sea lions lolled.

Under Lily's watchful eye, Cate collected what interested her, plunking little treasures in a pink plastic bucket. They studied the small universes in tide pools between the rocks, left footprints in damp sand, watched sandpipers scurry.

All around them the land sprang abruptly, dramatically from the sea, creating the breathtaking cliffs. Waves rushed and slapped the rocky coastline, carved out whirling pools, small, stony arches, and made this small slice of beach a private haven.

The kick of wind had Lily taking the scarf she'd tossed on and wrapping it around her neck for more warmth.

She couldn't claim a love of chilly beaches on a February evening, but anything that distracted the girl helped. For that matter, she wanted distraction herself.

God knew sunset over the Pacific provided a spectacular distraction, but with the brisk air whipping, she'd have preferred it from a seat by the fire with a cold, dry martini in her hand.

But her girl needed the air, the movement.

Regardless, now that the sun dipped closer to the sea, the light changing with the journey, they needed to start back.

As she started to call it, Cate looked up at her. Such big blue eyes, Lily thought.

"Do you miss Miranda and Keenan and all of them when they go home?"

"Sure I do. Especially now that Miranda's home is all the way in New York. But . . . I'm happy they've made their own lives. It means I did a good job, I guess."

She took Cate's gritty-with-sand hand, began to cross the beach toward the rise of stone steps carved into the bluff.

"And I'm going to have you and your dad around."

"We're going to live in your guesthouse for a while."

"That's going to be fun. We can work on meeting our goal of finishing a million jigsaw puzzles."

"Daddy said I could write down the things I want from the other house, and I don't have to keep everything. When we get a new house, we can get new things. So it's just ours."

"What's first on the list?"

"My stuffed animals. I can't leave them. He said I can pick some of them to go to Ireland, too, because we're going to go and help Nan be settled."

"You're going to be a big help to her."

Lily saw the lights starting to glimmer, inside, along the paths, around the terraces. And tried not to think of the panic, the outright fear she'd felt at the same time the day before.

She gave the hand in hers a quick squeeze, just to feel it.

Then that hand tightened in hers. "Somebody's coming. A car's coming."

Maybe she felt a flutter of fresh panic, too, but Lily only smiled. "Girl, you've got ears like a bat. There's a gate," she said in that same easy tone. "Your grandpa won't let anybody in unless he knows them."

Tugging her hand free, Cate ran up the stones until she could see. "It's the sheriff's car! It's okay, G-Lil, it's the sheriff."

Was it okay? Lily wondered as she followed Cate up. Would it ever be okay again?

CHAPTER SEVEN

By the time Lily caught up with Cate—the kid could move!—Cate stood at the top sweep of the drive, waiting for the car. She put an arm around Cate's shoulders, felt the trembling.

"Let's go inside, sweets."

"I want to know." Trembling or not, the words came fierce. "I don't want to get sent away again. I want to know."

She pulled away, marched right up to the car as it parked, blurted out the question as Red got out. "Did you catch them?"

He gave her steady look for steady look. "They're in police custody. We'll talk about it."

The sound escaping Lily's iron will was half sob, half gasp. When Cate turned to her, eyes wide and worried, she could only shake her head. "It's all right. I'm all right. I'm just relieved. Just relieved. Let's all go inside. It's turning cold."

She called out when Aidan opened the front door. "Have somebody put some coffee on, will you? And for God's sake, somebody mix me a martini. A big one."

"Are they in jail? Are they going to get out? Are they—"

"Slow down, tiger. I wouldn't say no to coffee," Red said to Lily. "I'd appreciate if we could talk to everybody at once, as we need to get back."

"Of course. I'll round them up. Most of us had to get back home, so it's just my husband and me, Aidan and Cate, Rosemary, Nina. You've had a long day, both of you," she added as she escorted them in.

"I'd say everyone has."

"Why don't you sit down. The fire's nice on a brisk evening. I think Rosemary's upstairs, and— Oh, Nina, would you go up and tell Miss Rosemary the sheriff and deputy are here?"

"Right away. Oh, Caitlyn, you need to wash the sand off your hands."

Hastily Cate wiped them on her jeans. "They're fine. Please."

Before she could insist, Lily tapped her own hand in the air behind Cate's back.

"I'll go tell Miss Rosemary, and get the coffee. Should I stay then?"

"I'd appreciate it if you would," Red told her, and nodded as Aidan came in. "Sorry to intrude again."

"Not at all. My father will be right in." He searched Red's face. "You have some news for us?"

"I do, and I hope it'll give you some peace of mind."

"They're in custody. He said they were, but didn't say how. I want to know—"

"Caitlyn Ryan." The quiet warning from her father had her straining, but silent. "Can I take your coats?"

"We're fine. We're not going to take up too much of your time." To get things rolling, Red sat, smiled at Cate. "Been down to the beach, have you?"

"I wanted to go outside. I like the beach."

"It happens to be my favorite place in the world. You surf?"

"No." Now she angled her head. "Do you?"

"Every chance I get. If it's cranking tomorrow, I may put on my steamer, grab my stick, and go on dawn patrol." He winked at her. "Surfer talk."

Intrigued, she sat on the floor, crossed her legs. "Did you ever see a shark?"

"See one? I punched one right in the face once."

"No, you—really?"

"Hand to God." He swiped one over his heart then pointed his finger up. "It wasn't a very big one, but I like to make him bigger every time I tell the story."

"Do you surf, too?" she asked Michaela.

"No."

"I'm going to teach her."

Michaela made a sound between a laugh and a snort. "No, you're not."

"You just wait."

Hugh came in with a martini glass in one hand, a glass of whiskey in the other.

"My hero," Lily murmured, took the glass and the first long, slow sip.

Hugh sat. "Nina's finishing up the coffee. I hope you'll come back, both of you, when you're not on duty so I can mix or pour you your drink of choice."

"I'll see we do." Red got to his feet as Rosemary came down the stairs. "I'm sorry to disturb you, ma'am."

"Not in the least." Rosemary took the whiskey glass from her son. "Aidan, be a dear and get Hugh another glass of Jameson's. I'm taking his."

"The sheriff said he punched a shark in the face."

Rosemary nodded, sat. "I'm not surprised to hear that. You're an avid surfer, aren't you?"

"Avid as they come."

Small talk, he thought, kept things smooth until.

Until Nina came with the coffee.

"Okay then. We wanted to come by, tell you that Grant Sparks and Frank Denby, suspected of kidnapping our girl here, are both in custody. The state police apprehended Denby in a motel room south of here."

"How did they know he was there?"

Red looked down at Cate. "Well, I'll tell you he wasn't too smart. We did our job, and got his name—"

"How?"

"Cate, it's rude to interrupt."

She glanced back at her father. "How will I know if I don't ask?"

"There's a point to that," Red agreed.

But when he hesitated, Michaela made a decision. The girl deserved to know. "Ms. Dupont gave us the name when we talked to

her. When we knew who we were looking for, we got some information. Like where he lived, and what kind of car he drives, and the
license plate. We put out an alert to other police. And the state police
spotted his car, the license plate, in the motel lot."

"Then he wasn't very smart."

"No," Michaela agreed, "he wasn't. But he wasn't very smart to
leave you that spoon, was he? And you were the smart one."

"That's a stone fact," Red put in. "As for Sparks, he was packed up
to take off. Didn't move fast enough, and the police in L.A. arrested
him. Both of them are being transported here, and we'll lock them
up, we'll talk to them."

"How long will you lock them up?"

"Well, that depends on the lawyers and the courts. Mic and me?
We don't get to decide. But I can tell you with the evidence and
statement and the case we've made? It's going to be a real long time."

"Like a year?"

"No, honey, a lot longer. Maybe twenty years."

"My mother, too?"

More cautious here, Red looked at Aidan.

"We've talked about it. Cate needs to know, we all do."

"Then I'll tell you. Because your mother gave us information on
the two men and information on what they all did, planned to do, the
state's attorney—that's the person in charge of trying cases like this—
made an agreement with your mother's attorney. It's called a plea bargain. So they made this bargain, and for the information, they eased
back on some of the charges, providing she says she did the things she
did. She has to go to jail, too, for ten years. She can get out in seven if
she meets the requirements, and the people in charge of that say she
can. But she has to go to jail for seven years for certain."

"She won't like it there," Cate said, mostly to herself. "She can't
go shopping or to parties or auditions. I don't have to see her." She
looked back at her father. "Even when she can come out."

"No."

"And we're divorcing her."

"Yes, baby, we're divorcing her."

"She doesn't love us. Nina's not in trouble."

"Not a bit," Red assured her. "We need to keep your phone in evidence for a while longer, Ms. Torez."

"I don't want it back, thank you. I really don't want it back. Caitlyn, now that you've talked to the sheriff, we should go up, get you cleaned up for dinner."

Not altogether satisfied, but calculating she'd gotten all she could—for now—she stood up. "Will you tell the people who helped me? Dillon and Julia and Gram?"

"It tells me about your character you'd ask that. It tells me good things. Yeah, we're going by there when we leave here."

"Will you tell them thank you again?"

"That's a promise."

"We're going to live in Grandpa's guesthouse for a while, and we're going to Ireland with Nan to stay there for a while, too. But will you tell me if you're right, and they have to go to jail for twenty years?"

"I can do that."

"Thank you."

"You bet."

"Thank you, Deputy Wilson."

"You're welcome."

As she went out with Nina, Red heard her say, "Will you stay with me while I clean up and change? Will you stay in my room?"

"She's afraid to be alone," Aidan said quietly. "She's always been so independent, ready to explore, or settle down on her own with a book or a project. And now she's afraid to be alone."

"I don't want to overstep, Mr. Sullivan, but it might be helpful if your daughter had some counseling."

"Yes." He nodded at Michaela. "I've already made some calls and contacts. She doesn't want to go back to our house in L.A., so as she said, we'll move into my father's guesthouse. And we'll spend some time in Ireland—get her away from any publicity for as long as possible. I know you both have work, and you've had a very long day. I don't want to keep you, but I need to ask. Will there be trials? Will Cate have to testify?"

"Ms. Dupont pled guilty, so no trial. I can't tell you about Sparks and Denby. I will say, while they're not all that smart, I think they may be smart enough to take a plea. We've got enough, if they don't, to push for life without parole. Twenty years is a hell of a lot better than life."

Red got to his feet. "We'll keep you updated. Are you heading back to L.A. soon?"

"I think yes, I think as soon as possible."

"I've got your cell. I'll reach out."

Red checked his watch on the way to the car. "I think we can mooch a meal at Maggie's when we fill them in. Let me tell you, Mic, both those women can cook."

Michaela considered it. "I could eat. Are we going to hit Denby and Sparks tonight?"

"Might as well strike while the iron's hot enough to burn their asses. You up for it?"

Michaela settled in the passenger's seat, looked back at the house, thought of the girl. "I'm up for this one."

Both men said: Lawyer.

Unsurprised, Red started the ball rolling for a public defender for Denby—who claimed he couldn't afford to hire one—and gave Sparks his call so he could contact his own.

With Maggie's exceptional chicken and dumplings—and a slice of Julia's spice cake—happily filling his belly, he huddled with Michaela.

Both agreed, of the two, Denby racked up more stupid points. They'd take him first.

Together they walked into the interview room. And though he restarted the recorder, Red held up a hand. "It's going to take awhile for the court to appoint your lawyer, and awhile for him to get here. You don't have to say a word, that's your right. We're just here to let you know it might take till morning, and to give you a little information."

"I got nothing to say."

"Nobody's asking you to, just making you aware that Charlotte Dupont's exchanged considerable information in exchange for a deal.

First come, first served—you know how it works, Frank. With what we got from her, and from other sources, the state intends to go for life, no parole."

"That's bullshit." But he'd gone sickly gray. "I didn't do anything."

"Not asking you what you did or didn't. Are we, Mic?"

"No, sir, the suspect has engaged his right to an attorney. Until that attorney—well, whoever the courts can scrounge up—gets here, we're not asking a single thing. Simply informing."

"I bet it's Bilbo." Red let go a snickering laugh. "With this guy's luck I bet it's Bilbo. Anyway, from what we already know, this was your operation, so you're likely to go down the hardest."

"Mine? That's a crock of—"

"Now, Frank." Red held up his hand again. "You don't want to say anything until you talk to your"—he rolled his eyes at Michaela—"lawyer when he gets here. Mic and I put in a long one today, but figure before we lock you up, get on home, we should let you know how things stand. The blonde? She rolled hard on you, Frank. And you were the one who had a gun in his possession. Then you got the blackmail."

"There wasn't any blackmail! That was bogus."

"Frank, if you keep saying stuff, we're going to have to put you back in your cell without giving you the information to help you decide how to handle things when your lawyer gets here tomorrow."

"Screw a lawyer. There wasn't any damn blackmail. I'm not going down for fucking blackmail."

"Look, if you've got something you want to say, something you want to tell us, you need to waive your right to an attorney. Otherwise—"

"Didn't I say 'screw a lawyer'?" His eyes darted back and forth between them, shooting out genuine fear. "I waive that shit then. Blackmail, my ass."

"Okay, the record shows you're waiving your right to an attorney and want to talk. You showed Ms. Dupont and Mr. Sparks photographs you'd taken of them in some very compromising positions."

"That's right, that's right. With Sparks's camera, for Christ's sake. Do you think I could afford one of those long lenses? Do you think I could've gotten inside the walls of that big-ass estate without him setting it up?"

Michaela didn't miss a beat, just cast her eyes to the ceiling. "Jesus, he expects us to believe Sparks set all this up? We're wasting our time on this one, Sheriff."

"He did! It's what he does, it's his game. He hits up rich women. He hits them up for loans, big-ticket gifts, cash, whatever. He'll honeypot them for more if he figures he can squeeze them."

"And you know this how?" Red asked.

"Maybe we ran a few together. It's not the first time he's tapped me for a game."

"Now they've worked together." Michaela kicked back, yawned. "Sparks makes good money as a PT for wealthy clients. Why would he risk that to hook up with a second-rate grifter like you?"

"Look, bitch—"

"Now, now," Red said mildly. "Language."

"He's got the style, okay? That's his gig. Sex, style, finding women who want some of both. Sometimes he wants somebody to hit the mark with photos. That's me. You squeeze a few thousand, and you move on."

"A few thousand? You were hitting for ten million."

"Ten—" Everything about Denby went dark, went ugly. "That son of a bitch. He said two. We'd split two. Biggest take ever. He had the woman wrapped. He saw how it was. The kid wasn't a big deal to her—but the kid was a really big deal with the father. And the father, he had the money. A hell of a lot of money. The fucking Hollywood Sullivans, right?"

He patted his chest. "Can I get a smoke?"

"No." Red just smiled. "Keep going."

"He says we'll go for the big one, the kind you retire on. I'm not kidnapping some kid, that's what I say. I mean whoa. But he's, like, he can get the blonde to set it up. If she balks, we walk. But if she bites, we're in."

"She bit." He leaned forward. "It's, like, I hit Sparks first, and he has to go to her, tell her. We meet up—she wears a wig, for Christ's sake, big sunglasses. Like anybody gives a rat's ass. I show the shots, she gets hysterical—'What'll it take? You can't sell these. My career, the press!' So I get how Sparks had it right. It's all about her, and that makes it easy. I say, like me and Sparks set up, how I'll let her know what it'll take, and it won't come cheap."

"You didn't directly demand the ten million?"

"No. Man, he said it was for two, so I say how I want two. They played me," he muttered, bitter. "Played me for a mark, went for ten. I figured she could get two, sell some shit or whatever, but he comes to me, says she can't get it, and how he talked her into using the kid. How she jumped on it."

He squirmed in his chair. "Look, if I can't get a smoke, can I get a Mountain Dew or some shit?"

"Finish it out, and we'll fix you up."

"Jesus, don't you see? He set me up. They fucking set me up. I'm not going down for all this. They worked out how to get the kid. He said she had the perfect time and place because they were having the party deal for the old man—the dead one—up in Big Sur. It'll be easy and slick. She knew about the house where we could keep her, that it was going to be empty. She knew it would be because they'd be out of town and wouldn't be coming to the party deal, got it?"

"Yeah." Enjoying himself, Red put his feet up on the table. "We're following you."

"I didn't snatch the kid. Sparks did. The blonde set up where, and he dosed the kid, loaded her up into one of those serving cart deals—with the storage? Into a van—we fixed it up like one of the catering deals—and just freaking drove away with her inside the damn van."

"How did the blonde set up where?" Michaela asked him.

"How the hell do I know? The two of them huddled about the details, right? I'm just supposed to get the room ready, get it, you know, secure, load in some supplies. I'm just babysitting, get it?"

"Did those supplies include masks?"

He squirmed again. "We don't want her to see our faces, right? Better all around. And I bought those damn masks out of my own pocket. Same with the food and stuff. I'm supposed to get paid back for it out of the take."

"Looks like a bad investment for you," Red commented. "Then again, you did a lousy job at babysitting."

"Who's gonna expect the kid to climb out the window? Makes a rope out of frigging sheets. Uses a damn spoon like a crowbar to pull the nails out of the window lock. Who expects that? Sparks beat the shit out of me like it's my fault."

He leaned forward. "What I'm saying is Sparks came up with the whole game, he's the one who brought the blonde in, and got plenty of sex out of it. The two of them worked out the details—and were goddamn cheating me all along. All I did was watch the kid."

"You were practically an innocent bystander."

Denby pointed at Michaela as sarcasm sailed over his head like a kite in a summer breeze. "Damn right."

"Okay, Frank." Red shoved a notebook and pen across the table. "Write it out, and don't spare the details. We'll see about that Mountain Dew."

By the time they'd finished with Denby—because he didn't spare the details—Red wanted a beer and a bed, in that order.

But he calculated the timing, and the fact Scarpetti loved playing the media like a fiddle.

He didn't know Mark Rozwell, the lawyer Sparks pulled in—and who was even now consulting with him. But he had to figure more media playing.

The more they nailed down before the morning news, the better.

Once again he dug into his supply of Cokes when he called Michaela into his office. "You're racking up the OT, Mic, and I'm going to ask if you're up for more."

"I can handle it."

"I believe you can." He tossed her the Coke. "We have to figure Scarpetti's going to call a press conference in the morning, do what he can to put Dupont in the light of a victim. The only reason I give two shits about that is it'll release the fucking kraken on the Sullivans, that little girl."

"So we get all we can get from Sparks, like we did from Denby, so he can't play into that before we do."

"That's the way."

"Do you think Dupont was in on the whole thing?"

"I'm fifty-fifty there. I'll weigh that again once we talk to Sparks.

Right now, I'm going to do a run on his lawyer to give us a sense of what we've got here."

"I already did."

He sat, tipped back in his chair. "You're an eager, enterprising soul, Mic."

"Just a cop. I Googled him, too, just to fill it out. California native, forty-six, married, one kid and one on the way. Did his law thing at Berkeley. He's worked at Kohash and Milford for ten years, and made full partner three years ago. He's a high-priced trial lawyer with a solid rep."

She took a long swallow of Coke. "He's a good-looking guy, and the camera loves him. He's not afraid of talking to the press. He's also written a couple of legal thrillers, but it doesn't look like John Grisham has to look over his shoulder.

"And Sparks is his personal trainer."

"There it is."

"There it is," she agreed. "No criminal on the run. Has a house in Holmby Hills, a beach house in Oceanside. He drives a Lexus, as does his wife—she's a freelance script doctor."

Red waited a beat. "That's it? You didn't get his shoe size, his political affiliation?"

"Registered Independent. I'd have to dig a little more for the shoe size."

He laughed. "Okay, I see we play this cards on the table. The man's got a rep, doesn't sound like an idiot, and has a law firm's rep to uphold. The guy's his trainer, not his brother, not his best pal. We've got him cold."

"You want to lay groundwork for a plea deal."

"I want that son of a bitch to live the rest of his life in San fucking Quentin, Mic. That's my personal want. And I have to hope I don't get it, because the idea of putting that kid—and the family, but that kid—through a trial just makes me sick."

Because her thoughts, her wants, ran the same, Michaela nodded. "I hate thinking he'll walk out one day, that all three of them will. But I feel the same as you do on this. Even so, it's not up to us."

"State's attorney will take twenty to twenty-five. We'll see if they do. Our job is to lay it out, make sure the lawyer understands the preponderance of evidence, and Sparks knows in his guts he'll face life, no parole."

"Got it. I'll ask the lawyer if they're ready to talk to us."

It took another twenty minutes, but Rozwell agreed to the interview. Since it wasn't Red's first day at the beach, he figured Rozwell assumed they'd all do a first pass, gauge the opposition, and restart in the morning.

Michaela had it right about Rozwell—a good-looking guy with a five-hundred-dollar haircut that allowed just a hint of silver at the temples, just a few strands of it through his dark brown hair. Dark brown eyes, smart, savvy. Clean-cut and handsome with a trim body.

But he paled against Sparks and his movie star gloss. Even a few hours in a cell, even the orange jumpsuit didn't dull it. Gilded sun-streaked hair with just a hint of curl fell thick around a golden tanned face with carved features—the cheekbones, the heavy-lidded brown eyes, the full mouth.

And all that on top of a sleek, muscular build.

He played it—because in Red's estimation of Sparks and his type, everything was a role to play—nervous, anxious, with no anger and just a hint of remorse and sorrow.

Red sat, turned on the recorder, read the necessaries in.

"Sheriff, Deputy, first, I appreciate you meeting with us tonight. I understand you've put in a very long day."

Rozwell's face stayed sober, his voice smooth. "At this time I'd like to inform you that I intend to file a motion for dismissal in the morning on a number of the charges made against my client. While my client is appalled at the part he inadvertently played in these events, any minor participation came at the behest and request of the minor child's mother, and with the belief said minor child was being abused by her father. As he was unaware of Ms. Dupont's scheme to extort from the Sullivan family—"

"Sorry, can I just stop you there?" He kept all the affable, just a county sheriff in his voice. "No point in wasting your time. Long day for you, too. So let me put some of that to rest. We have Charlotte Dupont's written statement, Frank Denby's written statement."

He smiled at Sparks as he said it. Red had been very careful to keep those arrests, interviews, deals under his hat. "There's direct corroboration in those statements, and evidence in hand supports that. As does the statement of the minor child."

"It's Mr. Sparks's contention that Ms. Dupont and Mr. Denby worked together on this scheme, duping him."

"Did they dupe you into sticking a needle full of propofol into that little girl's throat?"

"I didn't—"

"Cut it. You wore a wig—which we recovered—and sunglasses, but Caitlyn has eyes. Good ones. And ears. You spoke to her before you jabbed her, and you spoke to her behind the wolfman mask—also recovered—you used to scare a ten-year-old girl. You jabbed her, stuffed her into a serving trolley, then drove away from a good man's memorial, from an already grieving family."

"Sheriff, a child under such duress would hardly be able to, without a reasonable doubt, identify voices in this way."

Michaela let out a laugh. "You haven't met this child. Put her under oath, in a courtroom, I can promise you a jury will hang on her every word. The word of a child whose own mother plotted with her lover to use her, to drug her, to terrify her. For money. Your voice is on the phone, too, Sparks, demanding ten million dollars in exchange. They didn't call the police, but they recorded the calls."

"Your partners rolled and rolled hard. Denby's pretty steamed you made the deal with him for two million—fifty-fifty—when you asked the Sullivans for ten. That opened him up like a steamed clam. And if you actually think a woman who'd bang her personal trainer in the same bed she shares with her husband, a woman who'd trade her own daughter's sense of safety, allow that child to be drugged and terrorized, has any sense of loyalty, you're an idiot."

He shifted to Rozwell. "I'm laying this out for you because I'm tired, I'm disgusted, and I've used up my tolerance for bullshit today. Both Dupont and Denby have taken a deal. Your client's last in line, and I figure everybody in this room knows the last in line gets shit. Maybe this fuck gave you a sob story, played the horrified dupe, and how sorry he is about the poor kid caught in the middle, but we have evidence that blows all of that aside.

"To sum it up, your dickbag of a client spotted Dupont for a mark, the last in a long line of wealthy women he bled for money. We have names, and will get statements to corroborate that. With Dupont, he saw a big-ass payday, enough to retire in style, starting with Mozambique."

Layering it on, Red sent Sparks a pitying look. "You had a bunch of searches on Mozambique—no extradition treaty—on your laptop, asshole. He hooked up with his sometime partner, Frank Denby, to run the con. Blackmail—pictures taken with his camera, also now in evidence—of his mark and himself in—what's that phrase?—in flagrante delicto. Said mark, being the worst shit of a mother in the history of mothers, agreed to the kidnapping for ransom—Sparks and Dupont boosted the price to screw Denby. She set up the kid, told her where to go for a goddamn game of hide-and-seek, where Sparks was waiting with the needle, the trolley, the van."

As if revolted—not a stretch—Red rose, turned away. "Pick it up, Deputy. I need a minute to settle my stomach."

She did, and seamlessly, snapping out the rest, or at least the high points.

Rozwell's face showed little. Red figured he'd handle a poker game as well as he did a courtroom. But everybody had a tell. He had to look for Rozwell's, but he caught it.

Just the slightest tightening at the corner of the mouth, a muscle twitch that brought out a tiny dimple.

When Michaela finished, Red sat again. "There isn't a judge in the world who's going to dismiss a single one of the charges. There isn't a jury in the world that's going to look at that sweet little girl and not convict. And your client gets life without parole."

He glanced at Sparks. "Keep playing the game, and that's your grand fucking prize."

"I did it for love!" Sparks filled his outburst with grief.

"Jesus," Red muttered. "Same coin, same mold."

"Charlotte swore she—"

"Be quiet, Grant."

"Mark, you have to believe me. You know me. I would never—"

"I said be quiet." This time Red heard more than a hint of weariness. "I'll need a few moments with my client."

"Take it. I need some air anyway."

When he went out, Red realized he actually did. "I'm going to step outside and breathe a minute, Mic."

"Do you think he's going to bail? The lawyer?"

"I'd say he's considering it. Give me a holler when they're ready."

Outside, he looked up at the sky, found himself grateful the night was filled with stars. He might wish he still had the energy left to sneak into Maggie's bed for a late-night booty call, but since he didn't have the stores left, a star-strewn night sky would have to do.

It calmed him, reminded him life offered a whole bounty of good things from the simple to the amazing. You just had to take a few minutes now and then to find them.

He heard the door open behind him. "Be right there, Mic."

"Sheriff, your deputy's taking Mr. Sparks back to his cell for the night."

Red nodded at Rozwell. "All right then."

"I'll need another few minutes with him in the morning, and would like to meet with the prosecutor."

"I can arrange that. Let's say nine o'clock."

"That's fine. I'll be here. I wonder if you could recommend a hotel, motel, just a decent place to spend the night. I didn't have time to make arrangements."

"Sure can. Come back to my office. I'll give you a couple close by—if you're looking for close."

"Close would be great."

"You can call from here, make sure they've got a room for you." In his office, he scribbled names on a pad. "The top one? Good beds, good service, and twenty-four-hour room service if you need it. They charge for Wi-Fi though, which burns my ass."

"Thanks."

"Go ahead, use the room."

Red walked out, waited for Michaela, and considered he probably had the energy for that cold beer before bed. And a hot shower. Christ, he wanted the shower more than the beer.

Rozwell walked out.

"All set?"

"Yeah, thanks. I'll be here at nine. I left my cell phone number on your pad if you need to reach me." He started for the door, turned, looked Red in the eye. "I have a daughter. She's only four. I have a little girl of my own."

And when he walked out, Red knew they'd deal.

Michaela walked back—still spit and polish, he thought. And had to admire it.

"You settle him in?"

"He tried tears on me. Slow, soulful ones. He's good."

"We're better. Rozwell wants to meet with the prosecutor in the morning. I'm going to contact him on my way home. You can take tomorrow off."

"I'd like to see it through."

"Be here by nine then. I'll walk you out."

"We'll walk each other out."

"Works for me."

CHAPTER EIGHT

Dillon liked mucking out the stalls. He loved the romantic smell of horses—even mixed with horse-shit bedding. Every clear memory of his life involved the ranch, and his favorite ones included horses.

His favorite of favorites was the night he, his mom, and Gram watched Diva deliver her first foal. Some of it had been kind of yuck, but mostly just cool. They'd even let him name the foal, a pretty bay with four white socks and a crooked white blaze.

He'd called her Comet, because the blaze looked like a comet trail. Sort of.

And even though he'd only been six, they'd let him groom her and work with her on the lead line when she got old enough. He'd been the first to stretch his body over her back to get her used to weight. The first to ease a saddle on her, the first to ride her.

He'd helped train others since—and thought he was pretty good at it. But Comet was his.

And he'd been by her side when she'd had her first foal the previous spring.

He just liked being a rancher—an agricultural rancher, because they planted and grew and harvested and sold vegetables, had an orchard of fruit trees, even Gram's vineyard, though she mostly made wine for herself and friends.

He didn't mind all the chores (in fact, he liked chores a lot better than school). The planting and hoeing, feeding and watering stock, even making hay when the sun beat down, or helping run their stall at the farmer's market.

He liked living up high on the cliff, seeing the ocean every day, or walking the fields—even better, riding over the fields, into the woods.

Winter Saturdays meant a lot of chores he handled by himself, or with his mom giving him a hand where she could. Inside the house, Gram and his mom would be baking—bread and pies and cakes for the cooperative. From Friday morning into Saturday the house smelled really, really good.

Sometimes Gram made candles, too, from soy and put smelly stuff in them. She was teaching him how, just like they were teaching him how to bake bread and all that.

He'd rather feed the pigs and chickens, watch them scramble around, haul the feed to the troughs for the beef cattle, milk the nanny goats. And muck out stalls.

He'd finished most of the morning routine before eleven—real ranchers, Dillon knew, started early—and hauled the last wheelbarrow from the stalls to the dung pile.

He heard the car coming up the ranch road, looked up at the sky to gauge the time. His good pals Leo and Dave were coming over to hang, but not until the afternoon.

So too early for them.

He rolled the empty wheelbarrow back to the barn, stowed it, and, slapping his work gloves on his pants to clean them, wandered over to see who was coming.

In the way of boys, he recognized the shining silver vehicle as a BMW—a fanCEE SUV. He just didn't know anybody who drove one.

Seeing as he was the man of the house, he waited—legs spread, thumbs hooked in his front pockets.

And when he saw Hugh Sullivan get out, he walked the rest of the way over to say hello.

"Hi, Mr. Sullivan."

"Dillon."

In a way that made Dillon feel very much man of the house, Hugh offered his hand to shake before he just looked around.

"I didn't really take all this in when we were here. So much worry, and it was dark. You have a very beautiful place."

"Thanks."

Hugh gestured at the work gloves now flopping in Dillon's back pocket. "And I can see you work hard to tend it. I realize you must have a great deal more work to do, but I wonder if I could take a few minutes of your time, speak to you, your mother, your grandmother."

"Sure. I'm mostly finished with the morning chores. Mom and Gram are inside baking. They bake most of Friday for the co-op, but there's a special thing tomorrow, so they're baking more today."

Maybe he thought it was too bad Cate hadn't come, but he didn't say anything.

"Ah, the sheriff came over the other day to tell us they caught the guys who kidnapped Cate. That they were in prison and everything already. I'm glad," he said as he walked Hugh to the door. "The man who killed my dad's in prison."

Hugh pulled up short, looked back down at the boy. "I'm so sorry about your dad, Dillon. I didn't know."

"I was really little, so I don't remember him. But he was a hero."

After swiping his boots hard on the mat, Dillon opened the door. He remembered his manners. "I can hang up your coat."

"I'd appreciate it."

As Dillon took it, Hugh drew in a deep breath. "It smells like heaven should."

Dillon grinned. "It gets even better in the kitchen. Since you're here, they're going to ask if you want some pie or cookies or something. If you don't say no, I get some, too."

Charmed, Hugh put a hand on Dillon's shoulder. "I won't say no."

He led him back, through the scents of fresh bread, rising dough, baked fruit, and sugar to where the women, in their big aprons, worked a kind of production line.

Pies, loaves of bread, four unfrosted cakes, cookies spread out on cooling racks on a long counter. He saw a number of white bakery boxes with the Horizon Ranch label hiding their treasures on the dining room table.

A big stand mixer whirled some sort of batter while Julia—her hair bundled up in a small cook's cap—pulled another tray of cookies from the oven. At the island, Maggie cranked some sort of device to peel and core apples for the pie crusts already waiting.

Music pumped out of a boom box, shaking the redolent air with rock and roll.

Hugh thought the women were as graceful as ballerinas, as strong as lumberjacks, as focused as scientists.

"Mom! Mr. Sullivan's here."

"What? Have you finished with— Oh." Spotting Hugh, Julia set down the tray, dusted her hands on her apron. After tapping her mother's shoulder, she switched off the music.

"Sorry," she began, "for the chaos."

"It's not. It's amazing. I apologize for interrupting."

"I could use a quick break." Maggie rolled her shoulders. "Dillon, why don't you take Hugh into the living room?"

"I wonder if I could just sit in here?" Hugh closed his eyes, drew an exaggerated breath. "And get drunk on the scents."

"Sit right down wherever you like." Julia switched off the mixer. "Dillon, don't touch a thing. Go wash your hands."

"I know the rules." He rolled his eyes, walked out, because one of the rules meant he couldn't wash hands after chores in the kitchen on a baking day.

"I'm going to speak my mind," Maggie decided, "and tell you you look worn out, tired out. I'm not going to offer you coffee because sometimes what a body needs is a good herbal tea. I have just the thing."

Grateful, he sat at the table crowded with their baking tools while Maggie put on a kettle. And smiled when Julia put an assortment of cookies on a plate.

"Thanks can't possibly cover it."

"Yes, they can," Julia told him. "We're all so relieved the people responsible are in prison. How's Caitlyn?"

"She . . ." He'd planned to say she was doing well, but the worry, the stress simply spilled out. "She has nightmares, and she's afraid to be alone. Aidan, my son, he's going to take her to a therapist, a specialist, someone she can talk to."

He paused when Dillon rushed back in. "He said he wanted to talk to all of us."

"And I do. Maybe you can sit here with me, help me with these cookies."

"Go ahead, Dillon." As she spoke, Julia got a jug out of the fridge, poured a glass of goat's milk for her son.

"My wife—Lily—she wanted me to add her thanks. She would have come with me, but she went with Aidan and Cate back to L.A. They're going to stay in our guesthouse for now. Cate didn't want to go back to their house."

"Because her mother lived there."

"Dillon," Julia murmured.

"No, he's right. That's exactly right. My mother left for Ireland this morning. The house here . . . it feels too big for her without my father. Too full of memories of him that, right now, make her sad. Aidan's going to take our Catey there, away from all this. We all think it'll be good for her, and she wants to go."

"You'll miss them."

"Yes. My mother's turned the house here over to me. I hope Lily and I can spend more time here, but we have caretakers, the couple who've worked for my parents for many years, who'll look after the place while we're in L.A. or working."

Maggie set a cup in front of him. "See that you drink that."

"I will. I wanted to ask if when we are here, if you'd come, have dinner with us."

"Of course. You're alone here tonight?" Julia asked him.

"I have some things to deal with before I leave. Tomorrow afternoon."

"Then you'll have dinner with us tonight. Red's already coming, so we're putting a pot roast on as soon as the baking's done."

"I would . . . Thank you. I'd love to come to dinner." To compose himself, he lifted the tea, sipped. "This is good, and interesting. What is it?"

"Basil and honey," Maggie told him. "Holy basil it's called, with honey from our own bees. It helps with stress and fatigue."

"I want to say you're both amazing women who are, clearly, raising an amazing young man. I speak for my entire family—and we are many—when I say we are forever in your debt."

"There's no debt," Julia began, but Hugh grabbed her hand and stopped her.

"She is the world to me. I adore the children Lily brought into my life, and love them like my own. But Caitlyn is the only child of my only child. My first wife died," he said to Dillon.

"I'm sorry."

"Her middle name was Caitlyn, and I see her in Catey's eyes, in the way she moves. She is the world to me. I want you to allow me to give you more than gratitude. I know there's no price for what you, all of you, did for Cate, but I'm asking you to allow me to give you some tangible repayment for what can never be repaid."

"Your heart's in the right place." Maggie took a bowl, poured the mix in it over the apples. "We couldn't take money for doing what was right for a frightened child."

"The world to me," Hugh repeated.

Reading the emotion, the need, the pain, Julia made a decision. "Dillon, did you finish your chores?"

He stuffed the second half of a cookie in his mouth before it was too late. "Almost."

"Since you've bolted your share of those cookies, finish the almost."

"But—" He caught the look in his mother's eyes, the one that said: Argue with me, pay the price. He dragged himself to his feet. "I guess I'll see you for dinner, Mr. Sullivan."

"Hugh, and, yes, you will."

He waited until the boy went out the back. "You thought of something you'll accept."

"That depends. We had a dog. Dillon loved Daisy so much. She went everywhere he went—except school, and if they could've figured out how to manage it, she'd have been under his desk. We, my husband and I, got her before he was born, so he had her all his life. She died two months ago."

Her voice broke. "I'm not over it. But grieving time has to end, and I've seen when Dillon has computer time, he's been looking at dogs. He's ready."

Maggie lifted her apron, used the hem to wipe at her eyes. "I loved that damn dog."

"I'll get him any kind of dog he wants."

"There's a woman I know who helps with rescues and fostering. I've been thinking of this for a couple of weeks, but couldn't make myself pull the trigger."

"Because this is the trigger," Maggie put in, and rubbed a hand on Julia's back.

"It feels that way. She's just this side of Monterey, so not far. I can call her if you want to take Dillon and go see."

"Yes. If this is what you'll accept, this is what I'll do."

"One favor. Don't tell him where you're going. I think the surprise is part of the gift. It's a gift, not payment."

"A gift." Rising, he took Julia's hand, kissed it. "Thank you."

The next thing Dillon knew, his mom made him wash up— again—so he could help Hugh with an errand.

"Um, Leo and Dave are coming over in a couple hours."

"You'll be back by then, and if not, we'll keep them entertained."

She made him put on his school jacket instead of his work jacket—like anybody cared. Still, he didn't think he'd mind a ride in the fancy car.

"I appreciate this, Dillon."

"It's okay." After hooking his seat belt, Dillon brushed his finger-tips over the leather seat. Smoo—ooth. "This is a really nice car."

"I like it. Here, you can navigate." He handed Dillon the directions Julia had written out.

"That's Mom's writing."

"Yes, she's helping me, too. So tell me, Dillon," he continued before the boy could ask with what, "what do you want to do, to be, when you're grown-up?"

"A rancher, just like now. It's the best. You get to work with ani-mals, especially the horses. And you plant things."

"It must be a lot of work."

"Yeah, but it's still awesome. We get some help in the spring and summer when we need it, but mostly it's just me and Mom and Gram. You're going to turn left at the end of our road, head toward Monterey."

"Got it. You said especially the horses. Do you ride?"

"Sure. That's the best. But I know how to train them. I saw that movie you were in where you were a rancher, but you used to be a gunfighter."

"Ah. *Into Redemption.*"

"Yeah, that's it. You need to turn left again on that road coming up. You really rode good. Mom let me rent the DVD of this movie you made with Cate and your son, and I guess your dad. We watched it last night because it's not a school night. You all used accents, even she did. It was weird."

Hugh laughed, made the turn.

"I meant it was weird for me, I guess, because after a while I kind of forgot who she was, and you and her dad, because it seemed like you were the people in the movie. It's the next left."

Slowing, Hugh gave Dillon a long look. "You've just given me and my son, my granddaughter, my own father the highest of compliments."

It felt good to know he had, even if he didn't quite understand how. "Is it fun, being a movie star?"

"Not always, but it's awesome being an actor."

Dillon wasn't sure what the difference was, but it seemed rude to ask. His mom hated rude.

"Mom says it's the blue house on the left with the big garage."

"Looks like we're here then."

Hugh pulled into the drive behind a van, a truck. "I appreciate you coming with me."

"It's okay. Mom or Gram would have remembered to make me clean my room otherwise."

"Clever boy," Hugh murmured as they got out.

Outside the blue ranch house on the short front lawn sat a Big Wheel. A birdhouse hung from the corner eave, and in the front window sat an enormous tabby cat who looked bored at the idea of company.

When Hugh knocked, a din of barking erupted from inside. In the window, the cat yawned. The door opened almost immediately.

Dillon saw a woman older than his mother, younger than his

grandmother, with short brown hair and really red lips and really pink cheeks. She pressed a hand to her heart over a shirt with lots of color that looked too fancy for Saturday morning to him.

She said—pretty much squeaked—"Oh, Hugh Sullivan! I just can't believe—I'm so . . . Come in, come in. I'm Lori Greenspan. I'm just honored."

Hugh said polite stuff, taking her hand, but Dillon didn't pay any real attention. Because he got the movie star thing now. People, or some people anyway, got crazy eyes for movie stars. He guessed acting was just a really cool job.

"And you're Julia's boy."

"Yes, ma'am."

"You come right on in. I hope you'll excuse the mess," she said, giving Hugh the crazy eyes again. "I was just doing my Saturday cleaning when you called."

Not in that shirt, Dillon thought.

"Your home's just charming, and we appreciate you letting us drop in on your busy day."

Her already pink cheeks pinked up more at Hugh's compliment. "I'm never too busy for—" She seemed to catch herself, gave Dillon a quick look. "For good company. Please have a seat. I'll just be a moment."

When she scurried out, Dillon looked up at Hugh. "Do lots of people do that when they meet you?"

"Do what?"

Dillon did his best imitation of crazy eyes, adding rapid head shakes for impact. With a rolling laugh, Hugh gave Dillon a friendly punch on the shoulder.

"It happens."

"Do you ever—" He broke off when a couple of puppies, yipping deliriously, raced into the room.

Hugh watched the boy's face light up as he dropped into a crouch. The pups licked everywhere, paws scrambling as they tried to climb on the boy. Just as delighted, the boy stroked and petted everywhere at once.

Love at first sight, Hugh thought, personified.

"Aren't they sweet?"

"Yes, ma'am." Dillon's laugh wound in, around, through the words as the pups leaped, licked, tumbled. "What're their names?"

"They don't have any yet. I've been calling them Girl and Boy so I don't get too attached. You see, we foster animals—mostly dogs and cats, but you never know. Sometimes they're abandoned or mistreated, and we help take care of them until they find their forever home. These two were part of a litter of six. The poor mama was trying to take care of them as best she could. They were all living in a drainage ditch, poor things."

"You do kind and caring work, Lori."

"I just can't stand to see animals mistreated. Anyone mistreated, of course, but we're supposed to be stewards, caretakers for puppies like these, and their mama."

"Is she okay?" Dillon asked. "Their mother?"

The look Lori gave Dillon showed her heart, and made him forgive the crazy eyes. "She is. My husband took her to the vet today to have her neutered. We needed to wean her puppies first, and give her time to get good and healthy again. We've decided to call her Angel, because she has such loving eyes. We're going to be her forever home."

"But you can't keep the puppies?"

Lori smiled down at Dillon. "If I had my way, and had the room, the wherewithal, I'd keep every single rescue. But I think it's a good thing to share them. We already placed her other puppies with good homes."

She glanced at Hugh, got the nod.

"These sweethearts have a whole lot of energy. As best we can tell, Angel's got some border collie, some beagle in her. So taking after her, they're good with people, love herding and running and playing. They need somebody who can keep up with them, so I was hoping you'd take one of these home with you, be one of those good homes."

"Oh!" Dillon's face lit again, then he lowered his head, nuzzled puppies. "My mom—"

"Said yes," Hugh finished.

His head popped back up, with all that light shining on his face.

"Really? Really? Holy cow! I can have one? I can just . . . but how do I pick?"

Hugh crouched down, got his share of puppy love. "They're both great-looking puppies."

"They both have a lot of border collie in the look," Lori commented. "Girl has more brown on her face, but they both have pretty markings, that mix of black and brown and white. And the fluffy tails, floppy ears. And they both, I swear, have their mama's eyes. Maybe you're leaning more to a boy dog, or a girl dog."

Dillon only shook his head. "But they're family, and friends, too. You can see how they play together and, you know, kiss each other and stuff. If I pick one, the other gets left behind. It doesn't seem right to, you know, separate a brother and sister. It doesn't seem fair."

Dillon shot Hugh a look, a quick one before he buried his face in puppies again. But in that instant it filled with one heartfelt plea.

Blowing out a breath, Hugh stood. "I need to make a call. If you'd excuse me for just a minute."

"You go right ahead." Lori sat on the edge of a chair as Hugh stepped out. "I can see whichever one you take home, you're going to take good care, be a real friend. That means a lot to me."

"It's hard to give them to other people?"

"Well, not so much when you know it's the right person. Then it makes you feel good inside. That's how I feel now, knowing one of these sweeties is going to have a boy who loves and tends and takes real responsibility."

"Won't the other one feel sad?"

"I'm going to do everything to keep the one who stays with me happy and healthy until we find just the right person, just the right forever home."

Torn between his desperate wish for a puppy and the genuine guilt at leaving one behind, Dillon could only stroke soft fur.

Hugh stepped back in. "You're a fortunate boy, Dillon, to have such a wise and loving mother. With your approval, Lori, Dillon has permission to adopt both."

"Both? I can have both?" Face shining, Dillon did his best to hug both puppies. "They can both come home with me?"

"If Ms. Greenspan agrees."

"Please?" Arms full, heart in his eyes, Dillon turned his face up to Lori's. "I'll take good care of them. We have lots of land for them to run on. When I'm in school, Mom and Gram will look after them, but before and after, they can come with me while I do my chores. I'll feed them and make sure they have fresh water. I know how."

"I think the two of them already picked you. You know these are smart dogs, about as smart as they come. You're going to be able to teach them lots of tricks."

"It's okay? I can have them?"

Forgetting her careful makeup, Lori dabbed at her eyes. "You already do. I have a list of things you have to promise to do. They're up on their shots, but when they need more, you have to see to that. You've got a good vet—your mom told me who you use. I use the same, so I know she's a good vet. When they're old enough, you have to promise to take them to the vet and get them spayed and neutered. That's really important. And I'm going to warn you, while they're just about housebroken, taking them to a new home usually sets that back. You'll have to do some work there."

"I will. I promise."

"All right then, I'm going to get that list, and you can sign it. And I have a brochure to help you with tips on care and feeding and training. I always give my adopted humans a little care package—of treats and toys. And I'm sorry to say I'm going to need fifty dollars. That's to cover some of the expense from foster care."

"I don't have any money with me, but I've got allowance saved up. I can bring it to you as soon—"

"Dillon, this is my gift. My thank-you gift to you."

Torn all over again, Dillon had to shake his head. "Mom said—"

"That this gift was acceptable," Hugh finished. "It would mean a great deal to me if you said you accept it, too."

Hugh held out a hand to seal the deal, smiled when Dillon shook.

"Thank you. This is the best gift anyone's ever given me."

"You gave me the same. Lori, Julia said the rescue organization you're affiliated with is called Loving Hearts Animal Rescue. In addition to the adoption fee, I'd like to make a donation to your group."

"That's generous of you, and much appreciated I can promise you. We can take care of the paperwork right back here. Dillon, why don't you take your puppies out that side door? There's a little fenced yard. I'd say you'd be smart to take them out, let them do their business before you put them in the car."

It took nearly half an hour before Hugh helped Dillon load the puppies—in a borrowed crate—into the back of his SUV. Along with what Lori called a congratulations basket of dog food samples, treats, chew toys.

Since the puppies seemed happy—for the moment—to share a big blue bone-shaped toy, Hugh got behind the wheel.

"I guess the next step is for you to name them. Any ideas?"

"He's Gambit, she's Jubilee. They're X-Men, and pretty awesome."

"Gambit and Jubilee." Hugh glanced back at the dogs as he eased out of the drive. "Good choices. I think we have one more thing to do before taking them home. We should go buy some collars, leashes, beds, what have you. Part of the gift," Hugh said before Dillon could comment.

Dillon looked back, then at Hugh. "I'm never going to forget it."

Hugh turned, started the drive, and said simply, "Neither will I."

PART II

THE NEXT TURN

From fame to infamy is a beaten road.
—FRANCIS QUARLES

All the world doth practice stage-playing.
—MONTAIGNE

CHAPTER NINE

County Mayo · 2008

Cate stood by the lake watching the big black dog her nan had loved swim. Ducks scattered, quacking protests, while Lola skimmed through the water like a seal.

Overhead, the stacked clouds spat out a thin drizzle, but every day was a holiday for Lola.

Lola had grieved at first when Nan passed—quietly in her sleep like the man she'd loved. The dog had lain at the foot of Nan's bed for days, inconsolable until Cate tied one of Nan's scarves around Lola's neck.

A comfort in scent, Cate thought, until gradually Lola had regained her always happy demeanor.

Another funeral for the Sullivan clan—and the world. Another celebration of life for the family.

While she understood why the loss and the rituals brought back the nightmares, the anxiety, that didn't make them any easier to get through. Even now, with the dog splashing, with so many of her family inside the cottage, she caught herself looking toward the woods on the side of the lake.

In case she saw movement, in case someone waited.

She knew better—she wasn't a child anymore—but still she looked.

She knew those woods, just as she knew the garden, as she knew every room in the cottage. For most of the last seven years, this had been home. The time spent in L.A. was just visits.

The trips to England or Italy, just trips.

For the first year, her father had turned down every script, every offer, shielding her, she understood now, as much from the press as from her fears.

But she'd had Nan and Nina right there, and G-Lil and her grandfather in L.A. on those visits. Aunt Mo and Uncle Harry and the rest on visits to New York.

She'd been glad when Nina fell in love and got married, even though it meant she didn't live in the cottage or the guesthouse in L.A.

Now Cate couldn't live in the cottage either. Her nan was gone; her father had work. So now she'd live in L.A., and her time here would become visits.

At last Lola climbed out of the lake, shook off a wild torrent of water. Then she rolled around on the wet grass in pure joy.

"You're getting as wet as she is."

She broke out a smile—she knew how—for her grandfather. "It's barely a drizzle." When he put an arm around her shoulders, she dropped her head to one of his. "I know she was ready to be with Grandda. She talked about him so much the last few weeks. Sometimes . . ."

"Sometimes?"

"She talked to him." Looking up, she saw the rain adding yet more shine to his hair, that shining silver hair. "I'd hear her talking to him, half expected to hear him talking back. I didn't, but I honestly believe she did."

"They loved a lifetime." As always surprised that her head reached his chin now, he pressed a kiss to her temple. "It's hard on us being without them. I know it's hard for you to leave here now. You'll come back. I promise."

It wouldn't be the same.

"I know I can't take Lola. This is her home, and it wouldn't be fair. She loves Nina and Rob and the kids, so she'll be happy with them."

"What can I do for you, Catey? What can I do to make this a little easier?"

"Don't let Dad turn down good scripts because he's worried about me. I hate when I know he does. I'm seventeen. I need to know he trusts me to . . . to just deal."

"What do you want, for you?"

"I don't know, not exactly. But, well, I'm a Sullivan, so I think I should try, again, to do what we do."

"You want to act again?"

"I want to try. I know it's been a long time, but it's in the blood, isn't it? I mean, just some little part, some little thing. Get my feet wet."

"I might have just the thing. We'll talk about it on the flight home."

Everything inside her tightened and clutched. "Is it time to leave?"

"It's getting close."

"I—I want to walk Lola over to Nina's. Say goodbye to everyone."

"Go ahead. I'll tell your father. Caitlyn," he said as she started toward the dog, "life's a series of turns. This is another one for you."

She stood, dark hair damp with rain, eyes as blue as a summer sky. And as sad as a broken heart. "How do you know where it's going to take you?"

"You never do. That's part of the adventure."

What if she didn't want an adventure? she thought as she hitched on her backpack holding Lola's favorite toys. What if she wanted the quiet, the ordinary?

What if she didn't want to turn in a new direction?

With no choice—it grated to always have so little choice—she called the dog, and with Lola started down the path that skirted the woods.

The familiar path, one she'd walked countless times, often with Lola for company, sometimes just alone with her thoughts. Wasn't she allowed to hate leaving the familiar?

Where would she find these damp, green scents in L.A.? That simple pleasure of walking a narrow dirt path in a soft rain?

She heard the quick call of a magpie before she saw him dart into the trees. Just one more thing she'd miss.

Her turn happened when she'd been ten. Nothing had been the same since.

"No one talks about it, Lola." At the sound of her name, Lola scrambled back from sniffing at the fuchsia dripping from the hedgerow, danced back. "Not even me anymore. What's the point? But I can count, can't I? I know she's coming up for parole."

Shrugging, Cate shifted the backpack. "Who cares, right? Who gives a damn? If she gets out, she gets out. It doesn't change anything."

But she worried it would, if her mother walked out of prison, it would be one more change she couldn't control, would have to accept.

Maybe, just maybe, acting again would give her some control over her own bloody life. As much as she loved her family—and God, she did, both here in Ireland and back in the States—she needed her own.

Her own life, her own choices, just her own.

"I miss it," she murmured to Lola. "I miss acting, miss letting myself be someone else, miss the work, and the fun of it. So maybe."

And in a year, she reminded herself, she could make all her own choices. She could act her ass off, or she could come back here and live by the lake. She could go to New York, or anywhere. She could . . .

Take another turn.

"Well, shit, Lola, that's exactly what Grandpa meant. I kind of hate when they end up being right."

She took out her phone, framed a photo of the fuchsias, bloodred against the drenched green. Another of Lola, tongue lolling, eyes full of fun. Then another, another.

The old gnarled tree—under which she'd gotten and given her first kiss. Tom McLaughlin, she remembered, a fourth or fifth cousin, so somehow still all in the family.

The cow stretching its head over a stone wall to crop grass on the other side. Mrs. Leary's cottage, because Mrs. Leary had taught both Nan and herself how to bake brown bread.

She'd take all that with her to look at anytime she felt sad or lost.

Barely a half mile from the cottage, she turned down the bumpy lane. Knowing where they were headed, Lola let out a happy bark and ran ahead.

"Goodbye," Cate said, and let the tears come because Nina would understand them. "Goodbye," she said again.

She stood a moment, slim and straight, long black hair flowing down her back. Then followed the dog to make it official.

L.A. poured sunshine. The streets and sidewalks baked under it. Flowers bright and bold pulsed hot. Beyond the walls and gate of the Sullivan estate, traffic snarled and bitched.

In the trendy restaurants, beautiful people talked business over their organic salads and quinoa while beautiful people who hoped to break into the business served them.

The guesthouse had its advantages. She had a beautiful room, full of soft colors and shabby chic, her own bath with a generous shower that pumped out hot water as long as she wanted.

She even had her own entrance so she could slip out, night or day, without going through the main part of the house—a habit she developed and kept up even when her father was working.

She enjoyed the gardens, and seriously loved having a pool.

She could make her own meals if she wanted—Mrs. Leary had taught her how to make more than brown bread—or wander over to the main house to join her grandparents. If they had a dinner engagement, she could sit in the kitchen with Consuela, their cook and de facto housekeeper, beg a meal and conversation.

When her grandfather gave her the script for the part he had in mind, she read it, then devoured it. Then got busy on the work to transform herself into Jute—the quirky, careless best friend of the daughter of the single mother in a sharp little romantic comedy.

She'd only have a handful of scenes, but they counted. Because she respected his opinion, and she'd need his permission, she passed the script to her father.

When he knocked on her bedroom door, she stopped practicing Jute's walk, called a "Come in."

Her palms actually got sweaty when she saw he had the script in his hand.

"You read it."

"Yeah. It's good, but your grandfather's careful about projects. You understand they've already cast Karrie."

"I don't want Karrie. Not that it isn't a good part. I don't want to take that much on, not now. Not yet. Jute's better for me. She plays off Karrie's need to be perfect, and the way the mother's always over-compensating. She brings a little chaos in."

"She does," Aidan agreed. "She's got a mouth on her, Cate."

In response, Cate did a slow roll of her shoulders, eyes rolling up as she dropped into a chair, slouched. "Jesus, she's just, you know, like fucking expressing herself."

She saw his eyes widen, that instant shock, and wondered if she'd gone too far putting Jute on for size.

Then he laughed. He sat on the side of her bed, set the script down beside him. "It's no wonder Jute's parents are a little afraid of her."

"She's smarter and braver than they are. I get her, Dad." Cate leaned forward. "I admire that she doesn't care about fitting in. I think, I really think, if I can get the part, I'll be good in it. And it'll be good for me."

"You haven't wanted any of this for a long time. Or . . ." He looked away, toward her glass doors to where twilight crept. "I kept the door closed. Not locked, but closed."

"It's not on you. I never asked if I could open the door, and really only thought about it once in a while. Now I just want to see if I can, and how I feel if I do."

"You have to be prepared for questions, for the ones who'll rehash what happened in Big Sur."

She said nothing for a moment, just sat, held his eyes with hers. "Do I have to give up everything because of what she did?"

"No, Cate, no. But—"

"Then let me do this, let me try to get the part. Let me see what happens."

"I won't stand in your way."

She jumped up, threw her arms around him. "Thank you, thank you, thank you!"

He squeezed tight. "There are conditions."

"Uh-oh."

"I'll hire a bodyguard."

Stunned, appalled, she yanked back. "Come on."

"I'll get a woman," he continued. "We can say she's your PA."

"God, like I'd need a personal assistant. Dad, the studio has security."

"Deal breaker."

She knew that tone, the one calm and clear as water. He meant it.

"Are you going to worry about me my whole life?"

"Yes." Same tone. "It's part of the job description."

"Fine, fine. What else?"

"If a call runs late, you text me. And as we both might be working, I get a text when you're home if I'm not here."

"No problem. More?"

"You keep your grades up."

"Done. Is that it?"

"Other than the already in place no drinking, no drugs, yeah. That's it."

"We have a deal. I'm going to run over and ask Grandpa to set up an audition."

She raced off so fast he barely had a moment to feel pride she'd expect to audition. But he had plenty of time to worry about what she might face out in the world he'd kept her from for seven years.

But Cate thought only of now as she raced along the wide, pavered path toward the main house. It stood gloriously Georgian, magnificently ornate in the deepening shadows. Lights flickered along the path, and along other paths through gardens smelling of roses and peonies, inside the many windows, glimmered in the blue, blue waters of the pool.

And, she saw, washed over the big patio with its outdoor kitchen under a pergola of wisteria where her grandparents sat sipping drinks.

"Look who's come to call." Lily, her hair a flaming red swing around her face, lifted her martini in toast. "Get a Coke, darling, and sit with us old farts."

"I don't see any old farts."

She sat, on the edge of a seat because that's how she felt. On the edge.

"I didn't want to say anything until I got the check mark from Dad. We read the script for *Absolutely Maybe*. He said I could do it, and boy, I want to. When can I audition for Jute?"

Obviously pleased, Hugh studied her over his whiskey. "Honey, I'm not just playing Karrie's irascible grandfather, I'm executive producer. It's yours."

Her pulse did a quick dance, just as her feet wanted to. "Oh, man, I want it so much. It'd be so easy to take it that way. But no, please. I want to audition. I want to do it right."

"Hugh, set up the audition, and congratulate yourself on having a granddaughter with pride and integrity."

"All right, I'll set it up."

"Yes! I need to go prepare." She jumped up, then dropped down again. "I need . . . G-Lil, I need a salon. My hair. And I need some L.A. clothes. Can you tell me where, and can I use the driver?"

Lily held up a finger, then picked up the phone she'd set on the table. She hit speed dial. "Mimi, do me a favor? Cancel my lunch date tomorrow and contact Gino—yes, now, at home. Tell him I need him to take care of my granddaughter tomorrow. That's right, personally. We can work around his schedule. We'll be shopping most of the day. Thanks."

"You didn't have to do that."

"Have to?" She threw back her head, let out a hoot. "Does a rooster have to crow? I've wanted my Gino to get his genius hands on your hair for years. Now's my chance. Add shopping, it's a day at the damn circus for me. And I do love a circus."

"She does," Hugh agreed. "It's why she married into the Sullivans."

"That's the pure truth. Oh, Mimi's fast. Here's Lil," she said as she answered the phone. "That's just perfect. Yes, I've got it. You're the best, Mimi. Kisses."

She set the phone down. "Gino's going to come in early—for him—just for you. Be ready at eight-thirty."

"Mimi's not the best, you are." Cate sprang up again, gave Lily a noisy kiss on the cheek, then repeated one for her grandfather. "Both of you. I'm going to make you proud. Gotta go!"

As she raced off, Lily lifted her martini again. "I dimly recall having that kind of energy. You're going to need to look after her, Hugh."

"I know. I will."

It had been years since Cate walked into an L.A. salon, the exclusive type that served its clients spring water or champagne, infused teas or lattes. The sort with private stations and a menu of services as thick as a novel.

When she did, the scents—expensive products, perfume, fragrant candles—melded together and shot her back to childhood.

Back to her mother.

She nearly balked at the door.

"Cate?"

"Sorry." She pushed herself into a world of black and silver, of techno music pulsing low and bright chandeliers formed with curving silver bands.

A man in a shirt that might have been designed by Jackson Pollock manned a semicircle reception counter. His hair rose up in a wave, like a surfer's curl, over his forehead.

He had a trio of studs in his left earlobe and a tattoo of a dragonfly on the back of his left hand.

"Luscious Lily!" Popping up, he clapped his hands together. "Gino's already at his station. This can't be your granddaughter. You'd have been ten when she was born!"

"Cicero!" Lily exchanged kisses. "Aren't you the one? Caitlyn, this is Cicero."

"My sweet girl." He clasped her hand in both of his. "What a beauty! I'll take you right back. Now, what can I get you? Your morning latte, Lily, my love?"

"We'll both have one, Cicero. And how are things with you and Marcus?"

He wiggled his eyebrows as he walked them through the salon. "Heating up. He asked me to move in with him."

"And?"

"I think . . . yes."

There was a sweetness, Cate thought, in the way Lily put her arm around him, hugged. "He'll be lucky to have you. You know, Cate, Cicero isn't just another pretty face. He helps Gino run the business, and he makes the best latte in Beverly Hills."

"But he does have a pretty face," Cate said, and had Cicero beaming at her.

"Aren't you a darling!" He whisked a black curtain open.

"Gino, two gorgeous ladies for you."

"My favorite kind."

While Cicero was slight and slick, Gino hit big and muscular. He had a shock of black hair tumbling to the collar of his black tunic, big, heavy-lidded brown eyes, and a perfect two-day stubble.

He didn't exchange kisses with Lily, but picked her an inch off her feet in a bear hug. "*Mi amor.* You got me out of bed an hour early."

"I hope whoever the lucky woman was, she forgives me."

He offered a toothy smile. Then turned to Cate. "So this is Caitlyn. My Lily flower tells me about all her chicks." He reached out, took a handful of Cate's hair.

"Thick and healthy. Sit. Lily, my own, Zoe will give you a mani-pedi."

"I planned to sit and watch. Quietly," Lily insisted.

Gino raised both eyebrows, then just flicked a finger toward the curtain. "Close it on your way out."

Cate sat in the big leather chair in front of the big silver station with its triple mirror and Hollywood lights. "You must be a genius with hair because nobody flicks Lily out of the room."

"A genius with hair, and discreet as a sphinx. The secrets that whisper in here stay in here." As he spoke, he ran his hands through her hair, studied her face in the mirror. "You're a Sullivan through and through. An Irish beauty still in bud. It's not telling secrets to say Lily loves you with all her heart."

"It's mutual."

"Good. Now, do you know what you want for your hair, or will you be smart and let me tell you?"

"I think I'd be intimidated enough to go with the second, but I need to look a part. For an audition."

"All right then, that's an exception I believe in. Tell me."

"I've got a couple pictures."

As she got out her phone, Cicero brought in her latte, set it down, and whisked out again.

"Um. Hmm." Gino nodded as he studied the photos, narrowed eyes at her face in the mirror.

"I'm thinking sort of a combination. She's defiant and quirky and likes making a statement—her own. So if you could—"

He cut her off with another finger flick. "Now you leave it to me. One question. Since you have good, healthy hair you're giving up, will you donate it?"

"Oh. Sure. I hadn't thought of that."

"I'll see to it. Drink your latte and relax."

She tried to, but even though he turned her away from the mirror, she squeezed her eyes shut at that first, burning-bridges snip.

Done now, she thought.

"Now, let out your breath. Take another, let it out. Good. Tell me about your life."

"Okay. Okay. God. Whew. Well, I've been living in Ireland mostly since I was ten."

"I haven't been there. Show it to me."

So she closed her eyes, told him about the cottage, the lake, the people while he worked.

Fully two and a half hours later, he opened the curtain and let Lily come in.

Both hands flew to her mouth as if holding back a scream.

Cate sat in the salon chair, her hair a short wedge with the heavy mop pulled forward from the crown dyed a deep, vivid blue. At Lily's reaction, Cate's delight turned to distress.

"Oh God. Oh, G-Lil."

Lily shook her head, then waved her hands in the air, then turned around. Then turned back. "I love it! I love it," she repeated, waving her hands again. "Oh, holy heap of smoldering shit, Catey, you're a bad-ass teenager!"

"Really?"

"I read the script, too. And even without that, it's fantastic. Be seventeen, sweets. Listen to Mellencamp and hold on to seventeen as long as you can. Gino, look what you did for my girl."

"Did you doubt me?"

"Not for an instant. Get up, get up, turn around. I love it. Your father's going to hate it, but he's supposed to. Don't worry about that. Plus, it's Jute, so he'll swallow it. We're going to get you some clothes to go with that hair. And some bad-ass teenager boots."

Two days later, with her statement hair, her lace-up combat boots, ripped jeans, artfully faded Frank Zappa T-shirt, blue nail polish she'd scraped off in strategic places, an armload of leather and cloth bracelets, she clomped into the audition.

Her heart pounded, her stomach churned, and she felt her throat close as the director—a woman she respected—gave her a narrow stare.

"Caitlyn Sullivan, auditioning for Jute."

She felt the eyes on her, judging, assessing, let herself go.

She cocked her hip, made her own eagerness drain, filled it with Jute's bored defiance. She spoke with just the faintest hint of Valley Girl.

"So, are we gonna do this or not? 'Cause I've got a bunch of better shit I could be doing. You know, like scratching my ass or whatever."

When she saw just the hint of a smile in the director's eyes, she knew she'd stepped through the door again.

CHAPTER TEN

In the long gap between *Donovan's Dream* and *Absolutely Maybe*, Cate forgot how much she enjoyed being a part of a project, part of a community. But it all came back.

She didn't exactly dress in character for the table read, but the hair was the hair. Plus, putting on what she believed Jute would just helped her get into character.

God knew she'd worked on her voice—the pitch, the rhythm. And what Lily called "the 'tude."

She liked Jute's 'tude, and wished she actually had a good chunk of it inside herself.

She'd met Darlie Maddigan, who'd play Karrie, had run a scene with her to test chemistry. She liked Darlie's approach to the role— the wide-eyed, anxious perfection seeker.

They played it as opposites attract, and it worked.

In reality Darlie, a confident, savvy vet of eighteen, had snagged her first part at the age of three and never looked back.

She had a house in Malibu, preferred lunch meetings to nights at the clubs, and had recently inked a whopping contract as the face— and body—for a line of activewear aimed at the sixteen-to-twenty-five demographic.

Darlie, her long blond hair in a simple ponytail, walked into the read and straight to Hugh. "Gramps." She hugged him. "I'm going to say, again, how excited I am to work with you. How's it going, Cate? Are you ready?"

"Really ready."

"Good. I'm psyched. Let's have some fun."

It was—mostly. Cate sat at the table with the cast, the director, the money people, the writer, the assistant who'd read the stage directions. She met her movie parents for the first time, and the actor playing the top jock Karrie pined for, the awkward nerd who not-so-secretly pined for Jute, and all the rest.

"Karrie wails, throws herself on her bed and sobs."

Though Cate found the wail impressive, she was too deep in character to show it.

"Jee-sus, Kare, mop it the fuck up! You're embarrassing yourself. More important, you're embarrassing me."

"Jute drops down to sit on the bed. For a beat, her face shows sympathy, then she slaps Karrie on the ass."

"The guy's a dickwad, Karrie."

"Why won't he be *my* dickwad?"

"Karrie rolls over."

"I love him. I want to die. My mother's having sex with Mr. Schroder. She bought sex underwear! I'm getting a B—a B!—in calculus. And—and after I tutored Kevin for two weeks, after I spent hours with him, after I helped him get an A, it's just: *Thanks, glad that's over!*"

"Hence dickwad. Let's address, in no particular order. Your mom having sex with Schroder—who's hot for an old dude—is advantage Karrie. As long as she's having sex, thinking about sex, buying sex underwear, she's off your back. It's the dry spells, Kare, where they're all over us. Root for the sex and live free."

Karrie throws her arm over her eyes, sniffles. "I don't want to live free without Kevin. You're my best friend. You're supposed to take my side."

Rolling with it now, Cate jumped up, turned a circle, kicked an imaginary bedpost. "You want me to take your side? *You* take your side. Do you want that dickwad?" Shouting now. "Do you want that dickwad!"

"Yes!"

"Then mop it the hell up. Mop it now! Strap on your ovaries, hoist your tits up." Walking over, she pulled Darlie to her feet. "Strap those ovaries on tight. Hoist those tits high, and go get your dickwad."

"How?"

"Are your ovaries strapped?" Cate jabbed a finger in Darlie's belly. "Are your tits high?" Covered a startled Darlie's breasts with her hands and pushed up.

"Yes?"

"Then I'll tell you. But I need some nachos."

Applause and laughter broke out around the table.

"Can we keep that in?" Darlie demanded. "Can we keep in the poke and grope?"

"Already in the notes," the director said. "Good work, ladies. Next scene."

Cate all but bounced out of the read, and would have bounced right into the wardrobe meeting the next day.

But that night *Entertainment Tonight* broke the story of Caitlyn Sullivan's return—and rehashed the kidnapping.

Variety ran the story. *People*, the *Los Angeles Times*, *Entertainment Weekly* all hammered on the door for interviews, statements, comments, photos.

The internet exploded over it.

The refusal to give interviews or comments didn't starve the fire. During the first week of production, it only shot higher when someone managed to take a photo of Cate on the back lot and sell it to a tabloid.

They ran the picture of her dressed as Jute, flipping her middle finger, beside one of her taken when she'd been ten.

LITTLE GIRL LOST TO TEENAGE REBEL
Caitlyn Sullivan's Ugly Secrets

Social media picked up the theme, ran with it.

Stewing with resentment, Cate sat in Darlie's trailer on the back lot, waiting for a call to their next scene.

"I know how it works. I know why they do it. I just don't understand why anyone cares so much."

"Sure you do. You were a kid whose mother used her. I'm sorry if that chips the bone."

Cate shook her head. "I know what is."

"Well, it sucks wide. You're also one of the Hollywood Sullivans, and that's a BFD."

Darlie, looking her part in a red-and-white cheerleader outfit, gestured with her bottle of unsweetened peppermint tea.

"Even if you weren't, you're an actor, you're a performer. We're not-so-fair game, Cate. That kind of bullshit is part of the price."

Truth, the simplicity of it, didn't make it an easier swallow. "I knew it would happen. I figured it would hit, then fade off if nothing fed it."

"People feed it. People who click on the stories, who grab the trash at the checkout counter while the grocery store clerk's ringing up their cans of tuna."

"I know they do it to you, too."

"Yeah. I can usually ignore. But I had someone I was pretty serious about last year. I go out to dinner with my costar, and somebody gets a picture of us smiling at each other, and wham-bam, it's all over everywhere we're doing it and hard. I could shrug it off, but the guy I was seeing couldn't. Wouldn't. He more than half believed it, so . . ."

She shrugged, drank more tea. "That ended that."

"I'm sorry."

"Me, too. I really cared about him." Smiling, she poked Cate in the arm. "Even though he turned into a dickwad."

At the knock on the door, Darlie glanced over.

"You're wanted on set, Ms. Maddigan, Ms. Sullivan."

"Thanks! It'll fade off," she told Cate. "Somebody'll cheat on somebody or get knocked up with somebody's baby or get busted for a DUI. There's always something. So."

She rose, tipped her head right and left to loosen her neck. "Keep those tits high."

"They're high." Sliding out from the table, Cate gave hers a quick boost to prove it. "You've just got better ones than I do."

Lips pursed, Darlie looked down. "True. But you've got longer legs. Come on, girlfriend, let's take my tits and your legs and go nail this scene."

The work helped. Having someone outside family, someone close to her own age to talk to helped. Her small, supporting role wrapped in a matter of weeks—and Darlie proved right—the bulk of the media attention faded off.

With her father on location for at least a week, she waited until her grandfather had a day off the call list to corner him.

She found him in his office with its view of a three-tiered fountain and wide green lawn.

Piles of scripts and notes littered his desk where he sat in a pale blue polo shirt and khakis. He still sported Gramps's grizzly beard.

"Finally! Company to spare me from scripts that have me stupid enough to be seduced by a girl barely older than you for my money."

"Really?"

"That's before I end up strangling her." He tossed the script down.

"Maybe you'd read one that doesn't have you stupid. Or have a part for you at all."

He eyed the one in her hand. "But one for you?"

"I got three from my agent this week. But you probably know since he's your agent, too."

"I heard a rumor." Recognizing the question on her face, Hugh shook his head. "I didn't ask Joel to send you anything, or pull any other strings. But he mentioned three came in he thought you should read—and two of them specifically asked him to send you."

"That's what he said. This is one of the two. Can I leave it with you?"

"Of course you can."

Something, Cate thought. Something in his voice. "Is something wrong?"

"Why don't you put that on my stack here, then take a walk with me? I could use the exercise, the air, the gardens."

"Something's wrong." But she put down the script. "Did I screw up something with Jute?"

"You were perfect." Rising, he came around the desk, put an arm around her as he walked her out of the office. "We should wrap next week. On time, on budget. Small miracles."

They walked out over tiled floors the color of honey, under ceilings that soared. The Grand Salon, they called it, to highlight the baby grand piano, the silk-covered sofas, the Georgian antique tables and cabinets.

"I do have some news," he said as he steered her toward the arching double doors. "It's going to upset you."

"Is something wrong with G-Lil? With you?"

"No." He nudged her outside, across a patio to one of the garden paths. "We're healthy as horses. I thought I'd wait until your dad was back and Lily was here, but I don't want you to hear about it before they are."

"You're scaring me. Just tell me."

"They granted Charlotte parole."

"She's . . ." Everything in her went still for a moment. She saw a butterfly, so light, so free, flutter and flutter before it landed—yellow as butter—on a deep blue flower.

"I don't think she'll come back here, Catey. She has to stay in the state, for now, but I don't think she'd come back to L.A. There's nothing for her here but derision and embarrassment."

"How do you know she's getting out?"

"Red Buckman keeps us informed. You remember Sheriff Buckman?"

"Yes." And there was a dragonfly, quick and iridescent, just a flash of color, then gone.

"I remember. I write to him, and to Julia—to the family—at least once a year. Well, to Julia more than once a year."

"Do you?" He turned her to face him. "I didn't know."

"I wanted them to know how I am. I wanted to know how they are. I never said goodbye before we left. I wanted to keep that connection, I guess. Um. Dillon's in college. Red still surfs."

A bee, baby-fist fat, whizzed past a rosebush.

So much life, all around, everywhere. Why did it feel like hers had stopped?

She stumbled as the weight dropped on her, as her lungs shut down. "I can't breathe."

"Yes, you can. Look at me, come on, Cate, right at me. In and out. Just slow breaths, in and out."

He cupped her face in his hands, firmly, kept his eyes on hers, continued to tell her to breathe.

"Chest hurts."

"I know. In, nice and slow, out, nice and slow."

Years, he thought, at least three years since she'd had a full-scale panic attack. Goddamn Charlotte to hell.

"Let's go sit now. I'll get you some water."

"I don't want to see her."

"You don't have to. She'll never be welcome here, never come through those gates. Your father has full custody, remember?"

Grieving for her, Hugh walked her back toward the house. "You're nearly eighteen in any case. My baby girl's nearly of age."

"Sparks and Denby."

"Years yet. Years. And no reason to ever come near you again. Here, sit. We'll sit by the pool. Ah, Consuela."

She must have seen him supporting Cate as he would an accident victim, he realized, by the way she ran out of the house. "Would you bring us out some water?"

As she dashed back in, he eased Cate into a chair under an umbrella. "We're going to sit here in the shade, breathe some fresh air."

"I'm all right. I'm all right. I just . . . I convinced myself they'd make her stay in prison for the full ten years. It helped to believe that. But it doesn't matter."

She swiped at the cold sweat on her face. "It's not going to matter. Please, don't tell Dad I panicked like that. He'll worry for weeks, and I'm all right."

Crouched in front of her, Hugh rubbed her hands. "I won't say anything. Listen to me now, Caitlyn. She can't hurt you anymore. There's nothing for her in this town. She was a low-rent actress before she went to prison."

"I think she married Dad for the name, for the boost. I think she had me for the same reason. It's good press."

"I'm not going to disagree with you. Oh, Consuela, thank you."

He straightened as the cook, her worried eyes on Cate, hustled out with a tray—a pitcher of water with ice and lemon slices swimming, glasses, and a cold damp cloth.

She set down the tray, poured the water, took the cloth.

Gently, she dabbed the cloth over Cate's face.

"*Mi pobre niña,*" she murmured.

"*Estoy bien*, Consuela. *Estoy bien.*"

"You drink some water, my good girl." She pressed a glass into Cate's hand. "Mr. Hugh, please sit, please drink some water. I'm going to make a nice lunch for you both, and the lemonade my Cate likes so. You'll feel better."

"Thank you, Consuela."

"*De nada.*" She gestured for Cate to drink more water, then hurried back into the house.

"I'm okay. I'm better," Cate told Hugh. "And I know better, I do, in my head. She's never cared about me, so why would she want to or try to see me now? I know better. I'm sorry."

"No apologies. I'll say one more thing about Charlotte, then we're going to sit out here and talk of pleasant things. I don't know, and never have known, how such a small-minded, weak, no-talent, heartless bitch of a woman ever gave birth to someone like you."

It made her smile. "The Sullivan genes are strong."

"Damn right." He lifted his glass, toasted, studying her as he drank. "There's Dunn in there, too, because, my God, you look more like your grandmother, more like Liv, every day."

Cate tugged at her mop of blue bangs. "Even with this?"

"Even with that. Now, tell me about the part you're after."

"Well, she's nothing like Jute. She's the oldest of three, trying to cope when her widowed father relocates the family from an Atlanta suburb to L.A. for a job."

"Atlanta. Southern accent."

Cate cocked an eyebrow, and spoke in a smooth Georgia drawl. "I think I can handle it."

"You always could do that," Hugh said. "Nail a voice. All right, tell me more."

She told him, had her lemonade, shared lunch with him among the flowers and butterflies. And put all thoughts of her mother aside.

That night, half asleep, the TV on for company, the lights low, the phone still in her slack fingers let out the quick hip-hop riff signaling an incoming call.

Groggy, eyes still closed, she answered. "It's Cate."

She heard singing first—her voice, a child's voice. A couple of bars from the number she'd done with her grandfather in the movie they'd made in Ireland.

It made her smile.

Then she heard someone scream.

She shot up in bed, eyes wide.

Someone laughed—it sounded wrong. And over the laugh came her mother's voice.

"I'm coming home. Watch for me. Watch for me."

"Did you think it was over?" someone whispered. *"You never paid. But you will."*

Struggling to draw air, she dropped the phone on the bed. The weight, the awful weight on her chest crushed her lungs. Her throat seemed to compress to a pipestem.

Around her the room went gray at the edges.

Breathe, she ordered herself, and shut her eyes. Breathe, breathe. Imagined the cool, damp air by the lake in Ireland, imagined it over the cold sweat now slicking her skin.

Imagined drawing it in, slow, steady.

Imagined the comfort of the ranch house, the taste of Swiss Miss and scrambled eggs. The gentle feel of Julia's hands.

The weight eased, didn't vanish, but eased. She leaped out of bed, still sucking air in, hissing it out, to check the locks, every lock.

No one could get in. No one would.

She let her legs collapse, and sat on the floor with the now-silent phone.

If her father had been home, she knew she'd have run screaming to him.

But he wasn't home, and she wasn't a child who needed her father to chase away the monsters.

If she told him, told her grandparents . . . She should, she knew she should, but . . .

On the floor, she drew her knees up to her chest, let her forehead drop on them.

Everything would stop again. Her father would pull out of the film and come home. He'd refuse more scripts, maybe take her back to Ireland.

Though part of her yearned for that, for that green, safe place, it wasn't right, not for her, not for her father, not for anyone she loved.

A recording, just a recording. Someone, someone vicious and ugly who wanted to scare her, made a recording, found her phone number.

Fine, they'd succeeded.

She made herself get up, go into the kitchen. With all the lights on it was bright, shining. And safe, she reminded herself.

The walls, the gate, the security, the locks. All safe.

She got a bottle of water, drank long, drank deep until her throat felt cool and open again.

She'd change her number. She'd say a reporter—how did she know it hadn't been a reporter?—had mined it out.

She'd say nothing and simply change her number.

No one had to worry about her because she'd handle it.

And whoever had sent the nasty recording wouldn't have the satisfaction of scaring her.

She made herself turn off the kitchen lights, then turned off her phone in case that someone tried to call again. But in the bedroom, she couldn't face the quiet or the dark so left the TV and the lights on.

"I'm not locked in," she murmured as she deliberately closed her eyes. "They're locked out."

Still, it was a long time before she slept.

She told no one. After a day, after a quiet night, the edginess faded. That alone told her she'd been right to deal with it herself.

She had studying to do with her tutor, research to do on the part she wanted. Being a Sullivan, seventeen or not, she thought carefully about the career she wanted to build.

She prepped, and made a solo trip to Gino, as Lily had work. The mop of blue bangs turned into a sweep of fringe—with some blue streaks because she liked them.

If she signed on—because miraculously, it was up to her—she had time to let her hair grow out more, go back to full black.

And thrilled at the prospect of her first meeting with the director, the writer, she chose her outfit carefully. No ripped jeans, no clunky boots this time. For her first professional lunch meeting, she opted for a sleeveless sheath with fun, multicolored diagonal stripes, red sandals that laced to midthigh.

For the meeting, she was Cate Sullivan, actor. If she signed, she'd drop herself into character.

Because her father okayed the solo meeting if she took the car and driver, she gave herself one last study in the mirror, grabbed her bag—a wrist-strap clutch in a blue as bold as her streaks—and walked to the main house.

She needed to get her license, she thought. She'd driven in Ireland. Of course, now she had to learn to drive on the other side of the road, and in crazy traffic, but she needed to get her license.

And a car of her own. Not some boring old sedan. A fun, zippy convertible. She had money banked, and when—if, if, she reminded herself—she signed, she'd have more.

She'd suck up the bodyguard again, and Monika was okay, but she needed a car, some freedom.

But for now, it was probably better to have Jasper handle the traffic.

He gave her a smile, white and bright against his dark, lined face, as he opened the door to the shiny (boring) town car.

"All ready for you, Ms. Sullivan."

"How do I look?"

"A treat."

Good enough, she thought, and slipped into the back seat.

Still, she checked her face, added fresh lip gloss as he drove. Just a get-to-know-you sort of meeting, she reminded herself. And her agent would be there.

Plus, they wanted her for the part, and that took some of the pressure off. Even if this time she'd play the central character, it was still an ensemble movie.

When Jasper pulled over, she checked the time. Not early—embarrassing. Not late—unprofessional. "I'm going to be at least an hour, Jasper. More likely closer to two. So I'll text you when we're wrapping up."

"I'll be close by," he told her as he opened her door.

"Wish me luck."

"You know I do."

The spring to her step might not have hit sophisticated, but what the hell. Showing excitement, she thought as she passed through the archway into the garden bistro, was real and honest.

She wanted to build her career on both. And that's just what she was doing now. Building her career.

She walked to the hostess podium. "I'm here to meet Steven McCoy for lunch."

"Of course. Mr. McCoy is already here. Please follow me."

She moved through the flowers and greenery, through the subtle sound of water spilling into little pools, through tables covered with peach-colored cloths where people sipped sparkling drinks or studied parchment menus.

She felt eyes on her, pushed down, strongly down, nerves that wanted to bubble up. Part of the price, she remembered. Pay it or look for another line of work.

She recognized McCoy and, since she'd done an internet search, Jennifer Grogan, the writer. They sat beside each other at the four-top. So, she understood, they would face her and her agent.

McCoy stood when he spotted her. He hadn't yet hit forty, had a scraggly mop of wiry hair he covered with a Dodgers cap when he worked. Grogan peered at Cate through the square lenses of serious black-framed glasses.

"Caitlyn." He gave her a Hollywood peck on the cheek. "It's great to see you in person. Jenny, meet our Olive."

"I know your step-grandmother."

"She told me. She said she likes that you write women of layers and substance."

"Somebody's got to."

"Have a seat, Cate." McCoy pulled out her chair himself. "We've got a bottle of San Pellegrino going, but you can take a look at the water menu."

"No, that's perfect, thanks." She set her purse in her lap, waited until the server filled her glass.

"We're waiting for one more, but let's have some squash blossoms for the table. They're amazing," McCoy told Cate. "Stuffed with goat cheese."

"Save me from vegetarians," Jenny said. "At least bring some bread."

"Right away."

She gave Cate a sour look. "Or are you a tofu eater, too?"

"Not if I know about it first. I want to thank you, Mr. McCoy—"

"Steve."

"I want to thank you both for thinking of me for Olive. She's a terrific character."

"You'll have to work with a voice coach." Jenny snatched up a tiny sourdough roll the minute the basket hit the table. "The accent—and it can't be so hick-thick you need a hatchet to cut it—is essential to her character, and part of her conflict and culture shock. It has to be right."

Cate nodded, took a sip of water. And put Georgia into her voice. "I'd be more than happy to work with a voice coach if I take the part. Her accent, her speech patterns, her vocal rhythms are part of what, initially at least, makes her feel isolated. Or that was my read of her."

Jenny broke the little roll in two, popped half into her mouth. "Okay, that's good. Damn it. What am I going to bitch about now?"

"You'll find something. Here's Joel."

"Sorry, got hung up as usual." Joel Mitchell, short and round, kissed the top of Cate's head like an uncle. He dropped down in his golf shirt—as red as Cate's sandals.

He had twin fluffs of white hair divided by a wide swath of pink scalp, thick-lensed shaded glasses, and a reputation for squeezing every last drop out of a project for his client.

"So." He glugged down some water. "Isn't she all that and a chicken taco? Damn, girl, you're the spitting image of Livvy."

"Grandpa said that just the other day."

"Growing up on me. How about we order some real food—because

I see Steve's pushing his squash again. They make a hell of a burger here—a real one. Let's get some menus, then we can talk some turkey."

McCoy signaled the waiter.

Cate saw his hand freeze in midair, his eyes widen.

Before she could turn, see what had put the shock on his face, she heard her name.

"Caitlyn! Oh my God, my baby!"

The hands were on her, dragging her out of the chair, into a locked-arm embrace. She knew the voice, knew the scent.

Struggled.

"Oh, so grown-up! So beautiful." Lips skimmed over her face, her hair as Charlotte wept. "Forgive me, oh, my darling, forgive me."

"Get off me! Get away. Get her off me!"

Air backed up in her lungs, weight dropped onto her chest like stones. The arms around her became vises squeezing, squeezing life, identity, purpose out of her.

Seconds, it took only seconds to throw her back into a locked room with windows nailed shut.

Fighting for air, Cate shoved, broke free.

Saw Charlotte, eyes streaming, lips quivering, lift a hand to her cheek as if struck. "I deserved that. I did. But I beg you."

She dropped to her knees, pressed her palms together as if in prayer. "Forgive me."

"Get the hell away from her." Joel, already on his feet, surged forward.

In the chaos of sobbing, shouting, voices buzzing, Cate ran.

She ran as she had that night in the woods, away, just away. Anywhere else. At intersections, she bolted through, blind to the oncoming cars, deaf to the blasting horns, squealing tires.

Away, just away, the prey fleeing the hunter.

Ears ringing, heart tearing, she ran until her legs gave out.

Shaking, drenched in panic sweat, she pressed against a building. Slowly, the red cloud over her vision thinned, the sounds outside the screaming in her head eked through.

Cars, sun sparking off chrome, someone's car stereo blasting hip-hop, the clip of heels on pavement as a woman walked out of a shop carrying a pair of glossy shopping bags.

Lost, she realized. Like in the woods, but here everything was too hot, too bright. No sound of the sea, just the constant *whoosh* of traffic.

She'd left her purse—her phone—she had nothing.

She had Cate, she reminded herself, and closed her eyes a moment. Gathering herself, she walked on legs she barely felt to the door of the shop.

Inside the cool, the fragrant, she saw two women—one young, stick thin in candy pink, the other older, trim in cropped pants, a crisp white shirt.

The younger one turned, frowned as she gave Cate a quick once-over. "Excuse me just one moment."

Disapproval with a dose of disgust slapped out as she strode to Cate. "If you're looking for a public washroom, try Starbucks."

"I—I need to call someone. Can I use your phone?"

"No. You need to leave. I have a client."

"I lost my purse, my phone. I—"

"You need to leave. Now."

"What's wrong with you?" The older woman walked over, nudged the younger one aside. "Go get this girl some water. What happened, honey?"

"Ms. Langston—"

The older woman whipped her head around, bored holes into the younger. "I said get some water." Putting an arm around Cate, she led her to a chair. "You sit down, catch your breath."

Another woman came out of the back, pulled up short, then hurried forward. "What's happened?"

"This girl needs some help, Randi. I just sent that heartless, pinched-mouthed clerk you hired back to get her some water."

"Give me a minute."

Ms. Langston took Cate's hand, gave it a little squeeze. "Do you want the police?"

"No, no, I dropped my purse—my phone."

"That's all right, you can use my phone. What's your name?"

"Cate. Caitlyn Sullivan."

"I'm Gloria," she began as she hunted through a huge Prada hobo bag for her phone. Then her eyes narrowed on Cate's face. "Are you Aidan Sullivan's daughter?"

"Yes."

"My husband directed him in *Compromises*. Hollywood's a small, incestuous world, isn't it? Here's Randi with your water. And here, finally, is my phone."

The third woman—one between the ages of the other two—handed Cate a tall, slim glass.

"Thank you. I . . ." She stared at the phone, working to bring Jasper's number into her head. She tried it, closed her eyes in relief at Jasper's voice.

"Jasper, it's Cate."

"Oh, miss, thank God! Mr. Mitchell just got ahold of me. I was about to call your daddy."

"No, please, don't. If you'd just come get me. I . . ." She looked at Gloria. "I don't know where I am, exactly."

"Unique Boutique," Randi told her, and gave her an address on Rodeo Drive.

"I got that, miss. I'll be there in just a few minutes. You just sit tight."

"Okay, thanks." She handed the phone back to Gloria. "Thank you, so much."

"Don't you worry about it." Gloria turned her head, gave one long, dark look toward the back of the shop. "It's called being human."

CHAPTER ELEVEN

The networks, the cable channels ran video footage, recorded on someone's phone. Photographs of the forced embrace, of Charlotte pleading on her knees or holding a hand to her face as if Cate had struck her swarmed the internet, the papers.

In disgust, Hugh slammed down the national tabloid with its screaming headline.

A REPENTANT MOTHER
AN UNFORGIVING CHILD
Charlotte Dupont's Heartbreak

"She set it up. Someone told her where Cate would be and when, and when I find out who—" He broke off, hands fisted.

"Get in line," Lily told him, pacing his office as Aidan stood staring out the garden doors.

"Even after all she did," Aidan said quietly, "we underestimated her. Days after she's released, days, and she's using Cate for publicity. The photos, she had a paparazzo on tap for those. She had the story ready to go."

"We'll get a restraining order. That's the first thing," Hugh said. "It's tangible, and if she tries to get near Cate again, she'll be right back in prison."

"We're all too far into individual projects to walk away at this point. But as soon as I'm wrapped, I'll take her back to Ireland. We should've stayed there."

"I could take her to Big Sur now," Hugh suggested. "I can commute when I'm needed for postproduction work."

"No." Cate stood in the doorway. "No Big Sur, no Ireland, no anywhere." She shook her head as Hugh moved to cover the tabloid with a script. "I've seen it, Grandpa. You, all of you, can't protect me forever."

"Wanna bet?"

She walked to Lily, squeezed her hand. "I know I made a mess of this. I did," she insisted before all three could protest. "I should've stood up to her. If there's ever a next time, I will."

"There won't be. The restraining order's nonnegotiable," Hugh told her.

"I'm fine with that. I hope like hell she breaks it so she's back in prison. But I'm not going to let her make me a coward, and she did. If she wants this—this shitpile of publicity, she can have it. I know we're getting another damn shitpile of reporters pushing for my side, my statement."

"You're not talking to the press about this." Aidan walked to her, took her by the shoulders.

"No, I'm not. I won't give her the satisfaction. Everyone here, every one of you gave me what I needed to get out of that room all those years ago. And every one of you gave me what I need to do what I have to do now. I told Joel to accept the offer. I'm doing the film."

"Cate." Gently now, Aidan brushed a hand over her hair. "I'm not sure you know what you'd be exposing yourself to. Even with security, even if they agreed to a closed set, there'll be more stories, more photos."

"If I don't do it, there'll be more stories, more photos, because it's already out I was having a meeting on just this when she barged in. I walk away from this, she wins."

After touching a hand to her father's heart, she lifted her arms. "You, all of you can tell me I've got nothing to be ashamed of, but I am ashamed. I need to do this for myself, to prove I can no matter what she throws at me. It's not a movie anymore, or a project or a part. It's how I feel about myself. And right now? I feel small."

Aidan pulled her in, rested his cheek on the top of her head. "I won't stand in your way. But we have to work out what precautions to take."

"Publicity like this brings out the loonies," Lily pointed out. "I can be proud of you, and I am, for taking a good grip on your own life. But we're going to protect you."

"I'll take the bodyguard, I'll use a car and driver. I won't go anywhere alone. For now, it's here and the studio."

"Now I'm pissed off all over again." Her face stony with rage, Lily dropped into a chair. "The girl's hitting eighteen now, Hugh, for Christ's sake. We should all be worried about the bad boy she thinks she's in love with, the clubs she's sneaking into."

"I hope to get to all that." Cate managed a smile. "Maybe a little late on the schedule."

While Cate focused on preproduction, Charlotte made the circuit.

God, she'd missed the cameras, the lights, the attention. It didn't matter when she sat in hair and makeup before her segment on a talk show whether she felt disapproval or fascination in the air.

She was on!

She knew how to play the part. After all, she'd had seven years to refine it. Remorse over what she'd done, grief over what she'd lost, the faint, shaky hope for a second chance.

And just a thin line snaking through that pushed the real guilt on Denby and Grant.

They'd lied to her, terrified her until she'd done a terrible thing.

Before her interview—a third-tier gossip rag, but cover story—she perused her wardrobe.

She needed new clothes, a star's wardrobe, but at the moment, she needed to stick with the simple. Not quite dull, she thought, scowling at the meager selection in the small closet in the crap house she rented. She could never go all the way to dull, but simple, clean lines, no flash had to do for now.

So . . . the black leggings—she'd worked out like a fiend in prison to keep her shape—the scoop-neck tunic in soft blue.

No bold colors.

Laying out the choices, she sat down at the desk—the crap house came furnished—she used as a makeup table, switched on the good makeup mirror she'd invested in.

She needed a flash tan, but the pallor worked for now. As soon as she could spare a couple weeks, she'd have a little work done. Nothing drastic, but she was sick and tired of looking at the lines.

As with the mirror, she'd invested in good skin care products, good makeup. It didn't pay to be cheap. And she'd made a little extra doing makeup for other inmates on visiting days.

She spent an hour perfecting her face. The pure, no-makeup look took skill.

While she dressed, she rehearsed—and she plotted. This current run of interviews and appearances wouldn't last. She'd have to take one of the offers on her table. Lean pickings—straight to video for two, and the third wanted her to play some lunatic in a B slasher that had her cut to ribbons in the first act.

Bullshit on that.

Maybe she could find a way to juggle both other offers, get things rolling again. And that would boost up more press.

Make some connections. If she could find a man who'd back her career—and get her out of this crap house—she'd really be riding again.

An old, rich man, she considered. All you had to do? Lay them right, and you lived like a queen.

She couldn't get pregnant this time to pull another man into marriage—too late in the game for that even if she could stomach the idea of another kid. But sex, with generous doses of flattery, adoration, and whatever bullshit worked could do the trick.

She'd find one, the right one this time, one without all those sticky family ties and interference.

But in the meantime . . .

As she used a perfume sample on her wrists, her throat, she thought of Cate.

Maybe she hadn't ever wanted the kid, maybe she'd seen Cate as a means to an end—but she'd treated that selfish, ungrateful girl like a princess.

Beautiful clothes, Charlotte thought as she walked out into the tiny living room with its ugly navy sofa, its hideous lamps. The best clothes, a professional nursemaid. A nanny—and fuck that Nina sideways. Hadn't she hired a top designer for the kid's bedroom? Bought her the sweetest little diamond studs when she'd had the brat's ears pierced?

She made one mistake—and it wasn't even really her fault—but one mistake, and the Sullivans try to make her into a monster.

She looked around at the beige walls, the secondhand furniture, the view of the street barely steps away from the front door.

Her eyes shimmered with tears of self-pity. For years, she thought, she'd honestly believed nothing could be as bad as prison—the sound of cell doors locking shut, the smell of sweat and worse, the menial work, the disgusting food.

The utter loneliness.

But how much better was this?

Cate had a few hours—hours—in a room, and for that Charlotte had seven years in a cell, and now how much longer in this horrible house?

It wasn't fair, it wasn't right.

She felt herself sinking toward depression, then heard the knock on the door. She blinked back the tears, put on the brave yet sorrowful face she'd perfected.

And hit the mark for her next scene.

In her trailer, Cate poured two glasses of sparkling water. "I'm so glad you're here, Darlie."

"Like I said, I had a meeting, and thought I'd swing in. How's it going?"

Cate, wearing the fuzzy pink sweater for her next scene, sat with Darlie at the little table. "It's good. Steve, he's—well, he's just an awesome director. He can really pull it out of you. The two playing my brothers—especially the younger one—they're just terrific. And they're a serious riot. Plus, I have my own quirky BFF this time, and she makes me laugh on set and off."

"Excellent." Darlie took a sip of water. "Now. How's it going, Cate?"

"Oh, shit." Slumping back, Cate closed her eyes a moment. "It's a good part, and I think I'm doing good work. But she sucked the joy out of it, Darlie. I can't find the joy in the work. She's still pushing out stories. Doing some straight-to-vid thing. I know, like you told me once, it's part of the job, but I can't step outside. Telephoto lenses catching me sitting by the pool at my grandparents'."

"Were you naked?"

"Ha-ha."

Darlie gave her a pat. "See, it can always be worse."

"It got there. We needed to shoot some exterior scenes on location, and somebody leaked it. So they're swarming, and taking pictures and shouting questions because I made the mistake of thinking I could go with my movie brothers to this pizza place for lunch. Just to do something. But the worst? One of them harassed my grandfather's cook—the sweetest woman in the world—when she was at the market. He threatened her, Darlie, threatened to report her to immigration if she didn't give him access to me. She's a citizen, she's a goddamn US citizen, but he scared her."

"Okay, fuck it. None of that's part of the job. Not any of it."

"Maybe not, but I can't stop it as long as I'm in the job."

"Don't you give up, Cate. You're good, really good."

"Joy," Cate said and flicked the fingers of both hands. "Sucked."

"This blows. We need sugar."

Shock had Cate's eyebrows disappearing under her bangs. "You? Sugar?"

"Crisis food." So saying, Darlie dug into her purse. "My emergency stash."

Cate stared at the bag Darlie pulled out, opened.

"Reese's Pieces is your emergency stash?"

"Don't judge me." After popping one, Darlie offered the bag. "What are you going to do?"

"I don't know yet." But oddly, sitting there in the deliberately dopey sweater, eating candy with a friend, settled her.

"I'm going to finish what I started, and do the best work I can. Then I don't know. I can't talk to my family about this, not right now. Their worry's constant, and that's hard to deal with, too."

"Fuck 'em—not your family. The rest of them."

"I'm feeling sorry for myself," Cate admitted. "*Absolutely Maybe*'s about to release. I couldn't do the circuit. I can't go to the premiere, not without getting my family—and me—all stressed out."

"Not worth it."

"No, not worth it." She propped her elbow, rested her chin on her fist. "I haven't so much as kissed a boy—as me—since Ireland."

"Ouch."

Wallowing, Cate took a handful of Reese's. "I'm going to die a virgin."

"No, you won't. Not with that face, those legs, and your annoyingly positive outlook."

Cate managed a snort, ate candy.

"But you're overdue for some touch, even considering your tiny tits."

"Tell me." And she found herself able to smile and mean it. "I've really missed you."

"Mutual."

"And way, way enough about me. Tell me what's going on with you, so I can add envy to my list."

Cate glanced over at the knock on the trailer door. "You're needed on set, Ms. Sullivan."

"Sorry, damn it. I spent all this time crying on your shoulder."

"I'll go dry it off. Look, how about I text you, and we figure out some hang-out time. I can come to your place."

"That would be great. Seriously."

As they walked out together. Darlie put an arm around Cate's waist, and Cate returned the gesture. "I'd hang now, watch you work, but I have to book it. I have a date—a hot one—tonight."

"Bitch."

With a laugh, Darlie veered away.

Within twenty-four hours, a tabloid printed a grainy picture of the two girls' affectionate embrace with the headline:

ARE HOLLYWOOD'S SWEETHEARTS ACTUALLY SWEETHEARTS?
Darlie and Cate's Secret Romance

Within the speculative article, with suggestions that the two actors had fallen into more than friendship during the filming of *Absolutely Maybe*, Charlotte offered a quote.

"I support my daughter, whatever her lifestyle, whatever her orientation. The heart wants what the heart wants. And my heart only wants Caitlyn's happiness."

She swallowed it; what choice did she have? But it cut in ways she couldn't explain.

And when she flubbed her lines in a key scene five straight takes, she felt something break.

"I'm sorry." Tears pushed through the crack, began to rise in her throat. "I just need to—"

"That's lunch," McCoy announced. "Cate, let's have a minute."

She wouldn't cry, she promised herself. She couldn't, wouldn't cry and be one of those overemotional, oversensitive actors who couldn't handle a smackdown.

"I'm sorry," she said again as he moved to where she stood on the rapidly clearing kitchen set.

The set looked like she felt, she realized, total chaos. Which was the damn point of the scene she kept screwing up.

"Have a seat." He pointed to the floor, lowered to it himself, sat cross-legged.

Thrown off balance, Cate hesitated, then sat with him on the floor.

"I know the lines," she began, "I know the scene. I don't know what's wrong with me."

"I do. You're somewhere else, and you need to be here. Your head's not in it, Cate. It's not just the lines, you're not giving me the heart, the frustration, the pent-up anger that leads to the blow. You're walking through it."

"I'll do better."

"You'll need to. Whatever's pulling you out, I need you to get rid of it. And if you're letting that bullshit tabloid garbage get to you, you need to toughen up."

"I'm trying! She blubbers about me on *Hollywood Confessions*, I have to toughen up. She blubbers on *Joey Rivers*, toughen up, Cate. *Celeb Secrets Magazine* does a cover feature on her blubbering? Don't think about it, Cate, just toughen the hell up. And on and on and on."

She pushed to her feet, threw up her arms. God, she wanted to throw something, break something.

Break everything.

"And now this, after weeks of being hounded, this? I can't even have a friend? Someone I can actually talk to without that being tossed in the sewer? And what if I were gay, or Darlie was, and we weren't ready to come out? What kind of damage would that do to someone if they were still trying to figure out who they were?

"I know this kind of shit happens, okay? Toughen up? Goddamn it. My whole life is behind the walls of my grandfather's house and this lot. I have no life. I can't go out and get a pizza, or go shopping, go to a concert, the damn movies. They won't leave me alone. She makes sure of it. Because I'm still her goddamn golden ticket. That's all I ever was to her."

She stood, fists clenched, angry tears still streaming, breath heaving.

His gaze still on her face, McCoy nodded. "Two things. The first as a human being, a father, a friend. Everything you said is right. And you have a right to be sick of it, tired of it, pissed off by it. It's not fair, it's not right, it's not decent."

He patted the floor again, waited until she—with obvious reluctance—sat again. "I haven't said anything about Charlotte Dupont to you. Maybe that was a mistake, so I'll say this now. She's despicable. Every way, every level, every angle, despicable, and I'm sorry for what happened to you, what's happening to you. You don't deserve it."

"Life's not about deserve. I figured that out really early."

"Good lesson," he agreed. "But I hope she gets what she deserves. I'm more concerned with how somebody got that picture than the content. I want you to know I've had some strong discussions with security."

"Okay. Okay. I shouldn't have taken all this out on you. It's not your fault."

"Hold on. Second thing—and this is from your director. Use those emotions, the frustration, the rage, the fuck this shit. That's what I want to see. Go grab something to eat, get makeup to deal with your face, then come back on set and give it to me.

"Pay her back. Pay the assholes back, and give it to me."

She gave it to him, kept her head in the character, toughened up. And during the following weeks of production, made a decision.

She waited. An actor knew the value of timing. Besides, Christmas was coming, and this year, Christmas meant returning to the house in Big Sur for a big Sullivan clan celebration.

She'd avoided going back easily enough with work, school, her family's need to shelter her in Ireland, then L.A.

But this year, schedules meshed, and her grandfather's real joy at the prospect of holding a kind of full-scale holiday reunion gathered such steam she couldn't find the heart or the will to spoil it.

She'd never told anyone but her therapist that every nightmare she suffered started at that house with the ocean crashing, the mountains looming.

But if toughening up remained the goal, she had to face it.

Just like she faced learning to drive on the right side of the road—mostly practicing on the back lots—and going through the gates to

Christmas shop. Yes, it involved a decoy, a disguise, and a bodyguard, but she got out.

In any case, Christmas in Big Sur had to be more festive and less plain weird than Christmas in L.A. with the Santa Ana winds blowing in the hot and dry. Sweltering Santas in open-air malls, fake trees tipped with fake snow, shoppers in tank tops didn't bring on images of dancing sugarplums.

Next year would be different, she promised herself.

But for now, she packed for the trip and put on her shiny, happy face. And kept it on as she strapped in for the short flight.

"We'll get there first." Lily scrolled through the schedule her PA had put on her phone. "That gives us all time to catch our breath before the invasion."

Shiny, happy face, Cate thought, perfectly described Lily's. "You can't wait to see Josh and Miranda, the kids. I know you miss them." Timing, Cate thought, and segues. "You'll see a lot more of Miranda and her kids when you're in New York. A whole year."

"A year if the play doesn't bomb." Lily fussed a hand over her artistically knotted scarf. "If I don't bomb in it."

"As if. It's going to be awesome. You're going to be stupendously awesome."

"That's my sweets. I wipe at flop sweat every time I think about it."

"My G-Lil never flops."

"Always a first time," Lily muttered and reached for her Perrier. "It's been years since I did live theater, much less Broadway. But the chance to do *Mame*? I'm just crazy enough to go for it. Workshops don't start in New York for six weeks, so I've got time to get my pipes and my pins in shape."

Before Cate could launch, Hugh leaned across the aisle. "I heard her pipes in the shower this morning. They're in fine tune."

"The shower ain't Broadway, my man."

"They'll eat out of your hand. After all . . . Life's a banquet."

Lily gave her rolling laugh. "And most sons of bitches are starving to death. Oh, speaking of banquets, Mo texted me this morning and said Chelsea's decided to go vegan. We're going to have to see what the hell to feed her."

Since she'd lost the window, Cate went back to biding her time.

If her throat went dry on the drive from the airstrip, she knew how to hide it. She used her phone as a shield, as if reading and sending texts. The perfect way to avoid making conversation, or looking out at the sea as they traveled the winding road.

Since a second car had loaded up the luggage—and the mountain of gifts—she could and would busy herself unpacking as soon as they got to the house.

Her stomach lurched when they made the turn onto the peninsula. She put her hand over the hematite bracelet Darlie had given her for Christmas. A grounding stone, Darlie claimed, to help against anxiety.

If nothing else, it brought her friend close and helped Cate hold steady when the car slowed for the gate.

It looked the same—of course it looked the same—the beautiful and unique house cantilevered on the hill with its pale, sunlit walls and archways, its red-tiled rooflines. So much glass, open to the views, the roll of green lawn rising, the big doors under the front portico.

Christmas trees flanked the doors, rising out of red urns. More stood on the terraces, and lined like soldiers along the bridge. Still more shined behind the generous windows.

Sun shot down from a pale, winter blue sky, drenching the house, the trees, and striking the snow-laced mountains, turning them into a sparkle of shadow and white.

She wished, God she wished, that she couldn't see—so clearly— the girl she'd been, so young and trusting, walking with her mother across that rising lawn on a cool winter morning.

Her grandfather leaned over, kissed her cheek, and used the moment to murmur in her ear.

"Don't let her come here. This isn't her place. It never was."

Deliberately, Cate put away her phone. She spoke clearly, her eyes on the house. "When she woke me up that morning, when she took me out to walk, it was the last time I believed she loved me. Even at ten I'd hardly ever felt it from her. But that morning I believed it. I always knew the three of you loved me. I didn't have to believe because I knew."

She pushed open her door the minute the car stopped, got out quickly. The air hit her face—a strong breeze. She thought it tasted blue, like the ocean. Cool and blue and familiar.

She hadn't appreciated—what child could?—the engineering feat behind the design of the house, the way it jutted from the hill, its layers and tiers and angles both organic and elegant.

"I count at least two dozen Christmas trees."

"Oh, there's more." Lily shook her hair back. "I ordered one for every room. Some are just little things, some are as big as Jack's giant. I had one hell of a fine time planning all this." She held out a hand. "Ready to go in?"

"Yeah." She took Lily's hand, and went inside.

Cate decided her grandparents had hired an army of elves to deck the many halls, from the soaring tree in the main gathering room to the trio of miniatures on the windowsill of the breakfast nook. The house smelled of pine and cranberry, and looked like a Christmas card.

In the gathering room a second tree—a family tree, Cate realized—held bright red stockings. She smiled at the one with her name embroidered across the white top.

"What with Josh married again and bringing in a second family, and babies starting to pop out here and there, we've got too many of us for hanging stockings on the mantel." Hands on her hips, Lily surveyed the room. "Hugh came up with the family tree concept. I like it. It works."

Like Lily, Cate studied the room, with its trailing greenery, fat berries, gold-dusted pine cones, the towers of candles, pyramids of poinsettias.

"Just a simple Sullivan Christmas."

Lily let out her big, from-the-gut laugh. "You ain't seen nothing yet. I've got a couple things I want to check on. You go ahead up, sweets, get settled in. We're in Rosemary's rooms now. You're in the one we used to stay in. You remember where it is?"

Not the room she'd used as a child, Cate thought. Not the one her mother had taken her from on the worst day of her life.

"Sure. G-Lil." On a sigh, she moved in for a hug. "Thanks."

"We're exorcising ghosts here, just the dark ones. This is a good house, with plenty of love and light in it."

Exorcising ghosts, Cate thought as she went upstairs. Well, that was her plan, too, so she'd get on board Lily's Christmas train.

Home from college on winter break, Dillon fell easily back into ranch routine. His dogs, thrilled, followed him everywhere as he filled troughs, hauled hay bales.

Or sometimes when he just stood, looking out over the fields to the sea.

Everything he loved was here.

Not that he didn't like college. He did okay there, academic-wise, he thought as he listened to the chickens cluck madly while his mother spread their feed. He even got why what he learned—at least some of it—could make him a better rancher.

He liked his dorm mates okay, too. Though at times the air was so ripe with weed he got high just breathing. He liked the parties, the music, the long, rambling beer-and-weed-fueled discussions.

And the girls—or one girl in particular right now.

But whenever he came home, all that seemed like a weird dream, and one that bogged down his reality.

When he tried to imagine Imogene here, gathering eggs or baking bread for the co-op or digging in with him over the books, or even just standing with him, like this, looking out over the fields to the sea, he couldn't do it.

It didn't stop him from remembering how she looked naked. But he had to admit, he didn't miss her as much as he'd thought he would.

"Too much to do, that's all," he told the dogs as they watched him with adoring eyes. He picked up the ball they'd pushed at his feet, gave it a good strong toss.

Watched them race after it, bumping each other like football players on the field.

Imogene loved dogs. She had pictures of her fluffy red Pomeranian, Fancy, on her phone. And in fact, planned to bring Fancy back with her from winter break because she and two other girls were moving into a group house off campus.

She rode, too, English style. Fancy like her dog, but she rode and pretty damn well.

He couldn't stick with a girl who didn't love dogs and horses, no matter how she looked naked.

He figured he'd see a lot more of naked Imogene when she had her own room in the group house.

He tossed the ball a couple more times, then headed into the stables.

He led horses out to pasture or paddock, then took extra time with Comet.

"How you doing, girl? How's my best girl?"

When she nuzzled his shoulder, he rested his cheek against hers. Two and a half more years, he thought, and he'd be home for good.

He took an apple out of his back pocket, cut it in quarters with his knife. "Don't tell the others," he warned as he fed Comet half. He ate a quarter himself, gave her the last before leading her out.

He got a pitchfork and went to work.

His muscles remembered.

He'd grown another inch since he'd left for college, and figured he'd topped out now at six-one. Since he worked part-time at a riding stable, he kept those muscles in tune, earned some money, and got to hang with horses.

When he wheeled the first barrow out, he'd fallen into the rhythm, a nineteen-year-old boy who'd finally grown into his feet, leanly muscled in jeans and a work jacket, his boots mucked and muddy.

One of the cows let out a long, lazy moo. His dogs wrestled over the tooth-pocked red ball. A pregnant mare swished her tail in the paddock. Smoke pumped out of the ranch house chimneys, and the sound of the sea came to him as clearly as if he'd sailed a boat over its waves.

In that moment, he was completely and utterly happy.

CHAPTER TWELVE

After breakfast, with the smell of bacon, coffee, pancakes on the griddle still in the air, Dillon had a vague plan to text his two local pals, see if they wanted to meet up later.

It would give him time to saddle Comet, take her out for a ride, maybe check some fencing.

The women in his life had other ideas.

"We've got something we need to talk to you about."

He glanced over at his mother. She wiped down the counters and stove while he loaded the dishwasher. Gram—with the privilege of the breakfast cook—sat with another cup of coffee.

"Sure. Is something wrong?"

"Not a thing."

She left it at that.

She had a way, Dillon knew, of saying exactly as much as she wanted to say, and leaving you wondering about the rest. Poking, prying, pleading, wouldn't get another word out of her until she was damn good and ready.

So he finished loading the dishes.

Since he'd had enough coffee, he got a Coke. And since it seemed they were going to have a discussion, sat in Discussion Central.

The kitchen table.

"What's up?"

Before she sat, Julia gave him a hug from behind. "I try not to miss this too much when you're not here. The three of us sitting here after the morning work's done, and before we tackle the rest."

"I was going to take Comet out. She could use the exercise. I can check the fences. And I want to talk to you about maybe switching over to a floating diagonal system. Some of the posts we've got went in before I was born, and sure, it costs to put in a new system, but it costs to keep patching what's just worn out. And isn't as smart as it could be—environmentally or practically."

"College boy." Maggie sipped her coffee. She'd dyed a couple sections of her hair for the holidays, and sported a pair of braids—one red, one green—down the side.

"Yeah, I am, because my mother and grandmother made me."

"I've got a fondness for college boys. Especially pretty ones like you."

"We can talk about fencing," Julia put in. "After you've run the numbers on it, come up with a cost for labor and material."

"I'm working on it."

And he hadn't intended to bring it up until he had those numbers. He just hadn't perfected his mother's ability to hold back until complete.

But he was working on that, too.

"Good. I'll be interested to see what you come up with. Meanwhile, Gram and I have some thoughts about the future. You've still got more college ahead of you, but time moves. You'll have big decisions to make in just a couple more years."

"I made that decision, Mom. That hasn't changed. It's not going to."

She leaned toward him. "Owning, operating, running a ranch, being a steward for its animals, depending on its crops, it's a rewarding life, Dillon. And it's a hard one, demanding, physical. We didn't push you into college only for the education, though that's important. We wanted you to see other things, do other things, experience other things. To step out from the world we have right here, see what else there is."

"And to get you out of a household where two women run the show."

Julia smiled at her mother. "Yeah, that, too. I know—we know—you love this place. But I couldn't let it be the only place you really know. You're meeting different people now, people who come from different places, have other views, other goals. It's an opportunity for you to explore possibilities, potential, beyond right here."

He got a sick feeling in his gut, took a slow sip of Coke to settle it. "Do you want something different? Are you getting around to telling me you want to sell?"

"No. No, God. I just don't want my son, the best thing I ever did in this world, to limit himself because he didn't just look."

"I'm doing okay in school," he said carefully. "Some of it's a lot more interesting than I thought it would be. And that's outside the ag and ranch management courses. I like hanging out and talking about politics and what's screwed up in the world. Even if a lot of it's bullshit, it's interesting bullshit. So that's hearing other views. I see what some of the others are studying, what they're working toward, and I can admire it.

"This morning, I was just standing outside for a few minutes. Just looking, and feeling. I'm never going to be that happy being somewhere else, doing something else. I know what I want. I'll stick, and I'll get my degree because it'll only help me be a good steward. That's what I'm working toward because that's what I want."

Julia sat back. "Your dad loved this ranch, and he would've given it all he could. But it never had his full heart like it had mine. And like it has yours. So okay."

When she rose, walked out of the room, Dillon frowned after her. "Is that it?"

"No." Maggie studied him. "That was some smart talking, my boy. She knows, and so do I, that came from the heart. When you left for college, your 'I want the ranch' talk was more a knee-jerk thing, more a stubborn thing."

"I want it more now than I wanted it then."

"That's right." She poked a finger into his shoulder. "Because a couple women bullied you into college." She smiled as Julia came back in. "Now here's a reward for not being too much of an asshole about it."

Sitting, Julia laid a roll of paper on the table. "When you graduate, you'll be over twenty, and a man of that age shouldn't live in the house with his mother and grandmother. He should have some privacy, some independence."

"And he shouldn't have to tell the girl he hopes to get in his bed he lives with his mom," Maggie put in.

"So, what, you're kicking me out?"

"In a manner of speaking. We all work the ranch, we all live on the ranch, but . . ." Julia unrolled the paper. "We talked options to death and back again, and this is what we think is the best."

Dillon studied the sketches—obviously professionally done, as he could see the architect's stamp on the corner. He recognized the stables, but the drawing showed an addition on the far side.

"It's a nice little house," she explained. "Far enough away from the main house for privacy, but close enough to, well, come home. You can see from the potential floor plan, it's got two bedrooms, two baths, a living room, a kitchen, a laundry."

"Bachelor pad," Maggie said with a wink.

"Good windows, a little front porch. This is preliminary, so we can make changes."

"It's great. It's . . . I never expected— You don't have to—"

"We do. You need your own place, Dillon. I'm glad it'll be here, I'm glad you want it to be, but you need your own. And when you start a family, when in the far, far distant future, you make me a grandmother, we'll switch. Gram and I take the little house, you take this one. You want the ranch. I believe you. This is what Gram and I want, for all of us."

He felt what he'd felt standing outside before breakfast. Completely happy. "Do I still get to come to breakfast?"

Marking this as the best Christmas ever, Dillon headed out with the intention of saddling Comet, riding fence. He'd head into town later, meet his friends for pizza, catch up.

He pulled out his phone as he walked, read the incoming text. Imogene.

Crap, crap, he'd forgotten to text her, and tried to think of a good response while the dogs worked hard to herd him back to the house.

Miss you 2. Sorry my mom called a family meeting & I just got out. What else? he wondered. He had to think of something else. *Bet it's warm in San Diego. If ur hanging at the pool, send me a picture. Don't have too much fun w/o me.*

He sent it, hoped it was enough. Seconds later, his phone signaled again. With a selfie of Imogene, all that California blond hair, those big brown eyes, and that . . . Jesus, that body in a really, really tiny bikini.

Don't u wish u were here?

Man.

Sorry, did u say something? I think I passed out for a second.

Guess u know who and what I'll b thinking about all day. Talk soon gotta work.

He studied the photo again, let out a little groan. She'd put on that pouty look on purpose because she knew it killed him.

But when he tried to picture her there, right there with him, even with the amazing visual aid, he couldn't.

The dogs went on alert seconds before he heard the sound of a car coming up the ranch road.

He stuffed the phone back in his pocket, tipped back his hat, and waited.

He recognized one of the cars Hugh kept at Sullivan's Rest, the fancy SUV, and grinning, delighted, whistled the dogs back. To keep them occupied, he tossed the ball high and long in the opposite direction.

But when he turned back, it wasn't Hugh or Lily getting out of the car.

She carried an armload of red lilies. The wind caught at her hair, raven black, and tossed it back from her face. He'd never really understood what they meant when they said stuff like classic beauty, or good bones.

But he knew it when he saw it. Especially when she pushed her sunglasses on top of her head and those blue eyes—like laser fire—met his. Then her lips curved—really, really, really pretty lips—and she started forward.

The dogs charged, crazed, barking.

"They don't—"

Before he could add *bite*, she'd crouched down, angling the lilies away to try to pet both of them one-handed.

"I know who you are." She laughed, rubbed bellies. "I've heard all about you. Gambit and Jubilee."

She looked up at Dillon, still laughing. "I'm Cate."

He knew, sure he knew, even though she didn't look much like the funny weirdo she'd played in the movie he'd seen the month before. Or like the pictures all over the internet.

She looked, well, happy and, well, hot. Really hot.

"I'm Dillon."

"My hero," she said in a way that made his heart jitter around in his chest like his drunken roommate.

She straightened up, apparently not worried about how the dogs got mud all over her really sexy boots—the kind that went straight up to the thighs of long legs in tight jeans.

"It's been awhile," she continued because apparently he could no longer form a coherent sentence. "I haven't been back until now."

She pushed at her hair, looked around. "Oh, it's so beautiful. I never actually saw it . . . then. How do you get anything done?"

"It's . . . it's all right there when you finish."

"I'd half forgotten the views from my grandfather's house, and how they pull. I spent a lot of yesterday just looking again. But today the house is full of people, and I just wanted to get out. And I wanted to come by and thank you all again, in person. I email with your mother now and then."

"Yeah, she said."

"I— Is she home?"

"What? Yeah. Sorry. Come on in." He dug around for rational conversation on the way. "You lost the blue. In your hair," he added when she gave him a blank look.

"Right. Back to normal."

"I liked the movie. You don't sound like you did in it."

"Well, that was Jute. I'm Cate."

"Right." He pulled a blue bandanna out of his back pocket when they reached the porch. "Let me get that. The dogs messed up your boots."

She said nothing as he hunkered down, swiped the mud off the tops of her boots. It gave him a moment to gather himself.

"So you're here for Christmas?"

"Yes. All of us. A horde of Sullivans."

She stepped in when he opened the door.

Their tree stood in the front window, presents piled beneath, a star on top. The air smelled of pine and woodsmoke, of dogs and cookies.

"Why don't you sit down? I'll find the rest of us."

The dogs went with him, as if attached by invisible leashes. And she had a moment to breathe out.

No panic, and that was good, she thought. Nerves, a lot of nerves, but the dogs had helped distract her from them.

And Dillon. He'd looked so different. So tall now, and not so bony. She supposed he looked like a rancher—the young, sexy type—in his scarred boots and cowboy hat. So kind still, she thought, rubbing her bracelet. The way he'd bent down and wiped off her boots had made her eyes sting.

Just kindness.

She stood when Julia ran down the stairs. Hair in a messy ponytail, a plaid shirt over work jeans.

"Caitlyn!"

Open arms to take her in, to hold on.

"This is the best surprise." Julia pulled her back, studying, smiling. "You grew up and got gorgeous. Dillon's getting his gram. She's going to be thrilled."

"It's so good to see you. I never really— I just wanted to come by and see you." Cate held out the lilies.

"Thank you. They're spectacular. Why don't you come back in the kitchen, sit with me while I put them in water? I was hoping you'd come by when you wrote your family would be here for Christmas."

"It looks the same," Cate murmured.

"Yeah. I think about a kitchen remodel, but never get beyond the thinking."

"It's wonderful." One of her safe places when the panic struck. "I almost didn't come."

Julia got two vases—the girl must have bought every red lily in Big Sur. "Why is that?"

"I could bring myself back here, in my head—something my therapist helped me with—when I had nightmares and couldn't sleep again. If I came here in my head, I felt safe. I didn't know if I'd feel that if I came, or be able to feel that in my head if I didn't."

Julia turned back, waited.

"It's the same. I feel safe. It's the same," she repeated, "a remodel wouldn't change how it feels, or what it is."

"Don't rush me, boy." Maggie brushed Dillon back as she reached the bottom of the back stairs.

Once again Cate got to her feet. "Gram."

"Well, bring it in."

Steady now, really steady now, Cate walked into the hug. "I like your braids."

"'Tis the season. Dillon, get the girl a Coke and some cookies. I hope some of those flowers are for me."

"Do you see two vases here, Mom?"

"Just checking. You sit down now and tell me all about your love life."

Cate gave Gram a sorrowful look, made a zero with one hand.

"That's a sad state of affairs. I can see I need to give you some pointers."

She stayed an hour, enjoyed every minute. When Dillon walked her out, she paused again, to look at the fields, the cattle and horses, the sea.

"You're really lucky."

"I know."

"It's good you know. I have to get back, and you must have so much to do."

"I was just going to ride some fence. Do you ride?"

"I love to ride. I haven't done any since I came back to L.A., but when I lived in Ireland, we had neighbors with horses, so I rode whenever I could."

"I can saddle one up for you whenever you want."

"I'd like that. I'd like to ride again. I'll try to get back and take you up on it. I'm glad I saw this, all this, in the sunlight. Merry Christmas, Dillon."

"Merry Christmas."

He watched her drive away before he walked toward the stable to get a saddle.

He thought how funny it was that he couldn't picture Imogene on the ranch, but how easy it was to see Cate there. A movie star.

It was just weird to think about it, so he put it aside and picked out his tack.

Rather than feeding her anxiety, Cate found her visit to Horizon Ranch energized her. Timing, she thought yet again. Time to push forward with that energy.

Some of the older cousins waged a flag football war on the front lawn. It looked vicious, so she just waved off the shouts for her to join in.

She had her own battle to fight.

And when she found Lily, her aunt Maureen, and Lily's daughter Miranda in the gathering room, Cate prepared to suit up.

"Come sit with us. We're taking advantage of a temporary no-kid/no-men zone." Lily gestured her over. "Most of the youngsters are in the designated playroom, and you must've seen the gang out front determined to bloody each other over a football."

"We're prepared to offer first aid in both areas." Maureen patted the sofa beside her. "But for the moment, we're taking a break from 'I had it first,' video game central, and shouting about fouls." She gave Cate a one-armed hug. "I haven't had a chance to really catch up with you."

"Not much to catch right now."

"I can't imagine you'll be between projects for long, but I hope you'll take this break to have a little fun. Some of the girls are talking spring break in Cancún. You should get in on that."

"My Mallory's already making her pitch." Miranda, one of the calmest, most centered women Cate knew, continued to crochet a scarf in variegated tones of blue. She might have inherited her mother's flame-red hair, but she maintained a kind of island of peace and tranquility.

"She graduates in May—can't believe that. She's aiming for Harvard. You'll graduate this spring, too, won't you, Cate?"

"Actually, I finished all the required courses before the break."

"You didn't say anything!"

Cate shrugged off Lily's exclamation. "There's been a lot going on."

"Not enough to bury that. Sweets, it's a milestone, and we need to celebrate."

"It's not like I'll do the traditional march in cap and gown."

As her tiger's eyes softened with sorrow, Lily's smile faded. "If that's what you want—"

"It's not. Really it's not. I like having it done, you know, checked off." To prove it, she used a finger to make a check in the air. "Done and dusted. Dad'll get the full report and certifications after the first of the year."

Maureen exchanged a look with Lily. "So, are you thinking college, gap year, or a hard dive into the Sullivan family business?"

Lily spoke before Cate could answer. "You can take some time. Your grades have always been stellar. You have a million possibilities and choices."

"I'm not Harvard material."

"Don't devalue yourself," Miranda said as she worked hook and wool. "You're a bright, talented young woman. You've just graduated high school ahead of schedule, while working in a demanding career, doing good work building that career. And dealing with difficulties no young woman should have to face led by a criminally poor excuse for a mother who's a stone bitch."

She said it so smoothly, so conversationally, all without missing a stitch. At the silence, Miranda looked up. "What? Am I wrong?"

"Not in the least. I love you, Miri."

"I love you, Mama. Don't devalue yourself," she told Cate again. "Too many women tend to underestimate their own worth. I learned from the master to believe in myself and work toward what I wanted in life. You should have, too."

"Maybe a few more lessons are in order," Lily decided. "With high school in the bag, you can come to New York and visit me. Spend a week or two."

"I don't want to visit you in New York."

It didn't come out as she'd planned, but sharp, pointed, and on the edge of angry. And she saw the shocked hurt on Lily's face. "I don't want to visit you in New York," she repeated, dulling the point, but maintaining the firm. "I want to go with you to New York."

"You . . . you lost me, sweets."

"I want to move to New York, with you."

"Why, now, Catey, you know I'd love to have you with me, but—"

"No, no, don't tell me all the reasons why not. You have to listen to my reasons why."

"Stand up," Maureen murmured to her. "You're vibrating. Stand up, use the energy."

She stood up, paced a minute, got her breathing under control. "I can't stay in L.A. I can't go anywhere, do anything. Every time I think it'll ease off, she comes up with something else, and they're back outside the gates."

This time she saw the looks exchanged. "What? What is it now?"

"She's engaged," Lily said flatly. "To Conrad Buster, of Buster's Burgers."

"B-Buster's Burgers?" The sound that came out of Cate started as a squeak, rolled into a helpless laugh. "You're not kidding?"

"I wonder how many Triple B's with the magic sauce she had to scarf down to rope him in. The press is doing their share of snickering, too," Maureen added.

Miranda hooked another stitch. "I remember her giving me a lecture once on the evils of red meat. Now she's queen of Busterville."

"He's seventy-freaking-seven years old—ought to know better." Lily reached for one of the candied orange slices on the tray on the table. "He has two ex-wives but no children. He's obscenely rich and popped a twenty-five-carat diamond on her finger last night. The story broke this morning."

"Well, if I had a glass, I'd raise it," Cate decided. "Eating burgers and planning a wedding should keep her too busy to take any shots at me."

The beat of silence told Cate differently. "What? Let's just have it."

"She never misses a trick, sweets. Her hope, as she tells it, is that her daughter, her only child, will open her heart and stand as her maid of honor."

"She just couldn't leave me out of it. She's getting everything she could want—money, fame, a rich husband with no kids to get in the way. But she can't leave me out of it."

It fired her up again, all over again.

She paced the room where the fire crackled, the sea rolled outside the glass, the trees sparkled like wishes, and felt everything in her go hot, go hard.

"And it won't stop. If I try to work in Hollywood, in film, it'll never stop because I'm wrong, there's more she wants. She wants to crush me. She can't damage Dad's career, or Grandpa's, they're too big. But I'm just getting started."

"Don't let her take this from you, Catey."

"G-Lil, she already has."

She dropped down on an arm of a chair in front of the window where her great-grandmother had once looked out to see her doing handsprings.

"She's used what she did to me, twisted it around, and she's squeezed all the joy out of the work for me. I don't know if I'll ever get it back. I don't know if I want to try. I do know that I finished production because I was obliged, because I couldn't just give up. And I did the best work I could. I can't do it anymore.

"I need a life. I need to see what else there is. I don't know what I want to do or be, but I know I won't find it in L.A. I need to be able to walk outside without a stupid wig and a bodyguard. I want to sit around with people my own age, meet a guy who doesn't care what my last name is. Maybe I'll take some classes, maybe I'll get a job. I just want a chance to do something, be somewhere without everyone hovering and worried and putting up shields for me."

"There are paparazzi in New York, too," Lily pointed out.

"It's not the same. You know it's not. New York doesn't run on movies, who makes them, who's in them. I need this, and I'm asking you to give it to me. I can take it without asking when I turn eighteen, but I want you to give this to me."

The front door slammed, and the aggrieved shout of "Mom!" beat Miranda's youngest to the room.

"Flynn, there's an invisible wall in front of you."

"But, Mom—"

"It may be invisible, but it's also impenetrable. I'll let you know when I take it down."

With the abject disgust only a twelve-year-old could muster, Flynn stalked away.

"Sorry, Cate. You were saying?"

"I guess I said it."

"It breaks my heart," Lily began. "It breaks my heart what she's taken from you. You know how I love you—you're my girl every bit as much as Flynn's my boy. You did see he had a bloody lip," she added.

Miranda nodded, kept crocheting. "Wouldn't be the first."

With a nod, Lily looked back at Cate. "I'd love to have you with me. You understand how busy I'll be with rehearsals and meetings, even before we open. But you have family in New York, too. If this is what you want, I'll talk to your father."

"It's what I want. Right now, it's all I want. Thank you."

"Don't thank me yet." She rose. "Well, why put off the hard stuff?"

"I'll go out with you." Miranda put her crocheting aside. "Make sure Flynn puts some ice on that lip." As she passed, she gave Cate's arm a squeeze. "Well done."

"Let me grab a jacket." Maureen got to her feet. "And you and I can take a walk."

"Maybe I should go with G-Lil to talk to Dad."

"Leave this to her." She put an arm around Cate to lead her out of the room. "I happen to know a number of people around your age. So do Miri and her Mallory. Not all of them are actors."

"Any of them cute straight guys, say, eighteen, nineteen?"

"I'll see what I can do."

Cate knew Lily did what she could when Aidan knocked on her open bedroom door.

"Hi. I was about to go back down. Later," she added when he closed the door. She braced herself. "You're mad."

"No, I'm frustrated. Why don't you tell me when you're unhappy?"

"You couldn't fix it."

"How do you know what I can fix?" he tossed back. "Damn it, Caitlyn, I can't try if you don't tell me."

"You are mad, so fine, be mad. But I wasn't going to come crying to you. Again. I have a right to figure out what I want, what I need. And she's got a right to spout her idiot bullshit the press laps up."

"She doesn't have the goddamn right to make you so unhappy you'd talk about giving up what you want and need. I haven't pushed certain buttons because I thought it could make matters worse for you. But Charlotte isn't the only one who can use the press."

"I don't want that!" Even the idea turned her insides to jelly. "She would. She'd love that kind of attention."

"Don't be so sure of that," Aidan replied. "Just because I don't choose to play dirty doesn't mean I don't know how."

"You could hurt her," Cate acknowledged. "I think she underestimates you, all of us, really. She hates us, all of us, so she underestimates us. And . . ."

To give herself a moment to gather the right words, to find the right tone, she trailed her finger down the carving in the bedpost.

"I understand her better than you think I do. Lily called her soulless that day. A soulless excuse for a mother."

"You remember that?"

She met his eyes again. "I remember everything about that morning, from you holding me when I woke up scared, and G-Lil singing a duet with me while I showered so I'd know she was right there."

"I didn't know that," he said quietly.

"I remember Nina's pancakes, and starting a puzzle with Grandpa. The fire snapping, the fog burning away so the sea broke through. I remember the things she said, and I said, and everyone."

She sat on the edge of the bed. "So does she—in her own way. She'll have done a rewrite, cast herself as heroine or victim—whichever works best. But however she remembers it, however she rewrites it, for her it's not about me. It's how she can use me to hit at you, at Grandpa, at G-Lil, at the whole family, but especially you. You chose me over her."

"It wasn't a choice. You were never a choice, Caitlyn." As his temper drained, he took her face in his hands. "You were a gift. What if we went back to Ireland?"

"That's just hiding. It was right before, and it gave me what I needed when I needed it. It's not what I need now."

"Why New York?"

"It's as far from L.A. as I can get and stay in the country. That's one. G-Lil would have a place for me. There's Mo and Harry, Miranda and Jack, the New York cousins, and you know they'd watch out for me. Maybe I wouldn't be anonymous, not right off anyway, but I wouldn't feel stalked."

"And you do here."

"Yes, I do. Every day. I don't want to act, not now. I can't feel it, Dad, and it's never been just a job for any of us. I don't want it to be for me. And she'll think she's won. We'll know she hasn't, but she'll think she's won and maybe move on. A rich husband for as long as that lasts who can buy her a few parts, who has the money and influence to push her up the social ladder."

"You do know her." He walked away to her view of the sea. "I was with her more than ten years, making excuses, overlooking."

"Because of me. I know you loved her, but you looked the other way or made excuses because of me. You would never have given her all those years of your life otherwise."

"I don't know."

"You haven't had a serious relationship since, because of me."

He turned back quickly. "No, don't take that on. Because of me. Trust issues," he said, and walked back to her. "I think I'm entitled."

"I'd say you are, yeah. But you can trust me, Dad. Trust me enough to let me go."

"Hardest thing in the world." He gathered her in. "I'm going to be making a lot of trips to New York. You'll have to tolerate that. You already know your grandfather will—and doubly now, as it's not just Lily but both of his best girls on the other coast."

"My best guys."

"I need a text from you every day, and a phone call every week. The texts for the first month. The call for the rest of your life."

"I can agree to that."

He rested his chin on top of her head, and started missing her.

CHAPTER THIRTEEN

New York City

For the first few weeks in New York, Cate stuck to the Upper West Side, where Lily had her condo. When she ventured farther, she was with Lily or aunts or cousins.

Since the weather in late winter in New York came as a shock to her system, she didn't find sticking close much of a hardship.

After all, she did get out—and was so bundled up when she took a walk the possibility of being recognized hit zero. And she enjoyed walking in a city made for it. While a far cry from the paths and quiet roads of Mayo, the long avenues, the jammed cross streets, the myriad of shops, cafés, restaurants all invited exploration.

By the time the air hinted—pretty vaguely—of spring, she'd gained considerable confidence and learned to love the taste of freedom.

Through her cousins, she met people her own age. Most were far too jaded to be impressed by her lineage. And actors of her father's and grandfather's generation were as ancient to them as Moses.

She liked it.

She learned to walk fast, like a native, and after some missteps learned how to navigate the subway system. She preferred long walks or subway rides to cabs, found both full of fascination.

So many voices, accents, languages. So many styles and looks. Best of all, nobody paid any particular attention to her.

Since she'd put herself, once again, into Gino's hands before leaving L.A., she sported a sharp, swingy do with side-swept bangs.

At times, she barely recognized herself.

As Lily moved into rehearsals, Cate liked to drop into the theater once or twice a week, just hunker back in the house and watch the evolution. Voices again, big, banging Broadway voices, lifting up, lifting out, lifting back.

Lily's laugh, she thought, watching the stage, or Mame's laugh now, just rolling. Some actors were born to play certain roles. In Cate's opinion, Mame was Lily's.

She took out her phone—always muted in rehearsal—and sent a text to her father.

Today's news from NY. I'm watching the director and the cast adjust some of the blocking in Scene Five of the first act. Right now it's just Mame and Vera. Lily's wearing leggings, Marian Keene is wearing jeans, but I swear you can almost see them in costume. FYI, Mimi, Lily's PA, had to fly back to LA to help her mom. Mom broke her ankle. So for now, I'm filling in. Tell Grandpa Lily's excited he's coming out next week. She misses him, and me, too. And you. Btw, I'm getting tattoo sleeves and my tongue pierced. J/k. Or am I?

Grinning at herself, she sent the text. Then folding her arms on the seat in front of her, she propped her chin on them and watched the magic happen.

When they took five, and the director huddled with the choreographer and stage manager, Lily called out.

"Are you still with us, Cate?"

"Right here." Hauling up her massive tote bag, Cate got up, moved forward and into view.

"Come on up."

Cate headed to the doors, house left, went through, went up to where chorus members warmed up for the next number, stretching limbs, doing vocals. Already reaching in the bag, she walked on, stage right.

"Protein bar, room-temp flat water."

Lily took both. "Mimi's going to fear losing her job."

"Just taking care of my G-Lil until she's back."

"I can use it." Lily dropped down into a folding chair, stretched out her legs, rotated her ankles. "You can forget how physical live theater is—double it with musical theater."

"How about I book you a massage later? I can have Bill there at six—I already checked—and have some of the penne you like, a nice salad, delivered from Luigi's at seven-thirty. Carbs are energy's friend."

"My God, girl, you're a wonder."

"Mimi and her detailed list, her spreadsheet and endless contact information's the wonder."

"How did I end up with a masseur named Bill? He should be Esteban or Sven."

Cate wiggled her fingers. "Magic hands, if I remember right."

"He does have those. Book 'em, Danno. Now tell me what you think. How are we doing up here?"

"Dead honest?"

"Oh Christ." Braced, Lily cast her eyes up to the catwalk. "Hit me."

"I know you've never met much less worked with Marian before this. The same with Tod and Brandon, your young Patricks. The audience is going to believe Mame and Vera have been friends forever, and that Patrick is the love of your life."

"Well." Lily took a long sip of water. "It turns out I like dead honest. I'd just love to have me some more."

"It's so different from movies, G-Lil. You don't do a take, another, another, then sit, wait. Wait some more. Reaction shot, retake, wait. It all moves so fast. And when you're off-book, you'll have to remember every line, every gesture, every step, every mark to hit, every beat, start to finish. Not a run of dialogue, not a scene. All of it. So the energy's completely different."

"Catching the bug?"

"Me?" With a shake of her head, Cate moved deliberately to center stage, looked out. All those seats, she thought, from orchestra to the upper balcony, all those faces watching.

In the moment. In the now.

For fun, she did a quick side shuffle, tap, flung out her arms to sell it. Laughed when Lily applauded.

"And that's as close as I ever want to get. It must be really scary and—I guess the word's *exhilarating* to work live onstage. And you'll do it eight times a week, six nights, two matinees. No, not for me. They're both magic, right?"

She walked back to Lily. "Magical ways to tell stories. I think it takes the amazing to be really great at both types of magic."

"My sweets. You've pumped me back up a hell of a lot better than this weird protein bar." Rising, Lily rolled her shoulders. "Now, you're dismissed."

"Fired?"

"Not until Mimi's back. Go, text some of your friends, go shopping or meet up at a coffee shop."

"Are you sure?"

"Scram. Just text me if you make other dinner plans."

"I will, thanks. Break a leg."

Grabbing her phone to book the massage, she went out stage right. Then pulled up short when one of the chorus stepped in front of her.

She glanced up. "Sorry. Texting while walking."

"I got in your way. I'm Noah. I'm in the chorus."

She knew; she'd noticed. She'd watched him and the others rehearse numbers over and over, tirelessly—or so it seemed.

Up close, like now, he gave her stomach a flutter. That smooth skin, like the caramel coating on the apples Mrs. Leary had made for All Hallows' Eve. Golden eyes, sort of like a lion's, tipped exotically at the corners.

Inside her head, she went: Um, um, um.

But a Sullivan knew how to hit her mark.

"I've caught some of the rehearsals. I love the juggling bit you do in 'We Need a Little Christmas.'"

"My grandmother taught me."

"Really?"

"Yep. She ran away to the circus—seriously—for a few years when she was a kid. So, hey, I should be done by four. You want to get some coffee?"

Inside her head everything sizzled, then went blank.

"I was just heading out, but . . . I could meet you."

"Sweet. Like four-thirty at Café Café? It's right around the corner."

"Yeah, I know it. Okay, sure. I'll see you later."

She walked away, casually, all the way to the stage door, stepped out, walked another ten feet to be absolutely sure.

Then she let out a squeal, did a quick dance—an Irish pullback—right on the sidewalk. Since the sidewalk ran in the Theater District of New York City, barely anyone noticed.

She made the booking for Lily, set an alarm to remind her when to order dinner. Then texted her Harvard-bound cousin, one she considered the most reliable and least silly.

How soon can you meet me at Sephora? The one on 42nd?

While she waited, she wondered if she should go home and change, or just buy a new outfit.

Too much, don't be an idiot. It's just coffee. Do you want him to know he's the first male not related to you who's ever asked you to have coffee?

Last class done at 2:45. Around 3?

Perfect. See you there.

What's up?

I've got a date! Just coffee, but a date.

Awesome! See you there.

Since she had time to kill, Cate slowed her pace, worked out some areas of conversation. When she reached Forty-second, she went into Sephora, strolled the aisles.

Ended up filling a basket more from nerves than wants. And checked her phone half a dozen times even as she reminded herself Noah couldn't text her to cancel because he didn't have her number.

Should she have given him her number?

Then she yipped and jolted when her phone signaled an incoming text.

Just walked in. Where r u?

Meet me at the makeover counter.

She spotted her cousin, romantic strawberry-blond hair swinging, serious-minded black-framed glasses over hazel eyes, and a loaded backpack over her shoulder.

"Okay, who is he, where'd you meet him, and is he cute?"

"Noah, he's in *Mame*—chorus—and he's all-caps cute."

"A thespian, so some common ground. What look are you going for?"

"I—"

One of the roaming staff—a guy with a cloud puff of emerald green in jet-black hair, beautifully kohled brown eyes—moved in. "Good afternoon, ladies, what can I help you with today? I'd just love to do your eyes," he said to Cate. "And yours."

"It's her." Mallory pointed at Cate. "She's got a date."

"Oooh. A hot one?"

"It's just coffee."

"These things have to start somewhere. Sit down right here, and let Jarmaine work his magic."

She could do her own makeup, and thought she had a good hand with it. But for this . . . "I want to look like I didn't really bother, you know? Or only a little."

"Trust me." Jarmaine took Cate's chin in his hand, turned her face this way, that way. "You have some good choices in your basket. I can use some of those. So." Jarmaine whipped out some makeup wipes. "What's he like? Does he have a friend?"

He swept, buffed, brushed, lined while Mallory looked on.

"I like what you're doing with her eyes. They're already crazy blue, but you're making them, like, bolder."

"She chose a good palette, neutral but not boring. We're going for the *I didn't do a thing, I'm just this ridiculously beautiful*, so neutrals are best."

"I'm going to braid your hair," Mallory decided. "Just a casual, low, loose braid. It'll go with the makeup." Out of a section of her backpack, Mallory pulled a fold-up brush, a small rat-tail comb, and a little clear case holding a selection of bands.

Her mother's daughter, Cate thought.

"Hair and makeup." Jarmaine smiled at Cate. "Movie star treatment."

She smiled back even as she thought: Jesus God, I really hope not.

After Jarmaine deemed her done and gorgeous, after she checked out, she went out with Mallory.

"I'll walk with you part of the way, then cut over. I've got a boat-load of studying to do. But I still expect a full report."

"You'll get it. Thanks for coming with me. I'm stupid nervous."

"Just be Cate, and unless he's a moron, he's going to ask you out again. Unless his big cute hides a jerk, you're going to go out with him again. Slow down a little, you want to get there about five after coffee-date time. Not rude late, but not on the mark."

"I need to learn these things."

"Listen to me. I am the master."

Mallory hooked an arm through Cate's, gave her a hip bump.

"Don't stay over an hour, even if you're doing great. Maybe, in this case, an hour and fifteen—but that's max. Then you've got to go. If he wants more, and he will, he'll ask to see you again. But don't do the need to check your schedule deal—lame and pissy—unless you really have to."

"My social calendar is wide open."

Another hip bump, more forceful. "Don't say that! Just, if he says how about catching a movie tomorrow night or whenever, you can repeat the day. Friday? Sure, that'd be great. If he makes a move, goes in for a kiss, fine, if you want to kiss him. But no tongues, not over a coffee date."

"Jesus, I have to start writing this down."

"You're an actor, cuz. You'll remember lines and staging. I need to split. Remember those few simple rules, then relax, have fun."

Mallory caught the WALK at the intersection, moved with the throng to cross. "Full report!" she shouted.

Be Cate. Five minutes late, which wasn't Cate because she prided herself on being on time. Stay an hour to an hour-fifteen. Don't pretend to have a crowded calendar, and no tongues.

Following her director, she hit her cue, walked into the rumble and scents of Café Café.

The sofas and oversized chairs, always at a premium, were already filled, the baristas at the coffee bar already busy.

She spotted Noah at a two-top wearing a long-sleeve T-shirt instead of the tank he'd rehearsed in. Those beautiful lion eyes met hers as she started toward him.

"Hey. You look great."

"Thanks." She slid in across from him. "How'd the rest of rehearsal go?"

He rolled those eyes. "It went. We're getting there. Hey, Tory."

"Noah. What can I get you guys?"

When Noah looked at her, waited, Cate decided on the simple. "A regular latte."

"Skinny latte, double shot, thanks, Tory. I've got a dance class tonight," he told Cate. "I need the double shot."

"Teaching or taking?"

"Taking. Three nights a week. Can I just say, get it out of the way, Lily Morrow is a goddess."

In no way a moron or a jerk, Cate decided on the spot. "She's always been mine."

"Has to be mutual. She really lights up when you're in the house. What do you do when you're not—in the house?"

"Try to figure things out."

His smile, slow and sweet, did jittery things to her heart.

"Hey, me, too."

They talked, and it was easy. So easy she forgot to be nervous. Forgot about the hour rule until her phone alarm went off.

"Sorry, sorry." She pulled it out, shut it off. "That's to remind me to order dinner. I'm filling in for G—for Lily's PA for a couple of weeks. I, ah, need to get back to that. This was nice. Thanks."

"Listen, before you take off, there's this party Saturday night. Some of the cast—some civilians, too—just blowing off steam. Do you want to go?"

Repeat the day, she reminded herself as everything inside her cheered. "Saturday? Sure."

He held out his phone. "You could put your number in my contacts."

Of course, of course, she knew how it worked. She did it with friends all the time. Just never with someone who asked her for a second date. She passed her phone to him, took his.

"I can pick you up about nine." He passed her phone back. "Unless you want to grab a pizza first."

Oh God, oh God! "I like pizza."

"Eight then. Just text me the address."

"I will." When he didn't make a move, she wasn't sure whether to be relieved or disappointed. "Thanks for the coffee."

She strolled out, and when she did her happy dance well out of sight, Tory glanced over at Noah, lifted her eyebrows.

He mimed a huge sigh, and beat a hand over his heart.

Three weeks later, after pizza and parties, after dancing in clubs and long, desperate kisses in the sweet bloom of spring, Cate lay under him in Noah's skinny bed in his closet of a bedroom in the cramped apartment he shared with two Broadway gypsies.

In her first-time haze, the lumpy mattress was a billowing cloud, the punishing beat of rap pulsing through the wall from the apartment next door the song of celestial angels.

While she had no comparisons, she felt absolutely certain she'd just experienced the true meaning of every song, every poem, every sonnet ever written.

When he lifted his head, looked into her eyes, she was inside the greatest love story ever told.

"I've wanted us here since the first time I saw you. You had on a blue sweater. Lily was taking you on a backstage tour. I was scared to say anything to you."

"Why?"

He twined a lock of her hair around his finger. "Besides you're so damn beautiful? Lily Morrow's granddaughter. Then you started torturing me, coming to rehearsals, and I just couldn't take it anymore. I figured hey, if I ask her for coffee and she blows me off, at least I won't die wondering."

He lowered his head, kissed her lightly, lips, cheeks, eyes. Heart and hormones stuttered inside her.

"I was so nervous, then we started talking." She laid a hand on his cheek. "And I just wasn't. I was really nervous about this, then you touched me, and I just wasn't."

And still, her first.

"It was good, wasn't it?"

He gave her a considering look that rushed doubts to the surface. "Well . . . I don't know. I think we should do it again, just to be sure."

Doubts washed away in delight. "Just to be sure," she agreed.

Because Lily ruled a cab—no subway—if Cate stayed out past midnight, Noah walked her over to Eighth Avenue to hail one.

Walking—slowly—hand in hand with him, she thought New York looked like a movie set. The light drizzle was sheer romance with streetlights shimmering in thin puddles and on wet pavement.

"Text when you get home, okay?"

"You're as bad as G-Lil."

"That's what happens when somebody cares about you." He pulled her in for one more kiss. "Come to dance class tomorrow night. You've got the moves, and you know you like it."

She did. Maybe her muscles were rusty, but she'd enjoyed the two classes he'd already talked her into. Besides, he'd be there.

"All right. I'll see you there."

Now she pulled him in, then slid into the cab. "Sixty-seventh and Eighth," she told the driver as she shifted to keep Noah in view as long as possible.

Then she pulled out her phone, texted Darlie.

I'm not going to die a virgin!!!

She snuggled that knowledge to her, dreamed out the window as the cab made the turn, headed up Eighth.

She laughed out loud at Darlie's answer.

Welcome to the club, slut. Now gimme deets.

She floated through the spring, took dance classes, added yoga, and on a whim decided to take a scattershot of classes at NYU over the summer.

French, just because the sound of the language appealed to her; Film Studies, because she may not want to act, but the business still interested her; and Writing the Screenplay, because maybe she could.

And once a week, she and Lily had dinner, just the two of them, in the condo with New York beaming through the windows.

"I can't believe you made this."

Basking in the accomplishment, Cate watched Lily take another bite of the penne with basil and tomato. "Me, either, but it's pretty good."

"Sweets, it's as good as Luigi's—but don't tell him I said so. And you baked Italian bread."

"It was fun. Nan and I learned how to bake bread from a neighbor in Ireland. It took me back there, brought her back to me. Plus, I wanted to surprise you."

"I haven't been this surprised since I got my first gray hair—and this is a lot happier. I don't suppose you can do an encore the next time your granddaddy's here."

"I know you miss him."

"It's hard to find the time or energy to miss anything, but I do. The damn old goat's got his hooks in me."

"Did you always know?" Wondering, wondering, Cate toyed with the little gold heart around her neck Noah had given her for her eighteenth birthday. "I mean right from the start that you loved him?"

"I'd go with attracted to, which irritated the holy hell out of me. I'd had a marriage go bad, was hitting that age where Hollywood wants to flick you off if you're a woman. Actually, I'd been bouncing off that for some time. I've got two kids in college, and what I saw as the fight of my life to stay relevant as a film actor. Then he comes along."

"And he's so handsome," Cate said with wiggling eyebrows to make Lily laugh.

"Child, that man got a triple scoop of good looks out of God's goody bag. Now, being an actor of a certain age in Hollywood, I'm cast as the eccentric aunt—at least they didn't make me her mother—of his love interest. Nobody blinks that he's twenty years older, it's not even part of the story."

"But you got the hero in real life."

"I did, not on purpose, but I did." Considering her girl, Lily stabbed more penne. "You're old enough to hear I thought—we both thought—we'd just have some fine sex, then move on. God knows neither of us intended to ever get married again. I had the bad, he'd had the damn near perfect."

Pacing—the story, the meal—Lily set down her fork to take a tiny sip of wine. "Olivia Dunn was the love of his life. When we started realizing it wasn't just sex, however fun, between us, I had to give that fact some hard thought. Could I stick with a man who had that kind of love, still had that kind of love, in him for another woman?"

She took another tiny sip from the single glass of wine she allowed herself on the night before a dress rehearsal. "You know what I figured? Any man who had that kind of love in him, well, I'd be a fool to walk away from what he'd have in him for me. And my mama, she didn't raise a fool for a daughter."

"All my life, it was seeing how you are, the two of you, that showed me what love is, or, I guess, could be."

"Then we did something right." She set the wine down. "That leads me comfortably into a subject I'd hoped you'd bring up with me. But since you haven't, I'm just going to poke right in like the bear into the honeycomb. And hope I don't get my nose stung. It's charming, my sweets, that you and Noah think you're keeping your relationship on the down low."

"I . . ."

"I even understand why you're trying to keep it quiet—though for heaven's sake, Catey girl, it's theater. We're a gossipy bunch, and we dearly love sex and drama."

Trepidation about what would come tangled with relief of letting go of a secret. "I didn't know how you'd react."

"Then somewhere along the line I did something wrong if you don't know you can talk to me about anything."

"I do know. I'm sorry. That's not fair. Most of it's me. It's been so good, just so good not to have to worry about what people might read about me, or hear about me, or say. She's so into her engagement, her big wedding plans, she doesn't need me to get press right now, and I just don't want to give anybody anything. I did tell Darlie, and Mallory knows. And Noah's roommates. I started to tell you so many times, but . . . I didn't really know how."

"Let's start with this, and hell, I'm breaking my rule and having a second glass of wine. You can have one with me. It's an occasion."

Before Lily could get up for the bottle, Cate jumped up, brought it and a second glass in from the kitchen. "Am I like driving you to drink now?"

Lily patted her hand. "You're giving me an excuse to indulge myself. Did he give you that sweet necklace?"

"For my birthday."

"He earns points there. It's a thoughtful gift. I want to know if he's sweet and thoughtful with you otherwise."

"He is. He always walks me out to get a cab, waits until I'm driving away, and asks me to text him when I'm home safe. He listens to me, pays attention. He got me back into dance class, and I didn't know how much I missed it until he did. He's kept it quiet because I asked him to."

"I'm going to tell you I asked around about him—that's not only my privilege," she continued, when Cate's mouth opened, "it's my duty. So I know he doesn't drink or do drugs because he's serious about his work. He comes from an interesting family—which we southern ladies appreciate and admire. He works hard, I see that for myself. And he's good, he's damn good. He can go places."

It shined inside her, the approval she heard from the most important woman in her life. "He loves the theater."

"It shows. Now, the big one. Are you being careful, both of you?"

"Yes. I promise you."

"All right then, it's time he started coming to the door instead of you meeting him outside, or wherever. I haven't said anything to your father or to Hugh, and I won't, as that's for you. And I understand, I do, your need to keep it out of the press." She leaned over to take Cate's hand. "But it will get out, sooner or later. Both of you need to be ready for that."

"I'll talk to him about it."

"Good. When are you seeing him again?"

"I was going to meet him after rehearsal tomorrow, and . . ." She caught the arched eyebrows. "I'll have him come to the door."

CHAPTER FOURTEEN

It delighted Cate how easily Lily and Noah hit it off. How could she not love listening to two of her favorite people sit and exchange theater stories?

When Lily insisted he come for dinner, he brought flowers for both of them. And that pretty much sealed it all around.

She missed them both, almost painfully, when the play had its out-of-town openings in San Francisco and Chicago.

But they both had to focus, as she saw it. And it gave her several days to find out how she handled living on her own.

For the first time in her life, she thought, standing on the terrace in balmy air, eating Chinese takeout from the carton. No anxiety, no nightmares, just her own routine.

Good long walks every day and daily yoga practice. Dance class, though it made her miss Noah all the more. Afternoon research on the courses she'd take in a few weeks.

Two abortive attempts at writing a screenplay, both so bad she trashed them. She'd still take the course, she decided, but had a feeling her area of talent didn't extend to writing.

That was okay. Scooping up noodles, she walked to the polished concrete wall, looked down at the busy, busy world below. She'd find her place, eventually. In that busy, busy world or somewhere else. But now, right now, this quiet time, this interlude where she could stay anonymous, where she could walk by a newsstand and not see her own face, or some headline shouting her name, gave her all she needed.

Ireland had given her that as a child. She'd take it from New York now, and because she wasn't a child any longer, she'd use the time, the interlude to explore her talents, or lack thereof, her abilities, or lack thereof.

Maybe she'd take a photography course, or art lessons, or, or, or.

"I'll find out," she murmured as she went back in, closed the glass doors on the rumble of the city.

She settled down with her tablet, did some searching on photography. She did like looking at people, listening to them. She might be good at capturing images.

Freezing a moment, an expression, a mood. She could practice with her phone camera, just play around. She'd walk around the neighborhood in the morning before she headed over to NYU to orient herself a little.

When her phone alarm sounded, she snatched it up.

"Curtain."

She imagined the curtain rising on the stage in San Francisco, the lights, the set.

"Break a leg, everybody."

She tried to occupy herself with more research, just couldn't. She could hear the opening act, the notes, the beats, the dialogue, the voices.

Did the audience laugh here, applaud there? Were they charmed and engaged?

She imagined the whirl of backstage, the costume changes, the warm-ups, the rush to hit the cue.

Rising, she checked the locks, lowered the lights before going into her bedroom. To try to counteract the anxiety in her stomach, the not knowing, she rolled out her yoga mat, started a relaxation session.

She'd have relaxed more, she could admit, if she hadn't kept checking the time, but she got in thirty minutes.

Trying to stretch out the time as she had her body, she changed into a tank and cotton sleeping shorts, did a long, involved skin care routine.

Made it to intermission.

She switched on the television, flipped through stations until she found a movie in progress. One with car chases and explosions to take her mind completely out of musical theater.

Apparently, the yoga worked better than she'd realized, as she dropped off as Matt Damon's Jason Bourne disposed of bad guys.

The phone popped her awake. She scrambled for it, and the remote to turn off the TV. "Noah."

"I woke you up. I knew I should've waited until morning."

"I told you I'd mess you up if you did. I'm awake. Tell me."

"Some kinks we need to work out."

She could hear the noise, the voices, the *buzz, buzz, buzz* in the background. "Tell me," she repeated.

"It was awesome." The wondering laugh came through, warmed her. "It was freaking great. Full house, standing O. Twelve curtain calls. Twelve."

"I knew it! I knew it! I'm so happy for you."

"We have to see what the reviews say. Jeez, Cate, you should've heard the house explode when Lily came onstage. Your grandfather was out front. He's coming to the cast party. I miss you."

"I miss you, too, but I'm so happy for you. All of you."

"Feels like the best night of my life. Go back to sleep. I'll text you tomorrow."

"Go celebrate. And when you have your smash opening on Broadway, I'll be there."

"Counting on it. Night."

"Night."

She put the phone on the bedside charger, hugged herself.

Smiling, she snuggled in, drifted off. When the phone signaled again, she sighed into another smile. "Noah," she murmured when she answered.

"You didn't do what you were told."

The robotic voice shot her up in bed. "What? What?"

Music now. An iconic voice asking: *"Are you lonesome tonight?"*

Vises closing down her lungs as she fumbled for the light, wheezing as her eyes darted around the room.

Her mother's voice, whispering: *"You're alone."* Static, a change in pitch. *"You can't hide!"*

In a panic, she scrambled out of bed, fell to her knees.

Music again, the upbeat, cheerful sound turned to terror. *"Hold on. I'm coming!"*

A horror-movie laugh, the kind of greedy laugh that rose out of dark basements, through graveyard fog.

When the phone went dead, she burst into tears.

She didn't just change her number, she trashed the phone, bought a new one. She struggled over whether or not to tell anyone. Opening night loomed, so the timing couldn't have been worse. But in the end, she told Noah.

They sat in Café Café, his hands gripping hers. "It happened before?"

"Back in L.A., last winter. It was a recording. I mean, this one was different, but they're recordings."

"Why didn't you tell your dad before?"

"Noah, I've told you how he gets, how he worries and tries to basically throw a force field around me. And I thought, really thought, it was just some jerk playing a nasty game."

"But now it's happened again. We'll go to the cops."

"I trashed the phone," she reminded him. "Part of the panic, and stupid, but I trashed it. And what would they do anyway? It wasn't really a threat."

"Trying to scare somebody is a threat. Do you think it's your mother?"

"No, not that she wouldn't do something, but I don't think she'd have used her own voice. In the first, I know it was from a movie she did. I'm betting this one is, too."

"Cate, they knew you were alone."

"Yeah." She'd had time to think, time to calm and think. "I told you how it works with me. There have been a couple of squibs about me living in New York with G-Lil, even something about me registering for classes at NYU. The out-of-town opening got a lot of play, so . . ."

"You have to tell Lily. I'll go with you."

"What? Now?"

"Now."

"I don't want to upset her, and she can't—"

Noah tossed the coffee money on the table. "If you don't tell her, I will."

That flipped a switch. "That's not right. It's my business, my decision."

He simply rose, took her hand to pull her to her feet. "You're going to have to deal with it."

Furious, she argued, demanded, threatened, but didn't budge him an inch on the fast walk to the condo. Those golden eyes she loved stayed hard, his face implacable.

Lily's reaction didn't make things better.

"Son of a bitch!"

Fresh from her massage, still in her robe, Lily swirled around the living room.

"The second time? And you didn't tell me."

"I just—"

"There's no 'I just.'" Her eyes narrowed as she caught the resentful look Cate tossed at Noah. "And don't you take it out on him. Noah's done the right thing."

"There's nothing you can do about it," Cate began.

"You have no idea what I can do when I have to do it. But I can't do a damn thing if I don't know. I'm responsible for you, my girl. I don't give a single cold damn if you're eighteen or a hundred and eight. I'm responsible. And the first thing we do is report this to the police."

Panic wanted to rear back. "Would you wait a minute, please?" The fury flying off Lily burned so hot it took genuine effort for Cate to step to her. "What happens then? I got rid of the phone. I can admit that was stupid, but it's done. I tell them what I remember about the calls. Then what?"

"I'm not the damn police, so I don't know then what."

"I can figure out part of it. I file a report, and the report gets out. That's a little feast for the tabloids. Then it's public, and how many other calls do you think I'll get once it is?"

"Son of a bitch!" Robe flapping, Lily stalked to the terrace doors, threw them open. Stalked out.

"Happy now?" Cate tossed at Noah.

"It's not about happy, don't be an idiot. She's pissed because she loves you. So am I. So do I."

"That doesn't help right now." Though it did, more than a little. Gearing up, she walked outside.

"I'm sorry I didn't tell you. I didn't tell anyone the first time because I knew Dad wouldn't let me do the movie, and I wanted it. I needed it. He wouldn't have let me."

"Probably not," Lily muttered.

"I didn't say anything at first about this time because, G-Lil, you've got opening night."

Lily whirled around. "Do you think a play's more important to me than you? That anything in this world is more important to me than you?"

"No. It's the same for me. There was press about my mother getting out, about me, about the new project when the first one happened. And there's been a little about me going to NYU just recently, and all the interviews she's doing about her wedding. Somebody took a shot."

"She could have done it herself. I wouldn't put it past her."

"She could hire better."

The sun, as fiery as Lily's hair, shot light over the river, bounced it off steel and glass.

"They're recordings, G-Lil. I know a recording when I hear it. The overdubbing, the really crappy splicing. She has plenty of money now to pay for quality, and this isn't."

"That doesn't make it better."

"But I can't stop living my life because of it. I hate the way it makes me feel when it's happening, but I can't stop living my life."

Lily walked back into the shade, sat, drummed her fingers. "No one wants that, Catey. You have a point about the police. This time. If it happens again, we do this differently. You keep the phone, call the police, give them the phone, and let them do what they do."

"All right."

"For now, you'll write down whatever you remember from both calls so we have a record, if we need it. You're going to call your father and tell him."

"But—"

"No." Eyes glittering, Lily shot up a finger. "That's absolute. What we'll call unhealthy communications happen to people in our line of work—and you were in our line of work. But he needs to know. Then you'll make up with your boyfriend, because he did the right thing, and he did it out of love and concern."

"I don't like the way he did it."

Lily arched those eyebrows. "Enough to kick him to the curb over it?"

"No."

"Then go make up—get that done. Then have him get me—and himself—a nice cold Coke. We'll sit out here while you deal with your daddy. I'll back you up there," Lily decided. "Bring me the phone after you've gotten things started."

With no way out, she went back inside where Noah waited. "I don't like the way you did this."

"I got that."

"I need to be able to handle my own life, make my own decisions."

"This is different. You know it's different, but you're still too twisted up about it to admit it." He walked to her before she could snap back, put his hands on her face. "I can't stand seeing you twisted up. I can't not do anything when you are."

He brushed his lips over hers. "You're going to be less twisted up now that she knows."

"Maybe, but now I have to tell my father, and that's going to be a mess. She said to get some Cokes and go out and sit with her while I call my dad."

It was messy, and upsetting, and ultimately took that dose of Lily to close it off. But the worst Cate feared didn't happen. She wasn't ordered to come back to L.A.—an order she would have refused. And she had yet another chance to live her life.

Before opening night came final dress and a theater filled with the energy of family and friends. Cate had her first experience watching it all full out—lights, music, sets, costumes—in a theater jammed with people who wanted nothing more than the success of their loved one on the stage.

She met Noah's family, and that felt like another major step in her life.

On the preview night, the one critics attended, she stayed backstage. Critics and press meshed together. She didn't want to chance taking the spotlight off her grandmother, her boyfriend.

Still, she agonized with the cast in the wait for the early reviews, celebrated with the raves.

With Monday's dark theater, she took an early dance class with Noah, and he went with her to tour the campus she'd attend at NYU.

"It's so big," she said as they walked to the subway. "And that's just part of it. It feels overwhelming."

"You'll do fine. Better than fine."

Together they walked down the steps to take the train uptown.

"Private school, tutors."

"Poor rich white girl," he said, which made her laugh and give him an elbow jab.

"It's the vastness, I guess." They moved through the revolving gate. "And so many people. Even summer courses are going to have a lot of students. The advantage to that," she added, pulling out her Metro-Card, "is being able to more or less disappear. *Change of Scene*'s coming out in a couple weeks. The rest of the cast is already starting the circuit."

"We're going to see it."

"Oh, I don't know." She hunched, wiggled her shoulders as if shaking off an itch.

"No way out."

They waited on the platform with two women, one with a round-cheeked baby in a stroller. They spoke rapid Spanish while the baby gnawed ferociously on an orange teething ring. Nearby a man in a business suit used his thumb to scroll on his phone. Beside him, a short, squat man in baggy basketball shorts polished off a slice while bopping his head to whatever played through his earbuds.

The air smelled of the pizza, baked-in sweat, and someone's overdone onion rings.

"It ended up being a pretty crap part of my life."

Noah just trailed a hand down her arm. "Another reason we're going, so you can see how good you are even through the crap parts. We can catch a matinee." He took her hand as the thunder of the approaching train swelled through the tunnel.

The doors swooshed open, and people piled out, people piled on. "How about we hit the park?" He tugged her toward seats. "We can do the stroll-in-the-sun thing, grab a couple street dogs."

And keep his mind off tomorrow night. Opening night.

"I like the sound of that. I can drop the backpack off at the condo, change into stroll-in-the-sun shoes."

He looked down at his own beat-to-shit Nikes. "I could use some new shoes."

"We can add shopping to the stroll."

He shifted his gaze over. "How many shoes have you got?"

"Irrelevant," she said primly—so primly he grinned and kissed her.

They talked about potential shoes, strolls, maybe hooking up with some friends, maybe just going back to his place, since at least one of his roommates had an afternoon audition, and he thought the other one had a shift at his day job.

Living life, she thought. No ugly calls, no pushy press would stop her.

"We combine," she decided as they walked from the elevator to the condo. "Your place first, especially if it's empty, because that just never happens. Then the stroll, shoes to follow so we're not schlepping bags."

"Maybe." He slid his hand down her hair as she got out her key. "Or maybe we'll never get out of my place."

"You would think that."

Laughing, a little starry-eyed, they walked in.

"And here she is!"

Hugh stepped in from the terrace, absolute delight on his face as he opened his arms.

"Grandpa. You were supposed to come tomorrow."

She dropped her backpack on the floor, hurried forward for the hug.

"We decided to surprise you and Lily, and maybe catch you with some dancing boys." He gave her a kiss on both cheeks, looked over at Noah. "And we did! The juggler with the very talented feet."

"Yes, sir, thank you. Noah Tanaka." He shook Hugh's hand. "I can get more dancing boys on a couple minutes' notice."

Hugh let out a laugh, slapped him on the back.

"It's fine, Lily. I'll be fine."

Cate's head swiveled at the voice. "Dad."

She bolted to him, squeezed as tight as she was squeezed when he lifted her off her feet.

"Let me look at you. Pictures and Skype aren't the same." He drew her back.

However skillfully he masked it, she knew him too well and saw the worry.

"I'm fine, Dad. More than."

"I can see that. I've missed you."

"I missed you, too. We were all set for tomorrow. Having a late lunch, a fancy one, here before Lily had to go to the theater. Then we'd walk over and slip in the stage door."

"We'll do that, too. Dad and I decided we'd take more time, surprise you."

Lily looked straight at Cate. "Surprise. Aidan, this is Noah, he's in the chorus."

"He's not going to stay there," Hugh commented. "Boy's got presence."

"It's great meeting you, Mr. Sullivan. Both of you."

"Nice meeting you. Is this your first time on Broadway?"

"Actually, my third. I only put one in the *Playbill* because the other shut down after ten days. But . . . I should . . . take off."

"We're taking our two best girls to lunch," Hugh put in. "Why don't you join us?"

"Oh, well, thanks, but—"

Shit, Cate thought, shit. Take the next step.

"Lunch sounds great." Reaching out, she took Noah's hand. "Noah and I, we're together."

She saw surprise flicker over her father's face, and maybe a little distress. "I'm going to take a minute. New territory for me. 'Together' means . . ."

"Dad, I'm eighteen."

"Right. That happened. Well, it seems lunch is now required. I need to spend time grilling Noah." He made a warning sound, pointed at Cate when she opened her mouth to object. "My job. I'm just figuring out how to do this part of it. Lily, you said your place for lunch is only a few blocks away."

"That's right. A very pleasant walk."

Aidan gave Noah a wide, toothy smile. "For some of us."

Later, when she walked with Noah to the corner—in the opposite direction of her family—she covered her face with her hands.

"I'm so sorry!"

"No, it's cool. It's weird, but it's cool. Maybe a little scary at first. No, a lot."

He swiped a hand over his forehead as if swiping off sweat.

"So you know how he said he had to figure this part out? Well, he's a fast study, your old man. He practically twisted my life story out of me before we got to the restaurant. And he's all 'What's next for you?' and I'm, like, 'Ah, ah, I want to move up to principal dancer, and speaking roles and, okay, I want to headline. I'll work for it, but I want to headline.'"

"You will."

"I'm going to work for it. Anyway, he made damn sure I knew

he'd come like the wrath of all the gods on anybody who hurt his daughter."

As she had no problem hearing her father say just that, she clutched Noah's arm, clung to it. "They're protective."

"It's okay, I get it, and I said how I don't hurt people, especially people I care about. I think he liked that. I think he almost liked me by the time we finished lunch."

"You did great." She kissed him to prove it. "And I'm sorry I can't go back to your place."

"No, that would be weird, too, now. And, you know, disrespectful. Besides, I think I'm going to need a little recovery time after the grilling."

"You can take some comfort knowing I'm in for it next." She glanced back. "Might as well get it over with."

"Text me later?"

"Count on it. I'll see you tomorrow, backstage, and then I'll be front row center when the curtain comes up."

When she walked into the condo, she saw immediately her grandparents had cleared the field. Her father sat, solo, on the terrace.

She went out, sat in the chair beside his. Waited.

"I love you, Caitlyn."

"I know, Dad. I know. I love you."

"There's a part of me that's always going to look at you and see my little girl. That's how it is, that's the deal. And you know the reasons I feel the need to protect you."

"I do. I need you to know I'm getting good at protecting myself."

"That doesn't change my need. I'm not going to pretend those calls don't worry me, or to accept I can't just wrap you up and keep you safe."

"I know I didn't handle it well, but I will if it ever happens again. Not just because I gave you and G-Lil and Grandpa my word, but because I'm not going to let some faceless asshole scare me stupid again.

"New York's been good for me," she continued. "It's given me some distance—not from you, from everything else. I panicked because I thought it was Noah, and I was half-asleep."

"The first one came when you were alone and sleeping."

"Yeah, but that's easy to figure. People are more vulnerable late at night. Whoever it is had that advantage. I won't let him keep it. It was months between calls, and if he's not getting anything out of it, I think whoever it is will stop."

"If they don't?"

"I'll tell you. I swear it."

"The calls weren't the only thing you didn't tell me about."

"It's a little awkward for a daughter to tell her father about the guy she's involved with. You've met him now, talked to him now, you must know what a good person Noah is."

Saying nothing for a moment, Aidan just tapped his fingers on the arm of the chair.

Then relented.

"He seems to be. He can also have actual conversations, seems to know what he wants in life, has a work ethic. I still want to beat him off with a stick."

"Dad!" She snorted out a laugh. "Come on."

"That'll ease off. Maybe." He turned to her then. "I didn't ask him because there were a lot of other things to ask. How long have you been seeing him?"

"A couple of months."

"Are you in love with him?"

"It feels like it. I know being with him makes me happy. He got me back into dance class, something I'd forgotten I really enjoy. He's not why I'm taking the classes at NYU, but I think I built up the confidence to try that because, well, because of the normal. It's nice to have the normal."

Watching her face, he nodded, then looked out over the city. "It was hard for me to let you come to New York. It's not hard for me to say you were right. It's been good for you."

"That doesn't mean I don't miss you, and Grandpa. And Consuela. I miss the gardens, and the pool. Boy, I really miss the pool. But . . ."

She rose, walked to the wall. "I love walking wherever I want, meeting friends for coffee, or going to a club. Going into a shop for jeans or shoes, whatever. Now and then somebody will give me a look, or even say I look familiar. But nobody really pays attention."

"Your movie comes out soon. That could change things."

"I don't know. Maybe. I hope not too much or for very long. Either way, I don't feel as, I guess it's vulnerable." She turned back to him, smiled. "I've toughened up."

Charlotte had it all. She'd bagged a gloriously rich, indulgent fiancé who believed her the most charming, delightful woman in the world. Sex wasn't a problem—despite his age, he actually had some style there. Plus, the trade-off was well worth it.

She lived in the biggest mansion in Holmby Hills, all fifty-five thousand square feet, with its marble walls, twenty bedrooms, ballroom, two dining rooms—the larger boasted a custom-made zebrawood table for eighty—its hundred-seat movie theater. She had her own beauty salon, a dressing room suite attached to two rooms of closets, and a third dedicated to her shoes.

Her jewelry, and Conrad indulged her, resided in a vault.

More than six acres held a serpentine swimming pool, clay tennis courts, a two-level garage with elevator, formal gardens, six fountains—one that now centered on a statue made in her image—a putting green, and a small park with a koi pond.

She had a staff of thirty at her beck, including her own social secretary, two personal maids, a driver, a dresser, a nutritionist who planned her daily meals.

She had a media specialist under contract whose job it was to pitch and plant stories, to make certain she was photographed at every event she attended.

Of course, she had access to her choice of three private jets, the mansion on the Kona coast of Hawaii, the Tuscan villa, a castle in Luxembourg, and the manor house in England's Lake District. Not to mention the three-hundred-foot superyacht.

On Conrad's arm, she had entrée into the top levels of society, not only in Hollywood but anywhere.

He bought the rights to the script she personally selected, and would produce what she saw as her blockbuster return in a starring role that would, at last, bring her the fame and adoration she deserved.

It wasn't enough. Not when she sat in bed with her breakfast tray—Greek yogurt with berries and ground flaxseed, a one-egg spinach omelet, a single slice of sprouted grain toast with almond butter—and watched that two-bit director Steven McCoy drone on and on about Cate and her stupid movie on the *Today* show.

"It's very much an ensemble movie, a story of family, but Olive's the heart of it. Caitlyn Sullivan brought that heart. She was a joy to direct, professional, prepared. The Sullivan work ethic, well, it's legendary for a reason. She's carrying that through to the next generation."

"Bunch of bullshit."

She burned inside, burned so hot the fire pushed tears out of her eyes as they went to a clip.

And there was Cate, young, fresh, beautiful.

Bad enough, Charlotte thought, bad enough the damn trailer was all over the place, the reviews rolling out like slaps in her face.

She could fix that, she thought.

She picked up her phone. She'd see how the little bitch who'd cost her seven years liked the kind of press she could pay for.

The tabloids hit the day *Change of Scene* went into full release. Headlines shouting CAITLYN'S LOVE NEST and SEX IN THE CITY screamed from newsstands all over the city. Photos of the apartment building in Hell's Kitchen, of Cate and Noah caught in a kiss outside the stage door dominated the front page. Interviews with neighbors inside the articles reported on wild parties, speculations of underage drinking and drugs. Details of Noah's life, his family, sprawled through the column inches.

"I'm sorry." She stood with him in Lily's living room—or she stood, he paced.

"They went to my mom's house. They got Tasha—I dated her for like five minutes two years ago—to say I cheated on her. I didn't.

They're saying I use drugs—no, they don't actually say it, just hint at it. My mom's a wreck."

She said nothing as he paced, as he ranted. What could she say?

"They're hinting I got into *Mame* because of you. I didn't even know you when I auditioned. How you're turning down offers because I'm jealous, and you're, like, what, under my thumb."

When he ran out of steam, she said the only thing she could. Again. "I'm so sorry, Noah."

He scrubbed his hands over his face. "It's not your fault. It's just . . . they make everything ugly."

"I know. It won't last. It's all timed because of the movie. That's what Lily thinks, and I think she's right. I know it's awful, but it won't last."

He looked at her then. "It's easier for you to say that. Yeah, I'm sorry, too, and I know it's screwing with you as much as me. But it's Hollywood shit, Cate. You're used to it."

Everything inside her shrank. "Do you want to break up with me?"

"No. Jesus, no." Finally he went to her, pulled her in. "I don't want that. I just . . . I don't know how to handle this. I don't know how the hell you do."

"It won't last," she said again. But she was very much afraid her interlude of quiet had ended.

Grant Sparks knew how to run a con—long or short. After his initial terror and fury in prison, he calculated the way to survive meant running the longest continuous, multiarmed cons of his life.

Maybe of anyone's lifetime.

He kept the gangs off his back—and kept himself out of the infirmary—by smuggling contraband inside. That meant bribing a couple of key prison personnel, but he didn't have much trouble homing in on who he could get to do what, and what it took to incentivize them.

He still had contacts on the outside. He could order in a carton of reals, then jack up the price of an individual cigarette, split the profit with his source.

Booze and weed moved profitably, too. But he stayed away from hard drugs. Selling smokes would get him a slap. Selling smack? More prison time at best, a shank between the ribs at worst.

He took orders for items as diverse as hand cream and hot sauce, and earned a rep for reliable delivery.

He had protection, and nobody messed with him.

Making sure he also gained a rep for doing his assigned work without complaint, keeping his head down, following the rules came easily. He went to services every Sunday, after gradually letting the prison holy assholes convince him in the power of God and prayer and all that shit.

Reading—the Bible, the classics, books on self-awareness and improvement—helped him transfer from the prison laundry—a hellhole—to the library.

He worked out religiously, and became a de facto personal trainer, always helpful.

Because he needed to keep fully informed about certain people on the outside, he read smuggled-in tabloids, even read *Variety*. He knew the little brat who put him inside had made a couple of movies. He knew the bitch who'd screwed him over played the penitent mother with the press.

And it burned his ass to read about her engagement to some old, fucking billionaire. He hadn't considered she had that much grifter in her. Maybe he admired it, on some level.

But either way, payback would come.

He saw an opportunity when he read the brat was in New York banging some dancer (probably gay). He spent some time working out how to give the little bitch a shot, who to assign, how much to pay for the job.

Making connections with anyone up for release had paid off in the past. He saw just how it could pay off now.

It took Cate less than two weeks to realize she hated school. Sitting in classrooms hour after hour listening to her instructor talk about things that—it turned out—didn't interest her didn't really open doors, she discovered.

It just closed her inside rooms someone else had designed.

Except for her French course. She liked learning a language, practicing the sounds of it, making sense of its rules and quirks.

Film Studies bored her senseless. She didn't care about analyzing a film, finding hidden meanings and metaphors. To her, it dulled the magic that offered itself on-screen.

But she'd see it through, every course. Sullivans weren't quitters, she told herself as she sat through another lecture.

"They expect me to know stuff because I acted, because my family's in the business."

She cuddled with Noah on his little bed on what she thought of as Blissful Mondays.

"You do know stuff."

"Not the sort of things they want. In an acting class, I'd have more to say, I guess. But I don't know why Alfred Hitchcock decided to film *Psycho*'s shower scene in those quick cuts, or why Spielberg let Dreyfuss's character live at the end of *Jaws*. I just know they're both really brilliant, scary movies."

Lazily, he stroked her hair, now nearly to her shoulders. "Do you want to take an acting class?"

"No. That one's all yours. You're the one in the hottest ticket on Broadway. I—"

"What?"

She turned her head, kissed his shoulder. "Stupid to think I can't bring it up, since all that crap's faded off."

"You said it would." He turned to kiss her in turn. "I should've listened."

"It was a kick in your gut, Noah."

"Lower," he said and teased a laugh out of her.

"I was going to say that people at college—even the dean of students—have asked if I can get them tickets to *Mame*."

"We've always got a handful of VIP seats available."

She shook her head. "Do it once, it would never stop. Oh, I have to go. I have a class at ten tomorrow morning, and I haven't finished the reading."

"I wish you'd stay."

"I wish I could, but I have to finish this, and I told Lily I'd be in around midnight. It's already midnight."

She slid out of bed to dress, sighed when he did the same.

"You really don't have to walk me to a cab, Noah."

"My girl gets an escort."

Sitting, she pulled on her shoes, watched him pull jeans on that lithe dancer's body. "I really like being your girl."

He walked her, as he did every Monday night, to Eighth so she could hail a cab going uptown. She remembered the first time, after their first time, in the chilly drizzle, the shine of wet pavement. Now they walked through the heat of a long summer night, the humidity baked in by clouds that blanked out the moon and stars.

"Text me when you get home," he said, as he always did.

And they lingered over a last lovers' kiss.

As she always did, she watched as he stood on the corner.

When the cab drove out of sight, Noah slipped his hands into his pockets, pulled out his earbuds to listen to a little 50 Cent on the way home. In his head, he choreographed steps to go with the beat, with the lyrics, considered asking his dance instructor to help him refine them.

They jumped him on Ninth Avenue.

Cate sent the text as she rode up in the elevator—and didn't notice Noah didn't send his usual smiley-face emoji in response, as she saw Lily sitting out on the terrace.

"Are you waiting up for me again?" she asked as she went out.

"What I'm doing is enjoying this heat and humidity. I'm a southern girl, and it takes me back home."

"Is that why you have two glasses out here with that bottle of water?"

"Thought you might be thirsty when you got here." She poured a glass to prove it. "And that you might sit with me for a few minutes."

"Yes to both." Though she thought about the reading she had yet to do, Cate sat.

"How's Noah?"

"He's good. We're good," she added, knowing that the question lay under the terrace-sitting. "Things got messed up for a while, and I can't blame him. But it's eased off. There's no real story, and a lot of other drama to write about."

"All right then. I can cross that off my list. Now, just how much do you hate these summer classes?"

Cate blew out a breath. "So I didn't pull that one off. I don't hate them, say, with the heat of a thousand suns. Or even a hot summer night in New York. I just don't like them, or school. At all. I didn't know I didn't like school until I tried this. Oh, except for French. That's my bright spot. *J'adore parler français et penser en français.*"

"I got the first part—you like talking French."

"I do, and thinking in French. I have to think in it to speak it. It's only a few more weeks, and I want to see it through. Then, I think I might look for an adult ed class on conversational French, maybe take a course in photography, get back to dance class. I don't know what else yet, but I'm thinking about it, what to do with what I learn, what I'm good at."

"You'll figure it out."

She hoped so. One thing she knew when she settled in to do the reading, the analysis of same? It wouldn't be teaching Film Studies.

The call from one of Noah's roommates woke her just after six a.m.

CHAPTER FIFTEEN

Fear in every pulse beat, Cate rushed to the nurse's station. "Noah Tanaka. They said downstairs he's on this floor. He—he was attacked last night, beaten. I—"

Despite the sunniness of her scrub top of yellow daisies over a blue field, the nurse spoke briskly. All business. "Are you a family member?"

"No. I'm his girlfriend. Please—"

"I'm sorry. I can't give you any information on Mr. Tanaka. He's restricted to family only."

"But I need to see him. I need to know if he's going to be all right. I don't know how badly he was hurt. I don't know—"

"I can't give you that information. If you'd like to wait, the waiting room is right down there, on the right."

"But—"

"The waiting room," the nurse said, "where some of Mr. Tanaka's family is. His family isn't restricted on sharing his information."

That got through. "Oh. Thank you."

Another nurse stepped up to answer a phone. "Poor kid."

The first watched Cate race down the hall. "Which one?"

She saw Noah's younger brother, Eli, curled into a ball on a small sofa, earbuds in, sleeping.

"Don't wake him." Bekka, Noah's sister, stood by a little coffee/tea station. "He just finally fell asleep."

"Bekka."

"Let's sit over here." Dunking a tea bag in a paper cup, she walked to a pair of chairs.

She looked exhausted, her dark cloud of hair drawn back into a tangled pouf of a tail. Deep shadows dogged her eyes—gold like Noah's. She wore gray leggings and a black tee with COLUMBIA emblazoned over it.

She went there, as serious about her ambition to become a doctor as Noah was about theater.

"I only just heard, and I came right away. They won't let me see him, or tell me anything."

"Hospital policy. We can add you to the list. But right now he's sleeping. They can't give him much for the pain right now because of the concussion. Mom and Dad are with him. Grandma and Ariel just went down for something to eat."

"Please." Cate grabbed Bekka's hand. "Tell me how he is."

"Sorry. I'm a little punchy. The hospital called last night, or early this morning. The police were already here when we got here. Noah came in unconscious, but he came to, tried to tell the police what happened. He's got a concussion, detached retina, left eye, orbital fractures, both eyes, a broken nose."

Bekka closed her eyes, sipped at the tea. And a tear leaked out. "Fractured cheekbone, left again. Bruised kidneys, abdominal bruising."

She opened her eyes again, met Cate's. "They beat him, two of them. Just beat and beat him."

Both arms hugged to her belly, Cate rocked. "Is he going to be all right?"

"He's going to need surgery for the retina, and possibly on both eyes for the orbital. We're waiting for the specialist to examine him. He'll need surgery for the cheekbone fracture because there's some bone displacement. They need to wait until the swelling goes down, until he's more stable."

"Oh God." Breathing in, breathing out, Cate pressed her fingers to her eyes. "How did this happen? Why would anyone do this to him?"

"He said he was walking back after you got a cab."

"Oh God, oh God."

"He thought there were two of them, and that's what the witnesses who scared them off said. Two men, white men according to the witnesses. Noah doesn't remember much, just walking and something, someone hitting him from behind. He doesn't remember, or didn't, what they looked like. The witnesses had more, but not much because they were about half a block away. But they said, when they started to beat him, they . . ."

"What?" At the hesitation, Cate clutched Bekka's arm.

"They called him a nigger chink, a faggot, and they said he'd get more and worse if he tried to fuck a white girl again. They said if he ever put his hands on Cate Sullivan again, they'd cut off his dick."

"They—" She couldn't find words, not in her mind, much less voice them.

"That doesn't make it your fault. But . . . our mother, especially our mother . . . You have to understand how hearing that, seeing him, makes her feel."

She couldn't understand. She couldn't understand anything. "I don't know what to do, what to say, how to feel."

"The police are going to need to talk to you."

"I don't know anyone who'd do this to him. Bekka, I swear it."

"You don't have to know them." On the sofa, earbuds out, eyes open, Eli watched her. In those eyes, eyes of a fifteen-year-old boy, lived such bitterness. "They know you." He rolled off the couch. "I'm going for a walk," he said, and walked out.

But they don't, Cate thought. They don't know me.

"Eli's angry," Bekka began. "Right now he can only see his brother in the hospital, put there by white men over a white girl. He can't see past that yet."

Cate closed her hand over the little heart she wore every day. "Will your family let me see him?"

"Yes, because he's already asked for you. Whatever they feel, right now, they want only what's best for Noah. Wait here. Let me go talk to my mother."

Shaken, sickened, Cate waited. Because she knew Lily also waited, worried, she texted an edited version she'd expand on in person.

He's sleeping. Two men jumped him last night. He's hurt, but resting now. I'm waiting to see him, and I'll tell you everything when I get home.

Lily's answer came instantly.

Give him my love, and take some for yourself.

She got up to pace. How did anyone sit in waiting rooms? How did they stand that creeping, crawling time of waiting to see, to touch someone they loved?

Bells dinged, feet slapped the floor outside the waiting room. Phones rang.

She didn't want coffee, she didn't want tea. She didn't want anything but to see Noah.

His parents walked by. His mother kept her face turned away, leaning into her husband. His father, tall like Noah, lean like Noah, looked in at her as they passed.

She saw sorrow and fatigue in his eyes, but no bitterness, and no blame.

And that single glance brought on a rush of tears.

"I can take you to his room now." Bekka stood in the opening to the hallway. "He's in and out. And when he's awake, there's pain, so you can't stay long."

"I won't. I just need to see him. I'll leave after that, get out of the way."

"It's not you, Cate. It's the situation. I'm going to wait out here." She paused at the door, and her eyes—dull and weary—met Cate's. "As long as Noah wants to see you, I'll work out a kind of visitation schedule. I'm not going to put my mother through any more upheaval. I'll let you know the best times for you to come see Noah. For short periods at first. Rest, a lot of rest and a lot of quiet are what he needs."

"I won't stay long."

Bracing herself, Cate pushed the door open.

Nothing could have prepared her. Bruises violent as storm clouds covered his beautiful face. Swelling distorted its shape. His left eye bulged out, red and raw. More bruises, black, yellow, purple, surrounded his right.

He lay so still on the white sheets in a hospital gown of washed-out blue that showed more bruising on his arms, ugly scrapes clawing down his skin. For a moment she feared he wasn't breathing, then she saw the movement of his chest, heard the beep of the monitor.

Everything inside her wanted to rush to him, simply cover his body with her own and pour her heart into him. Give him strength, ease all the pain.

But she walked slowly, softly in the dim room with its single window shaded against the light. She took his hand, lightly, gently.

"I wish I could be here when you wake up, I wish I could talk to you. But you need to rest. I'll come every day, stay as long as they let me. Lily sends her love, and even when I can't be here, you have to know you have mine."

She bent down, kissed his hand, then left as she'd come in. Slowly and softly.

In the drugging summer heat, in the blast of summer sun, Cate walked the nearly thirty blocks home.

The early hour meant shops remained closed, most tourists had yet to venture out. It was a time, as she walked uptown, of dog walkers, nannies, joggers heading to the park, suits with early meetings. No one paid any more attention to her than she did to them.

She'd left him there, battered and broken, because he had a family who loved him. And one who now resented her. Even Bekka, she thought. What Bekka did, she'd done for Noah.

Cate couldn't blame her. Couldn't blame any of them.

How much, she wondered, would Noah blame her?

She walked from the heat to the cool of the lobby, to the elevator, down the hall, to the door. Inside.

"Catey. Oh, my poor baby. Come, come sit down. Did you walk? Let me—"

Shaking her head, shaking all over, Cate bolted to the powder room. The sickness she'd carried inside expelled, brutally, viciously, as Lily rushed in behind her, held her hair back with one hand, reached for a guest towel with the other.

"All right, sweets. It's all right."

She wet the cloth with cold water, laid it against Cate's forehead, then the back of her neck.

"Here now, you need to lie down. Come on now." She pulled Cate up, supported her as she wept, made soothing noises as she steered her to the bedroom and the bed. "I'm going to get you some water, some ginger ale."

She hurried out, came back with two glasses. "Water first, that's my girl." She propped pillows up, settled Cate back against them. "Slow sips, that's the way. When you're steady enough, you're going to take a nice cool shower, and I'll get you some fresh clothes."

First, Lily sat on the side of the bed, brushed Cate's sweat-damp hair back from her face. "Can you tell me?"

"Two men. His face, G-Lil, they beat him so bad. He's going to need surgery, more than one. Two men on his way home from walking me to a cab. They beat him. And they called him ugly names. They said because he's not white and I am. They said my name. He's just lying there, so hurt. His family blames me."

"Of course they don't."

"They do." Swollen eyes spilled more tears. "His mother wouldn't even look at me. His brother wouldn't stay in the same room with me. They said my name when they hurt him."

"Because they're ugly, racist, bigoted shitheels. Not because of you. His family's scared and worried, angry and worried. Give them time. What did the doctors say?"

"I only know what Bekka told me. They can't give him much for the pain because of the concussion, and he needs surgery. I saw him for just a minute, but he was sleeping. I couldn't stay because . . ."

"That's all right. He's young, he's strong, and nobody's in better shape than a dancer. Sip a little ginger ale now."

She urged Cate to drink, then nudged her into the shower, got her girl some fresh clothes. Checking the time, calculating, she put off calling Hugh. No point waking him so early with this kind of news. And the same went for Aidan.

She'd call her director as soon as she felt Cate was steady. Another hour before Mimi arrived, she thought. Considering, she texted her personal assistant, asked her to work from her apartment, and to hold any calls that weren't vital.

She'd make tea. She'd—

"G-Lil."

She turned to see Cate, wet hair pulled back in a tail to leave her face, so young, so sad, unframed.

"Why don't you lie down awhile, my sweets? I'm going to make us some tea."

"I'm all right. The shower helped. I guess throwing up did, too. I'm all right. I'll make tea. Being busy with something has to help, too."

She started to walk toward the kitchen, then stopped, pulled Lily into a hug. "Thanks."

"Nothing to thank me for."

"Only everything. You've been my mother, my grandmother, somehow both almost as long as I can remember. You're my G-Lil, and I needed you so much."

"Now you're going to make me cry."

"You didn't call Dad or Grandpa yet, did you?"

"I was going to give it another hour."

"Good." She stepped back. "I'll make tea, and maybe you can help me figure out what I should do."

"All right. I like figuring."

They started for the kitchen together when the house phone rang.

"I'll get that." Lily detoured, picked up the phone. "Lily Morrow. Yes, Fernando. Oh." She glanced toward the kitchen. "Yes, send them up."

In the kitchen, Cate studied a bright red tin. "Energy Boost Tea. Does it work?"

"Not especially. We'd better put on some coffee, too."

"You want coffee?"

"Sweets, that was Fernando in the lobby. Two police detectives are coming. They need to talk to you. I thought it best to just get it done."

"Yes." Cate put the tin back, turned to the elaborate machine Lily claimed she loved almost more than sex. "I want to help. I don't know how I can, but there may be something. I really am all right, G-Lil."

"I can see that. You've always been a strong one, Cate."

"Not always, but I remember how to be one. I'll make coffee for all of us." She managed a wan smile. "Do you think cops drink it black like in the books and movies?"

"I guess we'll find out. I'll go let them in," she said when the buzzer sounded.

Lily gave the living room a narrow glance as she walked through, worked out how to set the stage so she sat with Cate on the main sofa. If her girl needed some support, she'd be right there.

She opened the door.

Whatever she'd expected, it wasn't a middle-aged woman with gray-threaded brown hair worn Judi Dench–style short and a skinny black man sporting short, neat dreads who looked barely old enough to order a legal drink.

They both wore suit jackets—his a charcoal gray with a nice clean cut, hers black and dumpy.

And they both held up badges.

"Ms. Morrow, I'm Detective Riley. This is my partner, Detective Wasserman."

Riley, the woman, gave Lily a steady stare out of frosty blue eyes.

"Please come in. Caitlyn's making some coffee."

"Terrific view," Wasserman commented while his dark eyes scanned the glass doors and beyond, the room and, Lily realized, everything in it.

"It is, isn't it? Please, sit down." She gestured, very deliberately to the chairs facing the sofa. "We're both of us just sick about Noah. Caitlyn just got back from the hospital a short time ago. I hope you find who hurt that boy."

"You know him well, personally and professionally?" Riley took out a notebook as she sat.

"I do, yes. He's a very talented young man, and a very good young man. I'm very fond of him."

"Do you know anyone who'd want to hurt him?"

"I don't. I honestly don't. He's well liked by the company. I've never heard anyone say a bad word about him. When Cate started seeing him, I gave him a good once-over." She smiled as she said it. "He passed the audition."

Wasserman rose as Cate came in carrying the coffee tray. "Let me get that for you."

She handed it over, stood a moment. "I'm Cate."

"Detective Riley, Ms. Sullivan. My partner, Detective Wasserman."

"How do you take your coffee?"

"A little cream, no sugar," Riley said.

"Cream and sugar. Thanks," Wasserman said as Cate busied herself with the coffee.

"Noah's roommate called me this morning. I went straight to the hospital. I don't understand why anyone would do that to him, to anyone." She passed out the coffee, sat beside Lily. "Noah's sister told me what they said to him. I don't understand that either."

"How long have you been involved with Noah?" Riley asked.

"We started seeing each other early February."

"Did anyone object to that?"

"Our seeing each other? No. Why would they?"

"Maybe someone you'd been dating," Wasserman suggested, "someone Noah was involved with before you."

"He'd dated some people, but he wasn't seeing anyone when he asked me out."

"And you?" Riley prompted.

"No. I hadn't dated anyone before Noah."

Wasserman's eyebrows shot up. "Anyone?"

"I lived in Ireland for several years. We went out in groups. I never really dated solo. There's no jealous ex-boyfriend in my life. I don't know of any jealous ex-girlfriends in Noah's. I don't know anyone who'd do something so vicious and ugly. I'd tell you if I did, if I had even a glimmer of a thought of someone.

"You've seen him. You've seen what they did to him. They used my name when they did." She clutched the heart at the base of her throat. "I'm sure you know what happened to me when I was ten. I know cruel people and what they're capable of. But I don't know who would do this to Noah."

"Take us through Monday."

Cate nodded at Riley. "The theater's dark on Monday, so we spend time together. I had two classes at NYU, so I met him about one, at the coffee shop—the one where we had our first date. It's what we do. That's Café Café at Seventh and Forty-sixth. About one, I think. We went back to his place. His roommates have day jobs, so we could be alone. We met some friends for dinner. About eight, I think, at Footlights, that's, ah, Broadway and Forty-eighth. A lot of the gypsies go there. The chorus people."

She cast her mind back to what seemed like years ago, another life ago.

"Some of them were going clubbing after, but we . . . Monday night's the only night he's not onstage. We went back to his place. About midnight, he walked me over to Eighth to catch a cab. I had reading to do for a morning class. He always walks me to Eighth."

When her voice broke, Lily shifted closer, took her hand.

"Always to Eighth?" Riley repeated. "Would midnight be another routine?"

"Usually, I guess. I have class on Tuesday morning. He always walks me, and waits until I'm in the cab, waits until I drive away. I can look back, see him waiting on the corner until we're out of sight. He—"

She cut herself off, set down her coffee cup with a rattle. "It's routine, almost every Monday night. Oh God, God, they knew he'd be there, knew he'd walk back from Eighth, right around midnight, Monday night."

"Do you know if anyone threatened him?" To pull her attention back, Wasserman leaned forward. "If anyone made comments about him dating you specifically, or specifically a white girl?"

"No. No. He'd have told me. I'm sure he would. No one ever, ever said anything like that to me. The two people who helped Noah. Did they see the men who did this?"

Riley glanced at Wasserman, gave him the slightest nod.

"They'd just come out of a bar, and they'd had a few. When they turned the corner, they saw the attack. They shouted, started running toward Noah. The assailants ran east. The witnesses weren't close enough to get a good look, in the dark, from half a block, and after a few beers."

"But they stopped it," Cate murmured. "They called the police, called an ambulance. They stopped it. Noah—his sister said he didn't really see the ones who hurt him either."

"We'll talk to him again," Riley assured her. "He may remember more. Celebrities often get mail from fans, some obsessed fans, some who develop an unhealthy and possessive fantasy."

"If I get mail, it goes to the studio, or to my agent. I'm not really a celebrity."

"You've been in four movies," Riley pointed out. "And you've generated a lot of media attention. Your relationship with Noah generated quite a bit not long ago."

"If there's been any mail like what you're saying . . ." She gripped Lily's hand. "The call."

"What call?" Riley demanded.

"In June, when the company was performing their out-of-town openings, someone called on my cell."

She told them all of it, told them about the call over the winter in L.A.

"You no longer have the phone?"

She shook her head at Riley. "I realize that was a mistake, but I just—"

"Reacted," Wasserman finished. "Have either of you received any other calls that felt disturbing? Or wrong numbers, hang ups?"

"No, I haven't."

"Nothing like that," Lily confirmed. "Do you think the calls are connected to what happened to Noah?"

"It's something we'll look into. Any other attempted contacts?" Riley asked. "Anything that's made you uncomfortable?"

"No. I mean, people usually recognize Lily when she's out, and sometimes they'll come up to her. Since the last movie I did came out, I've had a little of that, but it's not mean."

"You're taking classes at NYU." Wasserman smiled at her, then glanced at his notebook. "Has anyone paid any particular attention to you, maybe asked you out?"

"A couple of people asked me out, but there wasn't any push after I said I had a boyfriend."

"You said he often meets you on campus. So you're seen together."

Cate looked back at Riley. "Yes. You mean a white girl and someone who's not white."

Riley met Cate's gaze steadily. "If this attack was racially motivated, it could make it a hate crime. We take that very seriously. If anyone makes a push now, we need to know about it."

"You will."

"And if we could have the names of the friends you had dinner with? Someone might have noticed something off," Wasserman explained. "Someone paying too much attention to you and Noah."

"Sure. I don't know all their last names."

"We'll take care of that." Riley set down her empty cup.

"Can I get you more coffee?"

"No, thanks. It's good coffee."

Cate gave them the names she remembered, rose when the detective rose. "I know you might not find them. I know things don't always, even usually, wrap up like a movie. It's just, Noah didn't deserve this."

"No, he didn't." Riley slipped her notebook back in her pocket. "Neither of you did. Thank you for your time. You've been very helpful."

"I'll see you out." Lily walked them to the door, then turned back to Cate. "Doing okay?"

"Yes. Even if it doesn't go anywhere, telling them everything I can think of, it's movement. It's not just letting it all push me into a corner."

"All right. I need to call your grandfather. You should call your dad. I'm going to call our director. He'll need the understudies for Noah and me tonight."

"Not for you, no. No."

"I don't want to leave you here alone tonight, sweets."

"And I don't want to disappoint a houseful of people coming to see Lily Morrow's *Mame*. The show goes on, G-Lil. We both know it. I'm okay. I'm hoping Bekka texts to say I can go see Noah. If not, she promised to put me on the list so I can at least ask about how he's doing. And I can send or take flowers so he knows I'm thinking of him."

"Tell you what, you come to the theater tonight. You can watch from the wings. Unless you're sitting with Noah, you come with me. That's a good deal."

"Okay. I'll go call Dad."

Bekka texted to come at four, to plan on a fifteen-minute visit.

She brought flowers, a cheerful summer bouquet. They kept the room dim, as before, the shades drawn. But this time his right eye slitted open, watched her come in.

She moved to him quickly, took his hand, kissed it. "Noah. I'm sorry, I'm so sorry."

"It's not your fault."

But that right eye looked away as he said it, and his hand lay unresponsive in hers.

In that instant, that hard line between what was and what is, she knew he didn't mean it. Knew he'd already taken the first step away from her.

Still, she went to see him every day. During his surgeries, she sat at home with her phone, waiting for Bekka to text his condition.

When he went home—to his parents' home—to recover, she texted once a day. Only once because she knew he'd taken several more steps away from her.

Summer blurred into an autumn that held the heat like a lover. She enrolled in two adult education courses. One for conversational French, one for Italian.

Language, she thought, pulled her in. She'd take the rest of her year, explore that, explore herself. Then she'd need to decide what to do with her life, her skills.

She was prepared when Noah texted her, asked to come by and see her on a Wednesday afternoon. A matinee afternoon, she noted, when Lily would be at the theater.

October brought the gorgeous dying color to the parks, that change of light that gleamed off the river. And since the day held balmy, she brought Cokes outside, drilled them down into the ice in a bucket. Unless that had changed since summer, Noah liked his Cokes.

She trapped nerves in a locked corner when she walked to answer the buzzer. Though prepared, her heart still stumbled.

"Noah. You look great. Oh, it's so good to see."

He'd grown some scruff, heavier on the chin and above his lip. He looked older, had lost some weight she hoped he'd build up again soon.

Though his eyes met hers, she read what was in them.

"Let's sit outside. It's pretty out, and I've got Cokes. Lily said you went by the theater last week."

"Yeah, I wanted to see everyone."

"You look ready to go back." She smiled at him as she opened the drinks. A Sullivan knew how to play a role.

"I'm not going back. Not to *Mame*. Carter's had the part for three months. I'm not taking it away from him. Anyway."

Since he didn't take the glass she held out, she set it down as he wandered to the wall.

"I know they never caught who hurt you."

"I didn't see them, not that I remember. Nobody did." He shrugged. "The cops did what they could."

Did he hear the thread of bitterness in his own voice? she wondered.

"Bekka says you still get headaches."

"Some. Not as bad. They're easing off like the doctors said they should. I'm back in dance class. Taking some voice because, you know, it gets rusty. I auditioned for *Heading Up*. It's a new musical. I got it. Second lead."

"Oh, Noah." She'd have gone to him, but felt the wall between them, as solid as the one at his back. "That's great, just great. I'm so happy for you."

"I'm going to be busy, with workshops, with lessons, then rehearsals. It's my first major part, and I need to focus on that. I won't have time for a relationship."

Prepared, she thought, she had been prepared. And still it cut so deep. "Noah, I'm happy for you. You don't have to use something you've wanted and worked so hard for as a reason. We haven't been together since that awful night. Sometimes one awful night changes everything."

"I know it wasn't your fault."

"No, you don't." Bitterness, yes her own thread of bitterness slipped out. She struggled to pull it in again, knot it off. "You were the one hurt, the one in the hospital, the one in pain, the one who lost a part he worked for. Part of you, at least, feels it's my fault. It doesn't matter that it wasn't my fault. It's what you feel."

"I can't do it, Cate. I can't handle the press—and they tried to keep it from me after, but I saw and heard the stories that came out after that night. They said your name when they were pounding on me. I don't know how to forget that."

"It matters to you, as much as what they did, it matters to you what they said. And the press matters to you. So you blame me."

"It's not your fault."

She just shook her head. "You blame me. Your family blames me. For a while I blamed myself, but I'm not going to do that. It's not my fault I fell in love with you. It's not my fault you've stopped being in love with me."

He looked away again. "I can't do this. That's what it comes down to. I can't do this."

"You were the first one who looked at just me, wanted just me. I'll never forget that. You can't feel that way about me now, so you can't be with me. I can't be with you, same reasons."

She took a long breath. "The person you are came here to tell me to my face. The person I am can let you go without blaming either one of us. So."

She lifted her glass from the table. "Break a leg, Noah."

"I better go."

He moved to the glass doors, paused. "I'm sorry."

"I know," she murmured when he'd gone.

Then she sat, shed a few silent tears over the sweetness faceless strangers had stolen from two lives.

PART III

TENDING ROOTS

To be happy at home is
the ultimate result of all ambition . . .
—SAMUEL JOHNSON

The voice is a wild thing.
It can't be bred in captivity.
—WILLA CATHER

CHAPTER SIXTEEN

As her grandfather had once told her, life was a series of turns. Most of her life, Cate felt she'd taken those turns at someone else's direction, or in reaction to another's action.

The day of her great-grandfather's memorial and the night that followed equaled a tectonic shift, forever altering her life's landscape. Still, in the midst of the quake, she'd turned toward courage.

Years later, she'd turned to fear after her mother's ambush.

Her loss of the joy and passion for a profession she'd loved, had intended to pursue, shifted her life yet again, and changed her direction to New York.

That first sweet coffee date with Noah turned her world yet again. Losing him forced her to take another turn.

It was time to stop reacting and choose her own direction.

When Hugh took a project filming in New York, settled into the condo, Lily extended her contract as Mame. And Cate began to hunt for her own apartment. It was time, she felt, she decided to claim real independence, and find out who she was living on her own.

At nineteen she could speak conversationally in Spanish, French, and Italian, and often volunteered as an interpreter, for the police—thanks to Detective Riley—for shelters.

She spent three months with her father in New Zealand while he filmed—on the condition she could serve as his assistant. She enjoyed every moment.

When she returned to New York, she continued the search for her own place, and turned twenty.

A new chapter, a new apartment, a new chance to explore.

But it was a chance encounter at a busy little bistro that shifted her life yet again.

She sat with Darlie—also filming in New York—over tiny salads and glasses of spring water. Over lunch, they caught up, Darlie's work and life in L.A., Cate's in New York.

"The physical training for this one's been killer. Three hours a day, six days a week."

"But look at those guns."

Her hair Tinker Bell short, her body seriously ripped, Darlie flexed, studied her biceps. "They are seriously awesome."

"I'll say."

"I have to admit, I like being strong, and doing an action film, playing an actual adult. I really get to kick some ass—and get mine kicked. We're shutting down part of Chinatown tomorrow for a scene. You have to come see."

"Text me the particulars, and I'll see if I can work it into my busy schedule."

"From what you've said, you are pretty busy. Learning Russian now?"

"Dabbling."

"Interpreting." Darlie nibbled on some arugula. "And you've moved into your own place. How does that feel?"

"Strange and wonderful at the same time. I stuck with the Upper West because it's close to my grandparents and made them feel better. Plus, I know and like the neighborhood."

Deciding a little flatbread couldn't hurt, Darlie broke a piece in two. "I like New York, but I'm a California girl. Anyway. No men squeezed into that busy schedule?"

"You sound like my new neighbor. 'Pretty girl,'" Cate said in an accent reeking of Queens. "'How come you got no boyfriend? How come I don't see boys knocking on your door?'"

Cate lifted her water glass. "And that brings another neighbor out.

'She maybe like girls.'" A Russian accent this time. "'It's okay if she likes girls.'"

Cate rolled her eyes as Darlie laughed. And back to Queens. "'You like girls? You got a girlfriend?'"

"I thought New Yorkers didn't interact so much."

"In my building they do. So when I explain, because they're both standing in their doorways waiting, that I like boys, but I'm just not seeing anyone right now, I realize too late I'm now a project."

"Uh-oh, not the blind date fix-her-up."

"'I got a nephew.'" Queens. "'He's a good boy. Smart boy. He'll take you to coffee.'

"'I talk to young Kevin who works at the market.'" Russian. "'He has a pretty face and good manners.'"

Enjoying herself, Cate gestured with her glass. "About this time, yet another neighbor—this guy who lives down the hall—comes out of the elevator with his little mop of a dog, George. George sees the first neighbor and starts . . ." Cate let out a series of high-pitched yips. "Because she always gives him a little dog biscuit. She pulls one out of her pocket, tosses it to George, and keeps talking about her nephew with the other one rooting for the guy at the market. So then George's dad, hearing all this, chimes in.

"'Leave da girl alone.'" She used deep, gravely New York now. "'She oughta play da field. Pretty young girls got oats to sow, too, amirite? Sow dose oats, girlie.'"

With an eye roll, Cate stabbed a grape tomato. "All this just because I took out the trash."

"Excuse me."

A man stepped up to the table. Somewhere in his middle thirties, Cate gauged, with a pleasant face made intellectual by horn-rimmed glasses.

"I'm going to interrupt. I was sitting just behind you, and heard. You have a serious talent with voices."

"I . . . thanks."

"Sorry, I should introduce myself. Boyd West." He looked at Darlie. "We actually met once, briefly. I don't expect you'd remember."

"Yes, I do. You're married to Yolanda Phist. I met you when we were working on *Everlasting*."

"That's right. Nice to see you. If I could just sit down for one quick minute."

He did, and turned his attention back to Cate. Shoving his glasses back up the bridge of his nose, he talked fast, a kind of whirlwind of words.

"I'm directing an animated short—a small but important project for me. We've cast most of the roles, but I haven't found anyone who works for me for the key. It's about a search for personal identity, finding your place in a chaotic world, and making that place matter. Have you ever done voice work?"

"No, I—"

"Sorry, I keep interrupting, but I just recognized you. You're Caitlyn Sullivan."

Her shoulders wanted to hunch, but he grinned, so open and delighted, she felt herself relax again.

Before she could speak, he plowed on.

"This is, well, kismet. I've admired your work, but I had no idea you had this kind of voice talent. I'd love to send you the script. In fact, I'm going to give you the script. I was just having lunch with my producers, and going over some things. Wait."

He got up, went back to the table where a man and a woman sat, grabbed a script, came back.

"Take this one, and my card." He pulled out a card case, scribbled on one of the cards. "That's my personal line. It's a small project, and I could only pay you scale, but it's an important one. I won't keep you, but read it. Just read it, and get back to me. Great meeting you, nice seeing you."

When he started back to his table, the other two rose. They glanced back at Cate before they left.

"That was . . . very surreal."

"Don't say no. Read the script," Darlie insisted. "He comes off a little jumpy and intense, but Boyd West has a solid reputation. He directs small, vibrant jewels. And you do have talent, Cate. You've had some really shitty runs, but that doesn't mean you waste what you have."

"But I don't know anything about voice work."

"You've got an amazingly fluid voice, you can act. West is a good director. If the script has any appeal for you, what have you got to lose?" Smiling, Darlie nibbled on another leaf. "Kismet."

Cate didn't know about kismet, but she knew a good script when she read one. And her life shifted again, with her at the wheel, when she took the role of Alice in the animated short *Who Am I Anyway?*

She found her place in sound booths, with headphones, in the closet she soundproofed and set up as a studio in her apartment. And in time she converted the second bedroom in a new apartment as work rolled in.

She found her place, her own *Who Am I Anyway?* in voice-overs for commercials, animated films and shorts, in audiobooks, in video game characters.

She found her identity, her independence.

She found her joy again.

The turn, the direction, the self-knowledge, and the years between made her a different person when she ran into Noah again.

Walking home with a market bag after a long day in the booth, she heard her name, glanced up, focused in.

He'd let his hair grow a bit longer; he'd added some scruff. And he still had those wonderful lion's eyes. She supposed any woman would feel a little heart-tug when face-to-face with her first love.

"Noah." She stepped forward, kissed his cheeks as pedestrians flowed around them.

"I was just— Doesn't matter," he said. "It's really good to see you. Are you busy? Can I buy you a drink? I'd really like . . . I'd really like to talk to you if you have a few minutes."

"I could use a drink. There's a place on the next block, if you don't mind doubling back."

"Great."

He began to walk with her. A hot summer night, she thought, not so different from the last time they'd walked together.

"I guess you still live in the neighborhood."

"Old habits," she told him. "My grandparents are back in California, but I stayed. I go back and forth more than I used to. How about you?"

"I have an actual bedroom that can hold an actual bed. In fact, I've got a town house. It's nice to have some room."

"Here's the place. Do you want a table? Want to sit at the bar?"

"Let's get a table."

The bar, several steps up from the coffee shops, pizza dens, Mexican joints they'd frequented once upon a time, offered steel tables, narrow booths, a long ebony bar.

Once they'd settled, she ordered a glass of cab, and he did the same.

"How's your family?" she began, and he looked deep into her eyes. "The Irish can hold grudges, Noah, but there's no need for it."

"My parents are good. They're in Hawaii for a couple of weeks—it's cooler there, and my mom still has family on the Big Island. My grandmother passed last year."

"I'm so sorry."

"We miss her. Bekka's a doctor. We're really proud."

He ran through his siblings until the drinks came.

"I need to say some things. I've started to call you I don't know how many times. I could never follow through. I didn't do the right thing by you, Cate. I didn't handle it right."

"What happened was beyond awful. There's no right way."

"It wasn't your fault. I said that then, but you were right, I didn't mean it. I do now. It was never your fault."

She looked into her wine. "It matters. Hearing you say that matters. We were both so young. God, the press afterward? Uglier yet, and we couldn't have handled it. It would never have worked for us."

She drank, studying him over the rim of her glass. "You were a key point in my life. I've been thinking about key points lately. How they all intersect or diverge. Being with you, then not. Key points. I've been to see every play you've been in since."

He blinked at her. "You have?"

"Key points, Noah. It was good to see someone who mattered to me doing what he was born to do."

"I wish you'd come backstage."

She smiled at that, drank again. "Awkward."

"I saw *Lucy Lucille*. Twice."

She laughed. "Spending Mondays at animated films?"

"You were great. Seriously. I guess . . . it was good to hear someone who mattered to me doing what she was born to do."

"You should hear my Shalla, Warrior Queen. You were never one for video games," she remembered.

"Who's got time? You look happy."

"I am. I love the work, really love the work. It's fun and challenging and, God, it's diverse. I'll say you look happy, too."

"I am. I love the work. And I just got engaged."

"Wow! Congratulations." She could mean it, Cate realized. And wasn't that a relief? "Tell me about her."

He did; she listened.

"If you decide to come to another performance, let me know."

"All right. And I'll try to come to another. I'm actually starting the process of moving back to California."

"Back to L.A.?"

"Big Sur. My grandparents are semiretired there. My grandfather had a fall, broke his leg last winter."

"I heard about that, but that he was okay. Is he?"

"Mostly, yeah. But he's getting older, whether or not he'll admit it. And G-Lil's waffling on doing a revival of *Mame* because she's worried about leaving him even for a limited run."

"So the rumors are true—Lily Morrow coming back to Broadway to revive her Tony-winning performance? Big buzz in my world."

"She'll do it if I'm with him, and I can do the bulk of my work anywhere. Or I can use a studio in Monterey, Carmel, San Francisco. I can make it work."

Would make it work, she corrected. She had the wheel; she chose her own turns now.

"And lately, I've been missing California. I feel like it's time to maybe change directions."

She angled her head. "Seeing you, talking like this, it's kind of closed a chapter—in a good way." When the waiter came by, asked if they wanted another round, Cate shook her head. "I've got prep to do. I've really got to go. I'm so glad we did this, Noah."

"Me, too." He reached over for her hand. "You were a key point for me, Cate. A good chapter in my life."

When she left him, she felt lighter. And knew as she walked home, as New York swarmed around her, she could leave without a single regret.

Because she had work, Cate flew into San Francisco. She'd forgotten how chilly November in San Francisco could be.

After a long, fraught decision-making process, she'd shipped ahead most of her possessions she'd opted to keep. Another selection went into storage for maybe later.

The rest she sold or gave to friends.

She'd thought it would make her feel lighter. Instead she felt weirdly empty, which wasn't the same at all.

Because she definitely wanted her own car and had already re-searched what would suit her best, she spent a day test driving, nego-tiating, and buying a nice little hybrid SUV. Not the convertible of her teenage dreams, she thought as she waited while the bellman at her hotel loaded it up.

She still had time to fulfill that dream.

Getting out of San Francisco put her very rusty, rarely used driving skills to the test. One she nearly failed twice on the steep hills, then again when she hit the twists of Highway 1.

To calm those rusty driver's nerves, she turned the radio up, did her best to mimic Gaga. She had decent pipes—not Gaga level, but who did? Still, she could sell it when called on.

And the views—the wild heights, the churning sea, the climbing cliffs. Yes, she'd missed this, somewhere deep inside. How strange it was, she realized, to be called back and find it a kind of coming home.

Even a year before she would have said, without hesitation, New York was home. Years before that, she would have said Ireland.

Didn't it make her lucky to finally understand she could put her heart into so many homes? And to find herself absolutely ready to come back to this one.

The thin November fog crawling in as she climbed only made it all the more beautiful.

When she passed the ranch road to the Coopers', she thought of them, all of them. She still kept in touch, but hadn't come back to Big Sur in years.

Maybe she'd bake some soda bread and take it over to them sometime soon.

Key points, she thought. They more than qualified as one of hers.

When she drove onto the peninsula, she felt nothing but excitement. She stopped at the gate, started to roll down the window for the intercom.

But the gates opened for her.

Video surveillance, she knew, and she'd described the car, in detail, after she'd bought it.

She climbed the road, thought of the beach, the rocks, the house, the everything.

The second gate—installed after her kidnapping—opened as well.

When she crested the last rise, her grandparents stood together under the portico with the house and all its fascinating levels behind them.

She nearly forgot to put the car in park, but avoided disaster before she jumped out and ran over to hug them both.

Lily's hair, still redder than red, waved the flames around her face in a new style. Hugh, with his trim little gray beard—a new style as well.

"We've been watching for you." Lily all but bubbled it. "Since you texted you were maybe an hour away. Come in, come in, don't worry about your things. All taken care of."

"How are those pins, Grandpa?"

He did a little soft-shoe. "Don't you worry about my pins. How was the drive?"

"A little nerve-racking at first. It's been awhile. But it comes back to you. Oh, everything looks so good. I've missed a fire in the fireplace, and this light. And— Oh, Consuela!"

She'd known the longtime cook had relocated with them as head housekeeper/cook now, but seeing her just made Cate's heart swell.

Beaming, Consuela rolled in a tray. *"Bienvenida a casa, mi niña."* She teared up a little at Cate's embrace. "Now you'll have some wine, some food, and sit with your grandparents. Your grandfather doesn't sit enough."

"The pair of them would have me propped up from dawn to dusk, then flat out from dusk to dawn."

Consuela only clucked her tongue, then, after stroking Cate's cheek, slipped out of the room.

"I won't say no to that wine. And look at that fruit. There's nothing like fresh California fruit. You two, sit, let me serve this up. I want to work out some kinks from the drive."

She poured wine, brought over the little plates, the fruit and cheese. Then paused just to look at the sea, the sky, the roll of lawn to the drop of cliff.

"You remember how beautiful," Cate murmured. "But memory isn't like seeing. It can't capture it, not all the way. Here's to Liam and Rosemary, their love, their vision, their gift to all of us."

"Without them?" Hugh clinked glasses. "None of this, no you, no me."

Cate tried a slice of mango, sighed. "And man, this is really good. It's another world here." She perched on the arm of his chair. "I'm ready for another world. I started dreaming about this house, this place."

Hugh rubbed a hand on her thigh. "Good dreams."

"Yes. Good dreams. Jigsaw puzzles and hunting shells on the beach, barking sea lions, waking up to the ocean, listening to Grandda's stories. He was so full of stories. I knew I wanted to come back, that I could."

"We want you to stay, but we don't want you to feel obliged," Lily added.

"I want to stay, and you'd better have my room ready because now you're stuck with me. Did you notice I bought a car?"

Hugh paused as he reached for the tray. "You bought the one out front?"

"Yesterday. That's no rental. Us California girls need our own wheels. And I may just buy me a hot convertible next summer."

"You always wanted one," Hugh murmured.

"Now's the time, finally. I've looked into studios in Monterey and Carmel, and I figure to talk you into letting me soundproof one of the big closets upstairs. I started in a closet, and it worked just fine. So listen up, I'm home to stay."

She reached for a sea salt cracker, topped it with some goat cheese. And grinned at her grandfather. "Too much Irish in me not to pay attention to dreams. I'm going to be looking out for you, pal of mine, while our Broadway babe hits the footlights again."

"Looking out for me," Hugh snorted.

"Damn right, so get used to it. I'd have come back either way, because dreams. But add broken leg—soft-shoe aside—and *Mame*? Too many signs pointing here for me to ignore. And just so you know, I'd started researching those studios before you decided to fall off that horse, cowboy."

"That does it." Lily slapped her hands on her legs. "Hugh, I can't wait another minute."

Cate reached for a slice of kiwi. "For what?"

"Bring your wine." Patting her leg, Hugh rose. "We'll show you your room."

When Lily led the way back outside, Cate shook her head. "You're kicking me out of the house before I even unpack?"

"A young woman should have her own space, should have some privacy. She may want to entertain a gentleman caller."

Now Cate snorted. "Yeah, I'm loaded with gentleman callers."

"You should be." Lily wrapped an arm around her waist as they crossed the side terrace, started down. "Hugh, you be careful on these steps."

"Nag, nag, nag."

"Bet your Irish ass. If you don't want the guest cottage, you can pick a room in the main," Lily continued. "I don't have to tell you you're free to come and go as you please. And watch out for the old man," she added, sotto voce.

"I heard that!"

They took the stone path winding through the gardens where roses bloomed madly, fragrantly, in the November cool. Toward the sea, the pool shined dreamily blue. Ahead, the guesthouse, built as an Irish cottage in a fascinating contrast to the contemporary splendor of the main house.

Deep green shutters framed the garden-facing windows, stood out against the cream-colored walls, the little stone steps. The charm of window boxes offered bursts of color, spills of greenery.

Cate knew the sea-facing walls were glass, to bring in the drama, but the rest spoke of quiet charm, green hills, sheep-dotted fields.

Rolling back through her memory, she decided she'd take the master upstairs, one with that glass wall, and the little fireplace, a square of light and heat built into an interior wall.

It had a good-size closet she could soundproof, and her clothes could go in the bedroom across the hall. Four bedrooms, she recalled. No, five including the one on the first floor they'd used more as a playroom/dormitory when the whole family came to stay.

Hugh took a key out of his pocket, offered it to Cate with a dramatic sweep of his hand.

"This is pretty exciting."

She unlocked the door, stepped in.

Fresh flowers, autumn blooms in milk bottles and mason jars— she'd expected flowers. She hadn't expected to see the few pieces of furniture she'd put in storage—unable to part with—mixed in with the rest.

"That's my coffee table, and my lamp! My hunt table, too, and my chair."

"A woman wants to have her own things."

She turned to Lily. "They were in storage."

"And wouldn't have been if they didn't matter to you."

"But how did you get them out of storage? How did you get them here?"

Hugh mimed brushing lint off his shirt. "We have our ways."

"Well, I love your ways. This is just so damn sweet, and everything looks great. And oh God, that view."

Breathtaking, she thought, with no obstructions to the hard blue of the sky, the wide, wide sea, the scatter of trees twisted by the wind into magical shapes.

"I'll never get anything done," she murmured. "I'll be drunk on the view night and day."

"The kitchen's been redone—it needed it," Lily added. "And you actually like to cook from time to time."

Soda bread for the Coopers, Cate thought, still dreaming.

"Pantry's stocked for when you don't want to come to the house for meals. Which we hope isn't often." Hugh walked over to join her.

She tipped her head to his shoulder. "You may have to come check on me, shake me out of my happy coma. I want to see the kitchen, and the . . ."

She turned, blinked. "I was so distracted I didn't see. You opened up some walls."

And the open floor plan brought the kitchen into view, separating it from the living space with a wide granite counter in myriad shades of gray and silver and hints of blue.

"It's fabulous. When did you do all this? I love it."

She walked over, skimmed her fingers over the granite. White cabinets—not sleek and modern but slatted and cottagey, a little distressed—hit just the right note against pale, pale gray walls. They'd gone with white, vintage-style appliances, added glass fronts on a section that held colorful glassware. Gleaming butcher block topped a small work island.

She admired the deep farm sink, opened the slatted door to a walk-in pantry. Stocked, she thought, to hold her through a zombie apocalypse.

She could eat on the rush-topped stools at the counter facing the breathtaking view, or snuggle into the nook with its benches as colorful as the glassware.

"What do you think?"

"G-Lil, I think I win the prize for grandparents."

"Combo laundry and mudroom through there." Lily pointed. "And I'm going to warn you, Consuela's going to come in twice a week to clean and do laundry. No point arguing," she added. "She's very adamant. Very."

"Okay, but I'll talk her down to once a week."

"Good luck with that," Hugh muttered.

"Either way, this is the sweetest kitchen I've ever seen. I'd have been happy in the main house, and I'd have felt at home. But this? Well, it's already home and I haven't even seen my bedroom."

"There's just one more little change down here, before we go up." Hugh hooked his arm with Cate's. "You've still got the half bath and reading room over there. And over here—"

"We called it the playroom, the older kids called it the dorm."

"We didn't think you'd need either of those," he said as he opened the door.

If she'd been dazzled by the changes so far, this knocked her speechless.

They'd given her a studio, fully equipped, soundproofed, complete with booth. Noise-blocking shades, up now to let in the light and the garden view, the rise of hills beyond, could be rolled down to give her complete silence during recording.

As with her furniture, the equipment she'd packed up, shipped out, wove in with new.

The mics, the stands, even the pop filters, her work comp, the headphones, the works. They'd put in a small, glass-fronted cabinet, stocked it with the water she needed to keep her throat, her tongue lubricated.

They hadn't missed a trick.

"I've got nothing," she managed. "I've got nothing."

"A professional needs a professional space to work."

She could only nod at her grandfather's statement. "And boy, is this one of those. It's got it all and then some. You even thought of the mirror."

"You said you practice expressions in character to help find the voice," Lily reminded her.

"I do." Stunned, she stepped into the little recording booth, looked at the equipment.

"And if you're doing a song, or an audiobook, especially, you like more isolation and control."

She nodded. "Yeah, a little quirk of mine, I guess."

"An artist isn't an artist without quirks."

She turned back to them. "This is the most amazing, most thoughtful, most absolutely loving gift from the best grandparents in the history of grandparents. I need to cry a little."

"I was hoping you would!"

On a watery laugh of her own, Lily pulled her in.

Cate reached for Hugh, made it a trio.

"And now, I have to squeal."

She did, added bounces, cried a little more.

And was home.

CHAPTER SEVENTEEN

She hadn't taken any work, had kept her calendar open for two weeks, calculating the time to settle in, to set up a home studio, check out the studios in Monterey and Carmel.

Now she opened that up by a week, let her agent know she'd be ready for offers. She still wanted the week to just be, to spend real time with her grandparents. To bake that soda bread.

They had a welcome-home dinner, a movie night. She worked out in the gym with her grandfather, who complained about it, but continued to work on strengthening his injured leg.

She worked out because he complained, and he couldn't shrug off the exercises under her eagle eye.

She walked the beach or just sat on the rocks.

Because it pleased them, she picked tomatoes or peppers, harvested herbs or whatever came to mind to take to the main kitchen for Consuela.

She read over some offers, considered, and decided to take them all. After all, why not? It's what she did.

One, a voice-over for a book ad, needed a quick turnaround, so she started her setup while her bread baked in the kitchen.

Since the client wanted warm, she chose a dynamic mic, used a pop shield, a shock mount to cut any rumblings. A fifteen-second spot still required all the tools. She mounted her mic, adjusted the angle. Satisfied, she checked her software, her monitors. Set up a second stand for the script.

After rolling down the shades, putting the RECORDING IN PROG-RESS sign on the door, locking it just in case, she put on her head-phones. Did the first run-through and playback.

Nearly a full second over. She could fix that.

But wow, the sound? Great. She couldn't have done a better job setting up the studio herself.

She ran through it again, nodded.

Warm, she thought, inviting. You know you want to read me.

She did four takes, punching different words, phrases. Ditched one because she'd gone more sexy than warm.

After two more, she listened to each, and chose what she consid-ered the best three. She labeled them, sent the audio files to the client.

If they wanted a different tone, she'd go back and do it again, but she'd given them warm, female, inviting. And considered her debut in her new studio a success.

Once her bread cooled on the rack, she grabbed a jacket, walked outside.

The breeze, a frisky one, carried the roses and rosemary, the sea and the salt. She wandered back toward where a little vineyard—another new addition—climbed the terraced steps in the cliff, where more roses smothered an arbor with pale peach blossoms and subtle scent as the leaves waved and whispered in the breeze.

Her grandfather sat in the sun. He wore a wide-brimmed hat to protect him against the rays. A mug, coffee no doubt, as no one could convince him to give it up, sat on the steel table beside him.

He had a script in his hands, and his reading glasses on.

"Retired, my butt."

He looked up, nudged the glasses down to peer at her over them. "Semi. I'm just giving it a read. It's not green-lit yet. It should be." But he set it aside. "Want coffee?"

"No, I'm good. God, what a gorgeous day. I hardly ever got up here in the fall. It's just glorious." She tipped back her head, closed her eyes, just breathed.

"If Lily sees you out here without a hat, she'll scold you. Take my word."

"I'll remember one next time."

"Big brim," he said, tapping his own.

"I only have ball caps."

"Get one. Trust me."

"Next time I'm out and about then. I did my first voice-over this morning. The studio rocks, Grandpa. It seriously rocks. I'm going to start rehearsing an audiobook read later today. I've read two of this author's books before, so I know her style, her voice when it comes to narration. I need to get a handle on the characters. It'll be fun."

She opened her eyes, reached out to tap the script.

"Who are you?"

"The freewheeling, slightly crazy grandfather trying to convince his straight-arrow grandson to cut loose. They're on a cross-country trip—Boston to Santa Barbara—because the old man won't fly. The daughter—the grandson's mother—is working on having the old man deemed nuts, and put in a nursing home. He ain't going without a fight."

"I don't like her."

"She's a former flower child who's converted to suburban matron. She believes she's doing the sensible thing. It's a romp, so far. Well done."

She tapped her finger at him. "I hear you, Sullivan. You're going to make sure it's green-lit."

"I may twist an arm or two. But I'll finish it first."

He turned his head, grinned when a couple of happy barks hit the air.

"When did you get a dog?" Cate asked.

"Not yet, but I'm thinking about it." He clapped his hands, gave a whistle from between his teeth. A pair of black-and-white dogs, with a few spots of brown for good measure, raced straight to Hugh, wiggled until he rubbed both of them.

"They—they can't be Dillon's dogs."

"They are. Not Gambit and Jubilee. They slipped away last fall. Meet Stark and Natasha."

They shifted attention to Cate, sniffing, rubbing, staring at her with soul-filled eyes. "Iron Man and Black Widow?" Laughing, she rubbed. "Sticking with the Marvel Universe."

"What can I say?" Dillon walked up the stone path. "I'm a fan. I brought you a basket of those fingerlings you like, Hugh."

"Hot dog—and I don't mean you two. Sit down, boy. I'll call in for coffee."

"Wish I could, but I'm on my way to the co-op with produce." But he pulled off his sunglasses, smiled at Cate. "I heard you were back. It's good to see you."

"You, too. You really can't stay for a few minutes?"

"With Hugh, I sit down for a minute and the next thing I know it's been an hour. Next time."

As he snapped his fingers for the dogs, Cate rose. "I promise I won't keep you an hour if you'd walk back down with me. I have something for you—your mom and grandmother."

"Sure. You're in the guesthouse, right? Well, I guess it's Cate's house now. I'll take that hour, Hugh, first chance."

"See you do."

"I guess you know," Dillon said as he walked with Cate, "you made Hugh and Lily about the happiest people on the planet when you said you were coming back to stay."

"It turns out it's making me pretty happy, too."

"Don't miss New York?"

"It's there whenever I need an East Coast fix. It was good for me. Now this is good for me. Tell your mom, and Gram, I'm going to come see them. I wanted to keep a close eye on Grandpa for the first few days."

"He needs one."

"I got that." She opened the door. The dogs rushed in, began their obligatory sniffing.

He walked around, looked around. "It looks good. I saw a couple of stages when they were changing it up. It really looks good."

So did he, she thought.

Obviously he didn't always wear a hat in the sun—wide-brimmed or otherwise—as that sun had spent plenty of time streaking through his dense brown hair and gifting it with a million highlights. It spilled around his face somewhere between a curl and a wave—an interesting medium she suspected would take her hours to perfect on her own rain-straight hair.

He'd fined down, too, looked honed, she decided, so his face was all planes, angles, shadows with an outdoorsman tan that added even more depth and color to his green eyes.

He had a body that seemed to have been made for jeans, work boots, work shirts. Tough and lean.

He moved, as he wandered her space, with the rangy kind of ease of a man who strode around fields and pastures.

She let out a half laugh. "It's central casting."

"What's that?"

He glanced back, and well, Jesus, the sun slanted over him like a damn key light.

She pointed at him. "Rancher. You nail the look."

He grinned, and of course, it was lightning quick and just the right amount of crooked. "I am what I am. And you're a—Hugh calls it— voice actor."

"That's right. They built me a studio in here."

"Yeah, they talked about it."

She gestured for him to follow her, led the way.

He stopped at the doorway, hooked his thumbs in his front pockets. "Well, wow, that's a lot of equipment. How'd you learn how to work it all?"

"Trial and error—a lot of both. It's not really as complicated as it looks. I worked out of my bedroom closet when I first started. This is a big step up."

"I'll say. I saw—heard—you in *Secret Identity*. You looked good as a superhero, and as her alter ego, the quiet, lonely scientist. The voices worked. Soft, like hesitant for Lauren Long, fierce and sexy for Whirlwind."

"Thanks."

"I figured you'd have to go into a studio, with a director, crew, all that stuff."

"For some things, yeah. For others? The bedroom closet works."

"This is some closet you've got here. Maybe sometime you can show me how all this works. But I have to get going."

"I can do that when we both have time. Let me get the soda bread."

She moved by him, realized he even smelled like a rancher: leather and fresh grass.

"Soda bread?"

"I made it this morning. I'd claim it as an old family recipe, which is true—just not my family. A neighbor when I lived in Ireland."

"You bake bread?"

"I do. It helps me clear out cobwebs, work on voices."

She got a cloth, took one of the loaves from the cooling rack, wrapped it. "I wanted to give your family something from me." She offered it.

He stood a moment, the wrapped bread in his hands, the dogs at his feet sniffing the air. His eyes held hers the way they had that night so long ago.

Direct, curious.

"Appreciate it. Come by. My ladies would really like to see you."

"I will."

He started for the door, the dogs at his heels. "We never had that ride. You still ride?"

It took her a minute. "Oh, sure. It's been awhile."

"Come by. We'll see if you remember how."

He started out, that easy, ground-eating stride, looked back. "You look good as Cate, too."

When he continued on, she stepped back, closed the door.

"Well," she said to herself. "Well, well, well."

Dillon did his rounds. Delivered to the co-op, hauled an order of hay and oats to a local woman who kept two horses, dropped off a half gallon of goat's milk to a neighbor who couldn't pick it up herself because her car was in the shop.

He got a couple of cookies as thanks, considered it a good deal.

Back at home, he parked the truck, let the dogs out to run as he went over his mental list of what he still had to do. The first? Deliver the bread and mooch some lunch.

He noted Red's truck, which meant he wouldn't be the only one mooching lunch. But when he went inside, he found only his mother and grandmother in the dairy kitchen.

His grandmother hung a cheesecloth bundle of goat's milk curds, the big bowl beneath it to catch the whey that would separate from the curds. His mother filtered another—and it looked like the last batch of milk.

The investment they'd made expanding their goat herd, adding a few milk cows—and adding the dairy kitchen—continued to pay off.

"Took you long enough," Maggie said.

"There were conversations." Opening the fridge in the main kitchen, he took out a Coke. "I took some orders—I'll get them up after the lunch I'm hoping for." He twisted off the top, gulped some down. "Where's Red?"

"She kicked him out." Julia nodded toward her mother. "He's out tinkering with the little tractor."

Dillon crossed one of the items off his list, as he'd planned to tinker after lunch.

"He was underfoot." Maggie, her hair in a burnt-orange-colored braid, walked down the row, checking the separation progress. "Just like you."

"But I come bearing gifts." He unwrapped the bread, sniffed it. "Smells good, too. It's from Caitlyn Sullivan. She baked it."

Lips pursed, Maggie crooked her finger while Julia worked on the last bundle. Like Dillon, she sniffed. "Irish soda bread? Lily said the girl could cook some."

"How's she doing, Dillon?"

Dillon gave his mother a winsome smile. "Maybe I could tell you over lunch."

Maggie flicked a finger at him. "Go tell Red to stop tinkering and clean up. We'll feed you."

Happy to oblige, Dillon went out. He needed to spend some time that afternoon working with a couple of the yearlings, and wanted to check on the pregnant mares. Then there were the fall crops to look over. And the stock.

His mother handled the afternoon milking of their three dairy cows.

And thanks to Red—who'd turned out to be a damn good mechanic—he might not have to spend any time on tractor repair.

He heard the engine turn over, run smooth, and smiled. Yeah, cross that one off.

He found Red sitting on the tractor, head cocked as he listened to the engine. His hair, stone gray, wound in a braid to just below the collar of his ancient denim jacket. He had an equally ancient ball cap over it.

He still surfed every chance he got, stayed trim and agile. Proved that as he cut the engine and hopped down, planting his feet in the peacock feather boots Maggie had given him for his birthday.

Because, she'd said, he thought he was the cock of the walk.

"Got her going?"

"Yep." Red swiped his hands over his jeans. "Timing was off mostly."

"Yours isn't. You finished up in time for lunch."

"That was my plan."

They walked away from the barn together. "I dropped by the Sullivans' on my travels this morning. Caitlyn's moved in."

Red nodded, paused by the old pump well to wash his hands. Considering those travels, Dillon did the same.

"How's she doing?"

"Seems good." They dried their hands on the towel hung for that purpose and changed daily. "Looks damn good."

Red's lips curved. "Is that so?"

"It's definitely so."

They rounded to the back, scraped boots, went in through the mudroom. Hung jackets on pegs. Removed hats.

Nobody sat at Maggie Hudson's table wearing headgear or with dirt under their fingernails.

In the main kitchen the smell of curds and whey fell under the aroma of soup on the simmer.

"Did you wash your hands?" Maggie demanded.

Both men held up their hands.

"Then you can have a seat at the big table. Soup's almost on."

Red snuck in a kiss to the side of Maggie's neck under her burnt-orange braid.

"Take that bread on the board in with you. We'll see how Cate's baking holds up to Julia's kitchen sink soup."

"She baked bread?" Obediently, Red picked up the breadboard.

"Says she learned how when she lived in Ireland, and how she can work on voices while she's making it."

The "big table" meant the adjoining dining room with its big walnut buffet that Dillon had helped his mother refinish when he'd been a teenager, and its view of the woods where Cate had run as a child.

Curious and damn hungry, Dillon cut a slice, sampled the heel. "It's good. Anyway, I didn't see Lily when I dropped off the fingerlings, so I went over to check on Hugh. He's looking good. Cate was sitting out with him."

"Dil says she looks good, too."

"And then some," Dillon added over another bite. "You guys should go over and see what they've done to that guesthouse for her. Really changed it up. And put in this whole studio deal."

"So she can work right there?" Julia brought in the pot of soup, set it on the big trivet.

"Yeah. She said she started doing all this in a closet. Well, this ain't no closet." Since his mother put out the crock of butter—made fresh at Horizon Ranch—he smeared some on the bite of bread he had left.

Even better.

Maggie brought in the bowls, began to ladle them up. "I feel good knowing she found her way, and found her way back. She needs to come see us."

"She's planning to."

"When I think about that mother of hers."

Red rubbed Maggie's shoulder, but it didn't calm her down.

"It just fires me up." She sat down to her own soup, wagged her spoon in the air. "That woman living like some queen after what she did. Even that rich asshole can't buy her into a hit movie, but doesn't she still swan around in them? Straight-to-video, made-for-TV, but she's still doing them, with a face so full of plastic she can barely blink her eyes."

"Rich doesn't mean happy, Mom."

Maggie spooned up soup. "It's a lot easier to be unhappy sleeping on silk sheets than it is sleeping in a cardboard box—which is what she deserves." She took the bread Julia sliced for her. "Don't worry, I won't say all this to that girl. I'm getting it out of my system."

She tried the bread. Chewed, considered. "Good consistency, nice flavor and texture. Damn it, this may be better than mine."

Holding back a smile, she pointed at Dillon when he just ducked his head. "It's a smart man who knows better than to agree with me."

"Here's what I have to say. Not about the bread," Red added. "Charlotte Dupont looks like what she is. A fake and a fraud. I know, because I've heard from Hugh, and Aidan when he comes around, that she pays to plant stories that take a poke at them, Cate especially. Still, after all these years, she can't stop taking those shots at them. She can sleep on silk in a bed of diamonds, she's never going to be anything but what she is. She's never going to have what she wants. She's never going to be happy."

He shrugged, ate more soup. "She paid her debt to society." Ignoring Maggie's hiss, he plowed on. "But if you ask me, she's still in prison. Her own making, and I get some satisfaction from that."

"What about the other two, Sparks and Denby? You keep your ear to the ground," Dillon added.

"All right, to clear all this out. Because he had the firearm, Denby's got another five years before any chance of parole, and his chances are slim there. Sparks? He's made himself a model prisoner from what my ear to the ground hears. He may get early release. That's a solid year off," he added as Maggie hissed again. "Prisons are crowded, and he's nearly served his minimum. It's possible they'll spring him in another year. Eighteen in so far, and that's a long stretch."

"It's hard to believe so much time's passed." Julia looked back toward the kitchen. "Sometimes it seems like yesterday Dillon brought me downstairs, and that little girl sat there."

"There's one more thing, because it might just happen. There's a true crime writer who's been interviewing him for months now. I don't know who else she's talked to—my ear doesn't reach that far—but I know she's talked to Denby. But she's spending a lot of time talking to Sparks. Since she's got a law degree and he's listed her as his attorney, I can't tell you what they talk about."

"Another bloodsucker," Maggie decided. "Who is she? I want to Google her."

"Jessica A. Rowe."

Sparks groomed himself for his visit with his lawyer/biographer. He worked some product into his hair, still thick, to add a sheen (subtle) of silver to the gray. He practiced his sad but adoring looks in the mirror.

He still had it.

Then again, Jessica proved to be one of the easiest marks in his long career. At forty-six, stout, saggy, plain as a plank of wood, she'd been ripe for a little illicit romance. Desperate for love.

He'd started her out with the repentant routine, shared details—some real, some fabricated—that hadn't gotten into the public trough as yet. Shyly, he'd confessed he'd tried to write his story himself, as a kind of penance, but he couldn't find the words to express himself.

He expressed himself with her, maneuvered her into using her very rusty law degree to represent him so they could talk confidentially.

Over weeks, then months, he'd primed her, reeled her in, wooed her.

Through the years, he'd had letters from, visits from, women drawn to men in prison. He'd considered many as liaisons to the outside. Rejected many as either straight-out crazy or simply unreliable.

But Jessie, oh, Jessie was another type altogether.

The rule follower fascinated with rule breakers. Because, his instincts told him, she wanted to be one.

The lonely middle-aged woman who believed herself—rightfully, in his opinion—unattractive, undesirable. The naive-to-the-point-of-stupid mark who thought of herself as insightful.

The first time he'd taken her hand, held it, looked into her eyes as he kissed her fingers in gratitude, he knew he could, and would, play her like a violin.

Now, after months of preparation, after stolen kisses, fraught embraces, after promises and plans to marry upon his release, came the true test.

If she failed it, he'd wasted his time. But she'd passed all the small ones. Reporting back to him on everyone he intended to pay back. He had other sources, and every bit of information she gave him matched. Right down the line.

And since she worked hard on getting him that early release—and might pull it off—it was time to act while he still had an ironclad (literally) alibi.

She was waiting when the guard took him into the conference room. They no longer shackled him. They would subject him to a search after—unless he bribed the handpicked guard.

But no need on this visit.

She'd changed her hair from the first time they'd met. Shortening it, coloring out the gray, trying to add some style. She used makeup now, though never lipstick. If they managed to kiss, there would be no telltale smear.

He knew she worked on exercise and diet, though her body, in his opinion, would never be anything but stubby.

Still, he gave himself full credit for her efforts, for the more stylish suit she wore—so much better than the brown bag she'd had on during that initial meeting.

"I've missed you. Jessie, I've missed you so much. All the years before you, I could deal with them. I deserved them. But now? It's torture just waiting until I can see you again."

"I'd come every day if I could." She opened her briefcase, took out a file, as if they had something legal to discuss. "But you were right. Too often and they'd wonder. I feel like I'm in prison, too, Grant."

"If only I'd met you all those years ago. Before I let Denby and Charlotte use me, manipulate me. We'd have made a life, Jessie. Had a home. We'd have had children. I feel . . . they stole all of that from us."

"We'll make a home and a life, Grant. When you're free, we'll be together."

"I think of the kids we'd have had. Especially a girl, with your eyes, your smile. It breaks my heart. I want to make them pay for what they took from us. For that little girl who'll never be."

She reached across the table for his hand. "They need to pay. They will pay."

"I shouldn't ask you to get involved in this. I—"

"Grant. I'm with you. You've given me more in these few months than anyone has in my whole life. I'm with you."

"Can you take this next step? Can you call the number I give you, say the words I tell you to say? Even knowing what it means? If you can't, I won't blame you. It won't change how I feel."

"I'd do anything for you, don't you know that? What they took from you, they took from me. A little boy, with your eyes, with your smile."

"Be sure, my darling Jessie."

Tears sparkled in her eyes. "For what they did to you, what they took from us, I'm sure. I love you."

"I love you." He kissed her hand, looked into her eyes. Gave her the number, gave her the words to say.

Twelve hours later, a guard found Denby's body, the shank still in his belly, in the showers.

When Sparks got the word, he smiled at the ceiling of his cell and thought: One down.

CHAPTER EIGHTEEN

After making a delivery—eggs, butter, cheese—to the main house, Dillon walked down to Cate's. Maybe returning her bread cloth equaled excuse, but it was her cloth. Besides, he had a little time, and wanted to see her again.

Nothing wrong with that.

Plus, he'd waited nearly a week—and he'd had to deliver the dairy anyway.

He glanced down at his dogs. "Right? Am I right?"

They appeared to agree.

The November wind brought a bite with it, and a light, steady rain. He didn't mind that. Not when it made everything on the peninsula look like a storybook.

The sort where witches lived in enchanted cottages and gnomes lurked among the denuded, twisted trees. And maybe mermaids with sinuous bodies—and sharp teeth—lurked under the waves crashing at the cliffs.

The ranch might be only a few miles away, but this was a different world. He liked visiting different worlds now and then.

And in the gray gloom, with the wisps of fog, smoke trailing up from the chimney, and flowers—still bright—in the window boxes, the guesthouse did look like an enchanted cottage.

It made you wonder, if you played around with the theme, if the woman inside was a good witch or a bad witch.

Then he heard her scream.

He bolted the rest of the way, the dogs racing with him, growls low in their throats.

When he burst through the front door, ready to fight, to defend, he saw her standing at the kitchen island, her hair scooped up, her eyes wide and shocked.

And bread dough in her hands.

He said, "What the fuck?"

"Back at you. You may have heard of this traditional gesture called knocking."

"You were screaming."

"Rehearsing."

Funny, he thought, his heart hadn't started hammering until after he'd run in and seen her. Before that it was just fight mode.

"Rehearsing what?"

"Screaming, obviously. Can't pet you," she told the dogs. "Hands full. Close the door, would you? It's cold out."

"Sorry." He closed it, changed his mind. "Not sorry. When I hear somebody let out a bloodcurdling scream, I react."

She kept kneading dough. "Did it hit bloodcurdling?"

He could only stare at her.

"Is that my cloth? You can put it down there. If you want coffee, you'll have to make it yourself. I'm a screamer," she added.

"I heard that. Loud and clear."

"Not all actors can scream realistically or pull off the type of scream the scene and character call for."

"There are types of screams?"

"Sure. You've got your heartbroken scream, your I've-just-stumbled-over-a-dead-body shriek—which could also be a caught-in-the-throat type—there's your I-just-won-the-billion-dollar-lottery scream, and the wet scream—filled with tears and vibrating—among scores of others. I need a bloodcurdling."

"Well, you hit it if I'm any judge."

"Good. I'm doing a quick job later, dubbing for a thriller. The actress and I share some tonal qualities, and she just couldn't hit the right pitch on the screams."

He decided he could use a shot of coffee, and since her machine was the same as the one Lily had given Gram, he could handle it.

"They pay you to scream?"

"Damn right. Three varieties for this job. I have to hit the pitch, the timing—as in six-point-three seconds for the bloodcurdling. I need to match the facial expressions of the actress for a good, clean dub. The director—I've worked with him before—likes three takes on each scream."

"Do you want coffee?"

"No, I stick with water before I work, and during."

"So you're screaming and kneading bread."

"Rehearsing," she corrected. "And making Italian bread because I'm having my grandparents over for dinner tonight. A pasta dinner. I don't have a deep culinary well, but I learned to make this meal in New York because it's one of Lily's favorites."

He leaned back against the counter with his coffee while she greased a bowl, turned the dough into it. She covered it with the cloth he'd brought back, then—just as he'd been taught—put the bowl in the oven with the oven light on to rise in the warm.

He studied the work island. "You're messy."

"Yeah." She went to the sink to wash dough off her hands. "And if I don't clean it up to Consuela's standards, I'll hear her clucking her tongue when she comes in to clean tomorrow."

He watched while she dealt with the excess flour first, dumped tools in the sink, put away canisters. Then got out a counter spray and wash rag.

She wore those leggings things, the ones that molded to—in her case—really nice, long legs. Over it a long blue sweater with the sleeves shoved up.

She'd let her hair grow long, had it pulled back into a tail.

Yeah, he thought again as she worked, she looked damn good.

"My mom's working on an organic cleaner."

"Really?"

"Yeah, like all-purpose to start, then laundry detergent and so on. You can't tell Gram to slow down on the physical work on the ranch. I mean you literally can't tell her, because she'll kick your ass."

On a laugh, Cate glanced back. "Experienced that, have you?"

"Oh yeah. So the connection between cleaners and ass-kicking is, if—no, when, because there's no 'if' with my mother—when she has it down, she'll turn it over to Gram. Like we expanded the goatherd, added a couple dairy cows a few years ago."

Frowning, Cate rinsed out the cloth in the sink. "That sounds like more physical work."

"It is, that's a trade-off. It also means butter and cheese, which are mostly Gram's areas."

"I've got your butter and cheese along with your eggs, milk in my refrigerator. My grandparents stocked me up. I'll be using your goat cheese on tonight's salad."

"I just delivered more up at the house."

She hit the counter with the clean cloth. "Are deliveries part of the service?"

"For special customers."

It fascinated her. The life the Coopers and Maggie lived had always fascinated her.

"Do you sell right off the ranch? Farm? Dairy?"

He smiled. "Sure. Something you need?"

"I will eventually. I'll be using a lot of those eggs later when I make a soufflé. I'm a little terrified as I've never made one before, and they've got to be tricky. But my grandfather has a real soft spot for soufflés. I want to—it's not pay them back. It's . . ."

"I know what you mean."

She rinsed out the cloth again, laid it out to dry before picking up her water bottle. Twisted the top off and on, off and on. "They've got their kid gloves on again, and I hate that. Frank Denby—he was one of the men who took me—somebody killed him. In prison. Stabbed him. And you already knew," she realized, reading it on his face.

"Red spends a lot of time at the ranch."

"They don't think I know, so we're not talking about it."

He'd already stayed longer than he'd intended, had a list of chores to start and finish, but she stood there twisting that damn bottle cap.

"From what Red said, Denby wasn't a popular guy in San Quentin. He had more than a few dustups that landed him in the infirmary, more bullshit that landed him in solitary. Hearing all this, well, it's bound to take you back, upset you, but whoever shanked him most likely did it because he was, in general, an asshole and, according to Red, was suspected of being a snitch."

She finally uncapped the bottle, drank. "I don't know how I feel about him being dead. I can't quite reach in and find what I feel about that. But I know I hate my grandparents giving off the worried-about-Caitlyn vibe."

"So you're showing them you're fine by making Lily's favorite pasta and Hugh's soufflé."

She tipped the bottle toward him. "Nailed it."

"If you want my opinion, which I'm giving anyway, that's productive and healthy."

"Since I like that opinion, I'm taking it. And I'm coming by next week. I was going to come this week, but dead kidnapper threw me off. Is any day better than another? I can juggle my schedule."

"Any day's fine. I've gotta get back. Thanks for the coffee." He added it to the dishes in her sink. "And you've got to scream."

"Yes, I do. Which reminds me, thanks for the rescue. The fact it wasn't needed doesn't negate the action."

"You're strangely welcome."

He crossed into the living room where his dogs piled together for a nap in front of the fire. He gave a short whistle that had them scrambling up and following him.

"Good luck with the soufflé."

"Thanks. I'm going to need it."

She moved around to watch through the wall of glass as he walked away through the whispers of fog, the thin curtain of rain.

She hadn't intended to bring up Denby, had done her best to lock even the thought of him away. But she supposed the odd bond forged when they'd both been children made it easy to say things she said to no one else.

"We don't even know each other. Not really."

Bits and pieces, she thought, from Julia's emails, from something her grandparents might mention.

Not altogether true, she realized, and took her water with her into the studio. Turned the RECORDING IN PROGRESS sign over, shut and locked the door.

She knew he loved the life he'd chosen because it simply showed. She knew he inspired loyalty—at least in dogs, as his clearly adored him. She knew he was the kind of man who'd rush through a door to help someone without thinking of his own safety.

All important aspects, even admirable aspects of the whole. Still a lot of blanks, she admitted. She'd have to decide how many blanks she wanted to fill in.

But right now, she had to scream.

With a successful family dinner and the beginning of a solid work-week behind her, Cate walked to the main house. She wanted to drive to the florist for some flowers, then to the ranch, finally.

She went in the house first, learned from the day maid Consuela supervised that her grandfather was in his office, door closed, and Lily had gone down to the home gym.

She went down the main stairs, turned away from the movie theater and toward the blast of grinding rock and roll. Inside the gym, Lily grunted her way through reps on the leg extension and curl machine.

Sweat gleamed on her face, on her really excellent calves as she pushed herself to match the beat of the music.

Always fashionable, she wore compression capris in a swirling pattern of blues and greens and a blue support tank that showed off damn good arms and shoulders.

It had Cate making a mental note to use the facilities more regularly herself.

With one last grunt, Lily closed her eyes. She swiped at her face with her wristband—green—then, pushing herself up, spotted Cate.

"Oh God, I want to kill myself with a hammer. You know what most women my age are doing right now? Turn off that damn music, will you, my sweets? I'll tell you what they're doing. They're playing with grandkids or knitting or they're curled up with a book or getting a facial. What they're not doing is sweating blood on a damn torture device."

Picking up her water bottle, Lily gulped some down while she scowled at the rest of the circuit machines, the dumbbells, the rolled-up yoga mats, the stack of floor mats.

"That's why you're ageless."

"Hah." On another long breath, she stood, then considered herself in the wall of mirrors. "I do look pretty damn good for an old broad."

"My word's *amazing*."

"I'm going to hold on to that because I'm only halfway done. Dear God, Catey, what made me think I could go back to Broadway, keep up that pace?"

"You'll kill it."

"If it doesn't kill me first. Well." She lifted her water bottle again. "What a way to go. And what're you up to?"

"I stopped in to see if you and Grandpa—or either of you—wanted to go with me. I'm going to pick up some flowers and go by Horizon Ranch."

"I'd love nothing better than to do that instead of this. But I have to stick. Then I have to shower and make myself presentable. I'm videoconferencing this afternoon. Technology's made it impossible to take a meeting in your pajamas."

Picking up a towel, Lily dabbed at her throat. "Tell Consuela to have the car brought around for you."

"G-Lil, I can handle the garage. I can handle it," she repeated.

"Of course you can. Say hey to everybody for me. Oh, and tell Maggie we need to have another In the Bag Night."

"'In the bag'?"

"A couple of old bags drinking wine and talking about their misspent youth."

"Old bags, my butt, but I'll tell her. Want the music back on?"

Lily sighed. "Yes. Damn it. Hit it."

Cate hit it, walked up to the side door and out.

The sun beamed and gleamed on the mountains. From somewhere close, she heard the small roar—a trimmer or edger one of the biweekly gardening crew worked with.

She crossed the patio, started down the stone path, well remembered, to the garage.

Maybe a flutter of unease, she admitted, but wasn't that normal? No panic, no terror, just the unease of old memories.

After it happened, she'd heard her grandfather talk about cutting down the tree, and had begged him not to.

She'd thought, such a young girl, the tree didn't deserve death. It hadn't done anything wrong.

So it stood, as it had, old and gnarled and simply wonderful.

She walked to it, laid a hand on the bark, rough against her palm. "Not our fault, right? And here we are, both of us. She couldn't knock either of us down."

Satisfied, steady, she hit the remote for the garage door.

When she parked at the ranch with her armload of fall flowers, she saw changes. Julia had told her they'd built a house for Dillon. She saw it on the far side of the stables, noted they'd made use of the space and location to give him privacy and a view. She judged it about the same size as her house, minus the second story.

She saw the goats, some sheep dotting the rising hills, cows on the flatland, horses in pasture and paddock.

And Dillon working with a horse, a young one, she thought, on some sort of line. With the distance and his focus on his work, he hadn't heard her drive up.

The dogs had, raced from where they'd romped among the cows to greet her. She took a moment to give them a rub while she watched Dillon.

With a gray hat low on his head, he urged the horse to circle at a light trot. Some sort of training, she supposed. She knew how to ride, how to groom a horse, but didn't know much about raising one, training one.

He clearly did, as—somehow or other—he had the horse turning, trotting in the opposite direction.

The dogs decided to herd her toward the house; she decided to let them.

Julia walked out of a barn.

It struck Cate that Dillon got that rangy build from his mother. She moved at the same ground-eating stride, her dark blond hair under a rolled-brimmed brown hat, work gloves tucked in the back pocket of her jeans.

A dozen twinges—longing ones—spread inside Cate when Julia spotted her and smiled.

"Caitlyn! You look like a photograph! *Young Woman with Flowers*."

She moved straight to Cate and without hesitation wrapped her in a hug. "Oh, it's been too long! Come inside. You look just wonderful."

"So do you."

With a laugh, Julia shook her head. "This is as good as it gets after afternoon milking."

"I'm sorry I missed that. Really, I've never seen a goat being milked. When I lived in Ireland, I saw cows milked a couple times. It's been awhile."

"Three times a day every day, except for the nannies and cows still nursing. We take those down to one or two milkings. So you've got plenty of opportunities to see how it's done."

As they walked, Cate looked around. The silo, the barns, the spread of the farmhouse. She echoed Dillon's thoughts. "It's like a different world."

"It sure is ours." Julia scraped off her boots at the door. "I hope now that you're living here, you'll come into it more often."

Inside, the fire simmered. They'd changed some of the furniture, gone for blues and greens to mirror the sea and pastures. But so much was, comfortingly, the same.

Did they still leave a light on low at night, she wondered, in case some lost soul wandered in?

"Come on back. Mom and Red should be in the dairy kitchen."

"Dillon said you added on."

"There's a good market for farm-made butter, cheese, cream, yogurt."

"I can see why, as I've been using some of yours myself. In fact, I need to get some cream, some butter, and . . . You remodeled."

Julia glanced around the main kitchen, the commercial range, double ovens. The big table remained, but they'd added more work space for baking days.

"It needed it, and we needed to step up to commercial grade. And now Mom and I don't bump into each other when we're working in here. Let me take those flowers—which are gorgeous—and your jacket."

Gleaming stainless steel, shelves of important-looking tools that were beyond her comprehension, the massive, shining vent over what looked like a massive range. Yet a fire still simmered in the little hearth, pretty potted herbs thrived on the deep windowsill.

"It looks professional, but it feels the same."

"Then it's a success. Mom and I debated, argued, and occasionally came close to blows over the design and layout." Julia crossed over to lay the flowers in a prep sink as she talked. Then went through the mudroom door to hang the jackets.

Cate moved through, trailing a hand over the table where she'd sat, where Julia had tended her cuts and bruises so long ago.

She stood, fascinated, in the wide opening that led to another kitchen. Not altogether a kitchen, she thought, though it had the range, the sinks, the work counters.

Bags of . . . something hung from wooden rods and dripped into glass bowls below. Big glass jars of—she supposed—milk stood on counters. Gram, orange braid bundled back, ran water in the sink, her shoulders moving as she pushed down. Red—yes, that was Red— poured milk into a small, shiny machine.

Through the big window over the big sink, Cate could see Dillon and the young horse.

Julia stepped up. "You won't get fresher butter and cream."

"Red's starting the last of the butter," Maggie said without turning around, "and I'm rinsing the last of the last batch. Check the curds on the stove."

"Will do. We've got a customer."

"Just have to wait until—" Still pressing, she looked over her shoulder. "Well, look here, Red. Somebody's all grown-up."

He switched on the machine, turned. "She sure is."

He walked over, held out a hand. Cate ignored it, hugged him. "It's good to see you, Sheriff."

"Just Red now. I thought I retired, but these women work a man to death."

"You look pretty healthy for a dead man."

Maggie cackled at that. "It's about time you came by, girlie. Once that last batch of butter churns and we finish it up, I'm ready to take a break."

Cate eyed the machine. "That's a butter churn?"

"You think we use a wooden bucket and stick?" Maggie cackled again. "We've come a ways since *Little House on the Prairie*."

"These curds are ready. Cate, why don't you have a seat, and we'll all take a break as soon as we're done here."

"She's got two hands, and we can use them. Are they clean?" Maggie demanded.

"I—"

"Wash them up anyway. You can help me wrap this butter."

"No one escapes," Red told her.

Curious, Cate walked to the sink, looked in. "Is that butter?"

"One more rinse and it will be. You've got to get the buttermilk out. Use the sink over there."

A half hour later when Dillon came in to grab a cup of coffee, he found Cate, wearing a big apron, her hair pulled back in a tail, wrapping rounds of butter.

"Don't you bring ranch dirt in here," Maggie warned him.

"I washed up at the pump. Hi."

"Hi." Cate smiled as if she'd just won the grand prize in a raffle. "I helped make butter. And mozzarella."

Transferring wrapped rounds of butter and cheese to the refrigerator, Julia saw her son's eyes, what was in them. Sighed a little inside.

"Why don't you help Red clean up the churn, and we'll get something going for lunch? Do you still eat meat, Cate?"

She'd only meant to stay an hour. Work waited. But . . . Well, she'd work tonight, she decided. "I do."

She sat down to leftover chicken stew with fresh dumplings.

"I saw you outside," she said to Dillon, "with the horse going in circles."

"Lunge line. It's training, and communication. That was Jethro. It's how they learn to switch gaits on command, to switch directions, stop, go."

"It takes skill and patience," Julia added, "which Dillon has in abundance."

"I'd love to see the horses next time I come."

"I can take you around after lunch."

"Workday for me—or should've been. Who knew I'd make butter? You can really do it just by shaking a mason jar?"

"If you've got the arm and the patience for it. I made it that way the first time when Julia was just—hell, about three, I guess."

"We used to use a tabletop churn—it's back there on the shelf. But we had so many people asking for it, we went higher tech when we expanded. Same with the cheeses. Remember, Mom?"

"My arm does. Now that this one's always underfoot?" Maggie elbow-poked Red. "He has to earn his keep. He's a half-assed rancher, but half an ass is better than none."

"She fills my life with grief." Red spooned up more stew. "And damn good dumplings."

"I need that soda bread recipe."

"I'll write it down for you."

"I know the basics, but there was something just a little different. A little sugar, right?"

"That's right, but the real secret is working the butter in with your fingers."

"With your fingers?"

"Mrs. Leary swore by it."

"Surprised you have time for all that," Red put in. "Hugh says you stay busy, in demand."

"Multitasking." Dillon shot her a look. "She gave me a heart attack last week when she's kneading bread and screaming."

"He gave me one back when he burst into the house ready to rumble. I do scream dubbing."

"That's a thing?" Red wondered.

"It is. Does anybody watch horror movies?"

Three fingers pointed to Maggie.

"Love them. The scarier the better."

"Did you catch *Retribution*?"

"Vengeful ghosts, ramshackle house on a cliff, troubled marriage they try to patch up by moving to a new place. It had it all."

"Anytime you heard Rachel—she was the mother—scream?" Cate tapped her throat.

"Is that right? I'm watching it again—I'll listen for you."

"I'm surprised any of you have time to watch anything. Milking and training and feeding and making and baking."

"If you don't take time," Julia said, "the work's just work instead of a life. More stew?"

"No, thanks. It was great. Everything was great. I have to get back and voice a snooty French swan for an animated short."

"What's that sound like?"

Cate angled her head at Dillon. "I think, it's along the lines of . . ."

As he watched, she changed posture, sort of lengthened her neck, and looked down her nose. And hit a snooty French accent on the nose. "'*Alors*, the duck, he is the disgrace, *non*? We have no room for so foul the fowl on our lake.'

"It's a sweet little story on bigotry and acceptance of the different. And I really have to get to it. Can I help with the dishes?"

"Red's got that."

"See?" He jerked a thumb at Maggie. "Works me to death."

"Let me put your order together." Julia rose.

"How do we do this? Do we run a tab, do I pay you now?"

"Your grandparents run a monthly, and you can do the same. But in this case, you earned the dairy."

"I'll take it, thanks. I'd love some of the mozzarella. Next time I break out a frozen pizza, I'll grate some on it."

There was a distinct hush.

"Ix-nay on the rozen-fay izza-pay," Dillon muttered.

"What?"

"She speaks like five languages, but doesn't get pig latin. It's too late for you."

"You don't know how to make a pizza?" Maggie demanded.

"Sure I do. You take it out of the freezer, put it in the oven. Or when I lived in New York, you pick up the phone and it magically arrives at your door."

"Next lesson, how to make an actual pizza instead of settling for processed sauce on cardboard." Maggie shook her head. "How do you expect to survive the zombie apocalypse if you can't make your own pizza?"

"I never thought about it that way."

"Better start."

"Dillon, take this out for Cate." Julia handed him a bag a child could've carried. "Her jacket's in the mudroom. You come back soon." She gave Cate a hard hug.

"I will. I hope you, all of you, come over to my place sometime."

Julia waited until she heard them go out, heard the door shut before she let that inner sigh out.

Maggie just nodded. "Yep, our boy's more than halfway gone."

"What do you mean?"

"Past smitten, rounding third, headed for home, Red. Didn't you see how he looked at her?"

"She's a knockout."

Now Maggie shook her head. "Men are just simpleminded about half of everything."

"She dazzled him," Julia murmured. "Not like any of the other girls—women—he's had an interest in. This one will either break his heart or fill it."

Outside, Dillon made sure they were well out of earshot. "You know the pizza that shall not be named? I keep one—hidden—in my freezer. For emergencies."

"For pizza emergencies?"

"They usually happen late at night."

"I can see that." She glanced back toward the house. "I was going to stay an hour, maybe have some coffee, tea, whatever. They pull you in. This place, your family, they pull you in."

"And before you know it, you're wearing an apron and working dairy."

"I'm not sure where making butter fits on my résumé, but I hope to work it in." She took the bag from him, set it on the floor of the passenger seat. "I really would like to see the horses, well, everything. And take that ride."

"Anytime."

She circled around to the driver's door. "I don't think 'anytime' works on a ranch like this. Is there a day you're not going from one chore to the next?"

"We try to slow it down some on Sundays."

"I could make Sunday work."

"Good. Around ten?"

"I'll be here. With my riding boots on." She hopped in behind the wheel. "I'm going to have a pizza emergency tonight. Don't tell Gram."

"Your secret's safe with me."

"See you Sunday." He closed the door; she started the engine.

She drove down the ranch road smiling to herself. She'd made butter.

Then as she turned on the highway she began a series of tongue twisters to limber up for her afternoon work.

CHAPTER NINETEEN

Her father came for Thanksgiving. Under Consuela's watchful eye, Cate made her first pumpkin pie. While she'd never again use the phrase "easy as pie," it turned out well.

Best of all, she walked Aidan down to her cottage, showed it off, showed off her studio before sitting with him in front of the fire.

They sipped whiskey after a long, happy day.

"I was going to feel guilty about nudging you to come back when I stayed in L.A. But it not only seems to be a good move for you, it feels like the right move."

"I was ready for it. What they did, with this house, with the studio? It's such a pleasure to live here, to work here."

"You're busy."

"Right now? Just the right amount." Thoroughly content, Cate curled up her legs.

Outside, the surf whooshed, and wind shivered through the trees. Inside, the fire crackled, and the whiskey went down warm.

"I'm starting an audiobook next week, and that'll be the biggest project I've taken since moving from New York. It still leaves me time to spend with Grandpa and G-Lil, and get out some. I went riding a couple of Sundays ago at Horizon Ranch. That felt good—until the next day when my muscles reminded me I hadn't been riding in a long time."

"And how are things with the Coopers?"

"Talk about busy. They've expanded—a whole dairy business. Dillon says they'll have some students come in over winter break. They train and work—and there's a lot of work. Same in the spring and summer. And they hire help during those busier seasons. Sheriff—just Red," she corrected. "Red's there a lot since he retired, and pitches in. Did you know Deputy Wilson is Sheriff Wilson now?"

"Dad mentioned it."

She studied her whiskey. Then her father. The years, she thought, just seemed to pile on more appeal when it came to Sullivan men.

"Since it's just you and me, should we deal with the elephant in the room?"

"Which one?"

"She does seem to have an endless supply. The one where I'm hiding out here because I've had a nervous breakdown. One partially brought on by being dumped by Justin Harlowe."

Her breath hissed out. Her own fault there, she reminded herself. And still. "I expect he's having a hell of a good time feeding that one."

"He's getting some play trying to boost his series and its sagging third season."

Irritated all over again, Cate shrugged. "He can get all the play he wants, and so can she. It doesn't bother me the way it used to."

"Doesn't it?"

"It bothers me," she admitted. "But not like it used to. I'm only bringing it up so it's, well, dumped. Like I dumped Justin months ago. I agreed to keep the breakup quiet because he was going into the new season, and he asked me to. I'm sorry I did, but it doesn't matter."

Aidan studied her face. "Does he?"

"No. He doesn't matter, and she doesn't matter either."

"Good. The rest will fade off, as it does. What about the calls?"

All right, she thought, get it all out of the way. "I haven't had one in nearly a year. As promised, I've told you about them, about all of them since I promised. And I reported all of them to Detective Wasserman."

"And no progress there?"

"What can they do, Dad? It's a prepaid cell, it's a recording. Months, even years apart. They're not going to matter either. I've got my family, my work, my life. I want you to know that. Especially since you'll be heading to London to shoot."

"I was going to see about you coming with me until I saw how happy you were here, how happy Dad and Lily are. Their gain, my loss. But it's not until February, so if you change your mind . . . Either way, I'm back here for Christmas and staying until after New Year's. I want some time with my girl."

"She wants time with you. How about saddling up and taking a ride while you're here?"

"Three's a crowd."

"No. It's not like that. We barely know each other. I don't think he's involved with anyone, but we're . . ."

"Before you say 'friends,' I'll point out you talk about your friend you barely know quite a bit."

"Do I?" Maybe she did. Maybe she thought of him quite a bit, too. "I guess it's a fascinating lifestyle. And the work ethic? Sullivans know about work ethic and passion for the work. I think it must take an innate kindness, and innate grit, to tend animals and the land the way they do."

She realized she was, again, talking about him.

"You know, I think Sullivans have either the best luck with relationships or the worst. So far my track record there's not so great. I think I'll focus on the work and making sure Grandpa behaves himself when G-Lil's in New York."

Shifting, she looked out the glass wall. "Moon's up," she murmured.

"I'm going to take that as my cue, get back up to the house." He rose, walked over to kiss the top of her head. "I like thinking of you sitting here, looking out at the moon over the water. Content."

She gave his hand a squeeze. "That's just what I am."

While he walked up the path, she sat, watching the moon. She thought she had a great deal to be thankful for. If some of her blessings had grown out of one horrible night, wasn't it worth it?

In the week before Christmas when the high hills carried a lacing of snow and the air snapped like a crisp carrot broken in two, Cate lit candles to fill the house with the scent of pine and cranberry.

She'd decorated her own little tree, had wrapped presents—poorly, but she'd wrapped them.

Her grandparents had taken a quick trip to L.A. for a holiday party—one she'd begged out of. Instead she settled into her studio to work, and didn't give L.A. a thought.

When she finished for the night, she shut down, checked her phone. Checked a voice mail.

"Ho, ho, ho!

Naughty, naughty. Didn't do what you were told."

Her own dialogue from her first voice job piped up. *"I know who I am, but who are you?"*

"Cate, Cate, where is Cate?"

Now her mother's voice, gleeful. *"Come out, come out, wherever you are."*

A scream, a laugh, and a final *"Ho, ho, ho."*

Weary, Cate saved the voice mail. She'd send it to Detective Wasserman for his files.

Okay, yes, her hands shook, but only a little. And she'd do what she hadn't done since coming back to Big Sur. She'd lock her doors.

But she'd wait until morning to call her father because why give him a sleepless night. She'd keep that upset for herself and do what she always did when the past crept into the now.

She'd find an old movie on TV, one with plenty of noise, and fill the night with sound.

And she'd wait to tell her grandparents until they returned from L.A.

The evening air held balmy in L.A. Holiday lights twinkled with the temperature hovering in the midseventies as the sun dipped down toward twilight.

Charles Anthony Scarpetti, retired from the practice of law, drew a hefty fee on the lecture circuit. He often appeared as a legal expert on CNN.

At seventy-six, with three divorces under his belt, he enjoyed the single life and the smaller home that required only two day staff and a weekly grounds crew to maintain.

He had a pool man, three times a week. He credited swimming, his preferred method of exercise, for keeping him in top shape.

Swimming, and a few careful nips and tucks. After all, he remained a public figure.

He swam every morning—fifty laps. He did another fifty every evening, with a top off in his whirlpool before bed. He'd given up cigars and refined sugar—both a sacrifice.

He slept eight hours a night, ate three balanced meals a day, kept his alcohol intake to a glass of red wine nightly.

He fully expected to live, healthily, into his nineties.

He was about to be disappointed.

At precisely ten o'clock, he stepped out of his house to cross to the pool. The underwater lights shined on the tropical blue water heated to a precise eighty-two degrees. He removed his robe, draped both it and his towel over the bright chrome curve of the ladder of the bubbling whirlpool area where he would end his last lap.

He walked the forty feet to the deep end, dived.

He counted off the laps, nothing but the water, the strokes, the count in his mind. He moved smoothly, steadily, as always in a strong freestyle.

As he counted off ten, fingers brushing the side, something exploded in his head. He feared a stroke—his housekeeper worried him constantly about swimming alone at night.

He tried to push up, push out, his eyes opening wide. He saw blood in the water, spinning like red spiderwebs in the pristine blue.

Hit his head, something had hit the side of his head. Confused, he struggled to surface, groping for the lip of the pool.

Something held him under, pushed him down.

Flailing, fighting, he gulped water. He clawed, pawed, felt his fingers break the surface. Hope cut through panic, but he couldn't find the side, couldn't pull himself up to the air.

When he tried to scream, water flooded his lungs.

Then the panic, the hope, the pain slid away as he sank.

Over her first cup of coffee, Cate tried to wake up her brain by going over her mental list for the day.

She'd voiced and sent the second set of five chapters on her audiobook job to the engineer and producer. Maybe she'd start on the next five. If she needed to do any fixes to the second set, she could just stop, fix, move on.

Or she could work on the couple of smaller jobs she had pending, wait to hear from the engineer.

The poor night's sleep nudged her toward the smaller jobs.

She should work out—it might get her moving. She really should walk up to the house—that was kind of a workout—then put in an hour . . . okay, forty-five minutes in the gym.

Maybe she should do that first and avoid her typical afternoon not-enough-time excuse.

Maybe she should have a bagel.

Obviously, she just needed more coffee. Her brain would wake up, and all would be revealed.

And when she felt fully awake and steady, she'd call her father in London. Keep her promise.

She started to shuffle back to the coffee maker, and through the wall of glass saw Dillon coming down the path.

She ducked back, even knowing that he couldn't see her through the treated glass. And looked down at herself.

Old woolly socks, old flannel pajama pants—the ones with frogs all over them—the sweatshirt she'd pulled over the T-shirt she'd slept in—tried to sleep in. The faded pink one with a hole under the left armpit and a coffee stain that resembled Italy's boot down the center front.

She kept meaning to toss it, but it was so damn soft.

"Really?" she murmured. "Just really?"

She swiped a hand over her hair. How bad was it?

Bad.

Merde!

No makeup either—and she probably had sleep crust in her eyes.

Mierda!

She rubbed at them as she crossed over to answer his knock. Ran her tongue over the teeth she'd yet to brush.

What sort of human being came knocking on a woman's door at eight-thirty-five in the morning?

She pulled out her most casual smile as she opened the door. And hated him, sincerely hated him in that single moment for looking just amazing.

"Hi. You're out and about early. Where are the dogs?"

"Back home. Sorry, did I get you up?"

"No, in fact, I was just going for my second cup of coffee." She walked back toward the kitchen, slapping herself for not putting on workout gear. Then she'd look athletic instead of lazy and sloppy. "You take it black, right? I could never manage that."

Wishing she could at least grab a mint, she reached for another mug.

"I need to talk to you."

"All right." She glanced back, mug in hand. Slowly turned all the way around as she saw what her obsession with her own appearance had blocked out.

The worry, the concern in the way his eyes scanned her face.

He didn't know about the call, did he? She hadn't told anyone about the call yet.

Then her brain cleared enough to remind her it wasn't always about her.

"God, did something happen? Gram, Julia?"

"No, no they're fine. It's nothing like that. It's Charles Scarpetti. The lawyer," he added when she only stared. "Your mother's lawyer from back then."

"I know who he is. He plays a legal expert on TV now. I know he wrote a book about some of his high-profile cases, and my kidnapping was one of them. I didn't read it. Why would I?"

"He's dead. They—the pool guy—found his body floating in his pool a couple of hours ago. It's going to hit the news if it hasn't already. I didn't want you to hear about it that way."

"All right." She set the mug down, then rubbed her hand over the bracelet she wore. Darlie's hematite for anxiety. "All right. He drowned?"

"The LAPD's investigating. Red has some connections there, and he got word. He—you should know he's still looking out for you."

"All right. Sorry." She dropped her hands to her sides. "I don't know what I feel. Are you saying he might've been killed?"

"I can only tell you what Red told me. His contact in L.A. says it smells—that's a quote. I just didn't want you to switch on the news and get hit with it."

"Because they'll bring up the kidnapping." Nodding, she picked up the mug again, went to the coffee maker. "And we'll start a round of poor, brave Caitlyn. Charlotte will do some interviews, weep Hollywood tears over the daughter lost to her. We'll have some speculation why I quit the business—or the on-screen aspect of it. And since the guy I made the mistake of getting involved with last freaking year is already using the breakup, months ago, to pump up some publicity, we'll toss that in."

Muttering curses in French, she paced a moment.

"Are those bad words in French?"

"What? Oh, yes. More impact."

After setting the black coffee on the counter, she opted for water. Her brain was definitely awake now, no more coffee needed.

"Okay. A man's dead, and I don't know how to feel about that. He was doing a job—that's all it was to him. Why should it have been anything else? It wasn't personal, I know that. In any case, she went to prison."

Since she didn't want the water either, she set the bottle down. "Did he have a family, I wonder? Children, grandchildren?"

"I don't know. The only thing Red got was he lived alone."

"Do you want a bagel? I was going to have a bagel."

"Cate."

"Sorry, I don't know how to feel. Somebody I never even met is dead, and you came over here to tell me because you know I'd have trouble with it. You know because you were part of it, the saving part of it. Like Scarpetti was part of it. And Sparks and my mother and Denby."

It struck her, drained the color from her face. "Denby. He was killed weeks ago, murdered in prison. Now the lawyer."

He'd been careful not to really touch her since she'd come back. And could admit the careful equaled self-defense mechanism. But he knew when touch was needed, for a person, for an animal.

He put his hands on her shoulders first, a kind of steadying gesture. "They'll probably go there, the press, maybe the cops. But Denby was in prison, Scarpetti in L.A. Both of them, considering career paths, had to have a list of enemies—different varieties."

"Professional criminal, defense attorney."

"I get they both connect to you, but—"

"To you, too." Struck by that, she gripped his wrists. "To you, your family. Have you thought of that?"

"We're fine. Our names don't sell papers or TV spots. Yours does, and I'm sorry about that. It blows."

"It blows," she repeated.

Responding to simple kindness, she moved into him, laid her head on his shoulder. When his arms came around her, the stress simply spilled out of her.

"It blows," she said again. "But I know how to handle it. Didn't always, but I know how to handle it. Oh crap." She sighed, stayed as she was because he smelled comfortingly of horses and man. "My grandparents. They were in L.A. yesterday, a party. They're due home this afternoon. I need to warn them. My father, too."

"I bet they know how to handle it."

"Yes, they do." Briefly, she tightened her grip, then released and stepped back. "We'll have family here starting tomorrow. Not everyone at once this year—too many scheduling conflicts—but most off and on until New Year's. That'll help."

He couldn't quite resist brushing tousled hair away from her face. "United front."

"We are that."

"Yeah, mine's the same."

"I want to stop by sometime tomorrow, drop off some gifts."

"Baking day," he warned her.

"Is it? Lucky me. You haven't had your coffee. Let me make you a fresh cup."

"It's okay. I've got to—"

"Get back," she finished. "I bet you've already put in a half day's work—what most would consider a half day's work. I haven't even brushed my teeth."

"That's the life."

"And you took time out of that to come here, get me over the first bump. I'm grateful. There are a handful of people outside of family I trust absolutely. You and your family take up most of the handful."

"You've got to get out more." He smiled when he said it. "I'll see you tomorrow if you get by."

"Baking day? Count on it."

As he walked back up the path, he wondered what the hell he was supposed to do when she said stuff like that about trust. She needed a friend, not some guy who wanted to get her naked. Even some guy, like for instance himself, who was willing to take his time, give her time, ease it all in by stages.

Maybe he wished he didn't have so many clear pictures of her in his head. The little girl trying to hide in the dark, the long-legged teenager holding red flowers, the woman in an apron ridiculously excited about making butter, the woman on horseback, laughing as she stretched a trot to a gallop.

Now add the sexily rumpled one opening the door to hard news.

Smarter, he thought when he reached his truck, to put those pictures away, at least for now.

She thought of him as a friend, and a woman didn't want a friend making moves on her. In the long list of ways to screw up a friendship, that had to be number one.

Thinking of friends, he decided he'd text two of his oldest, see if they wanted to hang out later, have a couple beers, play some video games. Might be tougher for Leo, since he had a wife, and a baby on the way.

But then again, he imagined Hailey might enjoy a night of quiet, which Leo rarely was.

He stopped at the gate, waited for it to open. A reminder about different worlds, he supposed. He did like visiting this one, felt welcome, but it remained a different world from the one he'd chosen.

Through the gate he paused again at the edge of the peninsula, waited for the second gate. He heard sea lions carrying on, and felt his spirit lift when he spotted a sounding whale out to sea.

Different worlds, maybe, but this was one they shared. He could picture her standing at the glass, looking out at the same wonder as he.

Maybe he'd keep those pictures of her after all. Time rolled, didn't it? And he had plenty of it.

About the time Dillon drove home, Sparks reported for work in the prison library. Due to his good record, he'd do some clerking at the counter today, probably restock some of the books returned by inmates.

He had a nice view from the window of the bay, the mountains. The freedom still denied to him.

Before Jessica, he'd spent time—as many others did—in the law library. He figured he'd educated himself there as well as any, so it began to piss him off he found nothing, no precedent, no loophole, no nothing, that might lead to overturning or shortening his sentence.

Charlotte had screwed him, and screwed him good.

He had access to computers—limited, of course.

When he had free time, he might sit and read some bullshit book or the *San Quentin News* or just shoot the shit with other inmates— had to keep things running smooth—with that view of San Francisco Bay mocking him.

Then Jessica, and after the wooing and winning, no need to waste his time on the goddamn law books. She'd handle that.

She'd handle what he needed handled.

He worked steadily through the morning. He'd wanted the library job because it was a popular place, a place to make contacts, make connections, make deals.

Close to the end of shift, one of his regular customers—two packs of reals a week—stepped to the counter to order a book as cover. He knew the illiterate asshole didn't read. He put in the order for the books, for the smokes.

"Hey, heard your name on the news."

"My name?"

"Yeah, some lawyer bought it. Was a lawyer for that rich bitch you used to bang, they said. The one who set you up for the kid snatch."

"Is that so? Scarpetti?"

"Yeah, that's the one."

"Fucker got her off in a walk when she flipped on me."

As Sparks finished his shift, prepared to take some time in the exercise yard, he thought: Two down.

Dressed in bold red, right down to the soles of her Louboutins, Charlotte angled herself toward the photographer. She had her hair styled in a loosely braided knot at her neck to show off the teardrop diamonds at her ears.

Her lips—plumped by her latest injection and as red as her dress—curved. But regally, she thought, with a hint of sadness.

Inside, she felt glee. It was about damn time she got solid press for herself, instead of for being the wife of an old man who could buy her a fucking country.

Which he would, had she asked. Conrad remained just that besotted. So anyone, any goddamn critic who claimed she couldn't act her way into a high school talent show could shove it.

The asshole lawyer had finally paid off. He just had to die to do it.

And not tabloids this time, but real press. She'd done the *Los Angeles Times*, the *New York Times*. When cable news came knocking, she opened the door.

Or the servants did.

Now, finally, the cover of *People*, and a four-page spread.

Sure, a lot of it meant playing the devoted wife, the reformed socialite, but now, at last, sitting in the sweeping parlor, the white marble fireplace simmering, the soaring Christmas tree—done in white and gold and shimmering crystal—dressed (intentionally) like a flame, she got down to the real business.

"Charles's death—the police say murder—is so shocking. I'm still shaken by it. Anyone who knew him must be. I remember, so clearly, his strength and support at the lowest point of my life."

She looked away, a hand to her throat as the reporter asked questions.

"I'm sorry. I was lost in the past. No, I'm afraid we didn't really stay in touch. I had to do my penance, of course, and Charles helped me understand that. I did ask his advice on how to adjust when I'd paid my debt.

"What did he advise?" Charlotte repeated to give herself time to make something up. "To give myself time, to forgive myself. He was so supportive, so wise."

On a quiet sigh, she touched a fingertip just under the corner of her eye as if to catch a tear.

"When I came back to Los Angeles, I wanted only to try to reconnect with my daughter, to find a way to earn Caitlyn's forgiveness. I hoped she'd find it in her heart to give me a second chance, to be her mother again."

Turning her head so the lights caught the diamonds, Charlotte put on that sad, brave smile. "I still hope, especially during the holidays, or on her birthday. I had to turn her rejection into my own strength. Rebuilding my life, my career. Wouldn't there be a chance she could see that, and consider forgiving?"

Leaning forward just a little, as if sharing a confidence, she added the slightest tremor to her voice. "I worry about her. I was deceived by men, used by them. I allowed myself to become so subservient I made the most terrible decision a woman, a mother, can make. She—my daughter—I'm afraid she's walking that same path."

Keeping the sad smile in place, Charlotte nodded at the reporter, used the response as her cue.

"How? Caitlyn's broken relationship with Justin Harlowe is just the latest, isn't it? Everything I hear makes it sound as if she's repeating my mistakes. Wanting too much, demanding too much, expecting—on one hand—a man to fill that void, and on the other allowing herself to be walked over because of that desperate need for love.

"If I hadn't found Conrad, learned to trust his kindness and his loving heart, I don't know what would have become of me. I can only hope that my daughter finds someone as loving to help her find her true self, her inner strength. Someone who might help her find that forgiveness."

As a flourish, Charlotte gestured up. "Do you see the angel on top of the tree? That's Caitlyn, my angel. One day I hope she'll wing her way back to me."

And scene, Charlotte thought.

CHAPTER TWENTY

Rather than push through it, Cate simply blocked out the noise. She kept the news, especially entertainment news, turned off. If she sat down with her tablet or computer to research, she restricted her use to the research or personal interests. No deviation, no giving in to the tug to check—just for a minute—on what someone said, wrote, blogged about.

She had her work and, through the holidays, a lot of family to keep her busy.

Before she knew it, the holidays slid toward February.

February always ushered in a period of bad dreams. Maybe, she could admit, they carried more intensity because she'd come back to where they'd started.

When she woke up, shuddering, breathless, for the third night running, she got up, went down to make herself tea.

The falling dream again, she thought. A popular favorite in her nightmare repertoire. Her hands, a child's hands, sliding, sliding helplessly on the rope of sheets. And all the fiercely tied knots breaking away.

Falling, falling, without even the breath to scream, with the second-story window changing into a cliff, the ground turned into the thrashing sea.

They'd pass, she told herself, standing with the tea, looking out at the sea. They always did.

But at three in the morning, they exhausted.

No pills, she thought, though February often tempted her. But no pills. Her mother had used them, and often as an excuse.

I'm too tired, Caitlyn. I took a pill to help me sleep. Go tell Nina to take you shopping. I need a nap.

Why, she wondered, did a child crave the attention and affection of the very person who routinely withheld both? Like cats who wanted the lap of someone averse to them.

That craving had certainly passed.

But since she needed to sleep, as Lily left the next day for New York—which meant she had to at least *look* rested for the morning goodbyes—she'd take her tea upstairs. She'd find a movie again, and hope she could drift off.

Since drifting off came in fits and starts, the wonder of makeup and a skilled hand did the trick.

"You two keep an eye on each other. I'll know if you don't." Lily gave Cate and Hugh a wagging finger warning. "I have my spies."

"I'm taking him to a strip club tonight."

"See that you have plenty of singles." Lily checked her purse, again. "Those girls work hard."

After shutting her enormous travel purse again, Lily put her hands on Cate's cheeks. "I'll miss that face." Then turned to Hugh, did the same. "And this one."

"I expect a call when you're settled."

"You'll get one. All right, here I go." She kissed Hugh. Kissed him again before enfolding Cate in a hug and subtle clouds of J'adore.

"Knock 'em dead, Mame," Cate murmured.

Lily touched a hand to her heart, to her lips, then slid into the limo.

With Hugh, Cate stood watching the car wind down to the gate. "Alone at last," she said to make him laugh.

"She is a presence, isn't she? How long is the list she gave you about keeping an eye on me?"

"It's lengthy. How about yours for me?"

"Same. So I'll cross an item off, ask you what you're up to today."

February had opted for balmy. It wouldn't last, but for this day, this moment, the air held the teasing promise of spring. Spears of bulbs, nubs of wildflowers poked up to bask in the sun. Out at sea, a ship, white as winter, glided toward the horizon.

There were times you really should seize the day.

"I worked a couple hours, and need a couple more. Audiobook, and it's going well. Then I think it'll be a really good afternoon for a walk on the beach. You could help me cross two items off my list. How about sitting in on the recording, then taking some sandwiches or whatever and walking with me."

"Oddly, that would also cross some off my list."

He took her hand, the way he had when she'd been a little girl. And she shortened her gait for him—as he'd once done for her.

"Have you heard from your dad?"

"I did, just yesterday. It's cold and rainy in London."

"Aren't we the lucky ones? Are you happy here, Catey?"

"Of course I am. Don't I look happy?"

"You look content, which isn't quite there. One of the items on my long list is to convince you to get out, find some people your own age. Lily suggests Dillon for that."

"Does she?"

"He's lived here all his life, he has friends. Work, for us, it's essential, but it can't be all."

"Right now, it's enough for me." At the cottage, she opened the door. "I'm enjoying the quiet, the same way I enjoyed the fast pace in New York."

"Has it been quiet?"

"Grandpa, I promised I'd tell you if I get another call, and I will. Nothing since before Christmas. Now, do you want some tea to take in?"

"Is Lily far enough away for you to let me have one of your Cokes?"

"Barely." But she went to the kitchen, got one for him. "Our secret. I'm using the booth, so you can be comfortable in the main studio, and won't have to worry about noise. And you can go in and out, no problem."

"I've never heard you work—just enjoyed the results. Expect me to stick."

"Then get comfortable." She handed him headphones, plugged them in. "I'm already set up from earlier. I'm going to voice a chapter. If there are any hiccups, I'll retake. If you need something, just signal."

He angled the chair toward the booth, sat. "I'm fine. Entertain me."

She'd do her best.

She closed herself in the booth, adjusted the mic, brought up her computer monitor, and below that the text on her tablet.

Room-temperature water to hydrate the throat, the tongue, the lips. Tongue twisters to loosen up.

"Susie works in a shoeshine shop. Where she shines she sits. Where she sits she shines. Eleven benevolent elephants."

Over and over, mixed with others until she felt smooth.

She took a moment, two, to put herself back into the characters, the story, the tones, the pace.

Standing close to the mic, she hit record.

Now she played multiple roles. Not just the characters she voiced, each one demanding a distinct vocal style, not just the role of narrator outside the dialogue. But she stood as engineer, as director, keeping herself in the story she read while scanning ahead to prepare for narration, dialogue coming next, while watching the monitor to be sure she didn't lose pitch or pop or slur.

Dissatisfied, she paused, backtracked, began the paragraph of description again.

Outside the booth, Hugh listened to her voice—voices—in his head. A born performer, he thought. Just look at her facial expressions, her body language as she became each character or shifted back to that smooth, clear narration.

Part of him might hope—an admittedly selfish hope—she'd step in front of the camera again. But his girl had found her place.

Talent would out, he thought, and sipped his Coke, let his girl tell him a story.

He lost track of time, found himself surprised when she shut down. He tipped one earpiece back as she came out of the booth.

"You don't need to stop for me. I'm enjoying it."

"For this kind of work, I need to take breaks. I'll start muffing it otherwise. What did you think?"

"What I heard of it's a damn good story. I'd say I want to read it, but I think I'd like to listen to the full audio. You've got a way, Cate." He set the headphones aside. "Did you use your cousin Ethan for Chuck, the obnoxious, noisy neighbor?"

"Caught." She pulled the tie out of her hair. "Ethan's got that—I think of it as a kind of pinch in his voice."

"It works."

"So, how about I make us some sandwiches? Consuela snuck some of her ham from last night's farewell dinner into my fridge, and I baked some brown bread this morning."

Since she'd been awake before dawn.

"Sold. I don't suppose I could get another Coke?"

He knew just how to put that charming innocence on. But Cate was no fool.

"No. I'm not willing to risk Lily's wrath. If she says she has spies, she has spies."

She put together a walking picnic of thick sandwiches, the baked sweet potato chips Lily—barely—approved of for Hugh's diet, a couple of Cuties, and water bottles.

She really wanted a Coke herself, but it didn't seem fair.

As they walked down the path, then the steps toward the beach, she relaxed. The man who walked with her still moved like a dancer. Slower maybe, she thought, but still with that same easy grace.

When they reached the beach, she aimed for the old stone bench so they could sit and eat and enjoy.

No bite to the wind today to stir up white horses on the water, but air that felt more of May than of February.

"I have this memory of sitting here with Grandda. It would've been summer, and he gave me a bag of M&M's. My mother wouldn't allow candy, so he'd sneak it to me when he could. It was the best candy in the world, sitting here that bright, bright day eating M&M's with him. We had sunglasses on—I still remember mine. I was in a pink-is-everything stage, so they were pink, heart-shaped, with little sparkles in the frame."

She smiled as she bit into her sandwich. "He said we were just a couple of movie stars."

"It's a good memory."

"It really is. Now I'll have this one, with you, on a cloudless, miraculous day in February."

The towering trees of the kelp forest waved, green and gold, in the shallows, and the strip of sand sparkled—like her long-ago sunglasses—with mica.

On a huddle of rocks at the far curve of the beach, sea lions lazed. Occasionally one slid silkily into the water. To swim and feed, Cate thought, in the forest of kelp.

One sat up, big chest rising, lifted his head to let out a series of barks. It made her think of Dillon and his dogs.

"Are you really thinking of getting a dog?"

"They do sound like them, don't they?" Hugh sampled a chip. He'd rather have fried, with a lot of salt. But a man had to take what he could get. "We always worked and traveled so much, it didn't seem fair. And now Dillon brings his to visit, so we have that. Still, I've been thinking about it. It might be time to think about getting a companion for our retirement."

"Retirement." She could only roll her eyes. "Lily's on a plane to New York to do Broadway. And I know you're going to sign on to that project you mention—every day. Crazy Grandpa road trip."

Grinning, he ate another chip. "It's a comedy jewel of a part, a good supporting role. Speaking of projects, do you know if anyone's bought the rights to the book you're voicing?"

She rolled her eyes again. "Retirement."

She stretched out her legs, began to peel one of the oranges to share with him. The sharp, sweet smell hit the air like joy.

"I'll find out," she told him.

The balm didn't last, but that made the memory all the sweeter. She worked through a day of slashing rain and wild wind, took her breaks just standing and looking out at the drama.

Hugh joined her for two more sessions, and she joined him for his Lily-assigned thirty minutes of cardio in the gym.

"The leg's fine," he insisted as he worked through a brisk walk on the treadmill.

"Ten more minutes."

He scowled over as Cate ran full out on hers. "Show-off."

"Oh yeah, and after this, it's strength training day. Fifteen minutes with the weights."

He scowled again, but she knew he enjoyed it—at least when she kept him company.

"We polish it off"—she had to pause to gulp down water—"with a good stretch, and Consuela, who is definitely one of Lily's spies—can report we did our duty."

"She can see for herself when I fly out to New York next week. Are you sure you don't want to come?"

"Gotta work."

When they hit the thirty, both reached for towels and water.

For the next fifteen, he used the weight machines, and she hit the free weights. She had to admit the side benefit of keeping an eye on him, keeping him company bled over into making her feel stronger. And sleep better.

Not just because February had, finally, whipped into March, but because she just moved more.

When they polished it off with stretches, she had to shake her head. "You're still Gumby, Grandpa."

With a grin, he looked over as they both did wide-legged forward folds. "Passed it on to you."

"For which I'm grateful."

"I'm going to be in top shape when I start shooting."

She angled over to her right leg. "You took the part."

"Signed on this morning."

"When do you start?"

"The first table read's in a couple of weeks. I can fly back whenever I'm not on call. Comedy jewel," he reminded her.

She angled to the left. "What does the boss say?"

"I knew you'd ask that. Lily's fine with it." He straightened, showed off his excellent balance as well as flexibility with a quad stretch.

"Now how about we get a nice little snack?"

"It's going to be fruit and yogurt. Consuela."

Sorrow covered him. "We deserve so much more. You got any ice cream at your place?"

"I might." They started up together.

"Maybe I'll come visit you later. If you're working, I'll just, you know, make myself at home."

"One scoop, no toppings."

"What sort of toppings?"

She shook her head at him as they turned toward the kitchen.

The dogs ran out to greet them.

"Look who's here!" Delight in his voice, Hugh bent down to rub. "Did you bring your boy or drive over yourself?"

The boy sat in the kitchen with a big mug of coffee and a plate—a whole plate—of cookies.

"I want some of those."

"You get one." Consuela eyed Hugh, held up a single finger. "With skim milk."

"I just did an hour in the gym. Who's the boss around here?"

"Miss Lily is the boss. You sit. One cookie, skim milk. Two cookies for you," she told Cate. "And milk."

"Can I have it in a latte? You know I don't really—"

"A latte," Consuela said quickly, remembering.

Dillon lifted his hands as Consuela poured skim milk for Hugh. "I had some errands. I dropped off some of the things Consuela ordered while I was out. Don't blame me."

"Didn't even know we had cookies," Hugh grumbled as Consuela set one on a small plate in front of him.

"I baked while you were in the gym because my young man said he would come see me." Consuela fluttered her lashes at Dillon. "And tonight, you can have one more cookie. And you'll have steak because my handsome boy came. Some red meat is good for your blood."

"I hear that."

"The hour in the gym looks good on you. Both of you."

"This one? He doesn't need the gym. He is a working man." To prove it, Consuela squeezed Dillon's biceps. "Such arms!"

"Made to hold you, Consuela."

She giggled like a girl, had Cate staring after her as she walked to the coffee machine to make the latte.

Dillon only grinned. "Haven't seen you around the ranch in a while," he said to Cate.

"I had two big jobs back-to-back." Since they were there, she took a cookie. "I was actually thinking I'd come by later today."

"My ladies would love to see you."

"You go. You take your cookie, your latte, and go take a shower, make yourself pretty." Decision made, Consuela switched the latte to a go-cup. "You don't go out enough. Young girls should go out. Why don't you take my girl dancing?" she demanded of Dillon.

"I—" It only threw him off stride for a beat. "I've been saving my dances for you, *amor mío.*"

Nice save, Cate thought as Consuela giggled again.

"Go, go." Consuela waved at Cate. "I have my eye on this one."

"Okay, all right." She grabbed up the latte. "I'll go clean up. I'll be over soon."

She didn't take long. Still, it surprised her to find Dillon just getting in his truck when she got back to the house.

"I stretched out the time. I haven't hung out with Hugh in a while."

She paused on her way to the garage. "I think that's an excuse for you to flirt with Consuela."

"Who needs an excuse?" He climbed in. "See you in a few."

Now he had another picture, he thought as he drove. Cate in a warm-up jacket open to one of those sports bra deals—blue like her eyes—and tight pants covered with blue flowers that stopped midcalf, and left a lot of midsection exposed.

Oh, well, what was one more?

He had had errands, and had wanted to see how Hugh was doing—plus, what guy wouldn't enjoy having a sweetheart like Consuela fussing over him?

And he'd hoped, maybe, to catch a couple minutes with Cate.

Done and doomed, Dil, he thought. You are done and doomed.

He parked at the ranch, waited for her to pull up beside him. Took the container of cookies out of the truck.

"These are mine, so don't get any ideas. I'm just going to drop them off at my place. You can go right on in."

"I've never seen your place."

"Oh. Sure. Well, come on over. But these are still my cookies."

"You're not the only one who can sweet-talk Consuela out of cookies."

"So. Busy?"

"Yeah." It smelled so good here, she thought. Different from the flowers and spice and sea of Sullivan's Rest, but so good. "Plus, I'm spending a lot of time with Grandpa."

"He looks great."

"He really does. You wouldn't know he'd been laid up last year. He's heading back to L.A. in a couple weeks."

"He told me. I'm supposed to keep an eye on you."

"Which one?"

"He didn't specify."

When Dillon opened the door, Cate stepped in, took stock.

"This is so nice."

A big Navajo-style rug accented dark, wide-planked floors. Paintings of rising mountains, of sheep-dotted hills, of wild orange poppies smothering a meadow hung on walls of dark honey.

He kept it tidy, she thought, and no-fuss male. No frilly throws or fancy pillows on the navy sofa or dark gray chairs. No fancy bits on tables other than a few photos, a polished wood bowl filled with interesting rocks, a few arrowheads.

"You never know what you're going to find," he said.

"I guess not. Terrific view, too. The paddock and the sea out the front."

She wandered over to the open kitchen—glossy white appliances, roomy counters that mixed the navy and gray. "Fields, hills, horses, and all the rest out here. It was smart to angle the house so you didn't end up looking at the side of the barn."

"Stables."

"Right."

He'd set up a little office space, the workstation facing the wall dominated by a calendar and holding a computer, some files, a mug full of pens and pencils.

A floor-to-ceiling set of iron shelves held books, lots of books, with a few more photos interspersed and what she supposed he saw as acceptable ornaments.

An old spur, some sort of odd tool, some X-Men action figures.

"No TV for you?"

"Are you kidding? I'm a guy." He gestured her over.

"It's two bedrooms. I sleep on that side. Planning for way into the future, my women wanted everything on one level, with each bedroom having its own bathroom. So if and when we ever switch houses they won't kill each other."

He led her in. "They figured I'd use this as a guest room—who for, I don't know—and office space. I had other ideas."

"Yes, you did."

She supposed it qualified as a man cave, though there was nothing cave-like with the views of the ranch out the windows.

He had a beer/wine fridge, a big chocolate leather couch, a pair of recliners. The enormous flat screen on the wall dominated everything.

She circled, noticed he had both an Xbox and a Nintendo Switch. And another floor-to-ceiling shelving unit holding—very, very organized—video games and DVDs.

"A gamer, are you?"

"Not like I tried to be as a kid, but if you don't make time for fun, what's the point? Especially on long winter nights. Anyway, I've got a couple of pals who game when we have a chance. Leo's got a kid coming in a few months, so he may fall out for a while. The other's actually a game programmer. Dave kicks our asses regularly. Always did," he added, "even when we were kids."

"You've known them that long?"

"Since first grade, yeah."

Something to envy, she thought, those roots, that continuity.

She trailed a finger over the games. "You play *Sword of Astara*?"

"Hot warrior babe, swords and battles and magic spells. What's not to like?"

"I voiced her."

"You did what? Shalla? Warrior Queen? She doesn't sound like you."

"No. But I can sound like her."

Turning, face suddenly fierce, Cate mimed drawing a sword, lifting it high. "My sword for Astara!" Her voice went as fierce as her face, deeper than her own and with a hint of the Highlands. "My life for Astara!"

He wasn't sure what it said about him that hearing that voice come out of her made him want to just grab her and dive in.

He tried restraint. "Well, holy shit. I've played you dozens of times. I didn't know you did games. What else have I got?"

"Let's see. Yeah, the bubbly fairy in this one, the wicked sorcerer queen in this, and, ah, the stalwart soldier here, the smart-ass street kid here."

She turned back, amused at the way he just stared. "One of the jobs I just finished was *Sword of Astara: The Next Battle.* I might be able to get you an early copy."

He finally found his voice. "I don't suppose you want to get married?"

"It's so nice of you to ask, but we haven't even been dancing. Instead, maybe I haven't missed the afternoon milking. I really would like to see how it's done. Who knows? I may need to voice a milkmaid one of these days."

"I can help with that." He started out with her. "Does Baltar the Conqueror come back?"

"He does."

"I knew it."

She milked cows. Well, the machines milked them, she admitted, but humans played a part. She hadn't been up close and personal with a cow since childhood, and only really to watch. She judged that washing and drying udders ranked about as personal as it got.

"Good work," Dillon told her. He took off his hat, plopped it on her head. "Next step is stripping before the machines take over."

Adjusting the hat, she gave him a long look. "I'm supposed to get naked to milk cows?"

"No. But now that's an image in my head. We prime the pump, let's say. 'Stripping' just means we help them let down the milk. Like this."

He closed a lubricated hand over one of the cow's teats, drew down. "Gently. Smooth. Anything that hurts her's wrong."

She watched with delight when milk squirted into the pail.

"How do you know if it hurts?"

"Oh, she'd let you know. Here."

Taking Cate's hand, he guided it, kept his over hers. Gentle, she thought, smooth.

A little thrill fluttered inside her as the milk squirted.

Maybe several little thrills, she realized, as he crouched beside her milking stool, his body close and warm, his cheek nearly pressed to hers.

He had strong hands, she thought. Strong, hard-palmed, calloused hands. Sure ones.

Mixed with the delight of a new experience twined the surprise of finding out a milking parlor that smelled of hay and grain and cow and raw milk could, in any way, be sexy.

"You've got a good touch."

Testing both of them, Cate turned her head so their faces were barely a whisper apart. "Thanks."

She saw his gaze flick down to her mouth—just for an instant, but she saw it—before he eased back. "You're good to go. Do you want to strip her other two?"

"I've got it."

He'd felt it, too, no question. And wasn't that interesting? Wasn't that fascinating?

He'd stripped the other two cows by the time she finished the one, showed her how to attach the machines. The cows seemed largely bored by the process. One buried her head in a bucket of grain.

"They tend to get hungry after a milking."

"How do you know when they're done?"

On cue, suckers released and dropped from one of the cows. "Oh, okay, that's how. And that was fast."

"Definitely a time saver, but we're not done. Now we wash and dry the udders again, clean and sterilize the machines."

"And all that three times a day. What happens if you miss a milking?"

"You're going to have unhappy cows," he said as he worked. "They'd be uncomfortable, even start hurting. They can get mastitic. If you're going to have milk cows, goats, it's your job to look out for them. It's your duty."

"Anything that hurts is wrong."

"There you go."

"It's a lot of work, what you do." She washed udders as he'd shown her—a completely different feel after milking. "Even just this part of it. Then there's the beef cattle, the horses, and all the rest. Doesn't leave you much time for recreation."

"There's always time."

Once he'd stored the tanks, he got to work cleaning the machines. Methodically, she thought. The man was definitely methodical.

"Since Red retired, he pitches in, and it takes some of the load off. I'm a decent mechanic, and so are my ladies. He's better than all three of us. He's damn handy in the dairy kitchen, too, so I mostly get a pass there."

"But you know how to make butter, cheese, and all that."

"Sure."

"No gender bias on a ranch?"

"Not on this one. We've got a system that works. The day starts early, but once the stock's fed and bedded down for the night, there's time for whatever."

Methodical, she thought again as he stored equipment, noted something down on a hanging clipboard. He led the cows back through the parlor door, back into the pasture.

"The Roadhouse just this side of Monterey's got a live band on the weekends. Dancing."

Oh yeah, he'd felt it, too. She kept her smile internal, just glanced up at him with mild curiosity. "Do you dance?"

"I grew up in a house with two women. What do you think?"

"I think you can probably hold your own."

"Dave can't dance worth dick, but he likes to think he can. He's seeing someone. Leo and Hailey might like to have a night out before the baby comes. Would you be up for that?"

"I could be. What's the dress code?"

"It's not fancy."

Amused, she took off his hat, rose to her toes, and dropped it back on his head. "I just helped milk cows, so I'd think you'd see fancy isn't one of my requirements."

"Good. I can come by, pick you up about seven-thirty."

"That'll work."

He walked her around to the mudroom rather than the front, and spotted his mother hoeing a row in the family garden. "She's tireless."

She had her hair bundled up under a wide-brimmed hat, a half apron with deep pockets over baggy jeans. The faded T-shirt showed the muscles in her arms rippling and flexing as the sun washed down over her and the turned earth, the tidy rows of vegetables.

"She's wonderful. I know you know how lucky you are because I see it. I envy it."

Following instinct, Dillon stepped back. "She'd like some company if you've got a few minutes. I've got some things I need to see to. I'll see you Friday."

"All right. I bet I can teach your friend to dance."

With a shake of his head, Dillon walked away. "Not a chance."

"Challenge accepted," Cate murmured, then walked toward the garden and the mother she wished she had.

CHAPTER TWENTY-ONE

Cate considered her choices of not-fancy attire on Friday. She'd considered them on Thursday, and maybe looked them over, briefly, on Wednesday.

She'd dated plenty, she reminded herself. But in New York, and that was just different. And she hadn't had a date in months. Or wanted one.

She couldn't be absolutely positive Dillon termed it a date-date. More of a night out with friends? That worked, too, because she wanted the room to decide if she wanted it to be a date-date.

Relationships were so damn fraught, she thought as she looked over her choices yet again. At least hers ended up that way.

The Coopers were too important in her life to turn this into something fraught. That, she decided as she took out one of her go-to black dresses—not fancy—hit number one in the against column.

She discarded the black dress. Not fancy, but too New York.

Balancing out the number one against? That moment in the milking barn. Definitely a moment, she thought as she considered black jeans. If you didn't test the waters, you never got to swim.

Problem there? Every time she decided to swim, really swim, she ended up sinking.

She grabbed the dress she kept coming back to, one she'd bought on impulse before she'd left New York because the orange poppies that covered it made her think of Big Sur.

Not fancy, but something she thought she'd wear to a family picnic.

She opted to leave her hair down, leave it straight. It fell past her shoulders now so the lack of fuss added to the lack of fancy. Low, casual espadrille wedges, her tiniest hoops for earrings.

Taking stock in the mirror, she put herself into the role. First maybe-date in the company of his friends, in a roadhouse for dancing.

She thought it worked, and the flow of the dress would have a nice swing to it on the dance floor. Not overdressed—she hoped—but showing she'd taken some care instead of just throwing something on.

Besides, she'd fiddled around so long she didn't have time to change.

She spotted him walking down the path—right on time. Jeans and high-tops—but not the sort she'd seen him wear around the ranch. A pale green shirt, open at the collar, but one she thought of as a dress shirt that would do fine under a suit jacket with a coordinating tie.

First hurdle—dress code—cleared.

She went to the door, opened it. And liked—what woman wouldn't—the way he paused, the way he looked at her.

"California poppies work on you."

"I was hoping." After closing the door at her back, she slung her little cross-body bag on. "You're prompt. I thought I'd head up to the house, save you the walk, but you beat me to it."

"Nice night for a walk."

"Nice night period. Do you do this often?"

"Do what?"

"Go dancing."

"Not especially." Jesus, she smelled good. Why did women make themselves smell so damn good? "Unless one of my friends says, 'Hey, let's hit the Roadhouse,' I don't think about it. I'm not big on the solo hunt."

He pressed a finger to his eye. "And that sounded all kinds of wrong."

"No, it didn't. Women have wingmen, too. So, you haven't been seeing anyone?"

"Not in a while, no."

He'd borrowed Gram's car—at her insistence. ("Boy, you don't take a woman dancing first time out in a pickup truck.") He opened the passenger door, waited until she'd pulled the colorful skirts inside before closing it.

"Because?" she said when he got behind the wheel.

"Because? Oh." With a shrug, he started the engine, headed down. "I was seeing someone last year for a while, but things get busy in the summer. It just didn't suit her, so we let that slide. Hailey, that's Leo's wife, she's always trying to fix me up. It'd be annoying if I didn't like her so much."

Pleased to find yet more common ground, she settled in.

"I got that back in New York. *Oh, you've got to meet this guy*, or that guy. And I'd think: You know, I really just don't."

He flicked her a glance. "Because?"

"I'd go out with somebody in the business, it ended up being a mess. I'd go out with somebody not in the business, it ended up being a mess. Fraught," she remembered. "*Fraught's* the word that comes to mind.

"So tell me about Hailey, and the woman your other friend's bringing."

"Hailey teaches fifth grade and hits that balance between sweet-natured and steely spined on the money. Smart, funny, seriously patient. We all went to school together back in the day. She and Dave were the ones always screwing the curve for the rest of us."

Fifth grade, she thought, her personal watershed year. One she'd ended with tutors—and no childhood friends to hold through life.

"You've all known each other that long."

"Yeah. You'd have thought, back then, Hailey and Dave would've hooked up. You know, nerd love. But that never happened. And she came back from college, and Leo dropped like a stone. They're good together. Probably have some fraught in there, but they're good together."

"And Dave's date?" Had to have a grip on the cast, after all.

"Tricia. She's a craftswoman, works in wood. Damn good at it, too. Artistic. Athletic, too. Likes to hike. She and Red hit it off because she surfs. I like her. She and Dave have a nice rhythm. Except Dave has no rhythm. He has algorithms."

"We'll see about that."

He turned onto a back road, pulled into the crowded parking lot in front of what really did look like a house. Single story, though long and deep, with a flat roof.

Big bulb lights strung their way across the front eaves over a porch where a number of people stood around drinking bottles of beer.

Since the doors stood open, she heard music pumping out.

"It's already busy."

"The band'll start soon," he told her. "It's early, I guess, by what you'd be used to, but we'll have a lot of ranchers, ranch hands, farmers, farmhands. They'll be up before dawn tomorrow, Saturday or not."

She got out before he could do as he'd been taught and come around to open the door for her. She gestured to the line of motorcycles. "Ranch hands?"

"Bikers like to dance, too."

A couple of people called out his name as they walked across the gravel lot. Some of the porch people wore Stetsons or ball caps, some wore bandannas and tattoo sleeves.

Inside she saw a lot of wooden tables crowded together, a decent-size dance floor, a long bar. And a stage at the front, raised up, equipment and instruments already waiting.

She felt some mild disappointment not to see chicken wire across it, *Blues Brothers* style.

Recorded music bounced off the walls—walls decorated with beer signs, bull heads, and cowhides.

"Looks like Leo and Hailey already grabbed a table." He took Cate's hand to lead her through the tables, chairs, benches, people.

His friend Leo wore his black hair in short dreads, looked over at their approach with big, appraising brown eyes. Hailey, her honey-blond hair cut in a side swing, had one hand on the mound of her belly as she studied Cate.

Decision pending, Cate thought.

"Hey, man." Though his eyes stayed watchful, Leo offered a smile.

"Cate, this is Hailey and the guy she married instead of me."

"Somebody had to. It's nice to meet you."

"It's nice to meet you." Cate took a seat. "Coming soon?"

Hailey gave her baby bump a pat. "Eight more weeks and count-ing. The nursery's finished, Dillon. You'll have to come by and see."

"I'll do that." With the ease of an old friend, he gave her bump a rub. "How's she doing?"

"So far, so perfect. If we don't count the times—you'll excuse me," she said to Cate, "she parks herself on my bladder."

"Do you have a name?" Cate asked.

"We think Grace because—"

"She's going to be amazing."

Hailey cocked her head, and the smile went all the way into her eyes this time. "That's exactly right."

The waitress stopped by.

"House nachos," Leo told her. "Four plates."

"I thought we were going to be six."

"Dave and Tricia are always late. With luck, we'll have polished them off before they get here. Want a beer?"

"I actually don't drink beer."

After a beat of silence, Dillon turned to her. "But you're Irish."

"And a disgrace to all my ancestors. How's the house red?"

"In my before memory?" Hailey wagged a hand in the air.

"I'll risk it."

Maybe in protest, Dillon ordered a Guinness. Then he smiled. "Hugh bought me my first legal beer. A Guinness."

"He would."

"So . . ." Leo lifted his own beer. "You do, like, voice-over work."

"I do."

"And Dil said you did the voice for Shalla."

Cate all but heard Hailey roll her eyes. She leaned forward, looked deep into Leo's, called up the voice.

"We do not surrender today. We will not surrender tomorrow. We will fight until the last breath, until the last drop of blood."

Leo pointed at her. "Okay. All right. That is cool. That is seriously cool."

The crowd whistled and cheered as a group of five—four men, one woman—hit the stage. With a crash of drums, a screaming guitar riff, the live music erupted.

Hailey leaned toward Cate, spoke directly in her ear. "Be grateful the music started, and it's loud. Otherwise, he'd have wanted to hear every video game voice you've ever done."

Twenty minutes into the evening, Cate learned several things. Hailey had been right about the wine—though so-so was generous. It wasn't hard for four people to polish off a plate of nachos before the latecomers arrived.

And Dillon could dance.

When a man knew how to rock to a hard, driving beat, and had the skills to hold a woman exactly right and move to a slow, sinuous one, a logical woman had to wonder about his skills and moves elsewhere.

Plus, he had the twirl-her-out-and-snap-her-back down to a science.

When he snapped her back, heated body to heated body, slow steps silky and smooth, she tipped her head back. Faces as close as they'd been in the milking parlor, music pulsing, other bodies swaying around them.

"Your ladies taught you well, Mr. Cooper."

"Could be they had my innate skill to work with."

"Could be. But a superior teacher can't be discounted. Which I'm about to prove."

She brushed her lips lightly over his, then pulled back and away before he could make more of it.

She was killing him.

She walked back to the table on those really terrific legs where Dave tried to convince Hailey they should name the baby after him because "I'm the one who convinced Leo to get his nuts up and ask you out the first time."

Cate leaned over Dave's shoulder, quoted an icon. "Shut up and dance with me."

"Who, me? Sure!"

Tricia, earrings sparkling with flowers and fairies to her shoulders, wildly curling burgundy hair spilling past them, offered a smirk. "I hope those shoes have steel toes."

Cate already found Dave, with his Elvis Costello glasses and Ron Howard freckles, adorable.

The fact that, with the beat hot again, he moved like a malfunctioning robot on crack just made him more adorable.

He flushed pink under the freckles when Cate gripped his hips. "Use these."

"Um." He glanced back toward the table.

"Not your feet, just your hips. Tick tock, loose in the knees."

She laughed when he obediently loosened his knees enough to sink three full inches.

"Not that loose. That's the way, but let's tick and tock to the beat. Let's try an eight count, go with me. One, two, three, four, five, six, seven, eight. Close your eyes a minute, listen to the beat, try it again. Keep going, add your shoulders, just a little bop to go with the hips."

He still blushed, but he followed directions. Potential, she decided.

"I'm going to do for you what Ren did for Willard."

Dave's eyes popped open, and the blush died on a wide grin. "*Footloose!*"

"I'm your Kevin Bacon. We're going to try a two-step. Anything's possible with a two-step. Look at my feet."

He did so with (adorable) intensity. "Just like me, and just your feet. There you go, there you go, on the beat. One-two, one-two, one-two. Add your hips, loose knees. Don't stiffen up. There you are."

She had his hands now, keeping the connection. "One-two, one-two, one-two, tick-tock, tick-tock. A little shoulder now, bop, bop, loose, loose. And you're dancing."

She sent a smug look toward the table where Dillon lifted his drink in acknowledgment.

"How the holy hell did she do that?" Tricia demanded, sending the flowers and fairies at her ears spinning as she jumped up. "I'm cutting in. This may never happen again in our lifetimes."

Cate strolled back to the table. Sat, shook back her hair. "I believe I deserve another glass of wine."

About the time Cate ordered another glass of wine, Red drove away from the ranch and along the coast. Maggie had her monthly hen party—not that he'd ever call it that within her hearing for the very basic reason he liked his balls just where they were.

Sometimes when the house filled with women, he hung out with Dillon, had a couple beers, watched some tube. But since the boy had himself a date—and anybody who hadn't seen it coming didn't have eyes in their head—he decided he'd spend a night at his own place.

He might even put on a wet suit and take his board out in the morning.

It suited him, just like it suited Maggie, for him to keep his own place. They'd been together, in their way, about twenty years now by his reckoning. And they liked their way just fine.

He had himself an independent, opinionated woman, and through her had the family he'd missed building for himself in his youth.

A part of him missed the police work, and always would, but he'd discovered a real affinity for ranch life. He'd come to depend on sitting around the table at the end of the day, eating things he'd helped raise and grow and make.

A bone-deep satisfaction.

He had the windows open to the sea-swept air, and found some classic Beach Boys on the satellite radio to put him in the mood for a morning surf. He had a pint of fresh milk in the little cooler for his morning coffee, along with some bacon, a couple of eggs he'd cook up after he caught a few waves.

He figured he'd stop by and see Mic before he headed home.

The little bungalow outside of town was his place. The ranch was home.

But part-time rancher or not, he'd been a cop a long time. Any cop with a brain knew when he was being tailed. Especially when the tail wasn't any damn good at it.

He watched the headlights in his rearview, how they kept the same distance whether he eased off the gas or punched it a little.

He figured he'd made a few enemies along the way, but none he could look back on who'd care enough to want to cause him serious harm.

Maybe somebody took a shine to his truck. Force him to the shoulder, rob him, leave him stranded—maybe kick his ass for good measure. Or worse.

Not the sort of thing that happened along this stretch as a rule, he thought as he took his nine-millimeter Glock out of the glove compartment, checked the load, laid it within easy reach.

If they tried anything, they'd be in for a hell of a surprise.

He considered calling it in, then considered he might be having a paranoid old man moment.

Then the headlights leaped forward, and he knew his cop instinct hit bull's-eye.

He punched it. He'd driven this road all his damn life, knew every curve and bend.

But he hadn't expected to see a man—black, red do-rag, indeterminate age—rear out of the passenger window with a goddamn semiauto.

The first volley shattered his rear window, peppered his tailgate.

Definitely not a carjacking. They wanted him dead.

He gripped and whipped the wheel, drove the accelerator to the floor. The car—a freaking Jag he saw now as it skidded on the turn—fishtailed, fought for control, found it.

Creek coming up. He envisioned it, the way the road would veer toward the canyon, ride the bridge, veer back toward the sea.

He gained a little distance there, just a little. But the Jag kept coming, and so did the bullets.

He had to ease off the gas to navigate one of the blind turns, then headlights streaming toward him blinded him for an instant. He watched the oncoming sedan swerve, bump the shoulder as he roared past.

And hoped they had the sense God gave a moron and called it in, as he was a little too occupied to do so himself.

The Jag had the speed, it had the muscle, but its driver didn't have the skill. The wasp-sting bite along his right shoulder told Red he needed to put that to the test.

He had the drop to the sea on his right, the cliff wall on his left, and a hairpin coming up only a desperate man would take at seventy miles an hour.

He took it at seventy-five, fighting to control the truck that tried to two-wheel it on him while his shoulder burned and bullets blew through the shattered window.

Behind him, the Jag lost its grip, overcompensated. And flew, just fucking flew over the guardrail.

His tires screamed and smoked when Red hit the brakes. He smelled burning rubber and blood—his own—as he battled the truck to a spinning stop. Behind him the smash and grind of glass and metal screamed. His hands trembled—he could admit that—as he loosened his death grip on the wheel, pulled over.

As he raced down the skinny shoulder, the explosion rocked the air. Fire seared it. He looked down at the twists of metal, the roar of flames, and calculated the chances of a survivor next to zero.

As cars began pulling over, he slid the gun in his hands to the back of his waistband.

"Keep clear," he shouted. "I'm a cop."

Or close enough, he thought.

He pulled out his phone.

"Mic, it's Red. I've got a serious problem out here on Highway 1."

And bending over, bracing his hands on his thighs as he pulled his breath back, he gave her the gist.

Along with cops, the fire department, paramedics, she came herself. Crime scene, accident detail, all of that went on around him. First responders, rappelling or climbing down the cliff to the wreckage, lights blasting and spinning.

She stood beside him while one of the medics treated his shoulder.

She had a husband now, and two kids—good kids—wore her hair in rows of braids that ended on a long tail of them.

And had put on the uniform before coming out. Because she was Mic, he thought, and would always choose structure.

He glanced down at his shoulder as whatever the medic did increased the sting. But he offered Mic a smile.

"Just a flesh wound."

"You really see this as the time to quote some old B Western?"

"I was going more for Monty Python. Just nicked me, and trust me, I know I'm damn lucky. Best guess is the shooter—black, slim build, passenger seat—used an AR-15. Tailed me a couple miles before they made the move. Can't give you dick on the driver, except he didn't know how to handle the Jag, so it's probably stolen. Add I don't know anybody who can afford a Jag who'd want to shoot me dead."

"You know anybody else who would?"

"Damn if I do, Mic." He closed his eyes a moment. The adrenaline was long gone. He felt shaky and a little sick. "They had to see me leave Horizon."

"You already said that. I've got men checking on them now."

"Right."

"You're a little shocky, Mr. Buckman."

Red studied the medic, remembered him as a teenager, skateboarder, a little bit of a troublemaker.

God, he was old.

"Getting shot at will do that. Sure could use a beer."

"Do you want to take him in?" Mic asked the medic.

"I'm not going to the hospital for a graze on the shoulder and some normal reaction for not getting a bullet in the head."

"He's okay, Sheriff. He shouldn't drive though."

"What am I going to drive?" Seriously aggrieved, Red pointed at his truck. "Look what they did to my baby. I only bought that bastard last fall."

"You know we have to take it in."

"Yeah, yeah. Thanks, Hollis," he said to the medic. "Good work."

When Mic's radio squawked, she stepped away while the once troublemaking skateboarder lectured Red about seeing his own doctor, changing the bandage, looking out for infection.

"I got it. I got it." Red pushed up, walked to Mic. "What's going on?"

"They've got a live one. He must've been thrown clear. He's uncon-scious, busted up, but he's breathing. Found the weapon, too. AR-15."

"I still got the eye." He sighed when the tow truck pulled up.

"Is there anything you want to get out of the truck before we take it in?"

"Yeah, I got a cooler in there, spare clothes. Fucking fuck, Mic."

"Get your stuff. I'll have someone drive you back to Horizon."

Maybe a little sick, maybe a little shaky, he thought, but goddamn. "Hey, I'm in this. I am this."

"Your family's going to be worried about you, Red. They're going to worry until they see you."

Family. She had it right.

"I need to—"

"You don't have to ask," she interrupted. "What I know, you'll know."

She insisted on structure, on procedure and discipline. But she reached out, hugged him hard. "I'm glad you didn't get shot in the head."

"Me, too."

CHAPTER TWENTY-TWO

By the time Dillon drove that stretch of road a couple hours later, only some barricade lights, some police tape, a single cruiser remained.

"There must've been an accident."

He nodded, and since cops remained, figured it for a bad one, one they needed to wait until first light to fully investigate.

"Red'll know. He's probably staying at his place tonight. My ladies had their monthly book club, political activist, feminist celebration tonight."

"All that?"

"And more. Red either hangs at my place or heads to his own."

"I may have to join. Gram mentioned it before, but . . . I'm usually not a joiner. Meeting your friends makes me think I could crack that window a little more."

"They liked you. I'd know if they didn't."

Curious, she studied his profile. "Would you tell me if they didn't?"

"No. I just wouldn't mention it."

Just lightly, just perfectly buzzed off cheap wine, she snuggled back in the seat. "I liked them, too."

"Would you tell me if you didn't?"

"No. I just wouldn't mention it. Seriously, it's just really lovely to have friends that go back so far with you, who've shared so much with you. And are still willing to open the door to new people."

When he paused at the gates, Cate used her remote to open them.

"You earned major points—like super points—for teaching Dave to move like an actual person instead of one without any working joints suffering an electric shock."

She had to laugh, as he'd slam-dunked the description—before her lessons. "He's got a sweetness. It's what draws the esoteric and freewheeling Tricia to him."

When he parked, she got out—deliberately, so he'd have to follow suit. "I'm sure your ladies taught you to walk a woman to her door."

"They did."

"It's so nice at night, isn't it? The sounds, the air. I never spent much time here during the spring. Just quick visits. I'm loving being here through the change of seasons, really seeing it."

Moonlight bathing the water, starlight sprinkled over the shadows of the mountains, the steady whoosh and slap of the sea.

They passed the pool, its little dollhouse, the charm of tangled bougainvillea.

"Your mother's going to show me how to plant some herbs, in pots, that I can play with. I've never actually planted anything."

"Watch yourself or she'll make a rancher out of you."

"No danger of that, but maybe I can keep a pot of basil alive."

The path lights gleamed low, as did the patio light she'd left on to show the way.

"Every time I see a light in the dark, I think of you and your family. That memory has been a light for me for a long time."

The truth of that had her taking his hand, his good, strong hand.

"And now you've added another. Dancing at a roadhouse, questionable wine, excellent nachos, really good friends."

She turned to him at the door. "I'm going to have to find a way to reciprocate."

"You could sleep with me and we'd call it even."

"Hmm." She opened the door she hadn't bothered to lock. "That's quite a bartering technique you have there. Does it ever work?"

"It's a trial run."

"Well then." With the door open behind her, she gave him a long study. "Let's test it out."

"I didn't actually—"

"Talk later." She took a fistful of his shirt, pulled him in.

Before he found his balance, she hooked an arm around his neck, shoved the door closed with the other. And latched her mouth onto his.

It was there, all there, everything he'd imagined too many times and for far too long. The give of her, the strength of her. The taste of her, too potent for sweet, and warm, already so warm it bordered on hot.

Nothing coy here, and everything that left a man aching for the rest.

He had to have the rest.

He swept her up, and for one terrible instant he feared he'd gone too far, too fast, because she stared at him with shock widening her eyes.

"Oh my God." Then her hands fisted in his hair; her mouth covered his like a fever. "Every man should be raised by women. Upstairs. First room on the right."

She slid her mouth down to his neck, used her teeth.

"You smell so damn good," he managed as he climbed the stairs. "Don't change your mind or I'll have to hang myself."

"But no pressure," she murmured, and moved up to his ear.

He turned to the right, to the view of the sea through the glass. He hit the light with his elbow, noted the dimmer, eased it down to a glow.

"Jesus, you're good." Already half-desperate, she scraped her teeth over his jaw. "We've barely started and you're really good."

"But no pressure."

He stood her on her feet at the side of the bed with its thick, towering, turned posts. A moment, he thought, he needed just a moment to breathe, to etch this new picture of her in his head.

Cate in her pretty dress with the night sky, the dark sea behind her.

He wanted to remember her, in this light, wanted to undress her and feel her skin under his hands.

He reached around for the zipper of her dress, forced himself to lower it slowly.

Her hands flew to his shirt, dragging buttons open. "Can we save slow for the second round?"

Possibly, just possibly, he fell the rest of the way in love with her at that moment. "I'm a hundred percent behind that."

They pulled at clothes, grappled with them, hands everywhere while mouths met, urgent and avid, parted with quickened breaths.

When the pretty dress dropped to the floor, she kicked it aside.

Hard, his body so hard, so roped with muscle. And his hands, hard, fast, deliberate. Those hands made her blood sing under her skin, reminded her what it was to crave another's touch. The way they closed over her breasts, the way his calluses slid rough over her nipples.

When she lay under him, the moonlight streaming, the sea whispering, she found his mouth again, poured that need into him.

"Now, just now. Don't wait."

"I want—" Everything, he thought. "Look at me. Look at me."

When she did, with those deep, deep blue eyes, he drove into her.

Heard her cry, the catch of her breath on the end of it. Saw her eyes go deeper yet as her arms, her legs locked around him.

Fast, driving her, driving himself as the years of pent-up fantasies ripped through him, then tattered in the wonder of reality. She raged with him, beat for frenzied beat even when her eyes glazed over with an orgasm.

She shuddered with it, but didn't stop.

Her hands clutched at his hair, dragged his mouth down to hers again. "More. More. More."

He gave her more, and more, still more until she cried out again, until her hands slid away and her body went limp. Then he buried his face against her throat, drew her scent in, and let himself break.

She lay sweaty, soft, and oh-so-wonderfully sated. She felt his heart pounding against hers, yet another wonderful sensation.

When he rolled over, bringing her with him, she realized she could breathe again. And her breath came out in a long, satisfied sigh.

"I've wanted to do that for a while," he told her.

"You're good at keeping things to yourself. I wasn't all the way sure until you were showing me how to milk—what's the cow's name I started on?"

"Bossie."

"You're making that up."

"There has to be a Bossie in a milk cow herd. It's the law."

"If you say so." Trailing a hand over his chest, she thought of the boy he'd been, the skinny build.

He'd filled out just fine.

"Until then."

"I didn't want to mess things up."

"Me either. We'll have to talk about that."

"Right now?"

"Maybe not right now, because I need about a gallon of water."

"I'll get it." He sat up, looked down at her. Another image for his collection, he thought. Caitlyn, naked in starlight. "I've got a lot of pictures of you in my head."

Her eyes, her lips gave him a sleepy, satisfied smile. "Do you?"

"This might be my favorite one. I'll be right back."

She lay as she was when he went downstairs, and realized she had a number of pictures of him in her head, too. Starting with the one of the skinny kid coming down the back steps to raid the refrigerator.

Something to think about, she decided. Later. She didn't want to think tonight.

She sat up when she heard him coming back up the steps, realized every inch of her felt soothed and smoothed.

He paused at the doorway, bottles of water in his hands. "You really are so beautiful."

She followed her heart, opened her arms.

His internal clock woke him before sunrise with Cate sleeping warm beside him. She had an arm flung over him, and he could smell her hair, feel the long length of her leg pressed to his.

There were moments, rare ones for him, when ranching had real disadvantages.

This ranked as number one.

But he slid out of bed to dress quietly in the dark. Because he couldn't quite remember furniture placement—he'd been a little pre-occupied—he sat on the floor to put on his shoes.

She stirred.

"It has to be the middle of the night."

"No, just really early in the morning. Go back to sleep."

"Count on it. Travel cups in the, uh, cabinet to the left of the coffee maker."

"Thanks." He got to his feet, leaned over the bed. Brushed at her hair, kissed her. "I want to see you again. Like this."

Shifting, she drew him down for another kiss. "Is tonight too soon?"

"Not for me."

"Good. You can experience my reasonably amazing pasta from my limited culinary repertoire."

"Really? You want to cook?"

"Tonight I do, because I want to see you again. Like this. And going out takes too much time."

"You're going to have to seriously think about marrying me. How about seven?"

"That works. Good night," she added and rolled over.

He went downstairs, made coffee. He drank it, thinking of her, on the drive home.

Maybe he'd toss out that marriage thing, all casual, now and then. That way she might not be shocked when he actually asked her.

She really needed to marry him. Not only because he was crazy in love with her, but because they just worked. If she needed time to fall for him, well, he had time.

He drove up the ranch road, caught the gleam of the downstairs light through the window. He'd never given a lot of thought to fate, but he decided fate had guided Cate toward that light so many years before.

To the light, and to him.

He parked, went into his house. As he showered, changed, grabbed something to eat, he went over the work for the day. Feed and water, move any stabled horses out to pasture. And it was time to herd the beef cattle from Marvel Field to Hawkeye Field, let them graze on fresh grass and get busy fertilizing.

He'd ride Beamer for that job, take the dogs. A good day for all.

He'd tap Red for washing out water tanks, mucking out the stalls, hauling some hay.

Then he had to supervise the seasonals with the plantings.

His mother would handle the pigs and chickens. And between her and Gram, they'd deal with the morning and afternoon milkings.

He'd take the evening.

Needed to put in some time working with a couple of yearlings, but he had it since his ladies handled the co-op deliveries most Saturdays.

He grabbed a light denim jacket, went out to start the day.

By the time the sun bloomed over the hills, he had the horses fed, watered, and out grazing. Since the dogs came running, he knew his ladies—who'd kept them for him the night before—were up and about.

When he opened the gate between pastures, the dogs knew just what it meant. They raced back, barking, scrambling to help herd the cattle.

Just as happy as the dogs, Dillon rode back at an easy trot to join the roundup.

It took a solid hour—there were always some who didn't think the grass was greener. He ditched the jacket in a saddlebag as the day warmed and his body heated.

The air filled with the mutter of equipment, the scent of manure as a couple of hands spread fertilizer over a field.

He heard the chickens humming and scratching at feed, the pigs snorting over their own. Over the rumbling roll of the sea, a gull cried before winging away.

From the saddle, he watched a falcon circle on a hunt.

His dogs wrestled in the grass while in the near pasture a couple of foals frolicked like any kid on a Saturday morning.

As far as he could see, his world was as perfect as perfect got.

He didn't see Red's truck, so figured his unofficial ranch hand either slept in or found a wave to ride. Which meant he'd start cleaning stalls on his own.

Beamer drank while he unsaddled him, toweled him down,

checked his hooves. He led him to the paddock, as he'd ride him out to check the fields later, then he headed into the stables.

He found his mother mucking out.

"I've got this," he began, only to feel a quick clutch in his guts when she turned to him.

For a woman of seemingly limitless endurance, she looked exhausted. Her eyes, bruised with fatigue, were sunken against a face pale from lack of sleep.

"What's wrong? Are you sick?" He took her arm with one hand, laid his other on her brow. "Is it Gram?"

"No, and no. It's Red. He's all right," she added quickly. "I need to work, honey, I need to work and keep my hands busy while I tell you."

She forked soiled hay into the barrow, the brim of her hat tipped low so he couldn't see her face.

"When he was driving home last night, two men in a stolen car . . . they shot his truck up."

She might have said aliens beamed Red up to Mars for the sense it made to him. "They—what? Is he hurt? Where is he?"

"They grazed his arm. He keeps saying it's just a graze, but we'll see for ourselves when we change the bandage. The police brought him back here because he wouldn't go to the hospital."

"He's here." Okay, that settled the worst fears. "Mom, you should've called me."

"Nothing you could do, Dillon. Really nothing we could do except look after him as much as he'd let us. He's more upset about the damn truck."

She stopped, leaned on the pitchfork. "He said they were shooting with one of those semiautomatic rifles, and trying to run him off the cliff."

"Jesus Christ. Does he know them? Does he know why?"

Her exhausted eyes on Dillon's, Julia shook her head. "They're the ones who ended up going over. One of them's dead, and the other's in a coma the last we heard. The police identified the one in a coma, and Red doesn't know him. It'll take longer to identify the other because he . . . the car exploded. His body's burned.

"It could've been Red down there, burned beyond recognition at the bottom of the cliff."

She cried without shame when happy, or deeply touched. But when immeasurably sad, she kept her tears private. Hearing them now, Dillon took the pitchfork from her, set it aside.

Gathered her in.

"He's like a father to me."

"I know." As he soothed her, a woman who so rarely needed soothing, he struggled to bank his own fear, and a terrible anger. "We'll take care of him, the three of us, whether he likes it or not."

"Or not." She managed a watery laugh. "Very seriously or not. I need to be grateful, we all need to be grateful he's alive and well enough to bitch at us because we're hovering."

She clung to Dillon another minute. "I'm so glad you're here."

"I'm sorry I wasn't."

"No, no, I didn't mean that." She drew back, laid her hands on his face. "But right now it's sure good to lean on my boy. You were with Caitlyn."

"Yeah."

When she nodded, reached for the pitchfork again, he stilled her hand.

"Is that a problem?"

"I already love her. She's easy to love, but even if she wasn't, I'd love her because you do."

"It shows?"

"I see your heart, Dillon, always have."

With her face tipped to his, she laid a hand over his heart.

"She's the only one I've ever known who could break it, because she's the only one who's mattered, really mattered to you. On the other hand, she's the only one who's ever put that light in you. So I'm torn between being happy and being worried. That's my job."

"I'm going to marry her."

Julia opened her mouth, then took a breath, scooped more hay. "Did you let her know that?"

"Did you raise a stupid son?"

Her lips curved a little. "I did not."

"I know how to take my time, and as much as she needs. The only way she'll break my heart is if I'm not what she needs. And I am."

"I also raised a confident son."

"I see her, Mom, who she is. She sees me. She might need some time to see us. I can wait."

He walked over, got another pitchfork. "I've got this. Go hover. I'll be along to take my shift there by lunchtime."

"Gram's got him for now. She's more pissed than he is, if that's possible. You and I know there's no fighting Gram when she's on a tear."

"He hasn't got a chance."

"Not in heaven or hell. So we'll get this done, then do a team hover."

Cate slept late—hello, Saturday—decided she'd go up to the main house. She'd talk her grandfather into a walk. Around the gardens, maybe down to the beach. She'd give him a break from the gym, but still have him moving.

They'd have some lunch before she came back, got some dough rising, looked over her next script. That would leave her plenty of time to fuss with herself, make the pasta—and maybe do the whole scene. Light candles, pick out some music, set a pretty table.

Maybe she'd been half-asleep when she'd asked him to dinner, but that was fine. They needed to talk, of course. And after the talk, after the meal, she wanted him back in her bed.

How nice to remember she liked sex, had some talent for it. And how being intimate with a man she cared about gave her all this positivity and energy.

She pulled on black leggings, a white tee that skimmed her hips, and old sneakers she wouldn't mind getting wet and sandy during that walk on the beach.

She grabbed her phone because Darlie had sent a little video of her baby—and Cate's unofficial godchild—Luke giggling when he knocked over a tower of blocks. Maybe she and Grandpa would make Luke a little vid. He was a year old now, and Cate wanted him to know her.

She thought of her friend as she walked up the path. And of the friends Dillon had held close most of his life. It took effort, she admitted, to hold friends close. Maybe she could convince Darlie to bring the baby for a weekend. Dawson, too, of course. Husbands couldn't be excluded.

But more, she wanted to see Darlie and the baby, show them the family home, show them the ranch. Introduce them to Dillon.

The more she thought of it, the more she wanted it. She started to text Darlie, just to put it out there. Then saw Michaela Wilson getting out of the sheriff's cruiser.

"Sheriff Wilson." Waving, Cate quickened her pace. "I don't know if you remember me."

"Sure I do. It's good to see you again, Ms. Sullivan."

"Come on. I'm Cate." Cate accepted the outstretched hand. "Absolutely Cate."

"And it's Michaela."

"Did you come to see Grandpa? I'll walk you in."

"Actually, I hoped to talk to both of you."

"Great."

She led the way in and over to the main parlor. "Have a seat. I'll go find out where he is. Would you like coffee?"

"If it isn't too much trouble."

"You'll give him an excuse to have some. I'll be right back."

Michaela didn't sit, but took the time to wander the space. She'd visited the house more than a few times over the years, at Hugh's or Lily's invitation. And often brought the boys swimming, again at invitation.

But she never failed to marvel at the place. The way it perched on the hill in its tiers and layers, the way it managed to exude a feeling of home and warmth even with what she considered the elegance.

When Cate hurried back in, Michaela thought much the same of her. A lot of warmth, and despite the casual clothes, innate elegance.

"Coffee's coming, and so's Grandpa." She nodded toward the window. "Never fails, does it?"

"No, it doesn't. It must feel good to be back, to be home, to see the ocean every day."

"Yes, to all of that. I honestly didn't know how much I missed it until I got back. Does it feel good to be sheriff?"

"Big shoes to fill. I'm doing my best."

"From what Red says, you fill them just fine." Cate gestured to a chair, but didn't miss the slight, the subtle change in Michaela's face. "Is something—"

She broke off when Hugh came in. Good stride, no favoring of the leg. And welcome all over his face.

"What a nice surprise! How are those boys of yours?"

"They're great, thanks. Their dad's in charge today. Little League game. I'm sorry to intrude on your weekend."

"Don't be silly." Waving that off, Hugh sat. "You're always welcome, and you know I expect to see those boys in the pool once it warms up a bit more."

"They'll love it. But this isn't really a social call."

She let that hang when Consuela brought in the coffee, along with a plate of bite-size pieces of coffee cake. "Good morning, Sheriff. Mr. Hugh, only one cake for you."

"They're small."

"Only one."

"I've got this, Consuela." Cate rose to pour the coffee. "And him."

"They unite against me." He waited until Consuela left the room. "Is this official business?"

"Yes. There was an incident last night. Red was injured. He's fine. He's at Horizon Ranch." She took the coffee from Cate. "Two men in a car stolen outside of San Francisco pursued him on Highway 1, northbound, after he left the ranch to go to his place. They opened fire on him."

"They—" The cup and saucer rattled together as Cate offered them to Hugh. "Shot at him?"

"With an AR-15. His truck's riddled. He sustained a minor wound to his left arm."

"He's been shot!" Hugh gripped the arms of his chair, started to push up.

"It's a minor injury. Hugh." Michaela's tone switched from objective cop to friend. "I can reassure you on that because I was there when he was examined, when the wound was treated."

"He could've been—"

"Could've been," Michaela agreed. "But he wasn't. We're still reconstructing, but from what we have, Red was able to outmaneuver them, and as they were unable to control the stolen car at such a high rate of speed, they jumped the guardrail, went over the cliff."

"We saw—last night Dillon and I were driving back from the Roadhouse. We saw the barricades. We thought there'd been an accident. He's all right, you said. He's really all right?"

"Minor injury, lower right shoulder, upper right biceps, treated on-site. The other two weren't so lucky. The first was DOS—dead on scene. The second died this morning in the hospital without regaining consciousness."

"There's a reason you're telling us," Hugh commented.

"We were able to identify the second man—the shooter—who died this morning. Jarquin Abdul. Is that name familiar to either of you?"

"No," Hugh said as Cate shook her head.

Michaela took out her phone, brought a mug shot on-screen. "This is Abdul. The photo's about three years old. Do you recognize him?"

Cate took the phone, studied the photo of an angry-eyed man of color with a shaved head and a thick goatee. With another shake of her head, she passed the phone to Hugh.

"I've never seen him before, or not that I remember. Should we?"

"He's out of L.A., has done some time. Gang related. He's been out about a year now." She took the phone back, put it away. "It'll take some time to identify the other man through dental records and DNA."

"That's not the answer," Cate murmured.

"I'm looking at some angles. There have been two murders and this attempted since November. Frank Denby was killed in prison. Charles Scarpetti was killed in his home in L.A. Now Red."

"They're all connected to me. To the kidnapping," Cate corrected.

She had to set her coffee down, grip her hands together to keep them still and calm.

"Almost two decades ago," Hugh pointed out. "Are you saying they were killed by these two men who tried to kill Red?"

"No, I don't believe that. But the connection's there. Whoever killed Denby was most likely another inmate, or someone in the prison system who had access to him. The LAPD has eliminated robbery as a motive for Scarpetti's murder. They're pursuing the theory of revenge killing. Someone he represented who got sent over, a victim of someone he got off. That's not panning out. With Red added, we're looking into the possibility all three were hired out."

Connecting dots wasn't hard when they stared back at you. "Someone who'd pay to have people connected to my kidnapping killed. But why?"

"Revenge still works."

Unable to sit, Cate pushed up, walked to the glass to look out blindly at the sea. "You think my mother may have done this."

"Has she attempted to contact you since you came back to Big Sur?"

"No. She knows better by now. She gets in little digs now and again, through the press. That's her way. I can't see her doing this." On a hiss of breath, Cate pressed her fingers to her eyes. "Then again, who would have seen her doing what she did to start all this? But . . ."

She turned back, looked at her grandfather. Hated to see the stricken look in his eyes. "She has all the money in the world now. It may sound dramatic, but if she wanted someone dead, she could hire a professional. She wouldn't need a thug from a gang in L.A. How would she know how to hire someone like that? And what does it gain her? She's about what it gains her, personally."

"There's a cruelty in her," Hugh said. "A calculated cruelty. But like Cate, I can't see her doing this, only because it offers her nothing. And if she wanted revenge? She wouldn't have waited so long."

"You're connected." Cate swung around to Michaela. "You, the Coopers. Gram. My God."

"I'm a trained police officer, like Red. And like Red, I can take care of myself. As to the Coopers, I'm going over to speak with them, with Red. But if Charlotte Dupont isn't involved, I'd look to her as the next target. You found the Coopers that night, Cate, they didn't find you. I'm not saying they shouldn't take precautions, be careful."

"Dad. G-Lil."

"Again, if Dupont's not involved, they didn't have a part in it. They'll be informed, this morning, but they weren't part of the kidnapping, they weren't investigators, lawyers. It's a theory," Michaela stressed.

"Grant Sparks."

"I intend to make a trip to San Quentin, speak with him. Get a sense. He has a record of being a model prisoner. I don't fully subscribe to model prisoners."

"But how could he arrange this from prison?" Cate demanded. "He couldn't even competently kidnap and hold a ten-year-old."

"What better place to hire killers than a facility that holds them? Again, it's a theory." Michaela set down her coffee. "And I know it's upsetting. If these were random, unconnected acts—"

"You don't think they are," Cate interrupted.

"I don't. I'll do my best to find and stop the source. Let me know if anyone contacts you, or attempts to, that feels out of line, if you feel uneasy about anything."

"The calls, Catey."

Michaela's eyes narrowed, flattened. "What calls?"

"They've been going on for years." Because she wanted to dismiss them, Cate reached for her coffee again. Calm and steady. "Recordings, various voices—my mother's is often in there, from movie dialogue—music, sounds."

"Threats?"

"They're meant to be threatening, meant to scare and upset me."

"When did they start?" The notebook came out.

"When I was seventeen, still in Beverly Hills. They come intermittently, months pass, sometimes more than a year. The last one came right before Christmas."

"Why didn't you report it?"

"I did. Detective Wasserman, in New York. I— Most of the calls happened when I lived in New York. I sent him the voice mail. The calls aren't long enough to trace, and they say it's a prepaid cell."

"I'd like Detective Wasserman's contact information."

"I— All right." Taking out her phone, Cate called up the number, gave it to Michaela.

"If you get another, I need you to inform me."

"I will. I'm sorry. I'm used to telling Detective Wasserman. I didn't think past that."

"No problem. You said your mother's voice is on some of them?"

"All, actually. Sometimes my voice—from a movie or my voice work." When her fingers wanted to twist together, Cate stopped them, ordered them to still. "I can tell you it's amateur work, poor overdubbing, a lot of noise, lousy splicing and editing. Still, they're effective."

"Other than these calls, have there been any threats, any attempts to harm you?"

"No, not me. The first year I lived in New York, two men attacked and beat up a boy I was seeing. They used racial slurs, they used my name when they hurt him. Detective Wasserman and—she's now Lieutenant Riley—investigated the attack, and I told them about the calls. They did what they could."

"Did they identify and apprehend the assailants?"

"No. Noah, the boy, couldn't remember what they looked like, wasn't sure he'd even seen them before they jumped him."

"All right." She'd get details from Wasserman. Michaela rose. "I appreciate the time, and the information. I need to follow up with Red."

"You tell him I'll be over to see him for myself, see if he's faking to get a bigger share of pie."

With a grin for Hugh, Michaela nodded. "He does love his pie."

"I'll walk you out." Cate got up, squeezed her grandfather's shoulder, then walked with Michaela outside.

"My grandfather's going to New York in a couple days, to visit Lily, take some meetings. My father's in London. I think they're all safer away from here."

"Do you feel safe here?"

"Yes. No. I don't know," she admitted. "I'd stopped thinking about it. But this is home now, and I need to stay."

"Whether I'm right or wrong, I'll keep you updated."

"Tell Red . . . tell him we're thinking about him."

As Michaela drove away, Cate looked toward the garage, toward the old California bay. One day, she thought, one moment, one innocent game.

How was it that day, that moment, that game never seemed to end?

CHAPTER TWENTY-THREE

She took the walk with Hugh through gardens so happy in spring they seemed to dance, but walked the beach alone to give herself time to think. To let the salty breeze off the Pacific clear her head.

Hide-and-seek, she thought again. Just a game. But then again, she'd done just that ever since. She'd hidden—or been hidden in Ireland. She'd hidden behind the walls of her grandparents' estate, behind studio security. She'd sought, yes, she had sought, but she'd hidden in the crowds and anonymity of New York.

She'd keep seeking—that was life. But she was done hiding.

She'd told Michaela this was home. She'd meant it.

L.A. would never be home, for so many reasons. New York had been a needed transition, an education, a place to come into her own.

Ireland was, and would always be, a comfort.

But if she stuck a pin on a map to choose a place to plant herself, to be herself, know herself? It would stick right here, here with the sea thrashing on the rocks, rolling green to blue. Here, with the kelp forest of her own pretty beach waving, the magic of seeing a whale sound or a sea otter sleek under the waves.

Here, with the cliffs and the hills, the chaparral and redwoods, the sight of a California condor winging across the wide, wide bowl of the sky, or a peregrine dive out of it.

Here was family—real family—and the chance to create the rest of her life. No one would drag her away from it again, no one could force her to cut and run again.

So she walked back to her house, did what made her happy.

She made bread dough, set it to rise. While it did, she closed herself in her studio to work for an hour, to do what actors did—become someone else for an hour.

She dealt with the dough, set it for a second rising, set her phone alarm to remind her before walking to the main house and enlisting Consuela.

If she was making dinner for a man she'd just slept with, it was going to be a damn good dinner. And that was no time to attempt to make tiramisu for the first time, on her own.

She ended up with a happy hour with Consuela in the guest-house kitchen with Consuela instructing, approving (or clucking her tongue), and guiding her through a process that didn't seem nearly as anxiety-ridden as she'd expected.

Consuela nodded (approval) at the loaves of bread cooling on the rack. "You do well making your own. It's . . ." She paused to think. "Therapeutic. That's a good word."

"It is for me."

"Next time, you make the tiramisu the night before. It's even better. Now, be sure you set a pretty table. He will bring you flowers."

"I'm not sure about that. It was a casual invitation." Before I really woke up, she thought.

Consuela folded her arms. "He will bring you flowers if he is worthy. If they're short, you put them on your pretty table. If they're tall, you put them there."

"I was going to go out and get some." At Consuela's fierce stare, Cate felt her shoulders hunch. "But I won't."

"Good. When he makes you dinner, you take wine. When you make for him, he brings flowers. It's correct. You have sex with him?"

"Consuela!"

The housekeeper waved away Cate's laughing exclamation. "He's a good man. And *muy guapo, sí*?"

Cate couldn't deny Dillon was very handsome. "*Sí.*"

"So I'll put clean sheets on your bed, and there you can put your own flowers. *Pequeña*," she added, using her hands to indicate small size. "*Bonita y fragante.* You go cut from the gardens while I change the sheets."

Experience told Cate that arguing with Consuela wasted time and breath and never resulted in a win. She went out to the gardens with her directive of pretty and fragrant for a small bedroom arrangement.

Baby roses, freesia, some sprigs of rosemary seemed to hit the mark—and met with Consuela's approval. And Cate pleased her by wrapping a loaf of fresh bread in a cloth and making it a gift of appreciation.

By the time she had her sauce simmering, Cate realized she'd spent the bulk of the day not thinking about the bombshell Michaela had dropped that morning.

So a good day, she decided as she set that pretty table. A good day at home, a good day just being Cate. She put some music on, opened some red wine to let it breathe.

Looking around, she caught herself nodding like Consuela. It made her laugh at herself as she went up to fulfill the housekeeper's last directive. She needed to change into something pretty, but not fancy, to make herself very attractive, but not too sexy.

She opted for a blue shirt, soft in both color and texture, stone-gray pants that cropped just above the ankle. She added dangles to her ears for pretty, and Darlie's bracelet for luck.

As she braided her hair—low, loose—she went over the conversation she needed to have with Dillon. The honest, she thought, the practical, and the realistic.

Because he was a good man, she mused as she went down, slipped on an apron. And she had lousy luck with men—good and not-so-good.

The knock came promptly at seven. When she opened the door she saw he held flowers. Sunny yellow tulips.

"I see you're worthy."

"Of what?"

"Of the dinner invitation, according to Consuela's standards. The flowers," she explained. "And they're just perfect. Thanks."

When she took them, he surprised her by framing her face with his hands, by kissing her first on the forehead, like a friend. That simple choice stirred her heart even more than the warm and lingering kiss that followed.

"I wasn't sure you'd be up for this. Making dinner," he added as she walked away to get a vase for the tulips. "But by the way it smells in here, I guess you were."

"I'm fine. How's Red?"

"Pissed. Mostly pissed. I can't tell you how much of a relief that is."

"You don't have to. More pissed than hurt's a big relief."

"Yeah, and still." Restless, he wandered to the glass wall, back again. "I was around when Gram changed the bandage, so remind me to avoid getting grazed by a bullet. It's damn nasty."

"Has he seen his doctor?"

"Gram didn't give him much choice there, so yeah. It actually is just a graze. His truck wasn't so lucky. It's toast. So more pissed off there."

"And he didn't know the man they identified."

"No. None of us did." He looked at her, into her eyes in that steady way he had. "How are you?"

To give herself a minute, she set the flowers on the island as Consuela had directed. "Wine?"

"Sure."

"How am I?" She considered as she poured for both of them. "Pissed, not mostly, but definitely pissed. First at what happened—worse, what could have happened to Red. And knowing it might have happened—a strong maybe—because of what he did for me years ago. For me, for my family. Add in frustrated, uneasy, and just plain baffled that anyone could and would carry such . . . is it hate? Resentment? Just a deep-seated need to, what, even the score?"

She handed him the wine. "It's not my mother." He just looked at her—that way of his again—said nothing, so she shook her head. "It's not that I don't think she's capable of hate or all the rest. It's just it's not her way of evening the score. Running me and the family down, finding subtle ways to do that while putting herself in the limelight. That's her way."

"And this doesn't do just that?"

"I— Oh. Wait. Hadn't gone there." Taking the wine with her, she walked over to—unnecessarily—stir the sauce. "No, I don't think so. It's possible, of course, what Michaela believes will leak, and then it's all splashing everywhere again. She could get some miles out of that. But Denby was killed months ago. It's too long for her to draw things out. She needs quick gratification."

"You don't really know her though. You haven't seen or spoken to her in years."

"But I do." She turned back to him. "Know your enemy, and trust me, I understand that's what she is. So I've made a study of her over the years. She's a narcissist, innately selfish and self-serving, has a child's need for immediacy and, well, shiny things. And has a complete lack of self-awareness, which is only one reason she's a mediocre actor. She's vain, she's grasping, she's a lot of unattractive things, but she's not violent.

"If I'd died during the kidnapping, she'd have played the grieving mother, but she wouldn't have felt it. She'd have believed she felt it, and that it wasn't her fault. She believed none of that would hurt me, or not enough to matter. She can't see past her own needs. Killing people doesn't serve her needs, and takes too many risks, takes too much time and effort."

"Okay."

She tilted her head. "Just like that?"

"I'm going to say this, then maybe we table it so it doesn't suck all the air out of the night."

Lightly, he laid a hand over the one she used to rub her bracelet for calm.

"I'm not much on hate. It doesn't get you anywhere, and tends to eat more at you than the other person anyway. But I carved out an exception for her a long time ago. I'm fine with that. But everything you just said fits into my opinion of her. So okay."

Turning her hand under his, she linked fingers with him. "She's not my mother in any way that matters."

"No, she's not. I guess I've got one more thing to say on it. I need to look out for you, and I need you to let me. You, Hugh, Lily, hell, Consuela. Toss in your dad when he's here."

She eased back, just a step. "That's a lot of looking after."

"We all do what we do. I figured I'd be subtle about it."

Now she smiled. "Sneaky?"

"That's a word," he agreed. "But why don't we be up front, you and me?"

"Up front's less complicated in the long run."

He brought the hand he still held up to his lips to brush them over her knuckles. "Your family matters to me and mine. You matter. Looking out for you just follows."

"Your family's connected to that night, if that's where all this comes from. How about I look after you and yours?"

"No problem there. Looks like we'll just have to spend more time together."

"That is sneaky." She got out the salad bowl, drizzled on the dressing she'd made, tossed it. "Let's eat."

Once they'd settled in with the salad, with hunks of bread, she decided to start the next conversation. "So, Consuela, who supervised, instructed, and eagle-eyed the making of dessert—"

"There's dessert, too?"

"There is. In any case, she wanted to know if we'd had sex."

He choked, grabbed the wine. "What?"

"She says you're a good man, and very handsome. And as she's one of my real mothers, she's really fond of you, I'd say she felt entitled to ask and advise. Just a warning the subject may come up the next time you visit her."

He honestly couldn't imagine it. Didn't want to. "Appreciate the heads-up."

"But while we're on the subject, there are some things I didn't take time to talk about last night because I was more interested in getting you in bed."

"Also appreciate that."

"You matter, Dillon. You and your family have always mattered to me. You matter, all of you, even more since I've come back. The time I've spent at the ranch with you, with your mom, with Gram, with Red, too? It's helped me come home, feel home. And I know how you feel about my grandparents. I've seen it for myself."

Not exactly a speech, he considered, but he'd bet good money she'd practiced that delivery, like she practiced her voice-overs.

He couldn't quite decide if that irritated him or touched him, so he opted—for the moment—for neutral.

"They're a big part of my life."

"I know it. We need to promise each other, and mean it, that whatever happens with us we won't push those parts of our lives away, or make it hard for each other to keep them."

He shifted from neutral into genuinely baffled.

"Why would we do that?"

"People get hurt, get angry when things go south. Relationships, for me, always end up a mess."

He decided to steer her in just that direction, and eat more bread. "It sounds like you've had the wrong relationships."

"Maybe, but the common element would be me. Up front," she repeated. "I've tried relationships with men in the business, and it gets complicated and falls apart. I've tried with someone out of the business, same thing."

"Yeah, so you said." Since he didn't intend for either of them to drive, he added more wine to both glasses. "Not very specific."

"Okay. The first, I loved him. I loved him the way you love at eighteen. Giddy and dazzled and without restrictions. He was a good man. A boy really," she corrected. "An actor—musical theater. So talented. And kind, sweet. One night when he walked me to a cab, as he always did, waited until I drove away, two men jumped him. They put him in the hospital."

"I read about it. I was in college."

"God knows it got plenty of play. So you know they used my name, the fact I was white and he wasn't to beat him unconscious. His family blamed me. How can I blame them?"

"How about because it wasn't your fault?"

"It wasn't about fault. I was the reason, or the excuse, or, hell, just the MacGuffin."

"What's that?"

"MacGuffin? It's a plot device, and it's often something that seems important, but just isn't."

"But you are," he told her, "important."

"Not necessarily to the two men who put Noah in the hospital."

Picking up her wine, she studied it, saw through it to that brilliant fall day on the terrace of Lily's condo with New York shining.

"He couldn't forgive me, not then, so it ended."

"He'd had a rough time he didn't deserve. But for Christ's sake, Cate, what was there to forgive you for?"

"MacGuffin." She lifted one hand, drank some wine with the other. "A handy device to put a twenty-year-old dancer in the hospital, to sell tabloids, to give the internet something to buzz about awhile."

"He was wrong, stupid wrong." Anger, sudden and hot, sharpened the words. "And don't claim it's easy for me to say. It's like if I blamed the shopkeeper for my dad getting shot, or blamed the women Dad died protecting. It wasn't their fault. It was the fault of the man with the gun."

"You're right, and still. Noah and I ran into each other not long before I came back to Big Sur, and we resolved things. I'm grateful for that. It took me a long time to want someone again, to trust someone enough between those points in my life."

She rose to clear the salad. "I'm going to plate the pasta because I'm fussy about the presentation. It's my signature meal."

"Fine with me."

"So. I met this man through a friend of one of my cousins. Law student, brilliant mind. Definitely not in the business, which I'd sworn off of. I'd dated once or twice between, but no heat."

She tossed, lightly, pasta and sauce as she spoke. "But something clicked with him, maybe because he didn't care about movies or TV or any of it. He didn't even own a TV. He read, extensively when he wasn't studying. Mostly nonfiction. He knew about art, went to galleries. Sophisticated, erudite."

"I'm getting the picture," Dillon told her. "Snob."

"No, he . . ." Then she laughed. "Well, yeah. He was, now that you mention it. Anyway, I put off having sex with him for about six weeks, I guess, and he seemed patient about it, willing to give me time. When we did sleep together, it was good."

"Good," Dillon repeated with the faintest of smirks.

"Well, it wasn't the angels singing, but good. He didn't care about the publicity when it came because he didn't pay any attention to it. He thought it was all low-class. He didn't think much of actors either—and I was doing voice work by then—but I was okay with that."

"And then?"

"Fresh Parm? It's yours."

"Sure."

"And then," she continued as she grated. "We'd been together about three months, talking vaguely about moving in together. I'd need a place with space for my studio—which didn't take much. That's when it started to go south. No way was I going to put some stupid soundproof room into his apartment, or any apartment. It was high time I gave up that ridiculous hobby anyway. It wasn't like I needed the money. When I objected, as you might imagine, he hit me."

"He hit you," Dillon repeated, very quietly.

"A solid backhand right across the cheekbone. Just once because once was all it took. I didn't panic," she murmured, thinking back. "I can panic in stressful situations, but I didn't. It was more like a wake-up call. So."

She shrugged that off. "He apologized, profusely, as I was walking out the door. He'd had a terrible day, he lost his temper, he loved me, it would never happen again."

She brought the pasta with its fresh basil and Parmesan to the table. "No, it wouldn't, because he'd never get the chance. I went home, took a selfie of my face in case. Which was handy, as he kept texting or calling, even coming by my apartment or showing up when I was out."

"He stalked you."

She knew tenors, pitches, pacing when it came to voices, and recognized a different kind of anger than before. This was iced fury, and definitely more dangerous than the quick, hot blast.

"Close enough. I went to the two detectives who'd investigated Noah's attack. I showed them the selfie, explained things, asked if they could, at least initially, just have a discussion with him, warn him off. If it didn't work, I'd file charges. It worked."

She rolled pasta onto a fork. "Try it."

He did. "I see why it's your signature dish. It's terrific. He didn't bother you again?"

"No. But about two years later, the female cop—she'd made lieutenant by then—she came by to see me, and to tell me he'd been arrested for battering his fiancée. She wanted me to know I'd made the right decision, and to ask whether, if it became necessary, I'd testify. I said I would, but God, I'm glad it wasn't necessary."

She ate some more, decided it really was terrific. "Which brings us to the third and last if you want to hear it."

"I do."

"Justin Harlowe."

"Yeah, I read about that, too. A lot of bullshit about that."

"Bullshit's what it was. We did click, and for a good stretch of time. He's talented, can be funny, is definitely charming. We had a lot in common, and he was riding high at the time, as his series was a hit. He didn't mind the publicity. Why would he, and half of it revolved around him anyway. He didn't much care for the Catjus shipping name, but he'd joke about it. We enjoyed each other. I didn't love him, but it was close. I felt good with him, and for a while it felt good to be able to talk to someone about the business. Someone who understood the demands, someone who actually appreciated voice work because he did some himself. Then . . ."

She shrugged. "The ratings dipped, and the feature he'd done over the season break wasn't getting good buzz. I didn't blame him for being moody—it's a bitch. Then I found out he was sleeping with his costar from that feature, and had been for months."

After winding more pasta, she wagged her fork. "Which, when confronted, he blamed on me. I hadn't been there for him, I wasn't supportive enough. I didn't like sex enough, name it. Toss in, it's only sex, it doesn't mean anything."

"If it doesn't mean anything, you're not doing it right. You dumped him."

"I did, but made the mistake of agreeing to keep it private while he was dealing with the series. It just didn't matter to me, but it did

to him. It mattered enough that my mother got wind, talked him
into taking some whacks in the press. Getting ahead of things by
claiming he dumped me because I was jealous, demanding, crazy,
and so on."

She picked up her wine. "So, three strikes."

"Not from where I'm sitting. The first guy—Noah, right? It wasn't
your fault or his. You didn't cause what happened to him; he couldn't
handle what happened to him. I'm giving him a pass on that, since
he was young and it seems like it was all too much at the time. The
second son of a bitch? A lot of women get fooled by men who'll hit
women. A lot of men manage to hide that long enough to cement a
bond. And you walked away, you took action. You did it all right. Not
on you. The last guy? A lot of people end up with people who turn
out to be cheaters and liars. And again, you walked."

"It's a crappy track record, Dillon."

"Two out of three turned out to be fucking bastards, and you
walked away. You said you ran into the first one and resolved things.
Is he a fucking bastard?"

"No, the opposite."

"Is there more of this?"

"Yes."

"I can get it," he said when she started to get up.

"Presentation." She rose, went to plate him a second helping.

"Do you want my track record?"

She looked over at him as she arranged the pasta. He sat so
relaxed—and confident, she realized—at her pretty table.

"It's not required, but of course I do."

"Not going into details because there've been more than three
women I've slept with."

She tried a Lily Morrow arch of eyebrows. "How many more?"

"What are numbers anyway? I've dumped, been dumped. There
was one I came close with, but I never tripped over the line into really loving her. They mattered, every one of them. Maybe I screwed
up, maybe she screwed up. Mostly, it just didn't stick, and we parted
ways. I never cheated, because that's weak. If you want somebody
else, you say so, you don't cheat. I've never hit a woman, and I hope

to Christ I've never mistreated one, because there are other ways to hurt somebody than with your fist."

"Yes, there are."

"I'll make mistakes with you. Bound to. You'll make mistakes with me."

"Bound to," she agreed, and brought over his second helping.

"But I don't hurt people, not deliberately. Not true," he said as he rolled another forkful. "I've punched a few guys along the way, and that was deliberate. But things happen."

She remembered the way he'd rushed through her door when he'd heard her scream. Yes, she imagined he'd punched a few guys along the way.

"I suppose they do."

"Anyway, I'll make you that promise because you need it. What-ever happens between us, you're part of our family. That's not going to change. And if you ever manage to shake me off, especially now that I've eaten this, I'm still coming to hang with Hugh and flirt with Consuela and Lily."

"You smooth me out, Dillon."

"That's fine. At the dinner table."

Laughing, she sat back with her wine. "I'll give you a chance to stir me back up, but I think two helpings of pasta equals a walk on the beach."

"It's damn good pasta. When we get married I'm going to expect it once a week."

"So noted. It's cooled off a bit. I'm going to get a sweater for that walk." She rose. "After the walk we can have dessert in bed."

"That schedule works fine for me."

"Be right back."

When she went upstairs, he rose to clear as his ladies would have expected.

And he thought of Cate and the three men who'd had the chance to love and treasure her. The three men who'd blown that chance.

He wouldn't blow that chance. He'd give her a little time to under-stand he wouldn't.

If someone out there killed to cause her grief and pain and trouble, if someone threatened her, well, he'd find a way to take care of that. To take care of her.

He knew no other way to be.

The first thing Michaela noticed when they brought Sparks into the interrogation room was he'd kept his looks.

An older version, yes, but Sparks retained that movie star aura, the middle-aged leading man type. Character lines fanned from his eyes, gray threaded through his hair, but he'd found a way to maintain both his face and his gym-rat build.

No shackles, she noted, as he wasn't considered dangerous.

The hell he wasn't, she thought. The cop in her smelled dangerous the instant he came into the room.

He sat down across from her, acknowledged Red with a nod, then looked straight into her eyes.

"I didn't expect to see either of you again."

"Our time's limited, so we'll get right to it. What do Frank Denby and Charles Scarpetti have in common?"

His brows drew together, a thoughtful yet puzzled look. "Obviously I know Denby, but the other doesn't ring right off. Denby was a stupid mistake inside a colossal one for me, but—"

He broke off, held up a finger. "I got it. That's the high-priced, fancy lawyer Charlotte hired to get her off. Didn't work out like she wanted, but she got off pretty light for somebody who arranged her own kid's snatch."

"They're both dead."

"I heard about Denby. The guy always was an asshole, and from what I heard didn't make any friends inside. Ended up shanked."

"Did you have contact with Denby inside?" As Red spoke, Sparks shifted his attention. "Talk about old times?"

"Hell no. You know how big this place is. We weren't in the same building."

"I know how big this place is, and I know there are ways."

"Why would I want to talk to that asshole? At first I was just pissed, so yeah, if it had been easy, I might've had some words for him. Look, I did what I did, I'm not excusing it, but like I said, stupid mistake. Denby's a bigmouthed junkie. Hang with somebody like that in here, you get your ass kicked, or worse. You've got to get through it, and you need to be alive to get out when your time's done. What happened to the lawyer?"

"Murdered."

"I don't get it. Denby gets shanked inside, some fancy lawyer gets killed outside. What's it have to do with me?"

"They were both connected to Caitlyn Sullivan's kidnapping. As is Sheriff Buckman." Michaela took a photo out of her folder, laid it on the table. "Recognize him?"

Sparks gave the photo a study, what appeared to be a serious one. "I don't think so. Why?"

"He's dead, too." Red leaned over, watching Sparks's face as he jabbed a finger on the photo. "So's his friend after they tried to run me off the road, after they shot up my truck."

"Well, holy shit. But again, what does it have to do with me? If you're thinking this all goes back to the kidnapping, that just doesn't make sense. That's a long time ago."

"Ever hear how revenge is a dish best served cold?" Michaela wondered.

He flashed a smile. "I like a hot meal myself." Let it fade, widened his eyes. "Jesus, you think Charlotte's doing this, like hiring people to kill? You think she'll go for me?"

Michaela didn't hide the smirk as she sat back. "Has anyone threatened you?"

"Not recently. Look, I keep my head down. I'm no Frank Denby. I work in the library, do the job, stay out of the heat. I do some coaching in the gym. You keep it cool, don't cause trouble, stay out of it, and you get through. I'm going to say Charlotte had a cold streak, cold as they come, but she's been making movies again, right? And she married that rich guy. The burger guy."

"You keep informed," Red commented.

"We get TV time in here. I don't know why she'd want to go after any of us over something that was her own fucking idea, whatever the hell she said to get a light touch."

"You didn't get such a light touch, did you?"

He looked back at Red. "No, I did not. I fell for the bitch, okay? Mistake on top of mistake. I got caught up, thinking of taking off with her and a pot full of money. I'm paying for it. The last thing I want is to go back there."

"Denby screwed things up. Scarpetti helped get Charlotte off with a handful of years. Sheriff Buckman made sure you're sitting just where you're sitting."

Sparks leaned back as if the air had gone out of him. "You think I'm involved in this? You've got to be fucking kidding me. I'm sitting where I'm sitting inside a maximum-security prison, for Christ's sake."

"So was Denby."

"That's right. That's right." A little outrage now as Sparks jerked forward. "And you think they didn't have a chat with me on that? Didn't find out where I was when it went down? I don't kill people, even assholes. I don't know this fucker." With a flick, Sparks tossed the photo across the table. "The lawyer didn't have dick to do with me. You had me cold because I was an idiot over a woman."

"The lawyer helped Charlotte put together statements that shoved you to the head of the train," Red pointed out.

"Yeah, that's right. Are you going to tell me I wouldn't have done twenty otherwise? That's bullshit. She got off light, but I'd have done the same time either way. What do I care?"

As if frustrated, Sparks threw his hands in the air, then dragged them through his hair. "Listen, for fuck's sake, I've got under a year to go till I'm up for parole. I've got a lawyer working on getting me that parole. I could be out in a year. Out of here. Nothing's worth more to me than that. No way I'd do anything to screw that up. And how the hell would I? What am I, Harry fucking Potter?"

"It doesn't take magic to get one inmate to shank another. A favor for a favor. You've made a lot of connections inside, Sparks."

"That's right. Connections help keep you out of the infirmary, out of solitary, out of the goddamn morgue. I order books. I help some of the cons who can barely write their name write letters to family on the outside. I help train in the gym. Denby's my past, and in here you'd better stay in the present.

"You think about this." He jabbed a finger that shook just a little at both of them. "If you've got anything on all this, I'm in the fucking barrel. I've got to watch my back until I get out. You do your time without moaning about it, and it's still not enough. It's never enough."

He looked back at the guard on the door. "I want to go back. I'm done here. I want to go back."

Michaela slid the photo neatly into the folder as the guard led Sparks out. "He's good."

"He is."

"It's hard to argue with anything he said."

"It made sense, right down the line." Red rose, rubbed lightly at his wounded arm. "And he's a sonofabitching liar."

"Oh yeah. He is."

PART IV

LOVE, DARK AND BRIGHT

Love sought is good,
but given unsought is better.
—WILLIAM SHAKESPEARE

Love is blind.
—GEOFFREY CHAUCER

CHAPTER TWENTY-FOUR

April slid into May, and the world filled with poppies. They waved orange and fire red in warm breezes, blanketing hills, smothering fields in color. Bluebonnets sprang up, adding some sassy charm, and lilacs sweetened the air everywhere.

Mornings brought fog sliding, smoking, sometimes so thick it hung a curtain over the world until the sun cracked through, burned it away, and turned that world to sparkling.

Cate threw open all her windows, potted herbs—under Julia's supervision—for her windowsill, set up a table out on her patio for breaks under the afternoon sun.

She watched the gardens surrounding her bloom and thrive, the crops at the ranch grow. The woods where she'd once run toward the light turned lush and green.

Of course the tourists came, and traffic on Highway 1 stalled like a clogged drain. But beauty had its price.

In the peaceful, blooming spring, she began to lean away from Michaela's theory. Coincidences happened, and the connection was vague and old in any case. The second man in the stolen car turned out to be a cousin of the first. And neither had any connection to anyone else.

She had home. She had work. She had a man who made her happy. Why look for shadows when she could stand in the light?

With another audiobook on her slate, she spent her morning in the booth, broke at noon.

Time to take a walk, clear the head, give the throat a rest. She decided to walk up to the main house, sit in the peace of the walled garden with its climbing roses and impossibly blue clematis, all its pretty flowers and benches.

She could mooch some of Consuela's excellent lemonade.

An hour break, she decided as she left the house. Another two hours in the booth. Three if she felt she had it in her. Plenty of time to fix herself up a bit before she drove to the ranch.

Dinner with Dillon, his ladies, and Red had become a weekly ritual, and a treat. And she'd stay at Dillon's for the night. If she managed to get there a little early, she might catch him working with the horses.

God, she loved watching him with the horses.

She topped the rise, stopped, stared as Consuela rushed out of the house toward the woman holding a baby on her hip beside a Lexus SUV.

"Darlie!"

She went on the run, barely beating Consuela to wrap her friend and the little boy in a hug. "Oh, the best surprise. The best surprise ever. Let me see him. Oh, hello, handsome!"

He tipped his head to his mother's shoulder, grinned at her. "Dog," he said, clutching a stuffed dog. "Mine!"

"And nearly as handsome as you. He got so big."

"He's walking now. R-running."

Cate heard the tremble in Darlie's voice, looked over, saw the tears welling in her eyes.

"I didn't know where else to go."

She didn't ask questions, not now. "You came to the right place."

"Come to me, my baby, come to Consuela. Can he have a c-o-o-k-i-e?"

"Of course. He deserves one."

"Would you like a cookie, *mi pequeño hombre*? Come with Consuela."

"Kee!" Luke threw his arms out to her.

"He probably needs a change. Let me—"

"No, no, Mama, give to me the bag and the baby. Consuela will take care of everything. That's right. Let's change your diaper and have cookies. Everything will be fine, you will see. Everything will be fine now."

"He's so friendly," Darlie said as the boy, chattering happily, let Consuela carry him into the house. "He's never met a stranger. Oh, Cate, everything is awful."

Those welling tears spilled; Cate wrapped around Darlie again. "Then we'll fix it. We'll fix everything. Did you drive from L.A.?"

Darlie nodded, swiped at tears sliding under her dark glasses. "I started last night. Luke slept through a lot of it. I just . . ."

"We're going to go sit down, have some lemonade. You'll tell me."

"Can we stay for a few days? I should've called first," she continued as Cate led her around to the kitchen patio. "I was so hell-bent on getting here, just getting here."

"You can stay as long as you want, as long as you need."

"It's beautiful here. I know you told me, but it's more than I imagined. And it's so away, and so secluded. I really need away and secluded. Oh, it's like a bridge."

Cate looked up. "It's a clever design, all the layers of it, the connections. Kind of like a village inside one house. Sit, breathe. I'll be right back."

Leaving Darlie at one of the tables under the pergola of rioting wisteria, she hurried into the kitchen.

Thought, Perfect, as she found a pitcher of lemonade. She heard Consuela making the baby laugh in her quarters. Yes, Consuela would take care.

And so would she.

She grabbed a tray, the pitcher, glasses, thought of tissues. Carried it all out.

"I bet you haven't eaten."

"I couldn't right now, but thanks."

"We'll get something later. You don't have to worry about the baby. Consuela's got him." She poured, sat. "Tell me."

"Dawson's having an affair with the nanny—and how clichéd is that?" In quick jerks she pulled out a tissue. "But he's not just having an affair with her, she's pregnant, and he claims he loves her."

"*Sukin syn.*" The Russian for *whoreson* suited Dawson best. "I should've gotten a bottle of wine."

With a watery laugh, Darlie snatched up more tissues. "Later, for sure. I found out yesterday. He confessed all, because rumors are grinding, and it's going to hit. He hopes I understand. So sorry, but the heart wants what the heart wants."

More tissues, snatched, swiped, wadded.

"The son of a bitch."

"I'm so sorry, Darlie."

"He's been sleeping with her in our home, Cate, with our son asleep in his crib. While I'm on set. Sneaking off with her on her day off. Luke's barely a year old, and he's got another woman pregnant. He wants to marry her."

"Does it help or hurt if I say I think they deserve each other?"

"Helps, because I think the same. How could I have had no clue, Cate? How could I have not seen what was happening right under my nose? How did I let my life become a frigging Lifetime Movie?"

"Don't you blame yourself, not for one minute. You trusted him, trusted them both—why wouldn't you?—and they used that. Love, my ass, Darlie. I don't care if they're Tristan and Isolde—and I wouldn't mind them meeting the same fate—they're liars and cheats. No excuses."

"Small wonder I came to you." Swiping her face with one hand, she gripped Cate's with the other. "Of all the places I could go, all the people I could turn to, you were the first and only one I wanted."

"I'm with you all the way. You're safe here, you and Luke. No one will even know you're here until you want it."

"Cate." Darlie's voice simply shattered on the word. "He said he'd give me full custody of Luke." Tears rolled again. She grabbed more tissues. "He said, he thought it was only fair, like our child is a bargaining chip. If I'd give him a quick divorce without any hassles, didn't blast him in the press, he'd give me full custody. He was having another kid anyway."

She knew what it meant to be disposable to a parent, and felt her heart break even as her blood boiled. "Listen to me. Anyone who could do that, feel that, isn't worth one more tear."

"Then why are you crying, too?"

"They're angry ones. Tits up, Darlie. Goddamn it, haul those tits up and take that offer. Take that offer right damn now and run with it. Because he doesn't deserve you, and he sure as fuck doesn't deserve that beautiful little boy."

"I thought he loved me," she murmured. "Maybe he did, for a little while. I thought I'd found someone to share my life with, to build one with. Now it's just another bad Hollywood story."

"You'll ride that part out. It's what we do, isn't it? Have you called a lawyer?"

"On the way here." Breathing out, Darlie mopped her face. "Because you're right about taking his offer and running with it. I want to get that written in blood—his—then he can have whatever the hell he wants. The only thing that matters is Luke."

"That's right. What we're going to do is get you and Luke something to eat, then we'll go down and get you settled at my place. You can count on me and Consuela to fight over the baby. Add my grandfather into that when he gets back. He's in New York for a few more days."

"I'm going to owe you for the rest of my life."

"Friends don't owe friends. Wait until I take you two over to see the ranch."

"And the supersexy rancher. Oh, Cate, we're going to be so in the way of that."

"No, you're not. You'll like him, and his family. And Luke is going to go crazy over the animals. I know he likes dogs—you said *dog* was his first word. Dillon has two sweet ones."

"We were— I was going to get him a puppy. I'd started looking at puppies."

"Well, he can have a trial run with Dillon's Stark and Natasha. Right now, we're going to have some lunch. And some wine with that."

"Oh hell, I didn't pack a high chair, or a crib."

"I guarantee you we have them in the house, and whatever else you need. The Sullivans are always having babies."

By midafternoon, she had Darlie settled, with the baby in the bedroom—facing the hillside—adjoining the seaside room by a Jack and Jill bath.

She had one of the high chairs in her kitchen, a bag of toys in her living area, and both mother and baby taking a much-needed nap upstairs.

She called Dillon.

"Hey, gorgeous."

"Somebody's in a good mood."

"Having a real good day."

"I'm having a busy one. My friend—my closest friend's here."

"Yeah? That's Darlie Maddigan, right?"

"It is. You pay attention. She needed a friend. Her marriage just went into the sewer so she came here with her baby. I'll give you details on that if she tells me I can."

"Got it."

"So, I won't be able to make it tonight."

"Don't worry about that. Can I help?"

"I actually think you can. When she's feeling steadier, I'd like to bring them over. He's about fourteen months old, loves animals."

"We've got a few of those."

"Dogs are the big love now. And I think your ladies will add something for Darlie. Just that female spirit."

"You know you can bring them, anytime."

"He's energetic," she warned.

"Bet we can wear him out. I'll miss you tonight."

"I'll miss you."

She would, she realized. She'd gotten used to seeing him almost every day, of sleeping with him almost every night.

Turning to the glass wall, she looked out. She wasn't ready to look past today, or maybe tomorrow on that part of her life. But she began to see that maybe, just maybe, it could roll like the sea. It could roll into forever.

Sparks worked out the timing and chose movie night. Well, movie on the communal TV night. And *The Great Escape* won the vote. Again.

He didn't give a shit.

What he cared about? A good group of inmates and guards in one place.

It wouldn't be easy doing what he had to do.

The cops had given him the idea, and the more he'd played with it, the more he saw it as perfect.

He'd already whined to Jessica about the police harassment, enlisted her—so fucking easy—to roll that over and add it to his pitch for parole. Maybe push that to early release.

Her client might be in physical danger. Police were investigating just that possibility. Not safe in prison, and blah yadda yadda.

Tonight would seal that one.

He'd figured to wait until the movie ended, and everyone filed out, then realized he might lose his courage.

Now or never, he decided.

He knew where to aim—personal trainer—and jabbed the shank into his side, toward the back, just above the waist.

He stumbled a couple of steps—motherfucker hurt—got an elbow, a shove. He managed to keep his grip on the shank, as if trying to yank it out. Went to his knees.

Blood, he thought. A lot of blood. His blood.

Seeing it, inmates scrambled back; guards pushed forward.

And there went movie night.

A baby changed things. A lot of things, Cate realized. It changed her friend. She witnessed for herself how completely Darlie focused on Luke's needs, his wants, his happiness.

The cuddles, the playtime, the feedings.

"You're a good mom, Darlie."

"I want to be. I try to be."

"You're a good mom. You've got a happy kid, healthy, charming. And he's easy with people because you let him be."

With Luke's hand in hers, Darlie matched Luke's toddling, then charging gait as they walked to Cate's car.

He wore a floppy navy sun hat, red Nikes, navy shorts, and a T-shirt that proclaimed him *wild thing*.

"I stayed home with him for the first couple of months, even with the nanny. Then I took them both to the set for a while, so I could nurse and see him. Then Dawson was between projects, so I pumped because I thought he and Luke should have a chance to just be together without me hovering. That didn't work out so well."

"Don't blame yourself."

"I'm not." When she shook her head, her long blond ponytail swayed. "Not even a little now. I weaned him just a couple months ago because it felt like he was ready. He's all about the sippy cup, and he's walking. Are you sure you want to haul us over there? We can stay here."

"We won't go if you're not ready."

"It's not that."

When they reached the car, Cate helped with the baby, the diaper bag, the car seat.

"I know we've sucked up time you'd have spent with Dillon. I don't want us to horn in on your afternoon with him."

"You need to strap him in the car seat. I'm not sure I'd do it right. He's a rancher, Darlie. And until I saw it all myself, I really had no idea how much work that means. Every day. He'll take some time today, but you'll see for yourself how much work there is. And his mother, grandmother? Those women are tireless. I don't know how they do it all. We're giving them a treat. This baby is a treat."

"He is for me." She secured him in the car seat with his beloved Dog. "Honestly, I think he's saving my sanity right now, if not my life."

She slid into the passenger seat, waited until Cate got behind the wheel. "I talked to my lawyer just before we left."

"And?"

"Dawson signed the custody papers. Just like that, Cate. Like it was nothing. My lawyer said his lawyer wasn't happy, but Dawson didn't care. So I file the standard irreconcilable differences, and that's the end of that. Except for the media storm."

"They can't bother you when they don't know where you are." She drove to the first gate, paused, then eased through when it opened.

"And you know what? The more you take the high road, the harder they'll be on him and his cheating slut of a nanny."

With eyes no longer red-rimmed and weepy, Darlie looked over with a smile. "I've thought of that."

"Of course you did. How else could we be friends? Traffic's going to suck, but it's not far."

"Cate, these past couple days. You saved my sanity, too."

"You sure as hell saved mine, more than once, back in the day."

"I haven't said much to you about her. Charlotte Dupont. Because I wasn't sure you wanted to hear it, or if it would just upset you. I've got a different take on that since I've been here."

"Different how?"

"We've kept in touch. Even managed a few face-to-face times, but mostly it's texts, emails, video chats. Spending even a couple days? You've got your tits up, pal. You're more comfortable with yourself, and happier. I'm going to say you looked good in New York whenever I got to see you. And I worried some about you coming back here. But I shouldn't have. You look even better here. Hell, you've got an amazing place, that rocking studio, you're having sex with a rancher. Why wouldn't you look even better?"

"I love it here."

"It shows. So . . . do you want to hear about Charlotte Dupont?"

"I'm pretty sure my family censors whatever they hear, whatever they know. So I'd like the uncensored version."

"Good, because that's the way I want to tell it. She's a joke in the industry. She gets work because her doddering, stupidly rich husband buys her work. Rumor is, and I believe it, he sometimes pays for reviews that don't skewer her. When he doesn't pay, they invariably do. And she's had so much plastic surgery I'm not sure how much of her is still organic."

Unable to help herself, Cate barked out a laugh. "Really?"

"Somebody—I wish it had been me—said she looks like Has-Been Barbie. Cold, but accurate. I've seen her a couple times, in person. Red carpet stuff or in a restaurant. I can tell you she doesn't know when to quit going under the knife, the injections, whatever the hell she's doing."

"Maybe you get the face you deserve in the end."

"Well then, wow. She's got the one she deserves." Shifting, she made faces at Luke to make him laugh. "She tried to talk to me once, at an event. Came over, with that face, diamonds dripping over her plastic boobs, tried to convince me to talk to you on her behalf. Sob story."

"I'm sorry."

"Forget that. I told her to fuck off. Just that: 'Fuck off,' and walked away. Felt good."

"I love you, Darlie."

"Love you back. Maybe I should buy a place up here. A getaway."

"You've got a place up here."

Reaching over, Darlie squeezed Cate's hand. "I do, don't I?"

Cate turned off the highway onto the ranch road. Started the bumpy drive up.

"Some road!"

"It's a ranch."

"Family ranch. I bet it's sweet. I can't wait to see how Luke reacts to ranch animals. And you helped make cheese and butter. What a riot. I've love to . . . This is not sweet," Darlie managed when the near pastures, the house, the barns, the rising hills dotted with sheep and goats came into view. "This is just, well, stunning."

"It really is."

"I thought family ranch, small and sweet. This is— Look at the cows, right there. The cows get a view. Look at the cows, Luke!"

At the moment, he continued an important conversation with Dog.

"Oh." Darlie gripped Cate's arm. "Is that the rancher? Tell me that's your rancher. On a horse, with a hat, and a body. A really good body."

"That's Dillon. He was probably checking fences."

"He's got dogs with him. Dogs, Luke!"

He looked up at the magic word, and his head swiveled from side to side. His reaction was a long squeal and an impatient bounce. "Out, out, out!"

"You bet."

Darlie popped out to free him when Cate parked. "Cows, baby, and horses, and sheep."

"Dog!"

He tried to wiggle free when the dogs ran over.

"They won't hurt him," Dillon called out. "They like kids."

Cautious, Darlie crouched with him, felt his joy when the dogs sniffed and licked. He shoved free, plopped right down on the lawn, gut-laughing as they wagged.

"Dog!" He did his best to hug them to him.

"Well, they're in heaven now." Dillon dismounted, wound the reins on a fence post. He walked straight to Cate, lifted her an inch off her feet, took her mouth.

"Missed you. Sorry," he said to Darlie.

"Don't be sorry. Do it again."

"Happy to." When he had, he set Cate back on her feet. "I already like your friend. Dillon Cooper." After pulling off a work glove, he offered a hand.

"Darlie, and Luke. *Dog* was his first word."

"It's a good one." At ease, Dillon hunkered down. "How's it going, big guy?"

"Dog," Luke responded in a tone of pure love. He spotted Dillon's horse. Eyes widened. "Dog!" As he scrambled up.

"Let's try this."

Dillon scooped the boy up, walked him over to the horse.

"Pet right here." He guided Luke's hand to the horse's neck, stroked it along.

Darlie looked over at Cate. Laid a hand on her heart. Rolled her eyes.

CHAPTER TWENTY-FIVE

Darlie couldn't get used to the glass wall of Cate's cottage. Luke loved it, evidenced by the little smeared fingerprints and mouth prints he left on a regular basis.

She appreciated the wonder it brought into the house, but it made her feel exposed, one-way glass or not. For Cate, she knew, it offered freedom.

Just as the open windows offered freedom and sea-tinged breezes. In L.A., even behind walls and gates, Darlie would never leave windows open through the night, or doors unlocked.

Seeing Cate's life here, sharing it with her for a few days, made her realize Cate made the right choice, for her, when she'd taken another path.

And now, Darlie thought, she had her own choices to make about direction. Just which path did she take now? Which path when she had Luke to think of, first, last, always?

She'd been an actor all her life, so she knew the roads, the obstacles, the tricky turns. Could she—should she—navigate all of that as a single mother?

So while her son punched every side of his music cube—again— and Cate closed herself in her studio to work, Darlie talked to her agent.

And her lawyer.

And her business manager.

Between conversations, she distracted Luke with other toys, put him in the high chair for a midmorning snack. Cleaned up the debris from the snack, and wondered how women ever managed to have more than one child.

Grateful to get off her feet, she stretched out on the floor to play with Luke and his building blocks, thought over her options. And watched her son.

He could say *Dada*—along with *Mama, Hi, Bye-bye, Mine, No, Out, Up, Cate,* and, of course, *Dog*. Since the ranch visit, he'd added *Cow* and *Horse*. All of those clear among a lot of chattering/babbling and half words she'd learned to translate.

But not once had he said *Dada* since they'd come to Big Sur.

Did babies forget so quickly—or had he never really bonded with his father? How could Dawson not feel what she felt, this overwhelming love for the wonder they'd created together?

"He doesn't, and that's that."

"Mama!" After pulling back her attention, Luke knocked over the short tower of blocks, and laughed like a maniac.

"That's right, baby. We knock it down and build it again. We just build it again. And better."

She pulled out her phone, redialed her agent. "Make the deal."

Determined, and a little terrified, she went back to building towers until the knock on the door jolted her.

Before she gained her feet, the door opened. Her heart flipped up, then settled again when she saw Dillon with a market bag.

Stark and Natasha raced in, and straight to the squealing, laughing Luke.

"Sorry. Delivery."

"Come in. You've just made my son's day," she added, grinning at the rolling, happy heap of boy and fur on the floor.

"Well, they figured it was time for another visit."

"It's good to see all three of you. Cate's recording."

"She usually is this time of day, so I just drop her order off if she's in there."

"I'll take it. What have we got?"

"Mostly dairy. My ladies sent some cookies for your boy. They're smitten."

Luke toddled over to Dillon, lifted his arms. "Up!"

"Want up here?" Dillon passed the bag to Darlie, picked Luke up, tossed him a couple times to make him laugh.

Seeing a man playing so easily, so naturally with her boy made Darlie's heart hurt a little. "You're good with babies."

"It's not hard."

"It is for some." And because it made her heart hurt, she repeated the old mantra.

Tits up.

"You're good with Cate, too."

"It's not hard," he repeated as he tossed Luke again, and Darlie walked over to unpack the market bag.

"Not if you love her."

Since Luke wanted down, Dillon gave him back to the dogs, then stepped nimbly around the scatter of toys. "Easiest thing I ever did. I don't suppose you'd tell me how close she is to feeling the same."

"I'll say, as her friend, you check a lot of boxes for me. You should come to dinner tonight."

"I should?"

"You should. She'll figure out something to make. Me, I stir and mix. I'm a mediocre chopper and slicer, but I excel at stirring and mixing." Puzzling on where to put the eggs, cheeses, creams, butters, milk, she glanced back at him.

"I've been an actor since I was about Luke's age. It's what I know how to do."

"You're good at it. But you know more than that. You know how to be a mom. How to be a friend. Those rank high on my scale of knowing."

No wonder he dazzled Cate. "Come to dinner," she repeated.

"Do you eat meat?"

"I've been known to."

"There's a grill out there. I can bring back some steaks."

"Steak." As she repeated the word, Darlie's eyes went wistful. "I don't know the last time I actually had steak."

"Break time." Cate opened her studio door. "Where's that baby? I need a fix. Oh, Dillon."

"He came with dairy," Darlie told her.

"Nice. And good timing. How about a walk on the beach?"

"I've only got a couple minutes. Catch the kid!" Snatching Luke up, he faked a toss, stopping Cate's heart, loosing Luke's gut-laugh. "Just kidding."

"He's coming to dinner, and bringing steak. We're going to make it a little celebration. I just told my agent to make the deal on an offer for a series on Netflix. Major project, starring role."

"Darlie! Break out the champagne!"

"I'll take it. Tonight. Think *Game of Thrones* meets the female, adult *Harry Potter*. The offer came in a few weeks ago, and I turned it down because it shoots in Northern Ireland, and that's six months on location for the first season. If it hits, that's half a year, every year for the three projected seasons. But now . . ."

She took Luke back from Dillon. "I think it'll be good for us. Meanwhile, I have a lot of things to tie up, more to plan out."

"The family base in Mayo's close. I'll come visit."

"I'm counting on it." Darlie gripped Cate's hand. "I'm seriously counting on it."

"When do you leave?"

"I'll go back to L.A. day after tomorrow, sew some things up. I'm going to get sloppy on you about that later, but right now I'm going to take this guy upstairs, change him, slather him with sunscreen like a good if obsessive mother, so we can take that walk on your beach."

She turned to Dillon. "Medium rare."

"Got it."

"I'll see you later. Say bye-bye."

Luke said bye-bye, waved over Darlie's shoulder as she carried him upstairs.

"You're going to miss her. And the kid."

"Like crazy. It's such a good move for her though. It's a smart one on so many levels." She moved to him, wrapped around him. "I wish you could take that walk."

"So do I." When he rubbed her arms, the way he rubbed them, she drew back.

"There's something else."

"I think we should keep tonight a celebration, so I'm going to tell you now, get it over. Sparks was attacked a couple days ago in prison."

She felt nothing, nothing at all. "Is he dead?"

"No, the shank missed vital stuff. He's hurting, from what Red said, but he'll make it."

When she let feeling come, all she had was mild anxiety and speculation.

"That's four now," she murmured. "I don't know what to think, Dillon. Who would do this? If it's my mother, she's not just selfish, greedy, and an all-out shit of a human being. She's crazy."

"I've got some thoughts on it. So does Red. We'll talk about it. You should enjoy your last couple days with your friend." He pulled her back. "I'll be back tonight." He kissed her, drew her up to her toes, deepened it. "I'll give you tomorrow night for a good farewell." Tugged her head back, changed angles, went deep again. "After that, you'll have to get used to being with me."

"It's been over a week, but I haven't gotten used to not being with you."

"Good." He started to the door, around the toys. "Darlie put the cookies my ladies sent in the fridge with the butter."

On a laugh, Cate walked over to rescue them.

Before she put them in a lidded jar, she took one.

Not her mother, she thought again. And not because she thought Charlotte wasn't capable of causing great harm, even for inexplicable reasons. But there had to be an upside for her to make the effort.

Nothing to gain by this, because if the publicity broke, it wouldn't flatter Charlotte. More likely, she'd become a suspect, which would only highlight the past in a harsh light.

She wasn't one to seek the harsh light.

Then again, maybe she hadn't thought about that.

"And I have to now," she admitted.

Because coincidence could only stretch so far. With this last attack, that band snapped.

She heard Darlie coming down, put it aside. She wouldn't mar her friend's last two days with worries and wondering.

Two days later, she stood with Hugh, watching Darlie drive away.

Hugh gave Cate a one-armed hug. "She'll be fine. More than fine."

"I know. She's already hired someone to look for houses in Ireland. She's going to give herself a month there before she's due on set to acclimate, to hire a nanny. She said she wanted to clone Julia. Someone kind and loving, who'd already raised a child well. She and her publicist worked on a statement about the divorce."

"Get out in front of it." Hugh nodded. "The smart way."

"Maybe I think it lets that bastard off too easy, but it's what's right for her and Luke. Anyway, I'm glad I had this time with her. I'm glad you had a couple days, too."

"That baby's a pistol. I'll miss having that energy around. We need to have a family bash when Lily gets home."

"We do."

"But for now, it's just you and me. Do you have time to sit by the pool with an old man for a bit?"

"No old man around I see, but I've got time to sit by the pool with my dashing grandfather. But tomorrow?" She poked a finger in his belly. "It's back to the gym for both of us."

"Slave driver."

She walked over with him, crossing the lawn, then over the stone path. She sat with the sun dancing light over the blue water of the pool, stretched out her legs. Barely had time to say *ahhh* before Consuela walked down from the bridge with lemonade.

"What? You're psychic now?"

With a mysterious smile, Consuela set down the tray. "Fresh berries—good for you. No phones," she ordered, and left them.

He adjusted his hat. "I might have mentioned I hoped to sit with you here for a while, and lemonade would go down nicely."

"That's a relief, because a psychic Consuela's terrifying. I think I'll start swimming during my afternoon break." She pointed at him before picking up her glass. "It'd be a good afternoon break for you, too."

"Give the weather another month. Still too chilly for me. Now." He picked up his own glass. "How are things going between you and Dillon?"

"We'll see tonight when he comes over for dinner." When her phone signaled a text, she winced.

"Cheat," Hugh told her.

"I just want to see— Oh, it's from Dillon. Hailey's having the baby. He's on his way to the birthing center. Hailey and Dillon are friends."

"Yes, I've met her, and Leo and Dave. Consuela's mother and Leo's grandparents came from the same area of Guatemala."

"I didn't know that."

"It's a small old world. Well, a toast to the new family on the way." He tapped his glass to Cate's. "*Sláinte*."

"*Sláinte*. Their lives will never be the same. I don't mean in a bad way," she said quickly when he blinked at her. "I saw, firsthand, how having Luke changed Darlie. Example: Before, she'd have skewered Dawson, then fried him up, chopped him to bits before feeding him to the wolves. But her son's more important than her pride, than slapping back at Dawson."

"If love isn't stronger than pride, it isn't love."

"That's . . . that's completely true. And I've seen that truth, firsthand, all my life. Like Dad did, Darlie's choosing her work differently. She said no to this series before because she wouldn't leave her son for weeks and months on end, and wouldn't take him away from his father for the same reason. Now she's a single parent with a disinterested ex, so she took it. And partly because it removes Luke from the media chaos, the gossip, the speculations. I admire that."

"So do I."

"Dad did that for me, gave me Ireland. And after, you and G-Lil juggled me with him. One or more of you would always be there."

"And now you're here for me."

"I sort of think we're here for each other."

Looking away from the sea, Cate scanned the vineyard, climbing up its tiered terraces, and the pretty little orchard where the April blossoms had fallen and the fruit began to form.

Season by season, she thought. Year by year.

"I never missed her, you know. I had such wonderful women stepping into the mother role for me. I hope Darlie finds some good men to do the same for Luke. She doesn't have a family like ours."

"Who does?"

Smiling, she toasted again. Then set down her glass when she saw Red walking toward them.

"Hi! Sit. I'll run and get another glass."

"I sure wouldn't mind it."

Consuela met her with one halfway across the bridge.

As she started back, she looked down, saw the two men in what read as heavy conversation.

Not a social call, she decided, though she'd expected just this.

She put on a casual smile as she walked down to pour Red a glass.

"Okay, now you can start over from the beginning. What do you think, feel, believe, suspect about Sparks, about all the rest?"

After fiddling with his Wayfarers, Red puffed out his cheeks. "I hate to pull you back into this, Cate."

"I've never been all the way out of it." Reaching over she rubbed her hand over Hugh's. "Stop worrying about shielding me."

"It's always the first instinct, even when I know better."

"Let's think about it this way. Forewarned is forearmed."

"I wish I had more facts," Red told her. "More definites to give you. I can start with some of those. Sparks was stabbed in a communal area, just before the start of a scheduled movie viewing, so you've got a lot of inmates coming in, milling around some before they settled in. The shank missed vital areas."

Demonstrating, Red tapped a fist to the left of the small of his back. "A couple inches over, it would've hit a kidney, and he'd be in more trouble. Sharpened toothbrush. He says he felt a sharp pain, reached back, got ahold of it, tried to pull it out. Went down."

"It sounds painful, if not lethal."

"Oh, he felt it. But a shank like that, you want to hit something important, and you want to hit more than once. If someone was trying to take him out, they did a sloppy, half-assed job of it."

"Do you think it was more of a warning? Something not a part of any of the rest. Just some prison problem."

Taking his time, Red drank some lemonade. "That's a theory."

She caught the tone, angled her head. "Not yours."

"He's got almost twenty years inside, never an incident. Mic and I go up and talk to him a few weeks ago, let him know we're looking at him. He gets shanked, sloppy and half-assed.

"Denby gets shanked, multiple stab wounds, gut wounds, heart wounds—nothing sloppy about it. Scarpetti's attacked, held underwater until he drowns. Clean, quick, done. The two who came after me? Bad luck for them I know the road better than they did, bad luck they boosted a car the driver couldn't handle. But they sure as hell killed my truck, and they sure as hell planned it out."

She spread her hands. "Leaving us with this being sloppy and half-assed. So different than the others."

"Could be whoever's behind this chose poorly this time out."

Reasonable, Cate thought, nodding. "But that's not your theory either."

"I'm thinking it through, running it through with Dillon after I got word on it. The morning after it happened. We're out there moving cattle from pasture to pasture. I'm saying it doesn't add up for me, doesn't smell right. And he says what I'm thinking."

Red leaned forward. "What if the son of a bitch did it to himself?"

"Stabbed himself?" The air went out of her at the idea. "But that's crazy, isn't it? You said he barely missed his kidney."

"But he did miss it, didn't he? The man knows his body. He's spent most of his life working on it."

"Sloppy's one thing. Jabbing a sharpened toothbrush into your own body, that's another. He could've miscalculated, or gotten jostled at the key moment."

"He didn't. He wasn't."

"Still an enormous risk," Hugh put in. "For what possible gain?"

"How I figure he figures? It takes him off the suspect list. 'Look at me, I was attacked, too.' The man's a liar, one who's run his life on lies and cons."

Face set, Red tapped a fist on the table. "I tell you as sure as I'm sitting here he lied to me and Mic when we talked to him. A load of horseshit about just wanting to do his time, how he deserved what he got. He made sure to shift some of the blame to Denby and Dupont, but claimed he'd put it behind him."

Red took another drink. "Horseshit."

"You really believe this? Dillon believes this?"

Red nodded. "It's what adds up for me. It smells right to me. Mic, well, she's about halfway there on it. The other half doesn't see him as having the spine to do it, to hurt himself."

"He's still in prison," Cate pointed out. "How could he do all this from prison?"

"Start with Denby. Nobody liked the bastard. He got his ass kicked regularly, did time in solitary. I'm betting you could barter his murder for a couple packs of smokes. With nearly two decades in, you can be sure a man like Sparks made connections, made friends, knows who'll do what and what they want to do it. Grifters, they're going to grift inside or out."

Hugh looked over the pool to the deeper, bolder water of the Pacific. "The others wouldn't be that easy."

"Connections. An ex-con doing a job, taking a quick score for it. There are ways to make money in prison, to get it in, get it out. Sparks would find ways. The two that came for me did time. Not in San Quentin, but you put the word out, order the hit."

Tapping that fist, Red scowled out to sea. "We'd have gotten it out of them if they'd lived. Sparks got lucky there."

"This isn't just a theory for you," Cate realized.

"It's a theory until I can prove it." Red reached into the bowl of berries, eating absently. "His lawyer? He hired this one over a year ago. She's a writer, too, one with a bad-guy fetish."

"I'm not sure I want to know what that means, exactly."

Red gave Cate a half smile. "A lot of women get hung up on men in prison. Write them, visit them, hell, even marry them. This one writes about them. She's got a couple of true crime books under her belt. I read one of them, and maybe it's just the cop in me, but my take? She leans toward the side of the criminal. She got clearance to interview Denby and Sparks for a book she's going to write, or is writing."

"What's her name?"

"Jessica Rowe," he told Hugh.

"That's familiar. Give me a minute." He rose, took out his phone, walked to the other end of the pool.

"I'm not playing devil's advocate, but it seems logical a criminal would want a lawyer who sympathizes with criminals."

"She's forty-six, single. Never been married. And don't give me grief for saying she's on the sturdy side, and plain-looking."

"And how is that relevant?"

"What's relevant to me is since she's been representing Sparks, since she's been visiting him at least weekly, she's spruced up. Taken off some weight, wearing better clothes, had the gray taken out of her hair, that kind of thing."

"You think she's doing that for him? That she's fallen for him, like my mother fell for him?"

"It slides right in to the adding up." He glanced over as Hugh walked back.

"I needed to check. Jessica Rowe contacted my publicist last year, and again six months ago, trying to arrange an interview. She pitched for an interview with you, honey, three times."

"I never heard of her."

"What have you told our mutual publicist to say regarding interviews or comments on the kidnapping?"

"The answer's always no."

"And she said no, every time. I'm going to assume she tried to contact Aidan, Lily, other members of the family."

"My mother."

"Most certainly. Charlotte wouldn't have said no if she saw any advantage."

"Which would connect her with Sparks again," Cate murmured. "I still don't see what this writer, lawyer, could mean in all this."

"What would you do for love?" Red speculated.

What would she do? Cate asked herself after she walked back home.

Not kill, not help to kill. Not kidnap a child.

But what other lines would she cross?

She didn't know. She'd never been tested.

Maybe because she'd learned—early—to take care with who she loved.

Her family, always her family. Darlie, who was the next thing to a sister to her. Luke, but who wouldn't love such a sweet, happy boy?

Noah. Oh, she had loved Noah, as openly, as freely, as fully as she'd known how. And if, in the end, he'd disappointed her, she'd never blamed him. Not fully.

She walked to the glass wall, looked out to sky and sea, so much blue, so much beauty, and searched her heart.

No, she hadn't fully blamed him, but a part of her had. Maybe still did. And fair or not, holding on to that part of her had made her wary of loving like that again.

She'd given her body if not her full and open heart to two other men who hadn't deserved it. Who wouldn't be wary?

After all, when a Sullivan loved, really loved, it was forever.

With that on her mind, she went upstairs to her bedroom, opened what she thought of as her memory box. *Playbills*—including the one she'd had signed by the cast and crew of *Mame*—ticket stubs, all the way back to her childhood, the recipe for soda bread—one she'd committed to memory long ago—in Mrs. Leary's careful handwriting.

And the little gold heart Noah had given her for her eighteenth birthday.

She hadn't worn it since the day he'd walked out of her life, and still she'd kept it.

Testing herself, she put it on, studied herself in the mirror, tracing the heart with her finger as she had so many times before.

A little pang for what had been, but no longing, and more important, no regret. It was only a memory, after all, a symbol of a sweet time. She had loved him, she thought as she took it off again, put it back in the box. As much as she'd known how at eighteen.

"But not forever, not for either of us."

What would she do for love? Maybe it was time to find out.

CHAPTER TWENTY-SIX

Work always helped. Closing herself in her studio, focusing, becoming took her out of herself. She knew something in the back of her brain would and could work on the problem—both problems—while she produced.

The external problem wanted to terrify her, and she couldn't let it. But the idea that someone—Sparks, if Red's instincts proved accurate—arranged killings, with her kidnapping at the center, rated some terror.

Revenge? It seemed like such a useless motive. He'd never get the years back. At the same time, he risked spending the rest of his life behind bars.

How could it be worth it?

She pushed herself through three hours in the booth, then deleted the last twenty minutes in edit.

Not her best work there, and the client always deserved her best.

By the time she'd finished, sent the file to the producer, she wanted a break like she wanted to breathe. A long shower did the trick, especially since she kept her mind as empty as possible.

A walk through the orchard over ground strewn with fallen blossoms polished it off.

In the kitchen, she followed Consuela's recipe for marinade—one with some zip—covered chicken breasts with it, put it aside. She made tortillas Consuela's way. They didn't look as perfect as Consuela's, but she hoped they'd pass the taste test.

She'd never asked if Dillon liked Mexican food, she realized as she chopped tomatoes for salsa. Well, she hoped he liked Mexican food, because that's what he was getting.

Chicken fajitas, frijoles, rice, salsa and chips, and flan to finish it off.

Considering the weather—pretty damn perfect—she set the small table outside, added candles. Why not?

She left the door open to the air as she sliced onions, peppers, took the chicken out, sliced it into diagonal strips.

Consuela had been very specific there, and—thank God—had been generous enough to make the guacamole for her.

She wasn't sure she was up for that.

By the time Dillon walked in, she had everything prepped for the cast-iron skillet (borrowed from Consuela).

And when he walked in with a handful of wildflowers, she realized the back of her brain, or some part of her, had worked on that internal problem.

He walked straight to her, wrapped around her, kissed her like a man who seriously meant it.

"You smell great."

"Is it me, or the salsa?"

He leaned down to sniff her neck. "Pretty sure it's you. From the field." He offered the flowers.

Everything inside her went to mush. "You picked them?"

"I didn't have time to buy any. One of the Angus cows decided it was a good day to calve. She needed a little help."

"First, wildflowers from the field are the best of the best."

"I'll remember that."

"Second, you helped deliver a baby cow?"

"Yeah. Usually they do just fine on their own, but now and then they need a little help. Good-looking bull calf. We may keep him that way."

She hunted up a vase. "What way?"

"A bull."

"What else would . . . oh." It genuinely made her shudder. "Ow! You do that?"

"You can't have a herd with a bunch of bulls, trust me."

"I bet the little baby cows trust you, too, right before you—" She mimed snapping scissors.

"If they were cows I wouldn't have to—" He mimed back. "Is this salsa up for grabs?"

"It is. I hope you like Mexican food."

With a tortilla chip, he scooped up salsa. "What's not to like? Pow," he said when he tasted. "I also like pow."

"Then you're in luck. I still don't like beer, so I'm having margaritas, but . . ." She got a Negra Modelo out of the fridge, poured it into a pilsner, added a wedge of lime.

After he studied it, he studied her. "You're the perfect woman."

"That'll get you all the fajitas you can eat."

"I can mow down some fajitas."

"Before I start on those, let's sit outside, with your beer, my margarita, and this salsa."

"Sounds good. Did Darlie and the baby get off all right?"

"Bright and early. She texted me awhile ago to let me know she'd stopped at a friend of her mom's. They'll stay there until morning rather than drive straight back to L.A."

"Better. That's a long drive with a toddler."

"And speaking of babies. Eight pounds even?"

Grinning, he hefted his beer. "On the nose, and from all accounts, Hailey had an easier time of it than my Angus. Four hours and there's Grace the amazing. The baby's a beauty, Hailey looked like a Madonna, I swear. Leo looked like a wreck. A really happy wreck. They're already home."

"Birthing center, midwife, easy delivery." Now Cate lifted her margarita. "Here's to all that."

"It's hard to believe, even when things go that smooth, they send you on your way that quick. My ladies are going to see them for a bit tomorrow, and the two new grandmothers are right there to help out."

"Here's to babies, each and every one." She tapped her glass to his. "I'd love to go see them, maybe in a couple days, once they're more settled."

"You can go with me."

"Let me know when, Uncle Dil."

He grinned again at that; she settled back.

"One day, I like to imagine we can sit out here like this—or sit anywhere for that matter—enjoying an adult beverage and some excellent salsa, and only talk about happy things."

"But not tonight. Sparks."

"Yeah, Sparks. Red told Grandpa and me what he thought, and what you seem to think."

"The guy gets stabbed in prison and only needs a few stitches? That doesn't work for me. It seems to me if somebody's going to stab somebody, they'd do a better job of it."

"I hadn't thought of it that way, but if you were nervous, or in a hurry—"

While butterflies fluttered behind him, Dillon tapped a finger on the table.

"First, you take the time to make the shank—and if you're caught with it, that's solitary. Second, you're so nervous and rushed you just happen to jab it into the perfect place? The place that causes little damage. Bleeds good, but that's about it.

"Bullshit."

Bullshit, horseshit. Either way, Cate saw he and Red had the same confidence.

"Wouldn't they fingerprint it?"

"Why do you figure he said he grabbed it, kept his hand on it? Smeared his hand and blood all over it? He's not stupid, Cate. He's no genius, but he's not stupid. He's calculating. I've thought about him a lot over the years."

"Have you?"

He met her eyes. "It was a turn for me, that night, Caitlyn. What you'd call a seminal moment for me, I guess. Up till then . . . I knew the world wasn't all rainbows, not with what happened to my father. But I'd never been close to violence, or fear. Watching you, watching my mom and Gram do what they did, your dad, Hugh. It all left a pretty big impression on me, so yeah, I've thought about Sparks over the years. And Denby, your mother. I feel like I know them on some level."

"Maybe you're right, you and Red. Maybe he's behind all this somehow, and for some reason. If he is, wouldn't my mother be his prime target?"

"She'd be harder to get to with a billion or so in security." He shrugged, drank. "But yeah."

"I don't feel anything for her, or about her. I haven't been able to work up a good rage in that area for a long time. But I wouldn't want her murdered."

"I'm a lot more concerned about you."

"I left my grandfather and Red this morning discussing tightening security here, adding to it. And since I can see you have other ideas, tell me what they are before I start dinner. Then we can close this door for a while."

"You could come stay on the ranch."

"I can't leave Grandpa, that's number one. Then there's my work."

"Figured that. So I spend my nights here. I need to be on the ranch early every morning, but Red's going to stay. He more than halfway does anyway, so he'll just put in the other half while I stay here."

Cate shifted, crossed her legs, then sipped at her margarita. "Do you think your ladies need a man to look after them? And I need one to look after me?"

A man could navigate a minefield if he knew where to step. And where not to.

"I figure my ladies can handle just about anything that comes. And you'd do a good job with that yourself. And yeah, everybody needs somebody, or ought to, who'll look after them."

"That's a damn good answer to a tricky question. And I won't lie. I'll probably sleep better at night with you here. Not just for me, but for Grandpa, Consuela."

"Then it's done. I've got one more thought before we close the door."

"All right."

"I don't see Hugh or Lily or your dad in this. They were set to pay the ransom. Nothing they did affected the outcome. If we're wrong, and it's Dupont behind all this, that changes. But it's not, because she'd have gone after your family first. And your nanny from back then."

Her heart jumped. "Oh God. Nina. I never thought of her."

"Red did. She's fine. You and the nanny are the ones who turned things on your mother. She'd have made moves there, and she'd have the means to do it."

"You do know her."

"As well as I can. It's a lot harder for Sparks to get to someone in Ireland, even to find her at this point. And for what? She cared enough about you, was afraid enough of your mother to keep her mouth shut about the affair. They set her up as a dupe, but you screwed that up for them, then Dupont finished it off."

"I'll feel better when I talk to her myself. I'll call her tomorrow. You don't mention yourself, your family?"

"I think we're low on possibilities, but that's why I want Red there, why we're hiring a couple of retired cops he knows to work on the ranch for the season."

"You cover your bases, Dillon."

"I take care of what's mine." He looked into her eyes in that way that always hit her heart. Right into them, right into her. "You have to know you're what's mine."

Nerves, sudden, intense, pushed her to her feet. "I need to cook."

She hurried inside, added oil to the skillet. As she gathered ingredients, she mumbled curses—self-directed—in Italian.

And felt the nerves ease off a little with movement, purpose. "You're going to let me get away with that."

He topped off her margarita from the pitcher she'd set on the island. "I know how and where to push when something or someone's being stubborn. You're not being stubborn, so I can wait."

"I'm trying to think what I did in this life to deserve you."

"Now, that's being stupid. I'm getting another beer."

"It's not." Rubbing her hematite bracelet, she turned to him while the oil heated. "It's not. And I'm not being stubborn. I need you to . . ." She pushed a hand in the air in his direction. "Keep your distance while I get through this next part."

Fascinated, he watched her, then poured the beer. "Seriously?"

"Yes. God, this is a lot of talk." She pushed at her hair, wished she'd tied it back out of the way. "I thought we'd get all that other business out of the way, eat, then have a lot of sex."

He lifted the beer, drank. "I said it before. The perfect woman."

"I'm not. So many parts of me are still a mess, and probably always will be. I used to have panic attacks, nightmares. I rarely do now, or in years now, but I know what they feel like, and I just came close to the panic attack."

"Because I'm telling you I'm in love with you? If you didn't already know that, I go back to stupid."

"Not stupid," she muttered, and added the chicken to the hot oil to sear it. "I didn't want you to."

"Love you or tell you?"

"Either, right now. *Foutre. Merde.*"

"That's French this time, right? I think I get the picture."

She pulled air in her nose, let it out of her mouth slowly. "I'm not cursing at you. I worried if things ever got close to that, I'd screw it up, or you would, we would. God, I don't want to screw it up. I just can't screw it up. I need you, Dillon."

Wasn't that, just that, enormous enough? That need for someone else.

"From where I'm standing, nothing's screwed up."

Not yet, she thought, and carefully turned the chicken.

"It may be self-defeating to jump to the what-if, but for me . . . I need you and your family. Since I was a child, since that night. Those emails with Julia helped me through the rough years, just that contact, constant, caring. A touchstone for me."

"We already made a promise we wouldn't mess with the family connection."

"I know. I know we'll try to keep the promise. I . . . My father took care of what was his, Dillon, and that was me. He gave up so much to take care of me, give me what I needed. I knew we'd both turned a corner when he felt able to travel for work again. I knew he'd stopped worrying, every minute, and that I was okay again. And even through all that, I had Julia. If I could wish for a mother, it would be Julia."

He laid a hand on her shoulder. "You're never going to lose her, or any of us."

"No?" She whirled around. "And what if I said I didn't love you? That I couldn't? That I wouldn't?"

"Then you'd break my heart. And the pieces of it would still love you."

Because her eyes filled, she pressed her fingers to them.

"Don't do that and expect me to keep my distance."

She pulled one hand away, firmly tapped a finger in the air three times to make sure he did.

"I need to cook," she said again.

Digging for calm, she took the chicken out to rest, covered it. After adding more oil to the pan, she sautéed the peppers and onions she'd already sliced.

Calmer, because she cooked and had to pay attention, she continued. "I told you about the three men I've been with."

"You did."

"With Noah, I felt some panic at first, but I recognized that as the normal nerves and excitement a girl, with very little experience, feels when a boy she's already noticed notices her enough to ask her out on her first actual date. I didn't feel anything like that with the others. Just attraction, interest. Normal, I'd say, if somewhat limited. I'd really hoped to keep it at that with you—with the addition of solid affection and friendship."

"That's not going to work out."

Without looking at him, she scraped up the brown bits from the chicken to coat the peppers and onions.

She let them cook while she sliced the chicken. "You're awfully sure of yourself."

"I won't settle for it. I don't know why you would."

"Because it's easy. Keep things on your own terms, within your own limitations, it's always easy. But you're right, it's not working out, not when you look at me and say I'm yours. Not when you say that, I see that, and hit the panic button."

Time for another shaky breath. "I didn't think I would, and I have been thinking about it, about you, about all of it. But I did panic, and not because I'm stubborn or stupid, but because while part of me wants it to be easy, the rest of me wants to be yours. Wants you to be mine."

He said nothing while she started one of her fancy arrangements of the food on a platter.

When he did speak, it was quiet, easy.

"It might've been that night when I wanted a drumstick, looked over, and saw you. But I really think it was when you drove up, got out of the car with an armload of red lilies. You had eyes like blue-bonnets, like spring in the dead of winter, and a smile that slammed straight into me, blew right through me. And those boots."

He paused, sipped his beer.

"Those really tall black boots. Man, I hope you still have those boots, because I like to imagine you wearing them and not much else. Anyway." He drank again while she uncovered bowls of grated cheddar, of sour cream.

"I'm pretty sure it was that moment when the rest of you got what it wants. I never got over it."

"You didn't even know me."

"Oh, for fuck's sake."

Now she blinked at him. He so rarely sounded impatient.

"You hadn't even seen me in years."

"I damn well knew you. Through the emails with my mom, through Hugh and Lily, through Aidan and Consuela. I knew when you fell for the dancer, how you studied at NYU, then otherwise, learning all those languages. You've been part of my life since I was twelve years old, so deal with it."

Carefully now, she pulled the tortillas out of the warming oven. "I think that's the first time I've seriously pissed you off."

"No, it's not. It won't be the last either. That doesn't change a god-damn thing."

"What if I hadn't come back?"

"You were always going to come back, but waiting for it was starting to wear some."

One more breath, and no more panic. "I was always going to come back," she agreed. "Even when I didn't know it." She laid a hand on his cheek. "I've got pictures of you, too, Dillon. I'm sorting them out."

"I told you I came close once, with one woman who mattered to me. But I couldn't get there. I couldn't because it was you, Cate. It was always you."

He set down the beer. "And I'm tired of keeping my distance. That food'll stay warm enough for later."

She smiled, expecting him to grab her into a kiss as frustrated as he looked. Instead, he scooped her up as he'd done their first night together.

"Oh. That much later."

"That's right."

"God, I've missed this." She set her teeth on the side of his neck. "I really don't think I have those boots anymore. It was years ago."

"That's a damn shame," he said as he carried her upstairs.

"But I'm a certified expert at shopping for boots."

"Black, up above the knee."

He dropped her on the bed, looked down at her as the light from the sinking sun spread gold over her.

She crooked a finger at him when he dragged off his shoes. When he lay over her, sent her shimmering with the first kiss, she chained her arms around him.

"I love you, Caitlyn."

So much spilled into her she didn't know how to hold it. "Give me time to say it back. It may be crazy or superstitious, or both, but I really do believe when I say it, when I mean it, it's forever."

"Since I want forever, and forever's what I'm going to have, take your time."

"That kind of confidence could be annoying."

"Be annoyed later."

He took her mouth again, but tenderly. So tenderly now. Offering love, she knew, and how could she resist it?

She opened herself to it, the simple and stunning gift of it. And opening, taking it in, she felt it smooth over old scars, ease away old doubts.

Take the gift, she thought, take it and give it back. If she couldn't yet say the words, she could give him what beat in her heart.

She could show him in the language of touch and taste that needed no voice. She could show him by the way she unbuttoned his shirt to skim her fingers over his chest, over those hard-ridged muscles of his back as she peeled the shirt away.

How she rose to him when he drew hers aside, followed the reveal of bare skin with his lips.

The golden light smoldered toward red as they undressed each other. The blue of the sea surging to and from the beach below deepened with it. And he felt her give, and give.

She had so much to give. More than she knew or believed. He'd seen it in her from the very first moment, and in all the moments he'd had with her since. When she trusted herself, trusted them, she'd give him the words.

For now, he'd simply love her, and know the heart beating under his lips held him in it.

When she rose over him, shook back her hair in the last pulsing lights of the sun, he knew he'd love her every minute of every day for the rest of his life.

She brought his hands to her lips, held them there as she took him in, slowly, slowly, slowly took him in. And when her head fell back from the pleasure of it, as her sigh shuddered out, she glided his hands down to her breasts.

Easy movement, slow again, and long and deep. Wave after wave of that pleasure, more pleasure, with the rise, the fall, the fall and the rise.

The light softened like a pearled mist, held and held there as she held him. And as night crept closer, as the first stars waited to wake, he lifted to her, wrapped around her to take them both over.

She dropped her head to his shoulder, let her body melt to his.

"I've never felt for anyone what I feel for you."

He stroked a hand down her back. "I know."

Melting or not, she laughed. "Confidence. Heading toward annoying."

"I know because it's the same for me. It's just fact I'm what you want and need. I can wait until you get there. It's not going to take much longer anyway."

"I'm seeing a new side of you." She eased back, tried to see his expression in the encroaching dark. "And it's leaning heavily toward arrogance."

"It's not arrogance to know what you know. No one's ever going to love you like I do, Cate. It's going to be hard for you to hold out against that." He gave her a quick kiss. "I'm starving. I'd say you are, too."

"I could definitely eat."

"See? I know what I know."

While Cate ate fajitas with Dillon in candle- and starlight, Charlotte stormed around her bedroom suite. She'd just had it redone, in gold, gold, and more gold, with emerald and sapphire accents.

She'd demanded opulent, and the decorator delivered with miles of fabric, acres of glittering crystals, including the seven-tiered chandelier imported from Italy.

Under its light she could—and did—lie in a bed draped in gold silk to admire the ceiling mural. Images of Charlotte as Eve, as Juliet, as Lady Godiva, as queens and goddesses gazed down to wish her pleasant dreams.

She had it all to herself now that Conrad occupied his own suite. The poor old thing had sleep apnea, required that awful mask at night. Poor ancient thing, she corrected.

Sleep apnea, two heart attacks, a bout of pneumonia over the winter, prostate issues, skin cancer that had required surgery and reconstruction of his left ear.

And he just kept ticking.

When would he just die, quietly, painlessly, of course, and free her to take a decent lover? The prenup—ironclad—left her nothing if she had even a tiny, little affair.

Which hadn't been a problem, or not much of one, up until the last few years. No, ancient Conrad could barely get it up now, and sure as hell couldn't keep it up.

She'd never expected him to live this long. Surely not long enough he had to use a cane to walk across the damn room, not so long his body went from robust to flabby, and she had to at least pretend to care about the pharmacy of drugs he needed to stay alive.

But at least she didn't have to pretend to want sex with him anymore. And he was sweetly grateful she "understood" he wasn't capable any longer—and remained his loving, devoted wife.

All the money in the world, and she couldn't afford to get a decent lay.

That wasn't the worst of it, oh, no, not nearly.

Having the cops come to her door—that trumped all. She hadn't spoken to them, of course. And damn well wouldn't. Her lawyers crafted a statement, her lawyers handled the idiotic police.

Imagine wanting to question *her* about murders and attacks that had nothing to do with her. About people she didn't give one good damn about.

Good riddance to that asshole Denby. And so what about Scarpetti, who hadn't been smart enough to keep her out of prison? Her only regret about that bastard hick cop? He hadn't plunged to his death. She hoped whoever had arranged it tried again, and did a better job.

And Grant? She wished he'd died choking on his own blood!

She paused to draw a finger down the gold silk drapes her maid had already pulled for the night.

No, she didn't. Not really. She still had a little, tiny soft spot for Grant Sparks.

She wondered if he'd kept that body in prison, if he'd kept his looks.

He'd be out in a couple of years, and if Conrad finally died, she might just have him brought to her. She'd even pay him to bang her brains out.

Just thinking about it, about the sex she'd had with him, made her hot and itchy.

She'd have the maid come back, draw her a bath, lots of oils. And she'd take care of the itch herself.

She paused to study herself in one of her dressing room mirrors. Thanks to implants, her hair remained lush and full. Regular tune-ups kept her face taut, smooth.

Admiring herself, she undressed, turned naked this way and that. Breasts full and high, ass high and tight. Implants and tucks worked wonders. She smoothed a hand over her belly—flat thanks to her last tummy tuck.

Smooth thighs, no wagging under the arms. The wonders of modern medicine—and the money to afford it, she thought with a slow smile.

She wouldn't have to pay Grant Sparks or anyone to get into her bed. To her eyes, she barely looked thirty-five, and with a perfect body. No one looking at her would believe she had a daughter over . . . how old was the bitch again? Who could remember? But no one would believe she had an adult daughter.

Maybe time to remind them, she considered as she reached for a white satin robe. Squeeze a little more juice out of that lemon. She'd get her publicist on that in the morning, but now, she wanted that bath, that self-release.

Then she'd take a pill, call it an early night.

She had a photo shoot the next day, had to look her best while she did the spread. Then a dinner party after where she could complain about exhausting herself for her art.

Really a perfect day, she decided as she rang for the maid.

The only thing that could make it better would be if poor old Conrad died in his sleep.

CHAPTER TWENTY-SEVEN

Relationships, Cate discovered, could offer a steady, satisfying kind of routine. Because she barely surfaced, if at all, when Dillon left each morning, she woke alone, took her time clearing her brain with coffee and the view.

Depending on her workload, she might put in an hour in the studio before walking up to the main house to nag her grandfather into the gym.

Better, as June hinted at summer, she nagged him into the pool.

She'd researched water aerobics.

"Swimming's supposed to be relaxing."

"It will be, when you finish those squats and biceps curls."

Standing in the shallow end, she did them with him.

"Whoever invented pool weights deserves to be shot." Sunlight beamed off his sunglasses as he curled the bright blue weights up through the water. "Then run over by a train. Then shot again."

"Consuela's making a frittata for breakfast." She squatted, curled, admitted a secret desire for that bullet and train. "But you have to earn it. *Fagfaimid!* Two more, Sullivan!"

"Now she throws Irish at me. I love my granddaughter, but my personal trainer's a pain in the ass."

"One more, and . . . done."

She laughed when he sank, Ray-Bans, sun hat, and all, under the water.

"Let's stretch it out," she said when he surfaced. "You're getting shredded there, Handsome Hugh."

He gripped the side, did the calf stretches, the hamstring, the quads. "A man my age should be allowed to get creaky and flabby."

"Not when he's my grandpa."

"Are you going to nag Lily into all this when she gets back next week?"

"That's the plan."

Hugh took off his hat, wrung it out, plopped it back on. "Might be worth it then."

Smiling, she pushed off to do a lazy reward lap, to float, to bask.

"Since Dad's due back from London soon, he'll come up for a while, and I'll get him in on this, too. We can work out a synchronized routine. Take that show on the road."

"The Swimming Sullivans."

On another laugh, she did a surface dive, skimmed along the bottom and to the ladder. Pulling herself out, she toweled off while watching boats ply the sea.

"Look." She pointed. "It's a blue whale. The first I've seen this season."

He stepped beside her in time to see the tail flip up, disappear.

"I remember watching whales sound from here when I was younger than you. And still, it never fails to pull me in. When my mother decided to move to Ireland, she asked which I wanted. The house here or in Beverly Hills.

"It was always this one. Always. Even when weeks, even months passed until I could be here and hope to see a whale sound, it was always this one."

"We're lucky, Grandpa, in our ancestors."

"That we are."

She hooked the towel on before dragging her hair back with her hands. "One problem with the location? Stylist. When Lily gets back, we're going to join forces and get Gino up here for hair. He'd come to Big Sur for Lily."

"You have beautiful hair."

She squeezed water out of it. "It needs something. A good, professional whack. There are only two people I trust to whack at it. Gino, and the woman I found in New York after many sad and failed attempts."

She turned, fluttered her eyelashes. "After all, I have a boyfriend now."

"You couldn't have chosen better." Hugh put on a white terry cloth robe.

"Sometimes I think fate did the choosing, but either way." She circled around to join him, hooked a floral sarong around her waist. "Come to dinner tonight."

"I'm not horning in on your time together."

"It's not horning in if I'm asking you."

As always, Consuela had already set the table for breakfast. A carafe of juice nestled in an ice bucket, an insulated pot of coffee stood ready.

Cate poured two servings of both.

"I'll ask Dillon to bring steaks—and your favorite fingerling potatoes if they have any. I could attempt my second soufflé."

On a happy sigh, Hugh sat. "You had me at 'steak.'"

"Good. He can bring the dogs, and we'll have ourselves a party."

"And what are you doing today besides making me dinner?"

"Singing for most of it. You guest starred on that series *Caper* a couple seasons ago, didn't you?"

"I did. Retired thief called back into action to help a friend. It's a solid ensemble show, cleverly done."

"And they're doing a kind of musical episode, but it turns out the lead actress can't carry a tune. Seriously can't. They'd planned to play that for laughs, but don't feel it worked. So I'm dubbing her songs. Two solos, a duet, and an ensemble."

"You'll have fun with it."

"I already am. And here comes breakfast."

Cate's smile faded when she saw Consuela's tight-lipped, hard-eyed expression.

"Is everything all right?"

"I don't want to tell you." With sharp movements, Consuela set down the tray. Lips compressed, she put two bowls of fruit and yogurt on the table, then the frittata. "But I must tell you."

Hugh rose, pulled out a chair. "Sit down, Consuela."

"I can't sit. I'm too angry to sit." On a rapid stream of Spanish, she threw up her hands, marched away and back again.

"That was too fast for me," Hugh admitted, "except for the curse words. I don't believe I've ever heard Consuela use those words."

"It's about Charlotte. On TV this morning. It's all right. It won't matter."

That brought another spate of furious Spanish. But this time at the end of it, Consuela crossed her hands over her heart, closed her eyes, took several breaths.

"I'm sorry. I will calm. That woman, she was on my morning show with her lies and sad looks, and her pretending to be a good person. She says—announces," Consuela corrected, "she is—has—established a big—much money—foundation. Her husband's money because she is a . . ."

Stopping herself, she shook her head. "I will not say the word she is. She makes this for—ah, I'm too upset for English."

"She's established a charitable foundation." Cate translated for Hugh as Consuela spewed in Spanish. "To help women, mothers, who are in or have been released from prison. To help them connect or reconnect with their child or children. Education programs, counseling, drug and alcohol rehabilitation, housing assistance, job training and placement. She's calling it A Mother's Heart.

"Yes, Consuela, I understand."

"But, *niña mío,* she says how her heart is broken because her daughter has never forgiven her. How this breaks the heart of all mothers. And she hopes to help heal the hearts of mothers who have made mistakes as she did.

"She has tears." Consuela tapped a finger to her cheek. "Lying tears that would burn her heart if she had one. She has no heart to burn, no heart to break."

"No, she doesn't." Rising, she put her arms around the furious housekeeper. "But you do. You are a mother to me, always. A mother in my heart," she murmured, kissing Consuela's cheek. "She's nothing to us."

"*Te amo.*"

"*Te amo,*" Cate echoed, and kissed her other cheek.

"Your breakfast gets cold. You eat. Both eat. I have work."

"She'll clean something within an inch of its life," Cate commented as Consuela marched off. "That's what she does when she's pissed off or upset."

When she sat, started to put a serving of the frittata on Hugh's plate, he covered her hand with his. "And you?"

"Me? I'm going to enjoy this excellent breakfast. The hell with her, Grandpa. Just the hell with her. And who knows? If she actually follows through with this, she may—inadvertently—help some women who need help."

"She'll make the rounds on this, milk some press out of it."

"I'm sure she will. I'm sure that's the point." She shrugged as she dished up the frittata. "I could do the same thing. I won't," she added when she caught Hugh's stare. "Because I think more of myself and my family than milking cheap publicity. But I've thought of it a few times over the years."

"If you wanted to make a statement—"

"I don't," she interrupted. "I made that decision a long time ago, and haven't changed my mind. And I have thought about it, considered it, weighed the upside of it. The downside, for me, is still heavier. I like the life I've built, Grandpa, the one I'm still building. I'm happy in it. And there's still enough in me to get real satisfaction from knowing she's not happy, not really, in the life she built."

"There's no revenge sweeter than a happy life."

"I bet she's not sitting by the pool on this gorgeous morning, with miles of sea and sky all around, smelling the flowers, feeling the ocean breeze. And eating the best frittata in California with someone she loves."

Cate went to work, miserably botched the first dubbing, and had to walk away, order her head to clear.

Bad enough, she thought, the timing on this song, the actress's lip movements, posed a challenge without letting Charlotte in.

Using the mirror, she visualized herself as the character, sang it out. Then she tried again.

Better, not best.

Five takes later, she felt the rhythm click, did two insurance takes. She played all three back, watching the monitor for any misses, decided the first insurance take actually hit the mark best.

Since she felt she'd found the groove, she worked on the second solo—a kind of anthem, lots of movement, considerable drama.

Tricky.

And the trick, Cate reminded herself, was putting herself into the role as much as the song.

By the time she broke for the day, she had three takes of each song performed, edited, and filtered. She sent the files. No point in going forward until she knew the director—and the actress—gave the thumbs-up.

Plus, she needed to pick up the order she'd sent Julia that morning. And she could use an hour at the ranch.

She joined the throng of tourists for the short drive—reminded herself she really wanted a convertible.

Yes, she thought as she drove up the ranch road, she could use an hour here. As much as she loved Sullivan's Rest, the ranch always gave her spirit a lift.

Hay, oats, corn climbed from the fields toward the sky, gold and green carpets waving in the breeze. Cattle and horses grazed in other fields, like a painting against the rise of the Santa Lucias. She heard the distant rumble of a tractor—or some machine—as she walked around to the family door.

She saw Maggie, a bright orange floppy-brimmed hat shielding her face, baggy overalls, sturdy Birkenstocks, staking tomatoes.

Bees buzzed in the hives on the far side of the garden. While Cate appreciated the honey, and all the work they did, she was more than happy with the distance.

"A pretty day to work in the garden," Cate called out.

Maggie straightened, stretched her back. "It's not half-bad."

"Everything's grown so much. I was here barely a week ago, and it's just running away."

"No poop like chicken poop for a garden."

"Apparently."

"Julia gave me your order. I can go grab it for you now if you're in a hurry."

"No, don't rush. I have some time. Can I help you?"

"Do you know how to stake tomatoes?"

"No."

"Well, come on over here and learn."

Cate stepped carefully between the rows and got an education.

"Julia's out in the fields somewhere, but she's due back about now. Red took the afternoon off to surf, and I guess he earned it. That's right, girlie, soft hands. You don't want to break the stems. If you're looking for Dillon, he's out shearing sheep."

"Shearing sheep?"

"We got a man to help him, knows what he's doing in that area. Better to have four hands than two when it comes to it."

"What do you do with the wool?"

"We used to sell it all, but this shearing, I'm keeping a quarter of it."

"For what?"

"Good job," Maggie decided after giving Cate's attempt a critical study. "And that does it. Come on in, and I'll show you."

They went in through the mudroom, where Maggie pulled off her gardening shoes, through to the main kitchen. Maggie signaled come ahead, so Cate followed her into a sitting room.

And stared.

"Is that . . ." She'd seen *Sleeping Beauty*. "A spinning wheel?"

"It's not a rocket to the moon." With obvious affection, Maggie stroked the wheel. "Got it on eBay for a damn good price."

"It's, well, it's adorable. What are you going to do with it?"

"What it was made to do. Spin wool."

"They shave—shear," she corrected, "the sheep, and you take the wool—"

"And wash it—wash it without washing out all the lanolin. Dry it on my old clotheshorse in the sun."

"Wash, dry, then put it on here, and it makes . . ."

"Yarn. Wool yarn for your crafting pleasure. Horizon Ranch

Wool," she added with considerable pride. "Pure. I may experiment some with natural colorings with some, just to see."

Like *Sleeping Beauty,* it struck Cate as something out of a fairy tale. "How do you know how?"

"YouTube." She took a hank out of a basket. "That was on a sheep a couple days ago."

Cate took it, felt it, marveled. "When the aliens attack, I want to be with you."

On a bark of laughter, Maggie led the way back to the kitchen. "We're having some raspberry sun tea."

"That sounds incredible."

She heard the mudroom door open.

"Mom?"

"Right here."

"We need to call the farrier. Aladdin threw a shoe, and while we're at it— Oh, hi, Cate. Sorry, I thought I'd be back before this, have your order ready."

"There's no hurry."

"I've got it put together back in the order fridge." Maggie handed her daughter a glass of iced tea.

"Thanks." She had her hair in a braid, wore jeans and a plaid shirt with the sleeves rolled to her elbows. Her skin, dewy from the heat, carried the glow of summer. "Thirsty work out there. And I'm ready to sit on something that isn't moving."

She dropped down, stretched out her legs.

After giving Cate a glass, Maggie skimmed her hand over Julia's hair, a gesture so casually affectionate it stung the back of Cate's eyes. "How about some apple slices and cheddar?"

Smiling, Julia tipped her head toward her mother's arm. "I wouldn't say no. My favorite after-school snack as a kid," Julia began, then saw the tear spill over onto Cate's cheek.

"Oh, honey."

She started to get up, but Cate waved her back down. "No, I'm sorry. That came out of nowhere."

"No, it didn't." Maggie got an apple, took it to the sink to scrub it nearly hard enough to remove the peel. "We get TV up here like everybody else. I didn't bring it up. I figured if you wanted to talk about it, you'd talk about it."

"It's not that. Or maybe that flipped a switch I didn't realize I hadn't shut all the way off again. It's—I see the two of you together, and it's so . . . the way it should be. You love each other, and show love in the simplest ways. I have that with my grandmother, with Consuela, with my aunts, so I know what it is."

"And she keeps finding ways to hurt you again."

"It doesn't hurt, not the way it used to."

"Keeps pushing it right back in your face." Maggie began to slice the apple as if hoping to see blood spill from its core.

"That." A relief to be so quickly understood. "Just exactly that. In all of our faces, not just mine. I'll probably have to change my phone number again because somebody always manages to dig it out, and the calls start. The stories will run, and I know they'll run their course, but for a while, it's front and center all over again."

She drew breath in, let it out. "I know how privileged I am because a song-and-dance man—boy, really—who could act got on a boat in Cobh and made his way to Hollywood. He met a woman—a girl—who was his match in every single way. Together they created a dynasty. Not just of fame and fortune."

"Of family, and ethics, and good work, good works," Julia said. "We've met a lot of your family."

"You had them over for a barbecue. I'm sorry I missed it."

"There'll be others. You're young, beautiful, white, wealthy, and talented, so yes, privileged. Being privileged doesn't negate trauma. Your mother doesn't see past the fame and fortune. Even though she has her own—"

"Infamous isn't the same as famous," Maggie pointed out as she sliced a cube of cheddar.

"True enough. She still wants a piece of yours, your father's, your family's. She still covets what you have, what you are. I'd like to kick her ass."

"That's nice of you," Cate said as Maggie cackled.

"Nothing nice about it. That's been top of my wish list since we found out she was part of what happened to you."

Fascinated, Cate studied the face she knew so well. "You always seem so calm, so level."

At that Maggie threw back her head, literally hooted before she set the plate of apple and cheese slices on the table. "Go after one of her chicks, my girl will kick a dozen asses, and won't bother to take names."

"Names wouldn't matter. She's not going to stop, Cate. I honestly believe she's not capable of genuine emotions, but only greed and envy. You have to face that. And still, the bottom line is she'll never have it. She'll never have any piece of you or your family."

"In fewer words, fuck her."

Julia shifted her gaze to her mother. "Well, those are fewer words."

"Why not be succinct?" And she touched Cate's heart when she skimmed a hand down her hair just as she had to Julia before she sat. "Now, put the cheddar on the apple, and eat something happy."

Doing what she was told, Cate ate the happy.

It didn't take long for a few enterprising reporters to dig their way to her phone number, her email. She blocked and ignored.

But the call she'd dreaded most came through.

Voice over voice—her mother's, her own singing a happy song from her first movie role, the horror movie laugh, whispers. Digitized, she knew, jerky. Layered together, inexpertly but effectively, into a clear message.

"You didn't do what you were told. Now people are dead."

"Blood is on your hands. More will die. Your fault. It's always been your fault."

She made a copy for herself before handing her phone over to Michaela. She'd buy a new one, again. Change her number, again.

It would be, she knew, the same as always. Bits and pieces from recorded interviews pieced together, layered together into a new recording, and sent from a prepaid cell.

"That's the best they can do?" Dillon demanded.

Cate bent down to pet the dogs who now had beds and toys at the cottage. "It's the reality of it. It's a crappy voice-over hack. Record a recording, pull out specific words or phrases, layer, merge, send. I could do a better job in my sleep, so it's an amateur. The recordings are always full of noise—static, vibrations, the echo of the room," she explained.

"I don't much give a damn about the quality."

"It probably lets my mother off the hook. She'd be able to pay for better. And as for Sparks, where's he going to get the equipment in prison?"

"These calls are threats, Cate. You need to take them seriously."

"It's a scare tactic, Dillon, and it's lost its ability to scare me. I'm taking Gram's advice on my mother, applying it here."

"Which is?"

"Fuck them."

It felt damn good to say it, to mean it.

"I've got a big, strong rancher and a couple of fierce guard dogs looking out for me. Lily's coming home tomorrow. I'm not letting anything spoil that."

"You didn't tell Hugh about this latest call."

"I will, just not right this minute." She got him a beer, poured herself a glass of wine. "Let's take the fierce guard dogs for a romp on the beach before dinner."

"Rain's coming."

Lips pursed, she looked out at the pretty summer sky. "I don't see rain."

"You will, but we've got a couple hours first."

Dillon didn't push—what was the point? But he cornered Red the next morning.

They stood on rain-soft ground in air fresh as a spring daisy pouring feed mixed with raw milk into the pig troughs.

"I never thought I'd get a charge out of feeding pigs, but here I am. Milk-fed pigs at that." He scratched his ear. "Nice soaker we had last night."

"We needed it. What do you know about these calls, these recordings Cate gets?"

Red glanced over where one of the seasonal hands fed the chickens. Since it was baking day, both women manned the kitchen.

He'd checked the daily work list, so he knew Julia had assigned others to muck out the stalls, but the horses had to be fed, watered, rubbed down with insect repellant before going out to pasture.

"Let's talk about this in my office. How's she handling this one?" he asked as they walked.

"Like it's no big deal, and it damn well is."

"You know she's been getting these calls for years now, so the impact's bound to fade."

"That doesn't make this one nothing."

When Dillon opened the stable doors, the air filled with horses, grain, leather, manure. All combined into a perfume he'd loved all his life.

Knowing the routine, Red took the first stall on the left, Dillon went right.

"Mic will do what she can, plus she's got the cop in New York. The FBI's on it, too. There's an agent who follows through on these whenever she gets one."

"How come they can't trace it back?"

"A lot of reasons." They both scooped out grain. "Recording's not long enough, it's from a drop phone. Whoever's sending it destroys the phone and battery right after—from what I'm told they figure. It's always recordings of recorded interviews or movie clips. They've actually been able to match some of those. Not the same message every time."

"Threatening her, scaring her."

"Yeah, same sentiment, you could say. One of the theories was some nutcase obsessed with Cate wanted attention. But that's thin now considering it's gone on for years."

"Her mother could be behind it. Cate doesn't think so because it's shitty quality, and the woman has plenty of money. But that could be a cover, something to make it seem like it's just some nutcase."

Red moved to the next stall. Every horse in the stables had its head out, watching. Like, Hurry up, man, I'm starving here.

It never failed to amuse Red.

"That's been my thought," he told Dillon. "Cate usually gets one around the time some story hits or Dupont gives some interview that gets a splash. It could be her way, her sick-fuck way, of taking an extra shot at Cate."

Dillon walked back to get the prenatals for the pregnant mare in the next stall. Once dispensed, he marked the clipboard outside the stall.

"If that holds true," he said, "it's not a real threat. Just petty and mean."

"Charlotte Dupont's got petty and mean to spare. I wouldn't put it past her to find someone to cause Cate real harm, but without Cate, she loses the easy lift."

Red frowned at the clipboard, turned. Dillon already had the horse pill punched into a quartered apple. "He won't take his med otherwise."

"I remember."

"Be sure he doesn't just spit it out. He's sneaky about it. What do you mean, 'easy lift'?"

"When she wants a publicity boost, she plays the sad, repentant mother with the unforgiving daughter. Some quarters buy that act."

"Because some quarters are idiots."

Red and the apple/pill-chewing horse eyed each other. "Plenty of idiots in this old world. And I got another on that. I think she likes it, likes thinking she's tormenting Cate, and the rest of them, too. I don't see her giving that up."

Dillon thought it over while they fed, watered, medicated.

"What if it's not her? Could Sparks pull this off?"

"I don't underestimate what Sparks could pull off." And Red believed wholeheartedly he had the scar to prove it. "I don't know what it gains him, but if there's an angle to it for him, I think he'd find a way."

They started the rubdowns, adding the scent of insect repellant to the mix in the air.

"He has reason to want to hurt her, just like it said on the phone. She didn't do what she was told, and he got caught."

"Then I guess we'll keep looking out for her."

Red glanced over, watched Dillon run his hands down a gelding's foreleg.

"You're what I'd call more conventional in some areas than your grandmother and me."

The statement brought out a grin as Dillon worked. "About everyone of my acquaintance is more conventional than Gram and you."

"That's why I've been crazy about her for going on twenty-five years now. You know she's got me rolling the yarn she's making. I'm trying to watch the ball game last night, and I'm rolling yarn like some pigtailed little girl in a pinafore."

"Well, that's a look," Dillon murmured.

"Listen, Dil, I'm not your father, your grandfather, but—"

Turning his head, Dillon met Red's eyes directly. "You've been the next best thing on both of those scores most of my life."

"Well then, I'm going to ask you straight out. Are you going to ask Caitlyn to marry you?"

Dillon coated a hind leg, moved around the back of the horse to the next side in a way Red never felt quite easy about doing himself.

"In due time."

"You've been in love with her for a while now."

"I more than half believe since I was twelve."

Red walked around his horse on the front side. "I think you're right about that. Any reason you're waiting now?"

"She'd say no now. She'd feel bad about it, but she'd say no. I don't see any reason to make her feel bad, so I can wait until she'll say yes."

"And you'll know when that is."

"Pretty sure I will. She's got tells."

"I never could beat you at poker, even when you were a kid. What tells?"

Dillon moved on to the next horse. "She's got a few. One's the bracelet—the one she wears a lot. She rubs on it when she's anxious."

"I've seen that."

"If she thinks she'll be anxious or nervous, she makes sure to wear it. She curses under her breath in foreign languages when she's frustrated. I don't know the language, but I know a curse when I hear it. When she's going to take a big step, she'll have that bracelet on. She might mumble under her breath something I don't understand, but it's not curses. It's more like I'd say a mantra."

Dillon coated the horse, taking his time, being thorough.

"So I'll know when."

"I'm going to bet you will."

CHAPTER TWENTY-EIGHT

As they had for Lily's departure, Cate and Hugh stood together outside waiting for her return.

"Any minute now." Cate checked her watch, calculated the time since Lily's text on landing. "Even with the traffic."

"She's bringing perfect weather with her. The air's bell clear. She'll want to walk around the gardens after being cooped up in the plane and the car all day."

"They've never looked better. Then she'll want a martini on the seaside terrace or up on the bridge."

"Most definitely." He slid an arm around Cate's waist. "We know our girl."

"We do. Oh, that's the gate. I heard the gate. I wish we'd hired a brass band!"

"I wish I'd thought of it. She'd love it. There she is."

They watched the limo, sleek and black, round a turn below. "Now I'll have my two best girls home."

The limo wound its way up, slid smoothly to a stop. Cate started to rush forward to open the passenger door herself. And her father stepped out.

"Dad!" Giddy with joy, she ran to him, jumped into his arms. Laughed as he swung her in circles as he had when she was a child. "Oh, what a surprise. What an amazing surprise. I thought you were still in London."

"I wrapped a couple days ago. Then Lily and I conspired." He swung her again. "I missed the hell out of you, Catey."

"Best surprise ever."

"What am I, chopped liver?"

Cate looked over to where Lily stood, holding hands with Hugh. "The finest pâté, with truffles." She turned into Lily's arms, breathed in her scent. "To quote another Sullivan, I missed the hell out of you."

"Mutual. God, it's good to be home! Oh, look at your hair! There's so much of it, and all beautiful. And smell California, feel that air. I love New York, but it was already eighty degrees and humid enough to bathe in when we left this morning. Consuela!"

She swung around, caught the housekeeper in an enthusiastic hug.

"Welcome home, Miss Lily. Welcome home, Mr. Aidan."

"It's so good to be home. To see you."

"I will see all the bags are taken in. Mr. Aidan, your room is ready."

"You knew?" Cate demanded.

Consuela simply zipped a finger over her lips, mimed turning a key.

"You're a treasure among treasures, Consuela," Lily told her, and left her to supervise the unloading.

"Did you?" Cate pointed at her grandfather.

"Not a hint. I married a sneaky woman." He embraced his son. "Stay awhile, will you?"

"I'm planning on it. You look very fit. I'd say Cate's been taking good care of you."

"If she's not dragging me into the gym every morning, it's into the pool. Water aerobics of all things."

"That I want to see." Lily rolled her shoulders. "But right now these legs need to walk off hours in a plane."

"We'll catch up," Cate said when Hugh lifted Lily's hand to his lips, when they started to walk away. "Give them a little room," she murmured to her father. "It's nice to see people in love after a couple of decades together."

"And it gives me a little room with you." Aidan took her hand in turn. "How's my girl?"

"Happy. Even happier right now."

"Water aerobics?"

"They're tougher than you think, but you'll find out tomorrow when you report at eight a.m., poolside. Everybody into the pool."

"Hmm."

"I'm giving you and Lily a small break while your body clocks adjust. Grandpa's an early riser. We usually start at seven-thirty. I'm a working girl, you know."

They wound around the front garden with its arching Japanese maple, with the formal roses perfuming the air, around the side with a flow of hydrangeas in heartbreaking blue, the Bloomerang lilacs that never gave up.

"I listened to one of your audiobooks on the flight from London to New York."

"That would be the author's book."

As Hugh had with Lily, Aidan kissed her hand. "Not to me. You well deserved the Audie for that performance. You have a wonderful sense of character, of pacing the narrative. It takes serious skills to embody not just one character, but all."

"I love the work. And my studio? It's a great place to work. I love the cottage, and being able to walk up to hang with Grandpa, or prod him into the gym or pool. Both of which he enjoys a lot more than he lets on."

"I wasn't blowing smoke when I said he looks fit. He looked better when I left for London, but not like this. I swear, he's shed years. You've given him a real lift, Catey."

"We've given one to each other. Can you really stay awhile?"

"I'm ready for some time off. I may have to fly down to L.A. a few times, but I'm planning on staying for the summer."

"The summer? Really?" Delighted, she leaned against him as they passed a small berm rioting with purple foxglove and wild thyme. "My happy quotient just spiked."

"I need time with you, with Dad, with Lily." He turned, looked back to the sea. "And time here."

"It fills me. Ireland, it made me feel safe, and it soothed. New York charged me when I needed charging. Helped me feel capable, helped me grow up. And this? Sea, sky, hills, quiet? It fills me."

"And do you feel safe?"

"Yes, and charged and soothed, all of it."

Knowing him, knowing his worry, she rubbed his arm.

"Let's get this out of the way because nothing is going to spoil this double homecoming. It upset me, her latest, but it didn't send me into a panic. You already know I had to change my phone number and email because I sent you the new ones. It's annoying, but so's a paper cut."

"A paper cut's more than annoying when someone squeezes lemon juice on it. She excels at that."

"I'm not going to say it didn't take a couple of days to ease the sting. But she's made so much noise about this foundation, and yes, I know she's having a gala in a few weeks to add more splash, she's boxed herself into doing some actual good. So there's your lemonade."

"It's a wonder to me she ever managed to produce someone like you."

"Sullivan genes are stronger than Dupont."

"Mackintosh."

"Sorry?"

"She changed her name at eighteen, legally, and went by Charlotte Dupont before that, but she was born Barbara Mackintosh."

"Like the apple?" For some reason, it made her laugh. "Why didn't I ever know that?"

"Didn't seem relevant."

"Well, Barb was downgraded to an occasional annoyance in my life long ago. As for the other, I do feel safe here. The police are investigating, and there are various theories we can talk about later. But I feel safe, and I feel happy, and I've got my dad for the summer.

"Now, I'll bet Lily and Grandpa made it around to the bridge, and Lily's sitting down with the view and a martini. We should join them."

"I could use a beer."

She took his hand again. "Let's go get you one."

After drinks, a light lunch, Cate went in with Lily to give father and son some time.

"You can keep me company while I unpack. I've pined for your company more than I pined for the emerald earring I lost last month."

When they walked into the master suite, Lily aimed straight for the dressing room. Stopped, shook her head.

No suitcases in sight, and her makeup case along with her signature perfume already on the dressing table.

"I should've known. I told Consuela not to bother with this."

"Bothering's her religion."

"Well, I'm not going to complain." She shifted directions to the sitting area, took one corner of the couch, pointed Cate to the other. She gestured to the forest of lilies set around the room. "You?"

Cate sent her an arch look. "Your lover."

Her eyes softened. "Knock me cold if I ever so much as think about taking a job that pulls me away for four months again."

"I actually think I would. We did fine, and I enjoyed having Grandpa to myself for a while. But you leave a hole, G-Lil. A really big hole."

"I'm selfish enough to like hearing that. And now that it's just us girls." Leaning forward, Lily rubbed her hands together. "Tell me all."

"Where do you want me to start?"

"Girls." Lily pointed to herself, then Cate. "With *your* lover, of course. Is he coming to the welcome-home dinner I know Consuela's planning tonight?"

"We'll feast on your favorite honey-baked ham with the brown sugar glaze—but don't let on I told you."

Lily copied Consuela's locked lips gesture. "And Dillon?"

"I couldn't budge him for dinner because he felt Grandpa and I should have that with you. And he added weight saying he should have dinner with his ladies and Red. But he'll come by about nine. He doesn't want me alone in the house until . . . well, until."

"I know I feel better with him there. It's just an extra precaution—with benefits." With a heartfelt sigh, Lily toed off her shoes. "I know he makes you happy because I can see it. And with him staying with you at night, you're taking him for a nice test drive."

"G-Lil." Cate lowered her head, shook it. "No wonder I've missed you."

"And how's the rest of the family? I need to get over there, have a gossip session with Maggie. There's nothing like sitting around a farmhouse table drinking homemade wine and dishing the dirt."

"They're all great. Really busy. They hire people on, take on students—I guess you know that. Still, there's so much work, all day, every day. It's a really full life, and one of them's always coming up with a way to add to it. Gram's spinning wool. Yarn. Wool into yarn. On a spinning wheel."

"I must've known that's how it was done, but I can't see it. I'm going to have to get her to show me. And Red's fully recovered?"

"Back to surfing, fixing engines, making butter and cheese and whatever else Gram points him at."

"No break, then, in the who, what, why, how of it all?"

"Not that I've heard, and I think they'd tell me. Dillon's half—more than half convinced me Sparks stabbed himself to give his lawyer another angle on early release. If you take that out, consider Red was the police and somebody could've had a grudge, and the same could be said about the lawyer, that Denby made enemies in prison, the whole connected thing gets weaker."

Lily rubbed Cate's leg with her foot. "Who are you trying to convince, sweets? Me or yourself?"

"Both, maybe," Cate admitted. "I know I have to live my life, be Cate and live it. That's a lesson I've had to learn a few times, but I've got it solid now."

"It's a good lesson, but I'm not sorry Dillon's tucked up with you at night."

"I can't be sorry about that either. You're tired. You need to stretch out, take a nap."

"I could use one. A nice little couch nap, right here."

"Then I'll see you for dinner." She got up, took the light throw to spread over Lily, kissed her cheek. "I'm so glad you're home."

"Oh, Catey, me, too."

Cate went out, back to the bridge. She saw her grandfather showing off his little vineyard to her father.

Leaving them to it, and to each other, she started back to the cottage. She'd live her life, she thought, and get a little work done before she changed for dinner.

Jessica Rowe stuck at average and ordinary all of her life. An only child, she grew up in a middle-class suburb outside of Seattle. She did well enough in school, but only by studying her brains out to push herself over that average line.

She'd never fit in.

The popular cliques ignored the slightly pudgy girl with her average looks, her awkward social skills, and dismal fashion sense. She wasn't nerdy enough for the nerds, geeky enough for the geeks. Without any affinity or talent for sports, she never caught the attention of the jocks or coaches.

No one bullied her, as no one noticed her.

She was the human equivalent of beige.

She loved to write, and used her abundance of free time to create fantastic adventures for herself in her journals. And shared them with no one.

She graduated a virgin, with no savvy, sassy, or sympathetic bestie to boost her standings.

College didn't throw open doors for her or change her status, as she simply melted away in the crowd. She aimed toward law only because crime interested her. Often she conjured up stories where she played the courageous heroine who foiled the master criminal. Or starred herself as the master criminal who foiled the authorities time and again.

She could admit, to herself, she preferred the latter. After all, she lived in the shadows as the best criminals did. The difference, as she saw it, was the courage—she lacked—to take what she wanted.

She graduated law school dead middle of her class, finally passed the bar on her fourth attempt. Meanwhile she had a brief relationship with another law student, gratefully lost her virginity, only to be dumped via text when he found someone more interesting.

She wrote a grisly short story about a woman's revenge on a faithless lover, and celebrated alone when a mystery magazine published it under the name J. A. Blackstone.

She wrote two more while she slaved at a very average law firm for very average pay without any hope of advancement.

All of her life she lived by the rules she dreamed of breaking. She arrived at work early, left late. She lived frugally, drank moderately, dressed modestly.

Some of that changed when her grandfather died and left her, his only grandchild, three-quarters of a million dollars.

Her parents advised—and fully expected her—to invest it. She fully expected to do so. Then she sold her first book. Not the fiction she used as an escape hatch, but a true crime work she'd spent nearly two years researching on her off time, her vacations.

She took the somewhat meager advance and her inheritance, quit her job, and moved to San Francisco. Never in her life had she done anything so bold. At the age of forty, she rented a modest apartment and, since she never entertained, set up her work space in the living room.

And there, thrilled with her solitary life, started on her next book. She found the courage to press for interviews—victims, inmates, witnesses, investigators.

An hour each day, as a reward, she worked on fiction where she became a female assassin who took lives and lovers as she pleased.

The modest sales of her first book encouraged her. By the time she'd finished her second, she felt more than ready to tackle the next.

She had Charlotte Dupont to thank for her inspiration.

She caught an interview over her usual Wednesday-night dinner of sweet-and-sour shrimp, began to take notes. Her initial thought to have the Hollywood actress, the mother, as the central figure flipped when she began more serious research into the kidnapping.

Grant Sparks leaped out at her. So handsome, so magnetic.

And what he had done for love! The price he'd paid for it.

Many, she knew as she dug in, saw Dupont as the dupe, but she followed a different angle. The rich, the famous, the beautiful woman had used Sparks, and continued to do so. Trying to profit off the bungled kidnapping while he remained in prison.

By the time she requested an interview, she was primed for Grant Sparks's smooth manipulations.

By the third visit she'd agreed to become his attorney of record. By the fourth she was deeply—and just as madly—in love with him.

He opened the doors for her, showed her the power and thrill of breaking the rules. She smuggled things in and out for him, passed messages to and from without a qualm.

She believed in his cause—as much as he allowed her to know of it. Crime—and hadn't she always believed it—sometimes had justification. And punishment too often fell on the wrong people.

She would help him correct that.

When she waited for them to bring him to her on a warm summer day a year and a half after their first meeting, the average, ordinary Jessica Rowe had long since crossed the point of no return.

He'd mentioned blue as his favorite color. She wore a blue dress. He'd been a personal trainer, and even now generously, selflessly offered his skills and advice to other inmates.

She couldn't quite make herself go to a gym, but bought exercise DVDs and worked out fiercely at home. She'd had her hair cut, colored, styled, had studied YouTube to learn how to apply makeup.

He'd transformed her. Though she knew she'd never rival someone like Charlotte Dupont, she'd found a new confidence in her looks, felt she wouldn't shame him when they built their life together.

Her heart pounded when she heard the locks give, the door open. She could barely breathe when he walked into the room, for that moment when their eyes met and she saw the love and approval in his.

Still, she nodded briskly at the guard, folded her hands over the file she had open. And waited until they were alone.

"I live for this," he told her. "For just this moment when I see you again."

Her already thundering heart swelled. "I'd come every day if I could. I know you're right when you said we need to stick to once a week. Maybe twice when it makes sense. But I miss you so much, Grant. Tell me first, if you've had any trouble, anything."

"No." His eyes cut away from hers as if he had to compose himself. "I'm careful. As careful as you can be in here. But I'm afraid she might try again. She'll wait for me to relax a little, for it to blow over, then she'll pay someone else to kill me. The next may have better luck."

"Don't say that, Grant. Don't." As her eyes filled with fear tears, she reached out, gripped his hands. "I'm still fighting for your release. I won't stop. I know you said no before, but I could hire a more experienced criminal attorney. I could—"

"I don't trust anyone but you." He looked into her eyes, deep, deep. "You're the only person in the world I trust. She could get to someone else, my darling. It's what she does. I know it's only months now until I'm up for parole. Now that I have you, I could do that time without a single regret or worry. To know you'll be waiting for me when I get out . . . But now it's *if* I get out. If I get out alive."

"Let me go talk to her. I always intended to for the book, but—"

"If she did anything to hurt you, do you think I could live with it?" He released her hands, used them to cover his face before dropping them.

"You can't worry about me, Grant. I know I didn't do a good job with that lying, conspiring sheriff, but—"

"That wasn't your fault," he said quickly. "I gave you the names of the men to hire. You stood up for me, Jessie, when no one ever has. But it did make me think . . ."

When he trailed off, she leaned close. "Tell me."

"It's a crazy idea. It's too risky. For you."

"I'll do anything. You know that. Tell me."

The excitement in her voice, the *eagerness* on her face told him he already had it in the bag.

"I had a lot of time to think after I was attacked. About what the cops said to me when they came here."

"Accusing you of everything." It lit a killing flame in her. "Always you."

"But there was some doubt there. I saw it. Especially with the girl cop. Women are more perceptive, I think. If there was a way to throw more suspicion on Charlotte, they might stop her before she . . . before she had a chance to go after me again. I could do the next eight months knowing I'd walk out and into your arms. I could do anything knowing that."

"But if I tried to hire someone to kill her—"

"No, darling, not her. And not hiring anyone. But no." He shook his head, looked away again. "I can't ask you to do something like this. I'll just have to watch my back until the doors finally open."

"I won't have you live like that. I won't live like that, afraid every day they'll call and tell me you've been hurt. Tell me what you want me to do."

"How did I live all these years without you?" Emotion—he could always call it up on cue—trembled in his voice. "You're my guardian angel. I'll spend the rest of my life trying to be worthy of you."

He took her hands again. Looked at her as if she was his only salvation.

She'd have done anything for him.

"Charlotte's having a gala in Beverly Hills next month."

It thrilled. For a woman who'd experienced little excitement, even the act of donning a wig—ash blond, a smooth updo—equaled the thrill of a lifetime. She wore the body padding as well, padding that added several of the pounds she'd so diligently taken off.

The understated (boring) black gown fit over the padding well. A few fake jewels—but nothing eye-catching. She shouldn't catch any-one's eye. She applied her makeup meticulously, following Sparks's instructions. Slipped on the black-framed glasses, then the mouth appliance that gave her a prominent overbite.

She looked matronly, something that would have upset her if not for the thrill. Her name fit the look. Millicent Rosebury. She'd paid for the fake ID, the credit card she'd used to buy the gala ticket.

She had those items, a lipstick, tissue, a small amount of cash, a pack of cigarettes, some already removed, a silver lighter, and what looked like a small perfume sprayer inside her black evening bag.

She'd left her car, as instructed, in a public garage blocks away. When she'd done what she came to do, she'd return to her hotel room, change, pack up Millicent in the single tote she'd brought with her, check out via the TV, walk to her car, and drive back to San Francisco.

It was all so simple really. Grant had such a brilliant mind.

Secretly, she worked on his story—*their* story. When finished, it would be for his eyes only once he lived free. Once they lived free together.

She walked to the Beverly Hills Hotel. Grant said to walk.

She struggled not to look awed—by the hotel itself, the glamorous people. After clearing check-in, she stepped into the ballroom. Had to muffle a gasp.

The flowers! White, all white, calla lilies, roses, hydrangeas, spearing out of gold vases on every table. Glittering chandeliers spilling sparkling showers of light. Champagne frothing in crystal flutes. Women in stunning gowns already seated or strolling.

Grant had told her not to come too early, not too late.

She knew, her greatest skill, how to be invisible.

Accepting a glass of champagne with what she considered a regal nod, she wandered. She didn't intend to sit at her assigned table, or if needed, not for long.

It only took a moment to spot Charlotte Dupont, flitting, swanning, holding court. She wore a sleek gold gown, like the vases. She dripped with diamonds, like the chandeliers.

Rage rose up inside Jessica. Look at the lying, deceitful bitch, she thought. She thinks she's a queen, thinks she's untouchable. She thinks this is her night.

Well, in a way, it would be.

Her husband, old, frail, and looking both, sat at the table in front of the stage. He sent his wife adoring glances, chatted with people who stopped by the table, with his tablemates—no doubt as filthy rich as he.

She bided her time, watched for her moment as she wandered closer.

There would be a speech from Charlotte—undoubtedly tooting her own brass horn, probably working up a few tears as she did so. Then dinner, an auction to raise more money, entertainment, and finally dancing.

The two women at the table rose, walked away. Ladies' room, Jessica assumed, and slowly moved forward.

While she could pick her time, Jessica felt the sooner the better.

Sooner came when one of the servers approached the table. She set something in a tall, clear glass with a lime on the lip in front of Conrad.

Slipping her hand into her purse, Jessica removed the top from the little atomizer, palmed it carefully as she stepped forward.

"I beg your pardon." She used the haughty voice she'd practiced, believed it came across well. "Could you possibly direct me to table forty-three?"

"Of course, ma'am. Just one minute."

As the server rounded the table to serve the other drinks, Jessica leaned down to Conrad. "I'd like to take this opportunity to thank you for the good work you and your beautiful wife are doing."

"It's all Charlotte." He beamed a proud smile, looking up as Jessica gestured upward with her empty hand. Misdirection, Grant called it.

"A beautiful setting for a beautiful cause," she said as she tipped the contents of the atomizer into his drink.

"Thank you for supporting it."

"I'm proud to be a small part of tonight."

She eased back as the server came to her side. "This way, ma'am."

"Thank you so much." With that regal nod, she followed the server. "Oh, I see it now. And my party. Thank you."

"Of course, ma'am."

Jessica continued toward table 43, walked straight past it.

Drink, she thought, drink, drink, drink.

She walked straight out of the ballroom, sliding the empty atomizer back in her purse, taking out the pack of cigarettes. She moved straight to the outside doors, fumbling out her lighter like a woman in need of a smoke.

Someone tapped her shoulder, making her jerk as if struck by lightning.

"Oh, I'm so sorry!" The woman in a bold red dress laughed. "I was hoping I could get a light."

"Of course." Jessica forced her face into a smile so they walked out like two friends. Afraid her hand would shake, she offered the woman the lighter.

"Thanks."

"You're welcome. Excuse me, won't you? I see a friend."

She moved away, taking her time until she saw the woman chatting with another smoker.

She kept walking. Kept walking. And realized her hand wouldn't shake. She not only felt steady, she felt triumphant.

She'd become someone to write about.

CHAPTER TWENTY-NINE

Because she wanted to keep her schedule light for the summer, Cate limited her workload to three hours in the morning. It gave her time to spend with her father, time at the ranch. Just time.

She loved watching the way her father interacted with Julia, Gram, Red, and of course, Dillon. And knew some of her favorite memories would come from that summer. Watching fireworks explode across the sky with the horde of Sullivans, with Dillon and his family, riding with her father and Dillon to herd cattle from field to field.

Something she'd never expected to do.

Walks on the beach, dancing at the Roadhouse, a visit from Gino—thanks to Lily—to add a little sass to her hair.

She imagined today would add more memories with the Coopers' big summer barbecue. She had a new dress, courtesy of a shopping trip with Lily. White might be a mistake at a barbecue, but it looked so fresh and summery with its floaty skirt and strappy back.

She hoped her contribution of bread and butter pudding held up to what she imagined would be amazing and plentiful food.

She'd just slipped it into the oven to bake when she saw her father through the wall of glass.

Opening the door, she called out, "Just in time! I put bread and butter pudding in the oven, and you can distract me from worrying about it. I dug out Mrs. Leary's recipe, but I haven't made this since I was a teenager. Why did I go with something I haven't made in over a decade?"

Then she saw his face, and the buzz of excitement over the day silenced.

"What is it? What's wrong?"

"You haven't had the news on?"

"No."

Her pulse shuddered. Someone else? Who? God, she'd convinced herself it was over.

As they stood in the doorway together, Aidan took her hands. "Your mother's been taken in for questioning over the death of her husband."

"But . . . They said he'd had a heart attack. I know it got Red's suspicions up again, but the man was, what, ninety? And he had medical issues."

"It seems he had some help with the heart attack. They found digitalis, a lethal dose, in his drink."

"God."

"Here." He slid an arm around her waist. "Let's sit down out here. In the air."

"Someone killed him. Poisoned him. They think she— But that doesn't connect with any of the other deaths or attacks. It was his drink? Not hers?"

"His, yes. A gin and tonic, apparently. She was drinking champagne."

"But then . . . It's not connected. She didn't even know him when everything happened."

"No. Do you want some water?"

"No, no, Dad, I'm okay. It's awful. A man's dead, a man's been murdered, and I'm relieved it isn't connected to me. Except, I guess it is," Cate murmured. "Is she actually a suspect?"

"The report said his death's been ruled a homicide, and that she was being questioned. I don't have much more than that."

"Daddy." She gripped his hands. "I understand neither of us really know her anymore, if we ever did. But do you think she's capable?"

"Yes."

No hesitation, she thought, and closed her eyes. "So do I. All that money, and she probably didn't expect him to live so long. Just give him a little nudge—can't you hear her think it—what's the real harm? Or do we think that because of what she did to us?"

"I don't know, baby, but it's for the police to figure out. I didn't want you to get blindsided."

She reached for the bracelet she hadn't put on, so just closed her hand around her wrist. "They've already rolled back to the kidnapping, haven't they?"

"Yeah, and it's going to get a lot more play."

"I don't care anymore. God, yes, I do. For what it does to you, Grandpa, G-Lil. How it'll upset Dillon and his family. Tell me the truth, straight, Dad. Should I make a statement?"

"Let's see where it all goes. She could be cleared, and quickly."

"She could be cleared," Cate agreed. "But having a second scandal like this? It's never going to go completely away. She'll know what that's like now," Cate said quietly. "If she's innocent, she'll know what it's like now to be hounded by something beyond her control."

Charlotte wanted to be angry, to be furious, but rage couldn't cut through the ice pack of fear.

They'd questioned her. True, this time she had a fleet of lawyers, the best money could buy, but they'd shot her right back to that horrible day after Caitlyn's incessant whining, to an interrogation room, to police accusing her of horrible things.

Her lawyers had done most of the talking, had called for a break when she'd dissolved in tears. Real ones, too. Not grief tears, but fear tears.

Wishing Conrad would just die didn't make her guilty of anything. She'd given him the best years of her life. She'd been a faithful and dutiful wife—there'd been billions riding on it.

Why, she hadn't even been at the table when he'd collapsed, but onstage, basking in the lights, making her selfless speech.

Hadn't she rushed to his side—after only the briefest of hesitations? Annoyed, justifiably, that he'd chosen that moment to take the spotlight away. But she'd rushed to him.

She hadn't expected him to die in her arms.

But, Christ, what a moment, she thought as she lay in bed, a cool eye pack over her aching eyes.

Thank God some of the press there had captured that moment. She could play off that for years.

But first, she had to get through this nightmare. The press again, crowding around, tossing questions, taking pictures as her lawyers and bodyguards surrounded her, pushed through them to get her inside her limo.

The way people looked at her, the way the reports added just that horrible touch of speculation and suspicion. They didn't care how she suffered.

She needed to order some new black suits, and a hat, with a veil. Absolutely needed a veil to showcase the grieving widow.

She would grieve—she'd show them! Once this horror passed, she'd give a memorial worthy of royalty—and she'd be the queen.

No self-tanner, no bronzer for at least two months to lend that pale, stricken look. She'd spend some time in seclusion, maybe traveling to their—her—various properties around the world.

Remembering the happier times with the only man she'd ever loved. Yes, she could sell that.

But she had to get through the horrible first. Then demand the police apologize for putting her through such trauma while she was mired in shock and grief.

She'd make them pay for it. And in private, she'd raise a glass to whoever the hell decided Conrad had lived long enough.

In her white dress, Cate carried her casserole into the Cooper kitchen.

Outside, smokers smoked, grills stood at the ready, dozens of picnic tables lined up. Inside, as she'd expected, Dillon's ladies prepared a banquet of sides.

"I knew you wouldn't need it, but I wanted to bring something." She hunted up space on a counter for her dish. "And get here early enough to, well, get in on some of the action."

"Grab an apron," Maggie advised, "or that white dress'll look like a drop cloth after the ceiling's painted."

Julia walked to her while Cate tied one on, cupped her face. "How are you?"

"I don't know what to think about it, about her, about any of it. So I decided not to."

"That's a good plan. It's a pretty day, and we've got enough food for a couple of armies. Maybe you could finish making that gallon of salsa. I've heard you've got a knack."

"Happy to. Dillon? Red?"

"Likely icing down the beer and wine and soft drinks," Maggie told her. "They gotta set up the horseshoe pit, and we usually have a bocce game going, pony rides for the kids. We'll have some dancing, too. A lot of musicians in the crowd. Whenever Lily and Hugh make it, they have to sing for their supper."

"I love hearing them."

"You'll have to get up there, too."

"Oh, I don't really sing." Cate glanced up from her chopping. "Other than voice-overs."

"What's the difference? Anyway, it's a kick-ass party, with good food, good people, music."

After an hour in the kitchen Cate accepted the reality. She would forever be an occasional cook. She watched Julia season a serious vat of baked beans while Maggie checked more items off the two pages on a clipboard.

"You know, caterers and party planners make good livings doing what the two of you are doing for fun."

Julia slid the beans into the oven. "If I had to do this for a living, I'd run away to Fiji and live on the beach. But once a year? It is fun. How're we doing, Mom?"

"Right on target. Time for party duds."

"I'll go see if I can help with anything outside."

When she stepped out, she smelled grass and herbs, horses and sea breezes. The dogs bolted toward her from whatever business they'd been about.

Bottles of beer speared through ice inside huge galvanized tubs.

Apparently a wheelbarrow had been enlisted to hold bottles of wine, and another for soft drinks.

A couple of hands kept busy stringing up party lights. In the distance came the rhythmic sound of metal striking metal and someone singing—slightly off-key—Tom Petty's "I Won't Back Down."

She let the dogs herd her toward the near paddock where Dillon patiently brushed out the mane of one of the two spotted ponies munching on a hay net.

He wore jeans—with a hoof pick in the back pocket—a chambray shirt rolled up to the elbow, a gray, rolled-brimmed hat, and well-worn boots.

She thought: Yum.

He paused, scratching the pony between the ears as he watched her approach. "Now, there's a sight."

She did a stylish turn. "Good for a summer barbecue at the ranch?"

"Good anytime, anywhere." He held up his hands. "I've been sprucing up these two, so I don't want to put my hands on you."

"That's okay. I'll put mine on you." She reached over the fence, gripped his shirt, tugged him over to kiss. "I didn't know you had ponies."

"We don't. We bring a couple in for this, take shifts leading the little guys around on them."

"They have sweet eyes." Cate reached out to stroke a cheek.

"They'll be bored brainless by the end of the day, but they know their job."

He gave the pony a pat on the flank before swinging over the fence. "You doing okay?"

"I just spent an hour in the kitchen with two women who leave my culinary and organizational skills in the dust, but otherwise, yes."

He lowered his forehead to hers in a gesture she found as sweet as the ponies' eyes. "I have to wash my hands because I need to get ahold of you."

As she walked with him toward the pump, Red came around the far side of the barn. "We got your horseshoes, we got your bocce, and some chairs set up if anybody wants to take a load off watching the play."

"Thanks, Red."

"*Woman in White,*" he said to Cate. "You're a straight-out vision."

"Aw."

"Now, do you want to hear it, or do you want to put it aside for the day?"

"I want to hear it, then put it aside for the day."

"You're a sensible girl, Cate. You always were. Okay, so I'll round it up. Dupont's up onstage, ballroom of the Beverly Hills Hotel for this high-class do to hype her Mother's Heart deal. She's been mingling around, like a lot of them, then she sat down by Buster at their table for a bit before going up to do her soliloquy. She's just over five minutes into it when, according to witnesses, Buster seemed to have trouble getting air. Then he keeled right out of the chair onto the floor.

"People scrambled, like you'd expect. It took Dupont a minute, but she scrambled, too."

"There must have been doctors there," Cate said.

"Yeah, there were. A couple of them got to him quick, got people to move back. Tried CPR on him, called nine-one-one. He went fast, nothing they could do. Dupont's wailing, dragging at him. Plenty of pictures of her holding him in her lap. Cops came in. It looked like a heart attack, and it wouldn't've been his first."

Red shifted, nudged at his Wayfarers. "But the cops came in, and a crime scene team. They covered the bases. Digitalis, killing dose, in his gin and tonic. Server's cleared, so's the bartender who mixed it. A lot of people milling around, like I said, and they'll do a lot of interviews. But the fact is, one person benefitted most from his death, one person sat right next to him at the table, had the easiest access, and that same person's already getting the eye from authorities on two murders, two attempteds. She's going to get a harder look now."

"Do you think she did it?"

"I can't give you a yes or no on that, but if you asked me do I think she's capable of it? You're damn right I do."

"So do I." Cate released a breath, one of cleansing. "I'm sorry the man died, and I'm sorry about the way he died. I'm not sorry she's back in the frying pan. If she's guilty, I hope they lock her up for good this time. If she's innocent, well, she's about to find out what it's like to do nothing wrong and still pay a hard price."

"Like I said, a sensible girl. You oughta know they're keeping an eye on Sparks, too."

"On this? But—"

"Cops are suspicious bastards, Caitlyn." He said it with pride. "So you have to suspect, if you're a cop, this whole thing is one big setup. What does Sparks do? What's his nature? He sets up marks. He's got plenty of motive to want Charlotte Dupont to land in that frying pan."

"If he could orchestrate all this from prison, if he could have two people murdered, why not just kill her?"

"If you kill somebody, it's done. Put them in that pan? They burn a long time. Trust me, high-dollar lawyers aside, she's sizzling now."

"Hey!" Maggie, grass-green braid dangling, shouted from her bedroom window. "Haven't you three got work to do? You expect people to eat out of serving dishes with their hands? Get those plates set up, and the flatware. Don't forget the damn napkins."

"Woman's a slave driver," Red commented when Maggie pulled her head back in. "But I just can't quit her." He turned back to Cate. "Put it away."

"Done."

As predicted, there was good food, good people, and plenty of music. Cate found it easy to embrace the moment. She sat with Leo and Hailey, cuddled Grace the amazing, watched wide-eyed kids circle the paddock on patient, plodding ponies.

It made her wish for Darlie and Luke even as she pictured them settling into their home in Antrim, with a puppy named Dog.

Watching her grandparents sing a duet, she tipped her head to her father's shoulder. "They've still got it."

"And know how to use it. They're never going to retire. Not all the way."

Even as he said it, Hugh walked over, took Cate's hand. "Remember that routine in the pub from *Donovan's Dream*?"

"Probably. Sure. Now?" Amused, more than reluctant, she tugged back when he tugged her hand. "Here? Grandpa, I was barely six."

"Muscle memory. Come on now, there's a fiddle player here who claims he knows the tune. You wouldn't let your old grandfather down, would you?"

"Oh, that's cheating. I was six," she said again, as Aidan helped by pushing her to her feet. "Oh God, I'm going to have to move to Fiji with Julia after this."

It was a quick, bright tune, and the fiddler played it well enough, and with plenty of enthusiasm. Cate tried to cast herself back, to remember the steps, the moves, the words.

Just a kind of strut to start while she held Hugh's hand. And into a five-beat riff walk.

He winked at her, just as he had then. And she was back.

Around them, people kept the time, let out whistles, even sang along. Through all of them, Aidan studied Dillon.

He knew it, of course, had seen it, heard it, felt it, every time he saw the two of them together. He knew the boy spent his nights in his daughter's bed, and felt, as the father of a grown woman, he'd adjusted well to that.

But here and now, under a bright summer sky, remembering when his girl had been a girl, just six, it both cracked and lifted his father's heart.

They ended as they'd begun, hand in hand, smiling at each other.

"That was one of the happiest times of my life," she murmured as she embraced Hugh.

"Mine, too. I'm not as young as I was."

"Me either!" Laughing, she led him back to the table. "Take ten, Sullivan."

"I'd take it better with a beer. It's a picnic."

When she got the nod from Lily, Cate kissed his cheek. "Then I'll get you one."

"Well done, Dad. I'll be back in a minute."

Aidan walked straight to Dillon, who still had his eyes on Cate and was obviously trying to extricate himself from a gaggle of people to get to her.

"Sorry." All charm, Aidan smiled, slapped a couple of backs. "I need to steal Dillon a minute."

"Thanks," Dillon began as they moved away. "I wanted to—"

"I know what you wanted. We need to talk first."

He walked toward the front of the house—fewer people. Still, some hung out on the porch, so he kept walking, heading toward the field where the cattle grazed. Where the woods lay behind them.

The woods where his little girl had run, lost and terrified.

"She's my only child," Aidan began. "I've had to fight the instinct to keep her wrapped up tight and safe, to keep her with me every second. It was my grandmother who pushed me to give her room, when we were in Ireland. She was right, my grandmother. But I knew when I wasn't there, right there, Nan was."

"I never met her," Dillon said carefully, "but I feel like I know her from the way Cate talks about her."

"She was a presence. When we came back to California, I knew my father and Lily were there when I wasn't. Even when Cate demanded, and Christ, did she, to go to New York, I knew Lily would be there. After that, Cate didn't give me much choice in it. She would live her life, and I want that for her. Love is letting go as much as it's holding on."

"I love her. I've loved her a long time, so I know that's true."

Aidan turned from the woods, looked into the eyes of the man he knew already held his daughter's heart. "You're both of age, but I'm going to ask what you intend to do about it."

"I'm going to take care of her, even when she doesn't especially want me to. She's a hell of a lot tougher than she looks, but she still needs someone to take care. We all do. I'm going to do my damnedest to make her happy, to work with her toward building the kind of life we can both be proud of. When she settles into all that, I'm going to marry her. We're both of age, but I'm hoping you'll give your blessing on that."

Slipping his hands in his pockets, Aidan shifted to look out at the ocean, to gather himself. "I've been grateful to you for nearly twenty years."

"It's not about—"

Aidan held up a hand to cut Dillon off. "I haven't spent as much time here as my father, as Lily, as Catey now, but I've spent enough to know your family is one I'd be proud to blend mine with. I've spent some time this summer keeping an eye on you."

"Yeah." Dillon shifted his hat back a fraction. "I felt that."

Pleased, Aidan shifted back. "So, if you want my blessing, you have it. And if you screw this up, if you hurt my baby, I'll kick your ass. If I can't do it myself, I'll hire somebody who can."

Dillon glanced at the hand Aidan held out, took it. "That's fair."

With a laugh, Aidan slapped his back. "Let's go get a beer."

Hours later, happily exhausted, Cate walked with Dillon toward his house.

"I don't know how any of you can get up before dawn in the morning after a day like this."

"Rancher's stamina. Let's sit out a minute. It's as pretty a night as they come."

They'd done most of the cleanup and hauling away, but some chairs still sat out, so she took one, sighed out at the sea, the stars, the fat ball of moon.

"Best moment of the day," she challenged. "Pick one. Don't think."

"I've got a couple of them, but we'll go with watching you dance with Hugh."

"One of mine, too."

From the hills, echoing, came the call of a coyote.

"You really don't want that?"

"Want what?"

"Performing that way. On the stage, or on the screen that way."

"No, I really don't." She tipped her face skyward, realized she was as thoroughly happy as she'd ever been. And understood exactly why. "It was fun, but I don't want it for my work. My father said today my grandparents will never really retire, and he's right. We Sullivans tend to pour it all in—like another family I know. I don't want to pour it all into that, and not because of childhood trauma, not anymore. Because I've found other things to pour it all into."

Brushing her hair back, she turned her face to his. "Would you like to know my best moment of the day?"

"Sure."

"I was bringing another load of buns out of the house. I saw you and my father, my grandfather, standing together at one of the grills. Smoke's rising up, you've got the turner in one hand, a beer in the other. Grandpa's hands are moving the way they do when he's telling a story, and you're flipping burgers and grinning at him while Dad's shaking his head. I don't have to hear him to know he's telling you to stop encouraging him."

She took his hand, brought it to her cheek to press it there. "And standing there with a tray of hamburger buns I thought, Oh, isn't that wonderful? Isn't that the best? Look at the three of them, through the smoke and the music, with all the people around, with kids riding ponies, and Leo dancing with Hailey while Tricia holds the baby. There are the three men I love. There they are."

His hand turned to grip hers, hard. His eyes never left her face. "If you say like a brother, it's going to kill me dead, right here, right now."

"Not remotely like a brother." She cupped the back of his neck with her other hand, locked her lips on his. "It's done now, Dillon. The switch flipped and there's no turning it off again. I love you. It's forever."

He rose, lifted her off the chair, off her feet. Took her lips again when she linked her arms around his neck. "This is officially the best moment."

"Mine, too."

Then he swept her up to carry her into the house.

"Spoke too soon," she decided. "Best may still be to come."

"I think we've got a lot of bests coming. Like the day you marry me."

"Marry? That's—that's fast. Like, boom!"

"Forever's forever."

"But—marriage is—" She felt the anxiety attack sliding in, reached to rub the bracelet she wasn't wearing.

"It's not boom. Breathe through it," he told her, calm as ever. "We're family people, Cate."

He was right about that, she couldn't dispute that. And yet. "Gram and Red, they love each other, but they're not married."

He shifted her to open the door. "Red is family, and Gram had raised hers by the time they got together. We have to make ours yet."

"Oh Jesus, oh Jesus. I'm not a rancher, Dillon. You can't think—"

He set her on her feet so abruptly her breath whooshed back in, and out again. "Is that what you think I want? What I expect? You'll marry me and start, what, milking the cows, mucking the stalls? For a smart woman, you sure can be an idiot. You've got your work, I've got mine. Why in the hell would I want you to give up your work, something that makes you happy, something you're so damn good at?"

"Okay, but—"

"'But,' my ass." He tossed his hat on the couch, dragged his fingers through his hair. "You've got that fancy studio, and you're going to want to use it, see your grandparents. I figure you'll need something here, for when you don't want to drive over there. So we add on here. We've got room. You know what you need for it. Hell, I can move into the cottage if that's a sticking point. What the hell does it matter? It's you I want, and I'm goddamned if you're going to tell me you love me, and it's forever, then make half-assed excuses about marrying me and building a life together."

When her eyes welled, he dragged all ten fingers through his hair. "Don't do that. I can't fight that."

"I'm not trying to fight. I don't want to fight. You'd build me a studio here?"

"We, Cate. We'd build it. Don't you understand the concept of *we*?"

"I haven't had much experience with this particular area of *we*, so give me a break on it. Besides." She drilled a finger into his chest. "You've obviously thought all this through."

"I've had years of thinking."

"And I've had about a minute."

Point made, and he couldn't deny it. "Okay. All right. I can wait."

"Dannazione!" She threw her hands in the air. Followed that Italian curse with a few others. "Screw that. I need to ask you one question. What do you see?" She tapped her hands on her heart. "What do you see when you look at me?"

"I see a hell of a lot, but I'll cut that down for now. I see the woman I love. I see you, damn it. I see Cate."

She stepped to him, pressed her face to his shoulder. "I've had about a minute. And I've waited my whole life for you."

"I've been here all along."

"I couldn't before. I couldn't until I realized, as I've started to over the last few months, that I've stopped letting what happened to me hurt the way it used to because it brought me to you."

"Is that a yes, or are we still going to dance around it?"

She drew back, framed his face. "What if I said I would turn that second bedroom into a nice, pretty guest room?"

"I'd say that's not even in the area of negotiable."

She smiled at him. "Good. Because I'd hate to marry a pushover."

"Wait."

She stared after him when he walked out of the room. Shook her head when he came back again. "I thought that was a moment."

"Here's another." He opened his hand, showed her the ring. The little diamond sat in a simple white gold setting. "It was my mother's, the one my father asked her with. She gave it to me when she knew how I felt, what I wanted. She said it was fine, she wouldn't be hurt, if you wanted something that suited you better, but you should have this so it got passed on."

She pressed a hand to her heart first, then held it out. "How could anything suit me better?"

CHAPTER THIRTY

In the morning, Cate found Julia in the henhouse gathering eggs.

"You're up early. And I'm a little on the late side." Julia added another egg to her bucket. "I missed Dillon before he headed out to the fields."

"I have to get back, but I wanted to . . ." She held out her hand with its small, winking diamond.

Even as her eyes filled, Julia's face went bright. She set down the bucket, managed an "Oh, oh!" before she pulled Cate to her.

"It means just everything that you'd want me to have your ring, that you'd want me to wear it."

Julia drew Cate back, then pulled her in again. "I need another minute. He loves you so much. I'm so happy for him, for you, for all of us."

Drawing back again, Julia took Cate's ring hand. "I'd hoped he'd ask you with the ring his father gave me. Now that he has, if you want something else, something new—"

Quickly, Cate interwove her fingers with Julia's. "My family values legacies, cherishes them. That's what this is to me. There's so much ugliness going on, and I don't know if it'll ever stop. But I have this, and I can look at it and know what really matters. I bring complications with me, and that's why I tried to say no—or at least slow it all down. Next steps are scary. But I love him, and if I didn't take the next step with him, I'd still be locked in a room, alone."

"Life brings complications with it, and the way I see it, you and

Dillon taking this next step together? It's a damn good way to give that ugliness the finger."

On a laugh, Cate looked down at their joined hands. "I hadn't thought of it that way, but now that I do? Yeah. Yeah, it is."

She drove back to Sullivan's Rest smiling at the thought. The hell with it, the hell with all that greedy, grasping, sensationalized bullshit. She'd take the next step, and the step after that, live her life, build a life with Dillon.

They'd build that life in a place that meant home to both of them, close to family that mattered so much. She'd have work that fulfilled and challenged her.

And if she wanted to milk a cow or make cheese now and again, well, she could do that, too.

Sky's the limit, she thought. And the limit was what you made it.

She parked, headed toward the main house, then spotted her father and grandparents at a table by the pool. Shifting directions, she started toward them.

Her father raised a hand in greeting, called out, "We weren't sure when you'd get here, but we got an extra cup in case."

"Excellent." She skirted the pool, took a seat at the table. "I'm ready for coffee. But I don't see bathing suits."

Hugh tipped his sunglasses down, peered over them. "We decided this was a day off."

"Yesterday was a day off." She added cream to the coffee her father poured for her. "But I'll tell you what, we'll change the schedule, have water aerobics late this afternoon. Say four-thirty. Followed by Bellinis. It feels like a Bellini kind of day."

"It's hard to say no to Bellinis," Lily began, then—as Cate hoped—spotted the ring. "Oh!" Her hand flew to her heart. "My baby!" And she was up, weeping and laughing, to wrap herself around Cate.

"That's a very enthusiastic response to Bellinis," Hugh commented. "What do I get if I add caviar to that?" He glanced at Aidan. "She loves the stuff, God knows why."

"Men." Straightening, Lily brushed at her wet cheeks. "They notice nothing that doesn't jump out naked and dance." She grabbed Cate's hand, thrust it out. "Our baby's engaged!"

Aidan simply stared. "He moves fast," he murmured. "I only gave him my blessing yesterday."

"Your blessing?"

He looked at his girl, his treasure, the true love of his life. "He asked for it, sort of."

"Shows respect." Hugh wiped at tears of his own, then laid a hand over his son's. "He's a good man, and he's the right man. I'd beat him off with a bat otherwise. Come around here and kiss your grandfather."

When she did, Cate added a hard hug. "I wouldn't have said yes if he wasn't a good man. He had a couple of high marks to reach, as I was raised by good men."

She turned to Aidan. "Daddy?"

"Part of me wishes I didn't know he was a good man, and the right one, then I could borrow your grandfather's bat." He rose. "But as it is . . ." Then took his daughter's hands, kissed them. "He loves you, and love's what I want for you."

"The hell with coffee," Lily said as Aidan held Cate, swayed with her. "We're having mimosas. I'm texting Consuela right now. Oh! Maggie, Julia, and I are going to have the best time planning a wedding!"

They certainly seemed to. Over the next few days, they held meetings, texted, sent emails—sent Cate texts and emails, with links to wedding dresses, flowers, themes.

She decided to embrace it, to ignore the ugliness still swirling— and embrace the whirlwind.

When she walked with Dillon on the little beach, watching the dogs chase the surf, bark at the gulls, she filled him in.

"I now have a big white binder." She spread her hands to demonstrate. "Courtesy of Lily, divided into categories, as I stood firm on no outside wedding planner. That might have been a mistake."

"I know eloping's not on the table, but . . ."

"I'm not breaking their hearts. And I'm kind of getting into it. I'd really like to get married here at Sullivan's Rest, and outside."

"That works for me."

"Good. Really good, because that's a big one. Or a big two. The place, and time of year. Does May work for you? I know it's busy season."

"Ranching's always busy. I can wait until May. It'll give us time to build your ranch studio." He scooped up the ball he'd brought down, gave it a toss so the dogs could chase it, wrestle over it.

"Friends and family? Considering the Sullivans that's already a horde. So we keep it to real friends and family?"

"That really works for me. I'd get through a Hollywood production considering the prize, but I like this better."

"There'll probably—likely," she corrected, "be press pushing at it."

"Don't care." He gave the ball another toss. "Do you?"

"Not anymore. So here, in May, friends and family. I can pass that to our ladies. I do want a fabulous, gorgeous, all-mine white wedding dress."

"I'll look forward to seeing you in it." He took her hand, gave it a swing. Stopped. "Wait. Does that mean I have to wear a tux?"

"It does. You'll look amazing in a tux."

"I haven't worn a tux since my senior prom."

"You told me you and Dave were best men at Leo's wedding."

"Suits, not tuxes."

"Suck it up. I'm going to hand you over to my men on that one. You, Leo, and Dave, since they'll be your best men. Darlie will stand up for me, and I'm stopping it there. If I start bringing cousins in, I'd end up with dozens of attendants. Do you care about flowers or colors?"

"Do I lose points if I say no?"

"In this case, you gain them. Big decisions made, which will please our ladies. With that done, what do you say we take the dogs back up, sit outside with a nice bottle of wine before we see how my attempt at making pizza dough and sauce work out?"

"Have you got frozen if it doesn't?"

"Always have a backup."

As they started up, the dogs raced ahead, barking.

"You must have a visitor," Dillon commented.

When they topped the rise, she saw Michaela, still in uniform, crouched down, petting the dogs.

The lift wedding talk brought plummeted.

"They're wet," Dillon called out as he gave Cate's hand a reassuring squeeze.

"That doesn't bother us, does it?" After giving a couple more rubs, Michaela straightened. "I'm sorry to cut in on your evening."

"Don't be." Cate stiffened her spine so she could mean it. "We were just about to sit out here and have some wine. Can you join us?"

"For the sit, not the wine."

"I'll get the wine. Coke?" Dillon asked Michaela.

"That'd be great, thanks." She took a seat. "How about showing off the ring?"

Obliging, Cate held out her hand. "It was Dillon's mother's engagement ring."

"I know—word gets around. That makes a nice circle. The ring, and you and Dillon. It's a nice bright ending."

"Is it ending?"

Letting out a sigh, Michaela sat back. "I wish I could tell you it was, and I am sorry to bring this in. But I feel I should keep you informed."

"I want you to. I appreciate that you do."

Dillon brought out the drinks, then pulled a couple of dog biscuits out of his pocket, doled them out. "That'll keep them busy."

"First, congratulations, best wishes, and all of that. Meant very sincerely." Michaela made a quick toast, then set down her glass. "So far, the investigation hasn't turned up any solid or substantial evidence against Charlotte Dupont. They're still looking, but the fact is, the motive's dicey there. She'd waited this long, and the man was ninety, his health deteriorating. There's no evidence—at all—she had affairs, money issues, no evidence they argued. Why kill him—and take that kind of public risk—when she could just keep riding the train, and wait him out?"

"Someone did," Dillon pointed out.

"Yes, someone did. At this point, they haven't been able to tie the other murders or attacks to this one, or Dupont to any of them. They're looking, believe me. You've got L.A. cops, San Francisco cops, our own department looking into all of it."

Michaela hesitated. "I want to say I don't think she's very smart. Cagey, yeah, but smart?"

"You don't think she could have pulled all this off?"

Michaela shook her head at Cate. "The more I look, the less I see her holding all these threads together. Because I do believe it's all connected. There are a couple other angles. They've questioned this guy who bullshitted his way into the gala. He's got a record—fraud, investment scams—but nothing violent. Do you know anyone named William Brocker?"

"No."

"It's not panning out, so far. The other is Millicent Rosebury. A ticket was bought in that name, on a credit card that turned out to be bogus. The address doesn't match. Same with the driver's license. They're running facial recognition there, but haven't hit. The server remembers—vaguely—a woman near the table asking for directions—she thinks to another table, but maybe to the restroom.

"They were busy," Michaela added. "The server hasn't been able to describe her more than middle-aged, blond, glasses, white. The security cameras caught a woman with that basic description walking out with another woman. She had cigarettes and a lighter in her hand. What they don't have is any view of her coming back."

Michaela sighed again. "It's thin. You should know Dupont's making a lot of noise about hiring her own investigators. I wish I had something more solid for you."

"First, I think you're right. She's not smart enough. And more, this isn't the kind of key light she'd want. She was having a big moment—why step on it? She'll play it up now, but she'd have ridden that big moment.

"Tell me honestly. Do you think it's Sparks?"

"I absolutely do. One hundred percent. But thinking it and proving it? Whole different thing. What I will say, and I hope this helps, is every death and attack links to Dupont. If we look at pattern, that's what this says. It's about Dupont, not you. Even the calls you've gotten for years now. Every one of them has your mother's voice on them at least once in the recording. It's about payback, about making us shine that—was it key light?—on her."

"It does make me feel better."

"If I get more, hear more, I'll let you know. Meanwhile, I'll get out of your hair." She rose. "I'm really happy for both of you."

As the dogs escorted her back to her car, Cate took Dillon's hand. "She's on the real friends list."

"Definitely."

At her weekly meeting with Sparks, Jessica dealt with the war of feelings churning inside her. As always, she knew the thrill of seeing him, hearing his voice, touching his hand. But gone was the excitement and anticipation of planning to do something vital and important to help him.

In its place lived fury and frustration.

"It's been over three weeks." Her hand balled into a fist, unballed, balled again. "She's making fools out of the cops, Grant. She's doing interviews, planning a big, elaborate memorial, making noise about hiring private investigators."

"Let her." Sparks shrugged it off.

"She's going to get away with it! They can't put two and two together and arrest her. Who else would want him dead, for God's sake? They need to arrest her."

He resisted reminding her he himself had wanted the old man dead, and that Jessica had killed him. The best cons, he knew, played out when you believed them.

"It's all that money, Jess. The fame. You did the best you could to make her pay. And she did pay. A little."

"Not enough, Grant. Not enough after what she did to you. I know I was close to getting you early release. I *know* it. And now they're questioning you. I know that's why you won't walk out with me today. It's not right."

"It won't be much longer." If he could stand the sight of her for that long. "The best we can do now is just wait it out. You did your best. Now we wait it out."

"You must be so disappointed in me."

"Oh, no, darling." She really was making him sick, but he took her hands. "What you've done for me, I can never repay."

His faith in her, his abiding love for her all but destroyed her. And obsessed her. She had to give him more. Had to show him there was nothing she wouldn't do for him.

Nothing she wouldn't do to see that Charlotte Dupont paid.

She thought of killing the bitch. Dreamed of it. She could get a job as a maid, gain access. Or impersonate a reporter.

There had to be a way to get close enough. A knife through the heart, a bullet in the brain.

But no, as much as the idea excited her, wouldn't the police continue to dig at Grant?

She needed to find a way to point the idiot police right at Dupont. And to keep Grant out of it entirely.

The way to do that? Go back to the beginning. Go back to Caitlyn Sullivan.

It took her weeks to work out all the logistics, and only great love kept her from telling Grant. She'd surprise him.

He'd be so proud of her!

She had tested telling him, just bringing up the idea of sending Cate another recording. But he'd been firmly against it. Wait it out, he'd said again, and had looked so tired and sad.

Once she'd done what needed to be done, once they locked Dupont in a cell, where she belonged, she'd tell him everything.

And she'd double her efforts for that early release. She'd demand one.

She knew the Sullivan estate well enough. How foolish of the rich and famous to allow photographers into their homes, or stories to be written about them.

And she could study aerial views on the internet to her heart's content.

She knew enough to understand the security—gates, cameras—the positioning of the guest cottage, and its famed wall of glass facing the sea.

Despite the cameras, she'd considered getting a boat, trying to get to the peninsula under the cover of night.

But she didn't know how to handle a boat, and she'd certainly set off alarms.

She didn't have enough time to learn how to bypass alarms like they did in the movies.

She considered killing one of the staff, and going in their place. But the cameras would spot her, and she didn't have the code for the gate security.

She could force one of the staff to take her through. But the cameras would see two people. Unless she hid in the back seat, with her gun pressed to the back of the seat.

But then what would she do with the driver? Couldn't kill him or her right there, couldn't let the person go.

Then, after reading an article in the *Monterey County Weekly* highlighting staff of prominent residents of Big Sur, she saw the way. One Lynn Arlow—part-time maid at Sullivan's Rest—had several quotes in the airy, soft news piece. Buried in the fluffy, Jessica found a few key pieces of information.

To help put herself through college (online courses), Arlow worked three and a half days a week at the estate. The article helpfully added Arlow rented a house with three other women in Monterey.

A little more research, and Jessica had Arlow's address. Risky, of course, it would be risky, but Grant was worth any risk.

She practiced, researched, studied, timed, traveled for on-site surveillance. She ran through every aspect she could think of, then ran through it again. As the first hints of fall freshened the air, she drove from San Francisco to Monterey, timing her arrival to the early hours of the morning.

She parked in a public lot and in the dark, walked the seven blocks to the little house Lynn Arlow shared with her sister, a cousin, and a friend.

Picking the trunk lock on the old Volvo posed no real challenge, since she'd practiced religiously. Armed with a penlight and a .32 Smith & Wesson, she climbed into the trunk.

To hold off quick panic, she concentrated on the glow of the internal trunk release. Before researching she hadn't known that safety feature existed—standard for nearly two decades.

For comfort, she put her hand on it, but resisted the urge to yank it. She couldn't smother, she reminded herself. Plenty of air. She had that glow, and her penlight.

True, she didn't like small, dark places, but she could stand it. She would stand it thinking about all the years Grant had survived in prison because of Charlotte Dupont.

Closing her eyes, she concentrated on slowing down her rapid breathing. She imagined walking on a beach in Hawaii with Grant, imagined him taking her into his arms under the moonlight with palm trees swaying. Imagined them making love, at last, for the first time.

With a smile on her face, she drifted off.

She woke with a jolt when the car bumped over a pothole. Panicking in the dark, she forgot where she was, what she meant to do, and for one horrible moment thought herself trapped in some sort of moving coffin.

When she remembered, her shaking hand dug for her penlight. In that little beam, she gasped for air, and calm. All at once, it fell over her, the insanity of what she meant to do. The average, ordinary rule follower she'd been reared up inside her and wanted to scream.

She had to get out, get out and run, go back to her quiet, solitary life.

The idea of being alone again, being nothing again, having no one again, stopped her as she started to yank the release.

She could never go back now, never go back to the quiet and solitary. She'd already killed, and knew how it felt—thrilling—to take a life. For love, but for justice, too. And still Charlotte Dupont, the true villain, hadn't paid the price.

She had to see it through. No matter how frightening it all seemed now, she would see it through. Closing her eyes, she thought of Grant.

The image of the love, the pride, the gratitude she'd see on his face when she told him steadied and strengthened her.

She was someone to write books about now, she reminded herself. And it was time for the next chapter.

CHAPTER THIRTY-ONE

Inside the trunk, Jessica switched off the light as she felt the car turn, stop at the first gate, then start to climb. She breathed carefully as it slowed, again, and saw the second gate in her mind.

Nine o'clock. She'd chosen Lynn Arlow's half day purposefully. It gave her four hours to make her way to the cottage, to kill Caitlyn Sullivan, to set the stage. Then she'd make her way back to the car, slip inside the trunk.

By the time anyone found the body, she'd be back in Monterey. Maybe even on her way back to San Francisco. On her way back to Grant.

Plenty of time. More than enough time.

When she finally felt the car stop, when she heard the engine cut off, the driver's door slam, she waited.

One full minute, then one more.

Now, she told herself. Do it now.

She gripped the interior release, pulled. Relief sweat drenched her face when she heard the soft *pop* of the trunk. Slowly, carefully, she eased the lid of the trunk up an inch. She heard the sounds—lawn mower? Weed whacker? The groundskeepers.

She just had to avoid them.

She eased the trunk up another inch, saw the back of a building. A garage, she decided after several sweaty minutes. She strained her ears for the sound of voices or footsteps, but heard nothing other than the distant sound of someone cutting grass.

Holding her breath, she scrambled out of the trunk, carefully eased the lid down before she crouched beside the car.

Between Arlow's car and another. Staff parking, she realized. And there was the groundskeepers' truck. There was the garage, the big tree.

Of course, of course, the staff parked in the back.

Staying low, she crossed a stretch of lawn not yet mown. She'd practiced moving fast and low in her apartment, but there were so many windows in the house, so much glass.

Her heart thudded as she dashed to a tree, green and leafy with summer, to shrubs wildly blooming. She'd studied every photo of the house she'd found on the internet. An architectural feat, they called it, with all its levels and layers, its famed bridge, its commanding views.

But it looked so much bigger in real life, sprawled in so many directions, and with all those sheer glass eyes. She didn't dare cross any of the patios or terraces.

It occurred to her she should've dressed like staff instead of in cat burglar black.

Work pants, a T-shirt, a cap so she'd look like one of the groundskeepers if anyone glanced outside.

Spotting the worker on the lawn mower, another with an edger, she dropped, heart thumping, thumping, onto a bricked path behind a rise of lilies. Overhead she heard a door open. Someone came out singing.

Lynn Arlow. If she looked down, she would see. But she didn't look down, only watered the pots of flowers and greenery on the terrace, singing all the while. Then went back inside.

Jessica took it as a sign, and ran.

She saw the bridge, but no one on it. The lawn mower engine became just an echo as she ran full out for the cover of the orchard.

Oranges and lemons and limes, bold colors, strong scents. Among them, she dropped to her knees to catch her breath. She checked her watch. It had taken her fully twenty minutes to get this far.

She had to be faster; she had to be braver.

Moving through the trees, she oriented herself. The hills rose to her left, the sea spread to her right. The cottage sat to the right and below. But before the cottage, the pool, more open ground.

She heard voices again, had to slow, move carefully.

Through the trees, she saw the pool below, the sunlight on its water. And the people sitting at a table, under a bright red umbrella.

The Sullivans. The old man, the father, the grandmother. And Cate. All of them, in their fluffy white robes, having breakfast, smiling, laughing while her Grant suffered in prison.

Maybe they should all die, she considered. Maybe they were all just as guilty as Charlotte Dupont. She couldn't get past them. No, one of them would surely see her if she moved out of the trees, started down toward the cottage.

Why should they sit there, enjoying the morning together with their coffee and omelets and fresh fruit when Grant had to endure the slop disguised as breakfast in San Quentin?

She imagined shooting them all where they sat, and found it didn't turn her stomach. Not at all. In fact, she found the idea, the images of it, immensely satisfying.

But it wouldn't help Grant.

She sat under the lemons and oranges and limes to wait.

"Two o'clock." Lily wagged her fork at Cate. "That gives you plenty of time to work before you indulge me."

"Who's indulging who?" Cate countered. "You're the one who commissioned wedding dress designs."

"And who can't wait to look at them with you. You've given me a good idea of what you want, but if nothing else, the sketches will give you a springboard for the most important wardrobe of your life."

Lily glanced at both men. "The two of you are excused."

"Good." Hugh lifted the coffeepot, and at Lily's warning eye, limited it to half a cup. "I have a script I want you to read, Aidan."

Cate put a hand to her ear. "Is that the sound of retirement shattering again?"

"Could be. Man doesn't live on water aerobics alone. Thank God."

He started to offer Cate more coffee, but she shook her head. "No more for me. I've got a couple of commercials to do this morning, and a video game character to study before I get to play with wedding dress designs."

"What do you say to dinner on the terrace tonight?"

She smiled at Hugh as she rose. "I say I'm in, and I'll let Dillon know." Circling around, she hugged Aidan from behind. "After all, I only have a couple more days before my dad's off and running again."

"Not far. And not for long."

"Two o'clock," Lily reminded her.

Holding up two fingers, Cate started toward her cottage.

"It's good to see our girl happy." Leaning back, Hugh sighed. "Through and through happy."

"It is." Aidan looked after her. "I'll be happier when this investigation's over. I've stretched things so I could stay a little longer. I can stretch them again."

"One minute I convince myself Conrad Buster's death has nothing to do with Cate, with us." Hugh pushed his coffee aside. "The next I'm convinced it has everything to do with her."

"She's a smart, sensible woman." Lily laid a hand over Hugh's. "We're smart, sensible people. We'll do what we always do, and look after each other."

"Spoiling the mood." Aidan pushed the coffee back toward his father. "It should be about wedding talk and scripts. Just what's this one about?"

Willing, Hugh picked up his coffee again. "Well, I'll tell you."

They lingered another half an hour before strolling back to the house.

Then nothing and no one stood between Jessica and the cottage. Excitement built as she covered the ground—but she covered it carefully. She had to avoid the sea-facing side and that impressive glass wall. So straight in the front door. Unless someone looked out from high in the main house, in just the right direction, at just the right moment, she was home free.

After one glance back, she walked to the front door. She took out the gun, turned the knob.

Nice she left it unlocked, Jessica thought. But why not? Secure estate, security cameras, staff all over. She took one big breath, leaped in.

Despite knowing about it, the sight of the Pacific rolling through that wall stunned her. Ordering her pulse to level—and being ignored—she crossed the empty living room, the open kitchen, trying to move with her gun the way they did in movies.

Competently, but carefully, sweeping from side to side.

She glanced at the stairs, but heard nothing. Absolutely nothing but the sound of the sea.

She saw the door, closed, with a sign on it that read: RECORDING IN PROGRESS

Angling toward it, she kept an eye on the stairs, just in case. Unlike the front door, this one was locked. Frustrated, Jessica stepped back, considered shooting the lock—they did that in the movies, too.

But she wasn't sure if it would work, and if it didn't, it might give Cate time to call for help.

Trembling a little, she checked the time. She'd eaten up more than an hour, might need that much time to get back to the car. That meant she still had plenty of time to do what she'd come to do.

Once again she waited, and as she waited scanned the cottage to decide just how to set Caitlyn Sullivan's final scene.

Cate completed two thirty-second spots. Edited them.

A productive hour, she thought as she sent them. She intended to have fun with the video game work and thought she had the character voice nailed down. But she wanted one more read-through, one more rehearsal. She decided half a Coke would set her right up, give her a little pump before the read-through.

And unlocked her studio door.

She didn't see the woman or the gun until she'd taken two full steps out.

"Stop right there."

Instinct had Cate throwing up her hands.

"I want you to walk right to the center of the room. Slow."

Two steps back, she thought. Could she make it? Then what? She didn't have a phone inside the studio. Out the window? Maybe, maybe.

"I can shoot you where you stand. I'd rather not."

The voice shook, but Cate couldn't tell, not yet, if it was nerves or excitement.

"Who are you?"

"I'm Grant Sparks's fiancée, and I'm here to pay back the woman who ruined his life."

Nerves, Cate decided. And some pride. "That wouldn't be me, since I was ten when they kidnapped me."

"Not you. You're the same as you were then. Useful. I'm going to kill you, and Charlotte Dupont's going to get the blame. She'll finally pay. Now walk over here."

"You want Charlotte to pay?" Cate smiled. A Sullivan knew how to sell dialogue, even on the fly. "Me, too. The bitch had me kidnapped, her own daughter! She's used me all my life. How the hell is killing me making her pay? She doesn't care about me and never has."

"They'll think she did it."

"Really?" Defiantly, Cate rolled her eyes. "They're going to think Charlotte Dupont figured out how to get through the security, came in here, and shot me? Why the hell would they think that? If you do this, they'll just look at Sparks again."

"No, they won't."

"Of course they will. She's got the best lawyers money can buy. She's spent years crying about how she wants to be my mommy again. And you want to give her an excuse to wail over her dead daughter? Sparks will take the fall."

"He won't!"

But Cate heard the doubt this time.

Take the spoon, she thought, and pry the nails out of the window locks. Take the steps.

"When you're dead I'm going to write her name on the floor with your blood."

"Please, that's just pitiful, and it'll never work. You know what will? A live witness." She wiggled a finger at her own head. "Telling the police some man broke in here, tried to kill me, and told me Charlotte hired him. Me, the poor, innocent daughter of the manipulative bitch. God, why didn't I ever think of this before? We can ruin her. Finally."

"You need to walk over here!"

"You need to listen to me." Risky, yes risky to put that much authority and anger in her tone, but she needed to dominate to survive.

Make a rope out of the sheets.

"You need me alive if you want this to work. Oh, put the gun down. A pro wouldn't shoot me." Cate waved a hand at the gun. "Somebody could hear. I may need you to hit me, leave some bruises. Or . . . How could we make it look like an accident? I mean that the hired killer tried to make it look like one? That's the way she'd want it. But I get away, and he has to run off, and he's told me she hired him."

"Why would you do that?"

"Why?" Fury erupted on Cate's face.

Climb down, climb down. Get out of that locked room.

"I was *ten*. And what did she do when she got out, after spending less time in prison than I'd been alive when she had me drugged and locked in a room? She used me again, and again and again. She terrorized me so I had to give up my career. Does she pay? No, never. Instead she marries one of the richest men . . ."

It wasn't easy to put admiration on her face when her heart raced. "Was that you? Holy shit, did you poison her meal ticket to try to pin it on her?"

"It should've worked!"

"Oh yeah, but she always slips through. Fucking snake. It took guts to do that. You must really love him."

"I'd do anything for Grant. He's the only one who's ever loved me. The only one who's ever seen me."

"I know how that feels. She used him just like she used me. He must be disappointed killing Buster didn't blow back on her."

"He is, but he's so brave."

"Did he tell you to come here and shoot me?"

"I'm doing it for him. He doesn't know. I can't stand seeing him so tired and worn out. We were so sure she'd pay. But none of it's gone right."

Time to run for the woods.

"Because there was no one alive to pin it on her. They'd believe me. Why wouldn't they? They'd believe me, and she'd finally get what she deserves. Now stop pointing that gun at me so we can think this through, work it out. I want a drink. Do you want a drink?"

Jessica lowered the gun. "I could just wound you."

"I'll take a punch, but I'd rather not get shot."

Keep running, keep running until you see the light.

"Let me just . . ."

Through the glass she saw the dogs, and Dillon with a market bag. Her pounding heart simply stopped.

"Wait! I've got it." Quickly, deliberately, she moved to the right so Jessica turned her back to the glass wall. "Simple, that's best. Simple, straightforward. I don't have to know how he got in or out. I'm hysterical. Say he tried to push me down the stairs, so it would look like I fell. He's wearing a mask so I don't see his face."

She couldn't run now, because the light was coming to her. So she had to take the wheel, make the turn.

"Oh, a clown mask, like that bastard Denby wore. You know, I think he worked with my mother to set Sparks up."

"He did!" Tears of gratitude sprang to Jessica's eyes. "Grant told me everything. He made a terrible mistake, but—"

"Yes, he did," Cate said as the door opened.

She lunged forward as the dogs ran in, as Jessica swung toward the noise, the movement.

Frantic, she grabbed Jessica's gun hand, yanked it up. The gun fired at the ceiling as Jessica struck out.

She took a punch after all, but kept both hands locked around Jessica's wrist.

Her hands, the wrist, both so slippery. She thought of falling, falling, falling, and gripped tighter.

Let out a scream, one of her best bloodcurdlings.

Then a hand, hard, strong, closed over hers, wrenched the gun away.

She went down in a heap, Jessica on top of her, wailing, flailing, then screaming as the dogs growled and snapped. Snarling herself, Cate tried a punch of her own, felt her knuckles sing as it connected.

She sucked in air, let it out in a stream of curses in every language she knew. Reared back to punch again, but hit air as Dillon dragged Jessica to her feet.

He shoved her into a chair. "Sit where I put you. Guard," he ordered the dogs, who sat growling while Jessica wept.

"Are you hurt, Cate?"

"No. No."

"You need to call Michaela now," he told her without taking his eyes off Jessica. "Can you do that?"

"Yes."

"It's not fair." Jessica wept into her hands. "She has to pay."

"She doesn't mean me," Cate said as she picked up her phone off the counter. "She means my mother."

"I don't care who she means. Lady, you put a mark on my woman's face, and I broke about a dozen eggs dropping that bag. I've never hit a woman in my life, but if you don't shut up, you're going to be the first."

Ignoring him, she raged at Cate. "I should've shot you! I should never have listened to you! You're a liar."

"No." The smile Cate sent her was fierce. "I'm an actor."

Instead of looking at wedding dress designs that afternoon, Cate sat with Dillon's hand over hers in the gathering room of the house her great-grandparents had built.

Her father paced. She wasn't sure she could have kept still if Dillon hadn't held her hand. Like an anchor right now, keeping her grounded.

Julia and Maggie sat together on one of the small sofas. Hugh sat in Rosemary's favorite chair, with Lily in the chair beside his.

Consuela, eyes red from weeping, came in with a fresh ice bag. "You put this on your face now."

Cate obeyed. Just a bruise, she thought. Not even much of one. But she could still hear that single gunshot. She could still imagine how much worse it could've been.

As if she'd had the same thought, Lily popped up. "I don't care how early it is, I'm having a martini. Anybody else?"

Maggie raised a hand.

"I'll mix them." Hugh rose, went to the bar on the far side of the room. "You think you've made a safe space," he said quietly. "You do everything you can to make a safe space."

Rising, Cate went to him. "She has to be crazy, Grandpa. And she got lucky to get as far as she did today. But I'm fine. Dillon's fine. And Michaela's got her in custody. Michaela and Red."

"You were smart and brave. You always have been."

Cate looked over at Julia. "I was scared. She was scared and stupid. That helped."

Julia shook her head. "Smart and brave. Both you and Dillon. Then and now."

"They were, but Cate's right about the stupid." Maggie hissed through her teeth. "I can't believe the woman's an actual lawyer and that bone stupid. And to start blabbing—that's what you said, Dillon—even before Michaela cuffed her."

"She was crying about how Cate bullshitted her."

"Please." Trying to make him, or anybody smile, Cate put on the haughty. "Acting's the highest form of bullshitting."

"You've always been damn good at it."

Hearing the strain in her father's voice, Cate went to him, wrapped around him. "I come by it naturally."

When she jolted, just a little, at the knock on the front door, Aidan tightened his embrace.

They both relaxed when Red and Michaela came in. "You pouring drinks, Hugh? As a retired officer, a consultant, I can have one. I damn well want one. Mic'll stick with coffee."

He stopped by Cate, took her by the shoulders, kissed her bruised cheek. "It's too bad, because she's earned a drink. She's about got this mess sewn up. I always knew Mic had potential."

"I'll bring fresh coffee. Does my baby want a Coke?"

Cate sat beside Dillon again. "That would be great."

"Pour Consuela a glass of red, Hugh."

"Miss Lily. I'm working."

"You can bring in more coffee and a Coke for Cate, then you're taking a break in here, with your family."

Michaela sat. "I should tell you we let your groundskeepers go, and I have a deputy driving Lynn Arlow home. We need to take her car into evidence. Rowe picked the lock on the trunk, hid in there to get through security. There's no evidence whatsoever Ms. Arlow was complicit."

"She closed herself in the trunk of a car?"

Michaela nodded at Maggie. "She did, and spent a good part of the night in it. She planned to get out the same way. She confirmed what you told me, Cate. She'd shoot you, then write your mother's name on the floor, figuring we'd snap Dupont right up, throw her in prison."

"Crazy and stupid," Maggie decided.

"It came too close to working." Julia linked her hands together.

"I don't think so. It's what she meant to do," Cate added, "but her voice was shaking. Her hand wasn't that steady either. And she's . . . gullible."

"Lethal enough to poison an old man in a ballroom full of people." Red took the whiskey Hugh gave him. "Bold as that was, it's different from looking somebody in the eye and pulling a trigger."

"And all to frame my mother."

Michaela waited while Consuela brought in fresh coffee, a Coke for Cate, and one for Dillon.

"Sparks convinced her Dupont was behind all of it, and he was just her dupe. He convinced her he was in love with her, that Dupont was the enemy. She helped him arrange Denby's murder, paid the kill fee herself. Same for Scarpetti's. She sees that as evening the scales. She doesn't believe he stabbed himself so I don't think he told her. She's convinced Charlotte tried to have him killed."

"Like Mic said, she helped with Denby and Scarpetti," Red put in. "Helped set those up, and helped set me up. She's made the last couple of calls for him, those recordings."

"For what she saw as love," Cate murmured. "She's not that different from my mother."

"She'll be doing a lot more time than Dupont." Red swallowed whiskey. "Conspiracy to murder, two counts, murder in the first, one count, attempted murder, one count. The break-in with a deadly today. She's cooked. There's another one in Sparks's column."

"He'll be doing a lot more time himself," Michaela added. "As in the rest of his life. My . . . consultant and I are going to enjoy paying him a visit."

"Bet your ass we are."

"We owe you again."

Red jabbed a finger toward Hugh. "Not a goddamn thing. The kids there took care of most of this mess themselves. I have a feeling Sparks is going to be pissed off his lawyer went out on her own this way." He downed the rest of the whiskey. "Are you ready to go find out?"

"More than."

"If you're back by seven-thirty, come to dinner. Your family, too, Michaela." Lily walked to her, took her hands. "All of you, dinner tonight at Sullivan's Rest. Family dinner. Bless your heart, Consuela, I'm going to help you cook."

"Oh, no, Miss Lily. *Por favor.*"

"We'd better get on our way then. Who's driving, Mic?"

"I'm the sheriff."

Cate got to her feet. "I could use some air, a walk. I'll help Lily help you later, Consuela."

"Muy bien."

"We'll walk." Dillon rose. "I'll be home in a bit to finish up."

"No. You stay." Julia went to him, hugged him. "Gram and I have it. You stay. We'll be back for dinner."

"Thanks."

Maggie snapped her fingers at the dogs, who scrambled right up. "Come on home. You can herd some cattle."

"Go on, take your walk." Aidan looked at Dillon. "You're in good hands."

So he walked with Cate, turning his steps toward the beach as he knew she wanted.

"Here's something I'm always going to see, and that's always going to make me feel safe," she said.

"What's that?"

"You, holding that woman's gun in one hand while you dragged her off me with the other. Just pulled her up one-handed, shoved her into a chair, and told the dogs to guard her. Up until that moment, everything I did was adrenaline fueled. My heart pounding, sweat going down my back. Then you did that, and everything just calmed down."

"For you, maybe." He turned his head, kissed her temple. "Scared the crap out of me."

"I know. I heard it. You were scared for me, but you didn't let her see it. I'm glad you didn't. And I didn't. I want them to both spend years in prison knowing we're not afraid of them."

She brought his hand to her cheek, turned her lips into his palm. "That part's over. But you have to know my mother's going to go full out on this. Sparks and Rowe handed her a gift. The publicity's going to be all over."

"I don't care about that." He paused at the steps of the beach, turned her to him. "Do you?"

She studied his face, let his voice play in her head. "You really don't?"

"I care about you, our family, the dogs, the ranch. I care about a lot of things. That one doesn't even make the bottom of the list."

"Then I don't care either. I really don't care. How about you marry me?"

"How about I do?"

She took his hand again, and together they walked down the steps, over the sand toward the sea.